The Book Of Legend

The Prophecies Of Fate Book One

T J Mayhew

For Alan...

Forever, and always, my Merlin.

Prologue

Britain, 539 AD

Life can change in a moment. We can be at our lowest ebb, lost and searching for answers, when suddenly, out of the darkness, comes a light: a hero who fights for the good, vanquishing the bad. For us, that hero was Arthur Pendragon, the High King of Britain. His destiny was foretold to me in the stars, just as his father's had been: two dragons in the night sky.

Under Arthur's reign, Britain was restored to the great nation it had once been under his father, the great Uther Pendragon, before the Sea-wolves had invaded, taking advantage of Uther's untimely death.

Now, death has come to this land once more and the country is mourning the passing of King Arthur who has left us to reside in Avalon. We are once again facing dark times; times when it may be easier to change allegiances or to run... run to save ourselves.

But there is hope, for nothing is ever truly lost if we believe there is a solution. Another will come to save us, to lead us, to make us great again, to put down any challenges and right the wrongs that have been done to us.

He will be as strong as his father, as compassionate as his mother and have a heart as brave and true as any of the knights of Britain. His name will be...

***

The man looked up at the sound of harsh voices, brutal in the stillness of the night. Quickly pulling his robes about him, he sat back in the shadows of the stones, at once merging with the darkness around him. He waited, hardly daring to breathe as the warriors passed by, towering over him as they sat astride their steeds, their fearsome black chainmail momentarily caught in the moonlight.

When certain they had gone, the man relaxed. He sighed; even this sacred place was no longer respected. He needed to hurry back before it was too late...

Kneeling down, he finished writing before frantically digging at the earth with his hands, hardly noticing as hidden stones cut his fingers. Finally, he laid the book in its resting place, satisfied no one would find it. Closing his eyes, he held out his hands and murmured words of protection before covering the book with soil. Casting one final ward, he stood and glanced around at his surroundings before clapping his hands and vanishing as if he had never been.

Chapter One

Cai Freeman hated himself; hated himself for being forced to hide out in the toilets like a scared little boy when he should have been in Maths, listening to Mr Carter's boring monotone as he droned on about algebraic equations. He knew he was going to get a detention for this, but there was nothing on Earth that would compel him to leave the safety of the toilet cubicle until he knew for sure the danger outside had passed.

But, as embarrassed as he was, to again find himself hiding in the toilets, he had to admit that ever since he had started at this stupid school, this had been his only safe haven. For some unknown reason, Ethan Nixon didn't feel the need to chase him all the way in, instead contenting himself to prowl the corridor until Cai dared to show his face. And Cai knew, beyond a shadow of a doubt, that

Ethan and his buddies were lurking outside now, waiting...

Ever since his first day in Year Seven, Ethan, along with his friends Charlie Slater and Aaron Wilson, had had it in for him. At first, it had started with shoving in the corridor but soon they had upped the ante and it wasn't long before they had found other ways to torture him. Not a day went by when he hadn't found his lunch tray 'accidently' slapped out of his hands or his PE kit hidden, forcing him to wear one of the reserve kits that Mr Grayson kept in his office, earning him the sniggers of the rest of the boys in his year.

The fact that he couldn't play sports only added to their reasons to persecute him. Whereas they were all members of the football and basketball teams, Cai couldn't even explain the rules, let alone play them.

He jumped as his phone vibrated in his pocket. Panicking as he tried to calm his racing heart, he reached into his blazer and pulled it out, sighing when he saw the caller ID: he really didn't need this right now. Reluctantly, he accepted the call and pressed the phone to his ear.

"Hello?"

"Hey, Cai, you in school?"

Cai rolled his eyes; where else would he be at eleven o'clock on a Wednesday? "Yes, Greg, I'm in school," he replied with forced patience.

"I'll make it quick then; I was just phoning to let you know that me and Jules will be out tonight, so get yourself dinner. OK?"

Cai rubbed his forehead. "Yeah, whatever."

"Great; see you tomorrow then."

Cai ended the call and returned the phone to his pocket. His foster parents were cool but they were enough to drive him crazy at times; every week they disappeared for a few days to attend some rally or protest, leaving Cai alone to fend for himself. Not that he minded; he preferred that to facing their endless questions about school or listening to their lectures about the latest cause they were fighting.

Knowing he couldn't stay in the toilets forever, he picked up his bag, braced himself and hesitantly unlocked the cubicle door. He shot a wary look around the room, checking he was still alone and that Ethan hadn't snuck in while he had been on the phone.

Satisfied, he stepped out, hitching his bag on his shoulder and caught sight of himself in the mirror. He tried to chase away the fear he saw in his eyes; it wouldn't do to let his tormentors know they had scared him. Walking over to the sink, he splashed cold water on his face, the shock making him catch his breath. After drying his hands and face, he gritted his teeth and took a deep breath.

"It's now or never," he muttered, running his fingers through his messy, blonde hair.

He placed a hand on the outer door, psyching himself up. Resisting the urge to retreat back to the stall, he pulled the door open and walked boldly into the corridor, fully prepared to run if he had half a chance. But, to his surprise, the corridor was empty. Looking around, he realised that his eyes weren't deceiving him; he was alone. Breathing a sigh of relief, he turned, eager to get to class, which, unfortunately, was on the other side of the school and would take a good five minutes to reach.

"Where *you* going, Loser?"

Cai froze; that voice, the voice that sent cold shivers running down his spine, could only belong to one person: Ethan Nixon.

Looking up, he saw Ethan step out from behind a bank of lockers, Charlie Slater by his side. He turned to retreat but Aaron Wilson now blocked his only way of escape; where he had sprung from, Cai couldn't say but he wasn't surprised. It was just his bad luck to find himself surrounded once more.

"There's nowhere to run, nowhere to hide," Ethan taunted menacingly as he slowly approached his cornered prey.

Cai took a step backwards, bumping into Aaron, who steadied him in a vice-like grip. Cai swallowed nervously as the other two boys advanced.

"Maybe it's about time we showed you what happens to people who run from us. What do you say, boys?" Although talking to his comrades, Ethan's eyes were firmly fixed on Cai, clearly sizing him up.

Aaron sniggered menacingly in Cai's ear, while Charlie slowly nodded in agreement.

Cai may not have been able to play sports but, after many years of this kind of torment, he could sure as hell run.

Summoning all of his strength, all of his courage, Cai stamped hard on Aaron's foot, eliciting a sharp cry of pain from his captor. As soon as he released his grip, Cai took off and, acting solely on instinct and adrenaline, pushed past the other boys, running full pelt towards the stairwell.

"Oh, you are *so* gonna pay for that!" Ethan snarled as he recovered from Cai's surprise attack.

But Cai wasn't listening; all he knew for sure was that he needed to put as much distance between himself and the others as possible because if Ethan caught him... Well, it didn't bear thinking about.

As he reached the door to the stairwell, Cai risked a backwards glance and was greeted by the sight of the three boys charging after him, Ethan leading the chase. Despite his head start, they were gaining fast and by the time Cai was through the door, Ethan was close enough to grab his blazer. As Cai twisted out of his grasp, he felt his foot slip off the top step; his arms flailed as he tried to find something to hold onto but it was no good...

... Before he realised what was happening, he was falling through space.

Chapter Two

Cai barely had time to register the shocked expressions on the other boys' faces, when the breath was knocked out of him as he landed flat on his back, his head hitting the tiled floor. He closed his eyes, wincing at the pain that shot through his body but didn't dare show any other sign that he was hurt; showing any weakness right now would definitely not help his situation.

Ethan recovered a lot quicker than Cai and hurtled down the stairs, Charlie and Aaron close on his tail. Grabbing the lapels of Cai's blazer, he pulled the injured boy up towards him, ignoring his gasp of pain.

"You're so pathetic," Ethan sneered maliciously. "You can't even walk down the stairs without falling, can you?"

Behind their leader, Charlie and Aaron smirked.

Reaching up, Cai grabbed hold of Ethan's wrists, desperately trying to prise him off, but the other boy's grip was like iron and wouldn't yield.

"What's the matter?" Ethan taunted, his eyes boring into Cai's. "This not comfortable enough for you? Let's see if I can help with that," he offered, relinquishing his hold. Cai dropped back to the floor with a yelp of pain. He immediately rolled over, trying in vain to scramble to his feet but was pushed back down again by Ethan, who now crouched over him. "You didn't really think it was going to be that easy, did you?" He grinned as he grabbed a handful of Cai's shirt, holding him firmly in place as he slowly pulled his right arm back...

Cai stiffened, closed his eyes and braced himself for the blow that never came.

"Shouldn't you be in class?"

All four heads turned in the direction of the voice. Mr Grayson, the boys' P.E. teacher, stood expectantly, his arms folded across his chest; if he was concerned that Ethan was about to punch Cai while the other two boys looked on, he certainly showed no sign of it.

Ethan immediately straightened up, pulling Cai with him, setting him on his feet. He draped an arm around Cai's shoulders and grinned confidently at the teacher. "Oh, hey, Mr Grayson," he said, oozing his usual confidence. "We were just passing by when we saw Cai fall down the stairs."

Cai glanced at the boy, amazed that he could come up with a story so quickly.

Mr Grayson, his gaze fixed on Ethan, nodded slowly, clearly not buying any of it. "And let me guess: you stopped to help."

Ethan nodded. "Sure, yeah, we stopped to help," he agreed.

"Regular Samaritans, aren't you?" Mr Grayson noted drily, his eyes studying each of the trio in turn. Glancing at Cai, he inclined his head towards the other boys. "This true?"

Cai hesitated for a moment; he knew this was his chance to end the terror, his chance to finally get the boys off his back for good. He glanced once again at Ethan, who shot him a warning glare. Turning back to the teacher, he nodded meekly. "Yes, Sir; it's true."

Mr Grayson held Cai's gaze for a moment before returning his attention to Ethan and his cronies. "Well, then boys; I'm sure Cai is very grateful for all your help, but maybe you should get to your classes now."

Ethan nodded. "Yes, Sir." He clapped Cai on the back, making him flinch. "See you 'round, Cai; we'll catch up at lunch, see how you are." Despite the friendly tone of Ethan's words, Cai heard the threat hidden in them: yes, they'd find him at lunch but it wouldn't be to check how he was: it would be to finish what they had started.

Cai watched as the others left, unable to hold back a sigh of relief; if Mr Grayson hadn't arrived when he had, he dreaded to think what might have happened to him. Now, at least, the interruption had served to buy him time; maybe he could sneak out of school for lunch...

Picking up his bag, he murmured his thanks to the teacher and turned to leave.

"Not so fast, Cai."

Cai turned, "Yes, Sir?" he asked warily.

Mr Grayson nodded towards the stairs. "Why don't you sit down?"

Cai shook his head. "No, I'm fine, thanks."

"It wasn't a request, Cai," he replied. "Sit."

Cai did as he was told, dropping his bag at his feet; Mr Grayson sat down next to him, resting his elbows on his knees as he turned to face Cai. Cai stared back, waiting for him to speak, unsure whether he was in trouble or not.

"Tell me what's going on."

"Nothing's going on, Sir," Cai protested, innocently.

Mr Grayson sighed. "I'm not blind, Cai; I saw what Ethan was doing. So tell me what's going on between you; I can't help you if you aren't straight with me."

Cai barely managed to stop himself from rolling his eyes; why was it that teachers always thought they could solve a problem when everyone knew they couldn't? The fact was that kids like Ethan were too good at what they did; they were too good at putting the fear of God into their victims so when someone did offer any help, it was already too late.

"How are you feeling?"

12

The question took Cai by surprise. "Um..."

"May I...?" Without waiting for a reply, Mr Grayson stood up and leant over Cai, checking the back of his head. He then placed his hands on either side of Cai's neck, gently moving his head from side to side, before sitting down again. "I think you'll be fine; no major damage, thankfully. You'll be a bit sore for a few days, but you'll survive," he added with a smile.

"Oh, good; I'm glad," Cai muttered sarcastically.

"Look," Mr Grayson continued. "I know what you're going through; it wasn't that long ago I was a teenager myself." He glanced at Cai. "I know you didn't just fall; I know Ethan and his friends were involved and, if you trust me enough to tell me what's going on, I will take action."

Cai stared resolutely at the floor. "There's nothing going on, Sir. Honestly," he added for good measure.

Mr Grayson was silent for a few moments. "Sixteen is a challenging time for anyone," he murmured. "It's always easier if you have someone to confide in; someone you can trust." Cai glanced at him and the teacher held up his hands in surrender. "But I know when to shut up; just promise me something."

"What?"

"That you'll think about what I said; even if you just tell someone at home."

Cai scoffed. He couldn't imagine sitting down with either Greg or Jules to talk about his problems; they'd probably suggest he meditate and give him some weird concoction of wheatgrass and jasmine to drink to 'calm him'.

But instead of arguing, he nodded. "Fine, Mr Grayson; I'll think about it."

Mr Grayson smiled. "Good."

"Can I go now?"

Mr Grayson frowned. "I hope you're not planning on going to class."

Cai frowned. "Why not? You sent the others," he protested.

"Well, correct me if I'm wrong, but the others haven't just taken a fall down a flight of stairs, have they?"

Cai couldn't argue with that. "So what do you want me to do?"

Mr Grayson considered his answer. "I would prefer you go to the hospital but I highly doubt you would agree to that; so, as a compromise, I'll take you to the Medical Room." He glanced at Cai. "The nurse can examine you."

Cai was about to protest when Mr Grayson held up a hand to silence him.

"This isn't up for discussion, Cai."

Cai's shoulders slumped and he sighed, frustrated. "OK, fine. Whatever you say."

Mr Grayson led the way, Cai following in silence. When they reached the Medical Room they found it empty.

Mr Grayson glanced at Cai. "I'm sure the nurse will be back any minute. Take a seat," he added, gesturing to an empty chair.

Cai obediently sat down as he tried to ignore the dull throbbing behind his eyes.

"OK, so…" Mr Grayson started awkwardly.

Cai looked up at him and got the distinct impression the teacher wanted to tell him something; something related to Ethan Nixon, no doubt. As he waited for Mr Grayson to continue, Cai braced himself for the worst.

Thankfully, thinking better of it, Mr Grayson muttered something about going to find the nurse and turned to leave.

"Sir?"

The teacher turned his head. "Yes, Cai?" he asked expectantly.

"Um… thanks for… you know," he finished lamely.

Mr Grayson nodded. "Don't worry; it's my job to care. And, remember, if you do ever need to talk about anything, you know where to find me."

As Mr Grayson left, Cai felt a pang of guilt; he was grateful the teacher wanted to help but he found it hard to open up to him or to anyone else for that matter.

Alone once more, Cai's mind started working overtime; if he stayed, he would surely have to explain how he had fallen down the stairs which would inevitably lead to more questions, questions that would lead straight to Ethan's door. He couldn't handle that.

Before he had a chance to think better of it, Cai picked up his bag and made his way to the nearest exit. Relieved no one was around to stop him, he hurried out of school, happy that he didn't have to worry about Ethan anymore; well, not for today, at least.

Chapter Three

Cai let himself into the silent house, dropping his bag in the hallway. One of the upsides of living with foster parents more concerned with saving the world than cooking him dinner was that he didn't really have to worry about keeping the house that tidy. According to Greg and Jules, there was no point worrying about the state of the house when there were thousands of innocent animals dying every day and the planet was in danger from global warming and all sorts.

That wasn't to say they lived in a pigsty, far from it; it was clean, just messy. Books and magazines littered every surface in the living room and it was often touch and go as to whether you could ever find the TV remote. Cups regularly littered the coffee table and today was no exception. Cai wandered into the kitchen casting an eye over the washing up that Greg and Jules hadn't had time to do before they had run off to wherever it was they were going that morning.

He opened the fridge and took out a can of Coke and the pizza box with last night's leftovers in it; cold pizza was never his first choice but it was better than nothing and he wasn't in the mood to cook.

He returned to the living room and switched on the TV to watch some mindless comedy that didn't require him to think too much. Kicking off his shoes, he put his feet on the sofa, munching on the tasteless, rubbery pizza and began sipping his Coke.

Although he had planned to go straight home, Cai had decided to go for a walk in order to clear his head; his headache had cleared up pretty quickly and he had decided to take advantage of his unexpected freedom. When he had finally headed home, he realised that several hours had passed and he was tired and hungry; the entire afternoon had passed him by and he couldn't remember a single thing he had done.

He threw the pizza aside; the thought of going back to school in the morning did not fill him with joy. Ethan would definitely be waiting for him, maybe even at the school gates, and would surely leap on him as soon as the opportunity arose; he may even be more vindictive than usual, seeing as he hadn't been around at lunchtime today. Cai briefly found himself wondering whether Ethan was at home now, plotting his revenge with Charlie and Aaron.

Pushing that thought aside, Cai turned off the TV and made his way into the hall to collect his bag. From the corner of his eye, he noticed the light on the answering machine flashing and he pressed 'Play'.

"Hello, Mr and Mrs Moore; this is Mr Grayson, one of Cai's teachers. I'm calling to let you know that Cai suffered an injury at school today but left before anyone could check he was OK. If you could please ring us back..."

Cai pressed 'Delete'; the last thing he needed right now was Greg and Jules knowing about his 'accident', let alone that he had skipped school. He just wanted to forget about today.

The machine clicked over to the next message and, this time, Jules' voice filled the room.

"Hey, C. Just to let you know, we won't be back tonight... There's some food in the fridge, I think... Greg says 'hi' by the way; hope everything was OK today. See you tomorrow. Byeee!..."

The answering machine fell silent as Cai made his way upstairs, his bag now forgotten; he needed to lie down and forget that he was alone once more. His foster parents hadn't always been as carefree as they were now; when he was younger, they had always been around, going to parents' evenings and sports days. All in all, they had been pretty responsible parents. But as Cai grew older, they had decided that giving him more freedom and responsibility would do him good, while also allowing them time to pursue their own interests. Since then, they had often taken off to save the world and Cai, being left alone, had found himself wondering about his birth parents.

He didn't bother turning on the light as he entered his room but just flopped onto the bed, allowing the stress of the day to leave his body; his back was beginning to ache again from the impact of his fall earlier and his headache had returned. After lying in darkness for a while, he turned over and switched on the bedside lamp. Catching sight of the silver torque bracelet on his bedside table, he picked it up and stared at the familiar dragon design etched into it.

Sixteen years ago, when his parents had left him at the hospital, he had had nothing with him, except this bracelet and a scrap of paper with the name 'CAI' written on it; the name Freeman, having been given to him by the authorities.

Greg and Jules had given him the bracelet on his eleventh birthday, the only real link he had to his parents. Therefore, whenever life became too much, he would find himself staring at it, wondering what his parents had been like and why they had given him away.

When he was younger, he had believed his real dad was Superman, flying off saving the world from bad people and that, one day, he would fly back and take him home to his mum so they could live happily ever after. But, as he grew up, he realised that was just a stupid kid's dream and it wasn't long before he had had to face the truth: his parents were never coming back for him and he would never know why.

But even now, knowing the reality of his life, he sometimes found himself looking at the bracelet after a bad day, hoping to feel just a little bit closer to them. He never made a habit of confiding in people but, in his head, he had already told them about Ethan and he couldn't stop the little boy in him from hoping his dad would come along and make the bullying stop.

Sighing, he returned the bracelet to its place on his bedside table and turned off the lamp. Lying on his bed, he watched as shadows played across the ceiling, an empty, hollow feeling in the pit of his stomach.

Chapter Four

Cai returned to school on Thursday to find the gates devoid of any threat. All day, he was vigilant, ever mindful that Ethan could jump him when he was least expecting it but, surprisingly, no attack came. When he did see him, Ethan made no attempt to approach or talk to him but he made sure he shot him glares that left Cai in no doubt he was biding his time and would, at some point, finish what he had started.

Cai's relief soon vanished though when Mr Grayson hauled him into his office to point out how idiotic he had been to leave school having just suffered a head injury. But this, and the detention he was served with, was a small price to pay considering the alternative.

Saturday found Cai sitting on the sofa, watching early morning cartoons as he devoured a bowl of cereal. Greg and Jules were up and about but had yet to come downstairs, so preoccupied were they with their early morning cleansing routine.

"Hey buddy," Greg greeted him as he entered the living room. "Have you seen my keys?" Despite having been up for hours, his hair was sticking up at odd angles, as though he had just got out of bed, and the shirt he was wearing was crumpled, as though he had thrown on the first thing that came to hand.

Cai sighed; this was always his first question. Greg would always start each day with a frenzied search of the living room before finding his keys in the usual place: on the table, in the hall.

Getting up, Cai went out into the hall and retrieved the keys. Returning to the living room, he tossed them to Greg, who caught them deftly and grinned.

"Cheers, mate, you're a life-saver. Hey, we're going down to Salisbury today; wanna come?"

Cai groaned inwardly; was it really that time of year again? Four times a year, Greg and Jules made their regular trip to Stonehenge to celebrate the Winter and Summer Solstice and the Spring and Autumnal Equinox and, every time, they tried to get Cai to tag along.

"Um, I just figured I'd stick around here today; catch up with some homework and stuff," Cai murmured, glancing at the floor.

"Oh, come on," Greg insisted, ruffling Cai's hair good-naturedly. "Blow off the homework for one weekend; it won't be the end of the world."

"I can't," Cai insisted. "I need to finish my History essay."

Greg scoffed. "You don't need to do it now though; it'll still be here when we get back."

Cai hesitated, his mind searching desperately for his next excuse. How could he tell him that the last thing he wanted to do was traipse down to Salisbury, a good three hours' drive away, and watch as men and women, dressed as Druids, took part in ceremonies? Frankly, it was just ridiculous.

At that moment Jules appeared, wearing a red and yellow tie-dye T-shirt and jeans, her hair pulled back into a messy ponytail. She looked expectantly at Greg. "Well?" she asked. "Did you ask him?"

Greg nodded. "Yeah, but he says he needs to do homework and stuff."

Jules scoffed. "Homework? You don't need to do homework."

"That's what I said," Greg agreed.

"You do when you're in Year Eleven and have a tonne of coursework and exams..." Cai retorted.

Greg and Jules shared a look before Jules rolled her eyes and sat down next to Cai on the sofa. "Sure, you could stay here, but think about all the interesting people you could meet; you need to get out and meet people, C," she declared decisively. Reaching out, she cupped Cai's face in her hands, looking at him intently. "You're sixteen, Cai; you need to live a little and experience life."

Cai frowned but said nothing; somehow he didn't think dancing around some old stones qualified as 'living a little'.

"And you've never been to an Equinox, have you?" she reasoned. "You can't learn everything about life in school, you know; sometimes you've got to get yourself out there and experience life itself."

Cai held her gaze for a moment; perhaps a couple of days away from his coursework and thoughts of Ethan would do him good. And maybe she had a point. After all, no matter how much he liked to scoff at some of the things Greg and Jules said and did, there was a small part of him that was curious about it; maybe, if he learnt more about their beliefs, it would bring them closer and he wouldn't feel so alone anymore.

"OK, fine; I'll come," he conceded reluctantly.

"Great!" Greg beamed. "It'll be like the old days: family road trip!" he cried, punching the air in excitement before giving Jules a celebratory high-five.

Cai grinned, touched by the excitement of his foster parents at the prospect of them spending time together as a family. As he went upstairs to pack some clothes, he realised he was quite looking forward to the trip, if only in the hope that it would take his mind off the events of the last few days.

***

"Ah, man, Logan will be so glad to see someone his own age!" Greg beamed.

"Who's Logan?" Cai asked.

"Blu and Sapphire's kid," Jules explained as she dumped her rucksack next to Cai's.

Cai suppressed a laugh; Blu and Sapphire? What kind of names were they?

"Yeah, it's always tough on Logan having to hang out with us oldies," Greg continued. "It'll be good for you both; he's a nice kid."

"So where will we be staying?"

"In the tent, of course; where else?" Greg replied, throwing the tent in the boot before slamming it shut.

"In a tent?" Cai echoed, horrified at the idea; this weekend was rapidly going downhill and they hadn't even got in the car yet.

"There's a field opposite the stones," Jules explained, opening her door.

"We're staying in a field?" Cai asked incredulously.

"What did you expect?" Greg asked, raising his eyebrows. "The Savoy?"

"'Course not," Cai replied. "I just thought we might be staying in a B&B or something."

Greg and Jules began to laugh, much to Cai's annoyance.

"Oh, that's a good one!" Jules giggled. When her laughter had died down, she continued, "You don't go to Stonehenge and stay in a B&B! You go to experience everything!"

"And that includes staying in a field, does it?" Cai mumbled as he got in the car. "I mean, how are three of us supposed to sleep in that thing?"

Greg waved his hand, dismissing Cai's concerns. "Oh, no probs; it'll be a bit of a squeeze, but we'll all fit in, don't worry."

Cai sighed, dropping his head back against the headrest; this was not how he had envisioned spending his weekend. Being squashed into a two-man tent with his foster parents, only to have to get up at four in the morning to run around some stones in a field, worshipping nature was not his idea of fun.

But, then again, it was better than getting beaten up by Ethan Nixon any day of the week.

Chapter Five

The sight that greeted Cai as he climbed out of the car the following morning was spectacular; he had never seen anything like it. The field they had camped in was chock-a-block full with tents, cars and colourfully decorated vans; people wandered about, eagerly reacquainting themselves with friends, their faces lit by the glow of campfires, as they grabbed a quick breakfast. There was a distinct buzz of excitement in the air; it wouldn't be long before they started the eagerly anticipated trek to Stonehenge.

"Hey, man."

At the sound of Logan's, now familiar, voice, Cai turned to see his new friend, still wearing the ripped jeans and oversized hoodie he had worn the previous day, climbing out of his tent; it seemed Blu and Sapphire had been far better prepared than Greg and Jules and had brought a second tent along for Logan.

Logan fought back a yawn as he ran his fingers through his unruly black hair and, pulling his hood up to ward off the early morning chill, he made his way over to Cai.

To look at, the two boys couldn't have been more different: whereas Cai was awkward, Logan was tall and athletic but, thankfully, had none of the arrogance that Ethan and his cronies had; where Cai was quiet and reserved, Logan's easy-going nature was apparent from the start and their conversation the previous night had been easy. Unlike Cai, he always accompanied Blu and Sapphire to these gatherings.

Cai grinned at his new friend. "Is it always like this?" he asked nodding in the direction of the crowds.

Logan nodded, his eyes taking in the sight before him. "Pretty much; always the same, every year." Logan clapped Cai on the back, his grin widening. "Except you, that is; glad to finally meet someone my own age at one of these things. I mean, don't get me wrong, this is all cool but..."

Cai glanced at him; he knew exactly what he meant. This may have been his first time but it was obvious they were the youngest ones here.

"Well, I'm off to freshen up," Logan declared, setting off towards the Portaloos that had been set up the day before.

Cai watched him go. Despite his initial doubts, Logan and his parents weren't that bad, as long as you didn't count their inexplicable liking for homemade dandelion and burdock drinks which, they claimed, cleansed the body. It turned out that Blu was quite a handy chef; someone you definitely needed if you were planning to spend the night in a field. He and Greg had spent the previous evening comparing various vegetarian recipes while Sapphire and Jules had spent the night giggling away like teenagers. All in all, it had been a fun evening.

On hearing rustling in the tent behind him, Cai turned to see Greg crawling out of it, an excited grin on his face.

The only thing that had really ruined it for Cai was trying to squeeze into a very small tent with Greg and Jules, finally resulting in him spending the night on the backseat of the car, his legs curled up in front of him. It wasn't the most comfortable of positions but at least he felt like he had retained some of his dignity.

"Morning, C," he said as he stood up, brushing the damp grass from his knees. He stretched. "God, smell that air!" he cried, taking a deep breath. "It's so fresh; so much better than at home." He came to stand alongside Cai, grinning enthusiastically. "Now, tell me you don't feel closer to nature, just by being here."

Cai said nothing, choosing instead to stare at the crowds; he would never openly admit it but things did feel different here and he found himself starting to understand what Greg and Jules had been talking about all these years. Somehow, it felt like he should be here, like he needed to be here, like he was meant to be here. It was beyond weird; he had never felt like this before. He shook himself, wondering what on Earth was going on with him. Were the stones, and what they stood for, really that powerful or was he just getting caught up in the excitement of it all?

***

Cai drove his hands deeper into his pockets, trying desperately to suppress another shiver as an icy blast cut across his cheeks; not only was it dark and cold, the air was also damp and, to top it all, his back was starting to ache, probably as a result of last night's sleeping arrangements. He looked around as best he could, unable to believe just how close he was to the stones themselves; the barriers had been removed, allowing the worshippers to descend upon the usually cordoned off monument.

Over the years, Cai had seen pictures of Greg and Jules' annual pilgrimages to this place but he had never thought it would affect him quite like this; it was overwhelming, to say the least. He stared up at the monolithic giants towering over the crowd, feeling insignificant in their presence. He shifted uncomfortably; he had the strangest feeling they were watching him but that was ridiculous, they were just stones.

"Bored yet?"

Logan's voice in his ear made Cai jump.

"Hey, whoa, sorry!" Logan apologised hastily. "Didn't realise you were away with the fairies!"

Cai shook his head. "I wasn't; I was just thinking."

Logan nodded, following Cai's gaze to the stones. "Yeah, that's how it gets you," he murmured thoughtfully. After a moment, he shook himself and glanced at Cai. "Come on; the ceremony's about to start."

Cai instantly perked up. "Really?" he asked eagerly; he was fed up with standing around in the cold, waiting for something to happen.

Logan chuckled. "It's OK, your first time's always the most boring; at least next time you'll know what to expect." He glanced at Cai hopefully. "You will come again, won't you?" His face fell as he saw Cai's hesitation. "I'll understand if you don't," he continued, shrugging his shoulders nonchalantly. "If you don't get it, you don't get it and nothing I can say will convince you otherwise."

"It's not that I don't get it," Cai protested, eager to reassure Logan. "It's just... I think I'd rather celebrate the Equinox by staying in a warm bed."

Logan held his gaze for a moment before collapsing in a fit of laughter. "Oh, man, I totally get that!" he cried. "That was a good one!"

Cai grinned, sorry that he would have to be saying goodbye to Logan and his family in a few hours; he had never known anyone quite like him.

Before any more could be said, however, the quiet of the morning was broken by the steady beat of a drum; a man seemed to separate himself from the crowd and was suddenly standing alone in the centre of a circle, his hands raised above his head.

Logan shook Cai's arm and nodded towards the man. "That's Merlin."

Cai stared at Logan in disbelief. "Merlin? As in King Arthur's Merlin?"

Logan snorted. "Don't be stupid! That Merlin would be thousands of years old! And you do realise he was just a character in a story, right? I mean he never actually existed." Cai felt himself blush at his own stupidity but said nothing. Logan watched him suspiciously. "You really aren't cut out for early mornings, are you?"

Cai returned his gaze to the man who was still standing in the same position, waiting for the excited chatter of the crowd to die down.

"It's not his real name, of course," Logan continued quietly. "But he is a Druid and, when he became our leader, he adopted the name. Makes sense really, considering what he looks like."

Cai couldn't have agreed more. The man had a grey beard and was wearing a collection of dark coloured robes; in his left hand he held a staff that he now tapped on the ground. As he did so, the crowd finally fell silent.

"Welcome." Merlin's voice rang out in the silence of the clearing. He looked round at the gathering and smiled. "It is good to see so many familiar faces amongst us, as well as some new." As he said these words, he seemed to look straight at Cai who swallowed nervously. "Before we begin, are there any announcements to make?" He looked around expectantly at the silent crowd. "Very well," he said, starting to pace slowly. "Join hands everyone; join hands with anyone you can, whilst we perform the Druid's Vow." He paused, allowing time for everyone to link hands.

Logan dragged Cai forward, propelling him into the crowd. Before he had a chance to recover, Cai's hands were grabbed by two strangers and held in a vice-like grip. Looking around, Cai saw Logan sandwiched between two people that looked like they had just walked off a medieval film set.

Cai watched as Merlin closed his eyes and raised his face towards the rising sun, holding his arms outstretched, his palms facing upwards.

"We shall repeat the Vow three times," he instructed. He paused briefly before beginning his chant. As Merlin spoke the words, a ray of sunlight appeared on the horizon, causing a surge of excitement to run through the crowd. Cai grinned; this really couldn't have been better timed.

As promised, the Vow was repeated three times and, during the second and third times, Merlin was joined in his chant by everyone gathered around, including Logan. Afterwards, a woman emerged from the crowd, beating a drum while everyone joined her in song. The crowd surged towards Merlin, who still stood looking up at the sky, a rapturous expression on his face.

Seizing his opportunity, Cai slipped silently away, not wanting to be caught in the middle of such an over-excited crowd. He wanted to be alone for a few minutes, away from everyone, to digest what he had just witnessed.

Normally, he would have thought that watching grown men and women in fancy dress, holding hands and chanting in a field would have been the most bizarre sight he would ever see but, actually being there and witnessing the spectacle first hand, it seemed like the most natural thing in the world. Everyone there truly believed in what they were saying and doing; who was he to rubbish their beliefs?

Away from the crowd, Cai breathed a sigh of relief, happy to finally be alone. Sitting down, he rested his head against one of the fallen stones and, closing his eyes, enjoyed the relative silence of this place. He was vaguely aware of the distant drumbeat and murmurings of the crowd but he was determined to tune them out and enjoy the peace and quiet while he could.

But something was making that very difficult. He sighed angrily and launched himself to his knees, determined to find out what was digging into his back; he frowned when he caught sight of it and leant forward to get a better look...

Chapter Six

With only his fingers, Cai frantically dug into the earth, ignoring the dirt that caught under his nails, desperate to free his discovery from its prison. Curling his fingers around its edge, he began to rock it back and forth until he felt it loosen under his grip. Bracing himself, he gave a final tug and grinned triumphantly as it was freed from the ground, the sudden release causing him to fall backwards.

Finding himself staring at the sky, he quickly scrambled to his knees, looking around to see if anyone had seen him. Realising he was still alone, he breathed a sigh of relief. Turning his attention back to his find, he frowned.

Who would bury a *book* at Stonehenge? For a start, how could they get close enough, considering there were usually barriers surrounding it? And *why* would they do it? What possible reason could there be for burying a book in the shadow of the ancient standing stones?

With the palm of his right hand, he rubbed the dirt from the front cover, looking to see if there was a title; there wasn't. The book was bound in dark brown leather, at least, he assumed it was brown; after all, it could just be staining from the mud. It was roughly A5 in size and was quite thick; it looked old, too. He heard the spine crack as he opened it; the pages had turned yellow-brown with age and damp. Flicking through, Cai noticed it was handwritten and that the author had used very tiny script; it was almost as though he or she had wanted to squeeze as much as possible onto its pages.

He squinted at the words, trying to make sense of them, but they kept swimming together making it impossible to read. He rubbed his eyes, but it was no good; he was too tired to focus.

Sighing, he closed the book and slumped back against the rock. What was he going to do with it? He knew what he *should do*: he *should* take the book to the manager of the site and tell him where he had found it. He *should* tell someone about it, even if it was just Greg or Jules…

But…

But there was a tiny little voice in his head that kept telling him he should keep this discovery to himself. He could hide it in his jacket until he got home where he could read it at his leisure, just to see what it was about. It would be an understatement to say he wasn't a little curious about its contents; after all, who wouldn't be? And that was assuming it was of any interest to anyone; it might be really boring... it could be someone's diary, detailing their daily routine or some other mundane activity. Who would be interested in *that*?

On the other hand, it *could be* quite a find and people the world over would be very interested in seeing it, in talking to *him*. It was only right that he hand it over to the appropriate authorities who could find out what the book was about and had people who would study it. Scholars dedicated their whole lives to finding artefacts like this; it wasn't fair that he'd just stumbled across it accidently.

Before he knew what he was doing, he had glanced around and, realising he was still alone, had unzipped his jacket and slipped the book inside, all the while, his heart beating like it wanted to burst free from his chest. He couldn't help himself; it was as though he was on autopilot. His curiosity had won out; he needed to read this book *himself*.

Having zipped his jacket up to his neck, he slipped his hands deep into his pockets and held firmly onto the book to prevent it from dropping out; he was mindful not to make any sudden moves for fear it would jut out at an awkward angle and raise unwanted questions. He looked down making sure that his fears hadn't already been realised.

"*There* you are!"

For the second time that day, Cai jumped at the sound of Logan's voice.

"You need to stop creeping up on me!" he exclaimed, trying to calm his racing heart while, all the time, gripping the book ever tighter.

Logan chuckled. "You need to stop being so highly strung, mate," he retorted. "And you could've
said you were going off; I'd have come with you."

"I was just heading back, actually," Cai said. "I just wanted to have a look around while I had the chance."

The two boys set off together back towards the gathering.

"It's a bit weird the first time, isn't it?" Logan began. "You probably think we're all a bit mad."

Cai chuckled, "Not quite. Actually, I think it's cool you all believe in it so much."

Logan shrugged. "Yeah, well you have to believe in something these days, don't you, otherwise what's the reason to get up in the morning?"

Cai was taken aback by his comment; it was the last thing he had expected Logan to come out with. But, he had to admit it was true. Cai's thoughts drifted back to Ethan; he always felt that no matter what Ethan had thrown at him, worse was yet to come.

"Anyway, the ceremony's over now, so..." Logan looked at him. "We're gonna be leaving; we have a long way to go."

"Yeah, us too."

They caught sight of Blu and Sapphire talking animatedly to Greg and Jules. Heading over to them, Cai felt his heart begin to beat a little faster; he had never been good at keeping secrets from his foster parents... well, apart from the Ethan thing.

"Thank God you found him!" Jules cried, hugging Cai.

"Yeah, he was just..." Logan began.

"Thinking," Cai interrupted quickly.

"Thinking!" Greg exclaimed. "You don't want to do too much of that, C."

"Could do some serious damage to your brain," Blu chipped in, laughing good-naturedly.

Cai smiled awkwardly, unsure how to respond.

"Well, I suppose we had better say our goodbyes," Jules said, a hint of sadness in her voice. "At least for another few months."

As their parents hugged each other and said their goodbyes, Logan turned to Cai.

"Maybe we'll see each other again, eh?" he asked hopefully. "Hey, you could come to the Summer Solstice!" he added enthusiastically.

Cai nodded politely, unsure if he was ready to do this all again so soon. "Yeah, maybe."

Logan held his gaze for a moment before nodding curtly. "Well... see ya!"

Cai watched Logan and his parents walk away, a strange sense of regret settling in his stomach. Why he should feel like that, he didn't

40

know; after all, he had only just met them. But he also knew that he was saying goodbye to the one person who had ever shown any interest in being his friend; a person he would probably never see again.

As he watched Logan leave, he couldn't help wondering if coming back for the Summer Solstice wouldn't be such a bad idea, after all...

Following Greg and Jules across the fields, he tuned out their excited chatter and focused, instead, on the book hidden in his jacket. He wouldn't be able to relax until he got it back home, where it would be safe.

At the car, Cai climbed onto the backseat, folding his arms in front of him in an effort to hide the mysterious book, determined not to fall asleep. However, due to his disturbed night and early rising, coupled with the excitement of the day, he soon lost that battle and succumbed to sleep.

Chapter Seven

The following morning found Cai hiding away in the library at break time, alone with the exception of Mrs Danvers, the sixty-year-old librarian, who was sure to leave him be as long as he remained quiet. And, seeing as he had no intention of talking to anyone about why he was there, that wouldn't be a problem.

He swung his bag onto the table and slid into a chair, cringing as the legs scraped along the wooden floor. Mrs Danvers' head shot up from the book she was reading and, in one swift, practiced movement, slid her glasses midway down her nose, her glare saying more than words ever could.

"Quiet!" she hissed.

"Sorry," Cai mumbled back, by way of apology.

Unzipping his bag, he rummaged inside and pulled out the book. He hadn't had a chance to look at it when he had returned home the previous day; he had spent much of his time sleeping and when he had been awake, Greg and Jules had insisted on talking to him about his experience of the Equinox so that he could 'process his feelings about it'.

He manoeuvred his bag so that it hid the book from Mrs Danvers' view. After a final glance around the empty room, he slid his eyes down onto the page and began to read...

***

Stories usually begin with a birth... mine began with a death.

My death.

I was but a boy when I was called to meet with Vortigern, King of the Britons. My confusion was plain for all to see and when I asked, the King explained that I was there because his Druids had told him to find me; I had a purpose. He sat me down and explained that he had been trying to construct a tower that would exceed the ones before it in strength and grandeur. He went on to tell me that every time his stonemasons built the tower a great rumbling in the earth would cause its collapse. I listened to this tale carefully, wondering how this affected me; in my youthful, foolish innocence, I could not see past my own fate.

When I asked the question, Vortigern told me that he had been consulting his Druids and Soothsayers and that they had told him that he needed to find a fatherless boy: me. I asked him why and he proceeded to tell me that he needed my blood; he needed my blood to sprinkle upon the earth as that was the only thing that would stop the tower from falling.

I said nothing; what could I say? It was not every day that I was told of my death. When I had fitfully recovered, I smiled.

"But, my Lord, your Druids have told you falsely," I said quietly.

Vortigern looked upon me as though I had grown two heads. "You accuse my Druids of falsehood?"

I shook my head, eager to explain myself. "No, I say no such thing, I assure you. I simply mean that they have misunderstood the stars."

Vortigern stared at me long and hard, trying to determine if the words I spoke were true. "How do you know this?"

I sighed. "I have long been in possession of a skill; the skill of prophecy. I tell you that shedding my blood on this ground will not have the effect you desire."

Vortigern narrowed his eyes. "Then what will?" he asked bluntly, clearly desperate.

I stood and looked down upon the site of Vortigern's tower; boulders and rocks lay everywhere, testament to all the failed attempts that had gone before. I pointed to the lake beside the ruins. "Drain the water from the lake," I instructed. "Underneath, you shall find two caves; one the home of a white dragon, the other the home

44

of a red dragon. They have resided under the earth for many years; they are the reason you cannot build your tower."

Vortigern stood and looked at me. He studied
me for some time and must have seen the truth of it in my eyes, for he said, "You shall remain here while my men work."

I watched as he turned and climbed down the mountainside on which we sat, down towards his expectant stonemasons.

I turned to find myself being watched by Vortigern's Druids; their eyes shone out from beneath their hoods, sending shivers down my spine. I turned back to watch Vortigern's men as they set about draining the lake.

Many moons later, the lake was drained, leaving behind an empty chasm in the earth. Vortigern stood on the shore, staring into it for a long time. Eventually he turned to me, threw his arms out to his sides and cried, "Where are your dragons, boy?"

I stood in silence, waiting...

"Well?" the king demanded, his impatience growing. "Answer me!"

I had no need to answer, for the earth did that for me. The ground had suddenly started to shake; it shook so hard that Vortigern was thrown off his feet onto his knees.

My hands flew to my ears as an almighty roar filled the air, joined by another soon after. I kept my eyes trained on what had been the lake and *watched as rocks started to break apart; it wasn't long before an enormous white claw broke through the ground followed, soon after, by a huge scaly head.*

On the shore, Vortigern let out a scream and began scrambling backwards, out of the reach of the white dragon as it let out another deafening roar, lifted its head to the sky and breathed fire up to the heavens. Lowering its head, it looked around before launching itself into the sky.

Suddenly, at the other end of the lake, the earth exploded and a streak of red flew up to meet the white dragon in the sky, immediately latching onto its back, scratching and clawing at it violently. The white dragon let out a cry of anguish as it tried to throw its attacker off. It bucked and jerked from side to side, eventually escaping the red dragon's hold.

The white dragon turned and dove towards its enemy, its eyes flashing menacingly. The red dragon, aware of this, turned and shot up to engage its foe. The two great serpents of the sky collided in mid-air, each tearing and ripping at the other's flesh. Soon both were covered with blood, their own and each other's; droplets fell from the sky like crimson rain.

They fought valiantly and the battle was great, until the red dragon could fight no longer. Letting out a great death cry, it fell heavily to the ground where it moved no more.

The white dragon, victorious in battle, snapped its jaws a final time before flying away, never to be seen again.

Below me, Vortigern crawled from his hiding place, too stunned to speak. Scrambling to his feet, he ran towards the edge of the lake, only to witness the vanishing of the red dragon.

Vortigern stared in disbelief. The lakebed was empty once more, devoid of all trace of the red dragon and the river of blood... as if they had never been. I sensed his confusion as he tried to come to terms with what he had just witnessed.

He looked up at me, our eyes met. I could tell he had many questions, questions that shone brightly in his eyes.

I stepped towards the very edge of the precipice upon which I stood. "The white dragon represented the Saxon invaders, the red dragon, the Britons," I explained, my voice ringing through the silence. "The victory of the white dragon shows that the Saxons will defeat the Britons."

Vortigern stared at me. "Is there nothing we can do?" he asked, his voice weak.

I could not help but notice that he was now seeking my insights; the insights of a seven year old boy! "You, my Lord, will be powerless; however, there will come a time for a great and noble leader to take the throne and he shall fight for us."

Vortigern nodded to himself, accepting his fate...

***

"Correct me if I'm wrong, Cai, but shouldn't you be in class?"

Cai jumped, slamming the book shut. He looked up to find himself looking into the eyes of Mr Grayson. He cleared his throat.

"Um, yeah, I should." He grabbed the book and shoved it into his bag, hastily zipping it up. Swinging it onto his shoulder, he turned to walk past Mr Grayson, muttering a goodbye.

"Not so fast." Mr Grayson nodded towards Cai's bag, a grin forming on his lips. "It must be some story," he commented wryly.

Cai looked at the floor, avoiding Mr Grayson's eyes; he had never been very good at lying. "Yeah, it's... good." He could have kicked himself for being so obvious.

"What is it called? I might try reading it myself."

Cai swallowed. "Um..."

Mr Grayson chuckled. "Relax, Cai; I won't keep you any longer. Get to class."

"Thanks, Sir," Cai mumbled, as he turned and hurried through the library, barely sparing Mrs Danvers a glance as he passed her desk. At the door, he looked back to see Mr Grayson watching him curiously.

Chapter Eight

As soon as the bell rang at the end of the day, Cai was out of his chair, heading towards the school gates, eager for the privacy of his bedroom where he could continue reading the book undisturbed. The close call with Mr Grayson that morning had unnerved him and he had decided it was too risky to read it at school; the last thing he wanted was for anyone to see it and start asking questions.

Ever since he had put the book away, he had felt drawn to it as if it had been calling to him, pulling at him with some inexplicable force. The yearning to read it was so strong he had found concentrating in lessons difficult and had to resort to clenching his hands into fists to stop himself reaching for his bag.

Arriving home, Cai dug into his rucksack, pulling out his keys; he unlocked the door and headed straight for the stairs, taking them two at a time.   Closing his bedroom door behind him, he threw himself onto his bed and slumped against the headboard, trying hard to control his breathing. When he had calmed down, he reached for his bag, took out the book and continued to read.

***

My powers were well known throughout the court, but none knew them better than my Lord and King. I have often used them at the request of my Lord and this time was no different.

When he approached me, I already knew of his question and my answer, but I let him ask anyway; it was important he felt he still had some measure of control over the situation, even though I knew what the result of this fateful night would be.

The door to my quarters opened and the King stood there looking at me beseechingly.

I stood and bowed deeply. "Sire."

The King was quickly fading; he was a shadow of his former self.   His love for the unattainable lady in question was taking its toll.

"The war is not going well, my friend," the King murmured as he closed the door.

As a result of his coveting the Duke of Cornwall's wife, the King had waged war but it was a fight that only one could win. It was episodes like this that made me glad I was above such human foibles.

50

"Is there nothing you can do?" the King pleaded.

I shook my head. "As much as it pains me, I cannot interfere in this war."

The King took my hands in his and fell to his knees, desperation in his voice. "But there must be something *you can do!*" he cried. "You have the *power to do* something!"

I thought for a moment; there was something I had been pondering for a long time, but I was not sure it would work. The risks were enormous for all involved and had the power to change things irrevocably.

I helped the King to his feet and pulled my hands away. "There may be a solution..." I began.

"Then do it!" the King ordered.

"But Sire, there are many risks involved, risks to yourself and your country..."

"Damn the risks!" the King cried, slamming his fist on a nearby table. "You know nothing of what I suffer! I want it to end! Do what you have to do!"

I thought for a moment. "Very well; but first, let me explain what I want from you, my Lord."

The King waved his hand dismissively. "Anything; I will give you anything! If it's gold you want..."

"It is not gold." I paused for a moment, holding the King's gaze. "As a result of your union with Igraine this night, she will conceive a child; your son. When he is born, I will come to you and you shall give him up to me so that I may choose

51

how he is raised to manhood." I held my hand out. "Do you agree to my terms?"

He seized my outstretched hand in his and shook it once. "I agree."

I smiled gravely and bowed my head. "Very well, Sire.   You shall have your wish; Igraine shall be

yours tonight."

I turned away from the King and readied myself, closed my eyes and started to control my breathing.   I turned slowly, imagining the Duke's face before my eyes, picturing his features; his bearded chin, the wild flow of his hair...

I opened my eyes and smiled; to all intents and purposes the Duke of Cornwall was now standing before me, in my chamber.

"How do you feel, Sire?"

The King considered his answer for a moment. "I feel well, my..." He stopped mid-sentence and looked at me. "Bring me a looking glass," he ordered.

I dutifully did as was asked of me and brought him a looking glass.

The King held it up to his face and gasped. He touched his face in wonder.

"The face of my enemy," he whispered.

"Indeed, my Lord," I agreed. "You shall visit with Igraine for she will know no better; she will see only her husband standing before her, returned from battle."

The King laid the glass aside. "What shall happen when the Duke returns and she realises she had not reunited with her husband?"

"Fear not," I murmured. "For tonight will be the Duke's last night upon this earth; one of your warriors will take his life. You have nothing to fear." I paused. "After a suitable period you could suggest a union between the Lady Igraine and yourself, one that will afford her some protection from the many unsuitable men that will surely court her."

The King nodded thoughtfully before grinning. "Very well; I shall take your advice into consideration. But for now, I must take my leave. Good day to you, my friend."

I watched as the door closed and I was left alone in my chamber once more, left alone to consider the turn of events.

That night ended exactly as I had predicted; the Duke was slain and a baby was conceived as a result of Igraine and King Uther Pendragon's union. Time passed swiftly and soon it was time for Igraine's confinement. I waited anxiously for the moment of the boy's birth, confident that all would work in my... no, in Britain's favour.

When at last the baby was brought to me, I took him from the knight and stared down at his sleeping form, innocent of his own destiny. I sent the knight back to the King with a message to tell him the baby would be gone by morning.

That night I took the boy, Arthur, to a family I knew of far away from his destiny, from the throne

53

he would one day sit upon. That night the future King Arthur, High King of Britain, found a home with Sir Ector and his wife, away from the pressures of the throne.

***

Cai tore his eyes away from the book in his hands. Was he *really* expected to believe that he was reading something written during the time of King Arthur? *The* King Arthur? He scoffed; that was just ridiculous.

He closed the book and tossed it to one side, shaking his head in disbelief. This was definitely a hoax, he was now sure of it. Maybe the author of the book wanted whoever found it to go to the authorities to report their find, just so they could have a laugh at their expense and make a name for themselves.

Cai glanced at the book and frowned. Snatching it up, he angled it towards the light shining through the window so that he could see what was embossed on the cover. It was a symbol; a symbol of a cross being held by a dragon, behind which was a circle. Whoever had done this had gone to a lot of trouble.

He sighed and shook his head, returning the book to his bag and taking out his iPod. Putting his earphones in, he turned the music on and pushed all thoughts of King Arthur, the book and the unexplained mystery out of his mind.

Chapter Nine

Over the next few days, the book's calling got worse the more Cai tried to ignore it; even in sleep, he wasn't free, with thoughts of dragons, wizards and kings invading his dreams. He tried to occupy his mind by burying himself in his homework, watching TV or listening to his iPod but nothing seemed to work. Greg and Jules, noticing that he was troubled, had taken him to the meditation room with the aim of 'calming him' and trying to 'focus his mind'; he hadn't the heart to tell them it was useless. He knew the remedy: he needed to read the book.

One day, after school, Cai found himself sitting alone at the bus stop outside his school; most of the kids had boarded the previous bus, but Cai, not wanting to be pushed and shoved on his journey home, had decided to wait for the next one. He sighed, trying to channel his mind, as Greg and Jules had tried to teach him, but it was no good; he had reached the end of his tether.

Unzipping his bag, he dug around inside, searching for the object he knew would ease the headache that had now settled behind his eyes. If he could just read a little more... Victorious, he pulled out the book, dropping the bag beside his feet. He was about to open it when it was suddenly snatched from his grasp.

"What's this then?" Ethan sneered nastily. "Your diary? Bit of a mess, ain't it?" He scoffed, glancing at his friends, before looking back to Cai. "Can't you afford a new one?"

Charlie Slater and Aaron Wilson grinned menacingly as they stood either side of Ethan, who was idly thumbing through the book.

"So, what do you write in here, then? How much you miss Mummy and Daddy?"

Cai stood up wearily and held out his hand. "Give it back."

Ethan glared at him. "Oh, so you *do* have a voice," he murmured sarcastically, studying Cai closely. "I was beginning to think you'd lost your tongue." He shook his head, meeting Cai's gaze. "It's not going to be that easy; you have to get it first."

Before he could respond, Ethan tossed the book to Aaron who jogged backwards a little, holding the book up to Cai.

"Come get it," he taunted, waving it about.

Cai pushed past Ethan and Charlie, focused solely on Aaron. Just as he got within touching distance of the book, Aaron threw it over his head; Cai spun round just in time to see Charlie catch it before tossing it on to Ethan.

Ethan grinned. "Watch it boys, I think he might cry in a minute!" He threw his head back and laughed mockingly.

Seizing his chance, Cai launched himself at Ethan. Ethan stopped laughing and threw the book back to Charlie, but was not quick enough to side-step Cai, who barrelled into him, knocking him to the ground.

"You're gonna bloody regret that, Loser!" Ethan growled, scrambling back to his feet.

He reached out, grabbing the front of Cai's shirt. Cai tried to twist out of Ethan's grasp, but his grip held firm. Ethan grinned wickedly, before bringing his right fist back and punching Cai full in the eye.

Cai fell to the floor, his vision swimming with unshed tears, determined not to cry out. He watched as Ethan snatched the book away from Charlie and stood over him menacingly.

"I think I'm gonna take this home with me," he said, holding the book up. "I reckon this'd make some good bedtime reading..."

But he was cut short when Cai launched himself at him, pummelling him for all he was worth. This wasn't about the book anymore; he just wanted to hurt Ethan as much as he had hurt him over the years.

Suddenly, he felt someone grab the back of his blazer and pull him away from Ethan who was now covering his face with his hands. Cai continued to hit out at his enemy, struggling against the firm grip at his back.

"Cai, stop it!"

Mr Grayson's voice cut through the red fog that had clouded Cai's mind. He stopped struggling, fighting to regain control of himself once more. He stood glaring at Ethan, breathing hard, a dull throbbing around his eye echoing the beating of his heart.

Mr Grayson turned Cai to face him. "It's OK, Cai..."

Cai met his gaze and nodded, as much to convince himself as Mr Grayson.

"Did you see that, Sir?" Ethan cried hastily. He touched his bleeding lip tentatively, glaring accusingly at Cai. "He just flipped out; he completely lost it!" He glanced pointedly at his buddies who nodded their agreement.

Mr Grayson scoffed. "Knock it off, boys. I wasn't born yesterday; I saw what happened." He held out a hand to Charlie. "Give me the book."

"But...!" Ethan cried indignantly, glaring at Charlie, silently forbidding him to do as the teacher asked.

Mr Grayson was firm. "No buts. Give me the book."

Ethan glared at the teacher; realising this was not a fight he could win, he nodded, granting Charlie permission to hand the book over.

Mr Grayson plucked the book from Charlie's hand and returned it to Cai, who clutched it gratefully; as soon as it was safely in his grasp, his need of it intensified tenfold but he willed himself not to acknowledge it.

"I want to see you three in my office at nine o'clock, sharp, tomorrow," Mr Grayson informed the boys.

Ethan went immediately on the defensive. "What? Why?" he cried. "*We're* the victims here!" he added, gesturing wildly to himself and his friends.

"It's not up for discussion," Mr Grayson informed him firmly. "I'll speak to your teachers and make them aware of the situation. Now, go home." He watched as the boys collected their bags. "Oh, and if you think you'll get out of it by skipping school, I'll be speaking to Mrs Gardiner."

Cai couldn't hold back the wry smile that crept across his lips as he saw Ethan pale at the mention of their head teacher; over the years, she and Ethan had had many run-ins and it was common knowledge that she was fast losing patience with him.

As soon as Ethan and his cronies were out of earshot, Mr Grayson turned to Cai. "You OK?"

Cai nodded. "Thanks," he mumbled.

"Any time." Mr Grayson stood awkwardly for a moment, obviously trying to decide how best to proceed. "So... do you want to tell me what that was about?"

Cai shook his head. "Not really."

Mr Grayson ran his fingers through his short, dark hair. "Cai, I can't help you if you don't tell me what's going on," he pointed out exasperatedly.

"Nothing's going on," Cai protested weakly, unwilling to meet his teacher's gaze.

"So, you're telling me it's just a coincidence that Ethan and his friends were around when you just *happened* to fall down the stairs last week and, now, I see them taunting you about a book you're willing to *fight* them for?"

Cai shrugged; there was no way he was about to grass on Ethan, he'd never live it down if he did.

Mr Grayson smiled wryly. "I'll say it again: must be some book."

Cai met his gaze defiantly. "Can I go home now, Sir?"

Mr Grayson nodded reluctantly. "But on two conditions: you let me phone your foster parents to come get you and you think about what I've said."

Cai rolled his eyes. "But I've already told you..."

"I know; nothing's going on." It was clear from his tone that he didn't believe him, no matter how much Cai protested to the contrary. "I'm just saying that if there *was* and if, after some thought, you decide you want to speak to someone, you can come to me. OK?"

Realising Mr Grayson wasn't going to give up his crusade, Cai nodded obediently. "OK."

"Good; now come back to school and I'll ring your parents."

Collecting Cai's bag, he led the way back to school, leaving Cai with no choice but to follow.

Chapter Ten

Cai was aware of Mr Grayson's watchful gaze upon him as he stared resolutely out of the window at the car park. He silently cursed Greg and Jules for the time they were taking to get here; he knew it wouldn't be long before Mr Grayson started asking awkward questions again, and he was running out of ways to avoid answering him.

He pushed himself away from the wall as he saw Greg's car pulling into the car park.

"They're here," he announced, glancing at Mr Grayson.

Mr Grayson nodded and followed Cai out of the building. They reached the car just as Greg climbed out, his eyes fixed questioningly on Cai. Cai said nothing by way of explanation and he watched as Greg and Mr Grayson exchanged a pointed glance before Greg headed over to the teacher.

Cai continued to watch them for a moment before settling himself in the passenger seat; he waited in silence, all the while becoming more aware that the book was in his grasp once again and he desperately needed to read it. Only half an hour ago he had been about to satisfy that need and now... now he was back at square one. For some inexplicable reason, the book felt like it was becoming part of him and that feeling was becoming more intense the longer he had it.

Cai was about to reach for his bag when the door opened and Greg climbed in, barely able to hide his disappointment.

"*Fighting*, Cai?" he asked in disbelief.

Cai said nothing; he could hardly deny it.

Greg shook his head. "This isn't you, C; you don't *fight.*" Receiving no response, he sighed, before starting the engine. "Aren't there enough wars in this world, already? Do you really need to start your own?" He put the car into gear and began to drive out of the car park. Once they were heading away from school, Greg glanced at Cai. "Mr Grayson said there's a chance you're being bullied. This true?" Cai continued to stare out of the window afraid that, if he said anything now, it would all come flooding out. Greg sighed. "Cai, if it's true, you need to tell us; we can't help you if we don't know there's a problem."

"Look, I already told Mr Grayson: I don't want to talk about it."

Greg held up a hand in surrender. "OK, OK; I'll back off. But if you *do* want to talk..."

Cai rolled his eyes. "I know, I know; I can talk to you guys."

Greg glanced at him briefly before returning his attention to the road ahead.

The rest of the journey was spent in silence and it was all Cai could do to stop himself from snatching the book out of his bag and reading it right there and then. He had never been a big reader but this book, and the world within its pages, appealed to him like nothing he had ever experienced before and he longed to be back there once more.

The usually short journey home seemed to take forever but, eventually, Greg pulled into their drive; Cai immediately unclipped his belt and, grabbing his bag, reached for the handle.

No sooner had Greg switched off the engine than Cai was out, heading for the front door. He was about to unlock it when Jules appeared, enveloping Cai in a bear hug.

"Are you OK?" she asked, holding him at arm's length, searching for any obvious signs of injury. Noticing his black eye, she gasped and reached towards his face. "Oh my God, are you...?"

Extricating himself from her grasp, Cai began to move towards the stairs. "I'm fine," he murmured. "I just want to be alone."

Jules began to protest but Greg put a hand on her arm and shook his head.

Cai hesitated a moment; he wanted to say that he was fine and they shouldn't worry, but he couldn't find the words. Instead, he turned and headed for the sanctuary of his room.

With the door closed, he upended his bag onto the bed and grabbed hold of the book. Holding it at arms length, he gazed at the now familiar leather cover and smiled to himself; laying down on the bed, he found his place and continued to read.

***

Life can change in a moment. We can be at our lowest ebb, lost and searching for answers, when suddenly, out of the darkness comes a light, a hero who fights for the good, vanquishing the bad. For us, that hero was Arthur Pendragon, the High King of Britain. His destiny was foretold to me in the stars, just as his father's had been: two dragons in the night sky.

Under Arthur's reign, Britain was restored to the great nation it had once been under his father, the great Uther Pendragon, before the Sea-wolves had invaded, taking advantage of Uther's untimely death.

Now death has come to these lands once more and the country is mourning the passing of King Arthur who left us to reside in Avalon. We are once again facing dark times; times when it may be easier to change allegiances or to run... run to save ourselves...

***

Cai paused, closing his eyes for a moment; his head was aching and he was suddenly feeling exhausted. Every muscle in his body ached and he longed to sleep but he also *needed* to continue reading; he *needed* to keep going.

He opened his eyes and looked at the book; every word seemed to swim together. He squeezed his eyes shut and shook his head before forcing himself to resume reading; he only had a few more lines to go, then he would rest...

***

...But there is hope, for nothing is ever truly lost if we believe there is a solution. Another will come to save us, to lead us, to make us great again, to put down any challenges and right the wrongs that have been done to us.

He will be as strong as his father, as compassionate as his mother and have a heart as brave and true as any of the knights of Britain. His name will be...

***

"What the...?" Cai stared at the words on the page in front of him, unable to believe what he was reading.

He sat up, frantically flicking through the book, searching for an explanation. Flipping once more to the page he had just read, he stared at the tiny handwritten words, a thousand questions running through his mind.

Suddenly, the letters began to swim and merge together, blurring into nothingness; he squeezed his eyes shut but, no matter how much he tried to cling to wakefulness, it was no good. He soon lost his grip on the world around him and knew no more.

Chapter Eleven

Cai opened his eyes to find himself staring up at a canopy of leaves, casting cold, dark shadows all around him; he shivered against the damp air as his senses took in his surroundings. He tried to sit up but a sharp pain, unlike anything he had felt before, shot through his head and stayed, throbbing, behind his eyes. He raised a hand to his left temple but winced, his touch aggravating his black eye.

Realising he was somewhere other than his room, but too tired to care, he dropped backwards, groaning, and pinched the bridge of his nose; his eyes grew heavy once more as he prayed for this weird dream to end...

***

Opening his eyes, Cai felt a wave of nausea wash over him; before he knew what was happening, he leant over the side of the bed and threw up, retching until his stomach was empty. Wiping his mouth, he propped himself up on his elbow and looked around.

No, this couldn't be...

He was lying on a makeshift bed in a clearing in the middle of a forest; there was a fire set up in the middle of the 'camp', the flames dying out. Another bed was set up across from him, on the other side of the fire, but this was empty. Whoever was sharing this camp with him was not here at the moment; he was quite alone.

He sat on the edge of the bed, resting his head in his hands, trying to regain some sense of reality. He had no idea what had happened to him or why he was here, for that matter. He forced himself to breathe deeply, trying to clear his head and make sense of it all.

He tentatively reached for his eye, recoiling as he touched the bruise; so his fight with Ethan hadn't been a dream. But that didn't explain what he was doing here, in the middle of nowhere.

He frowned; did he have concussion? Had he collapsed and gone into some kind of coma? He knew that concussion could seriously mess with a person's head, Mr Grayson had already made that perfectly clear... and that would certainly explain the way he was feeling now and why he had been sick... He felt his heartbeat quicken as fear took hold of him but he fought against it; he couldn't freak out now. He had to stay calm and figure this out.

The last thing he remembered was sitting on his bed having just finished reading the book. He stood up, remembering something, and immediately sat down again, regretting the sudden movement as the world around him spun; he really shouldn't have moved. His heart began to race once more as he recalled the last thing he had read in the book. It couldn't be true... *could it?*

Resting his head in his hands, he cursed the day he had found that bloody book; it had turned his life upside down and been nothing but trouble. As he sat in the silence, he realised that this was the first time he had been able to think clearly since he had found it.

He quickly looked up as he heard leaves crunching underfoot and stared as a man appeared from the trees making his way into camp. He was middle-aged, wearing a black tunic and trousers. His black cloak, draped around his right shoulder, was held together with a silver brooch in the shape of a dragon.

Cai frowned, instantly recognising the design as the one on his bracelet at home.

Noticing Cai's gaze, the man offered a brief smile. "You're awake then?" he observed, sitting down on the empty bed opposite, watching him carefully.

Cai glared at him suspiciously but said nothing. Questions began spinning in his head: who was this man; why was he wearing the same design as on his bracelet? Did it mean something and, if so, what and to whom?

Cai shook his head, trying to regain some sense of control but the questions just kept on coming, wave after wave of them: where was he? How did he get here? Why was he here? How was he going to get home? And why did he feel so weird; had this man drugged and kidnapped him?

Studying the man's face, Cai knew he had the answers to most, if not all, of his questions but knew, instinctively, that he had no intention of explaining anything, anytime soon, if at all.

So he just sat and watched, trying to order his thoughts, trying to focus on something other than the pain and confusion in his head. As he watched the man busy himself turning the fire with a long, heavy branch, an icy fear settled in the pit of his stomach. Occasionally, the man looked over at Cai, as though waiting for him to say something, as though he knew Cai had questions for him.

"What?" Cai asked eventually, unable to keep the defensive tone from his voice.

"How are you feeling now?" the man asked quietly.

Cai snorted. "Like you care," he muttered.

The stranger put the branch aside and stared at Cai. "Oh, but I *do* care actually; it's more than my life's worth to make sure you arrive safely."

"What's *that* supposed to mean?" Cai demanded.

71

The man rested his elbows on his knees and met Cai's gaze. "What do you remember about the time before you woke up?"

Cai thought about that for a moment. Shrugging, he said, "I remember I had a fight with Ethan... a boy in my school," he added by way of explanation. He rubbed his forehead, trying to order his thoughts. "When I got home, I was reading and then..." He met the man's gaze for a moment before searching amongst his blankets; surely it was here somewhere...

"Is this what you're looking for?"

Cai looked up to find the man holding the book in his hand. He held his hand out, a sudden need to possess the book, once more, rushing through him. "Give it back," he demanded.

The man made no attempt to return it; instead he studied the cover reverently. A smile crept onto his face as he gazed at it. Cai stared at the man, trying to figure out his strange behaviour; it was weird as though he had been reunited with something he had been missing for so long.

He glanced at Cai, as if suddenly remembering he was not alone. "It feels good to finally have this back again," he murmured, running his hand over the cover.

Cai frowned and his body tensed, preparing to run. "Who *are* you?" he asked warily.

"Who *I* am can wait," the man replied. "You've been asleep for two days; you need to rest tonight before we start our journey in the morning."

"I'm not going anywhere with you," Cai announced. Then he frowned, the man's words finally reaching him. Shaking his head in disbelief, he said, "Hang on a minute..." He met the man's gaze. "I've been out for *two days?*" he demanded, his anger flaring. He ran his fingers through his hair. "But I was *just* in my room... now I'm God knows where and you're telling me I've been out of it for *two days*?" he raged. He stared at the man, at a loss. "What about Greg and Jules? Do *they* know I'm here?"

The man held up a hand. "Do not worry about your foster parents, Cai..."

"What do you mean *'don't worry about them'*?" Cai retorted angrily. He stood up, trying to work out the best way back to civilisation. "They'll be worried about me; I need to..."

"Cai."

Cai stopped short and looked at the man, taken aback by his commanding tone; he stared at him, transfixed by his gaze, suddenly unable to look away.

"What do know about this book?" the man continued pleasantly, as if Cai hadn't even spoken.

Cai shook his head, frowning. "Nothing; it's just a book," he replied dismissively. But even as he spoke the words, he knew they weren't true; the book had a power, it had a power over *him; he* knew it and he suspected this man knew it, too. He shrugged, trying to appear nonchalant. "It's just a story," he added for good measure. "Why?" he challenged mockingly. "Are you going to tell me it's something else?" He attempted to smile at such an absurd idea.

"I might wonder, if you believe it is nothing more than a story book, why you would ask such a question." He studied Cai carefully. "You sense its power, don't you? In your heart, you *know* this isn't just a story," he stated. The man took a moment before continuing. "The book is a portal, Cai," he explained.

Cai stared at him. "A what?" he asked blankly.

"You were always meant to find it," the man continued, ignoring his question. "And it was always meant to bring you *here*," he added, indicating the forest around them. "I have been waiting for you; we *all* have."

Cai shook his head, trying to clear the grogginess that was settling behind his eyes once more. Was he really expected to believe all this? That the book was some kind of magic portal that had transported him to this place, wherever 'this place' was? He gazed around the camp; everything about it was alien, so different to anything he had experienced before.

The trees cast deep shadows around the camp that even the campfire found hard to penetrate. Cai suppressed a shiver; the last thing he wanted was to appear weak in front of this man.

Cai fixed him with what he hoped was his most determined stare. "Who *are* you?" he demanded. "And how do you know my name?"

The man held Cai's gaze. "There are things you need to know, Cai, and you need to believe what I tell you, no matter how strange they may sound."

Cai narrowed his eyes suspiciously. "How do you know my name?" he repeated, his voice hardening.

Once again, the man ignored his question. "This is not the world you knew; this is..."

Cai frowned. "What...? The future? D'you really expect me to believe that?" He scoffed at the idea.

"Try the *past*, Cai."

"The... *what*?"

"The past," the man repeated. "This is the year 555 AD."

Cai laughed in disbelief. "You've completely lost it! There's no way we've travelled back in time! It's not possible." He laughed, a harsh sound in the silence. "Do you *honestly* expect me to believe that?"

"You have to," the man replied simply. "Because all of this... is *your* destiny."

"My... *what*?"

"Your destiny."

Cai couldn't believe what he was hearing. Not only was this man telling him things that sounded like they belonged in a movie, but he was saying it with a straight face, with not a hint that he was joking.

Standing up, Cai began to pace. "This is ridiculous; I want to go home. *Now*."

The man watched him calmly. "Cai, sit down. Please."

Cai rounded on him. "No way; look, I don't know who put you up to this or for what twisted reasons but it stops now, OK; the joke's over. Take me home."

"I wish I could," the man murmured. "But I cannot; like I said, this is your destiny and you can avoid it no longer." The man stood and approached Cai, holding his gaze. "You know I speak the truth, don't you?" he asked, his dark eyes boring into Cai.

Cai shook his head and began to protest but was interrupted by the man.

"You must know I speak the truth because you are here; you unlocked the book." He stepped closer, forcing Cai to move backwards. "Tell me what you read in the book, Cai."

Cai's determination wavered as his gaze flicked to the book in the man's hand. He swallowed fearfully. "I... I don't remember." He cringed inwardly, hating that he sounded so small and scared.

"Answer the question, Cai," the man commanded.

Unable to withstand the man's penetrating stare any longer, Cai spoke. "It said... it said something about Britain facing dark times; that the King was dead... but that someone was going to come to make everything right again," he explained, tearing his eyes away from the man's gaze, afraid of what he might see there.

"And can you recall *who* that someone was?"

Cai looked up, his head spinning, afraid to answer; terrified of saying the words aloud for fear they were actually true. As it turned out, he didn't need to say anything; the man was only too willing to fill in the blanks.

"It's *you*, Cai," he said, placing his hands on Cai's shoulders and looking deep into his eyes. "*You* are the one we have been waiting for; *you* are the son and heir of King Arthur Pendragon; *you* are the High King of Britain."

Chapter Twelve

Cai stared at the man, blood rushing in his ears, causing his head to throb all the more. This couldn't be true... it was ridiculous. He was no king; he was just a normal teenager trying to keep his head down. This was all just the ramblings of an old man...

"You're mad," he accused. "You must be if you expect me to believe this."

A faint smile touched the man's lips. "But you knew, when you read those words... it spoke of you."

Cai shook his head, wishing the man would stop talking. "But my name is Cai *Freeman*..."

"*Your name is Cai Pendragon,*" the man insisted.

"No... it's *not*," Cai protested, unwilling to believe what he knew to be true; the book had shown him this.

The man continued, "I did not expect you to believe me, Cai; not without proof." The man turned away and made his way across the camp.

"Please; just take me home," Cai pleaded, wrapping his arms around himself, fighting the urge to shiver, suddenly very aware of how cold he was.

The man turned to face him. "Perhaps I should explain some things to you," he conceded, totally ignoring Cai's discomfort.

Cai shook his head. "What, like this game you're playing? Telling me that I'm the son of some mythological man who never even existed?" He shook his head dismissively, still desperate to deny the truth.

A shadow crossed the man's face; Cai had obviously hit a nerve. "That is where you are wrong, Cai," he murmured darkly. "Arthur most certainly *did* exist; you are proof enough of that." He paused, allowing his words sink in. "I was honoured to serve both him *and* his father before him."

Cai rubbed his forehead, wishing this man would just let him go home and return to normality. But he continued, not allowing Cai's tired mind a moment's respite.

"Everything you've read in this book is the truth, Cai," the man explained, holding it up. "I was there for everything that is described in its pages; for *I??* was the one who wrote it."

Cai was unable to find the words to protest anymore; his head hurt, he felt like he was being pummelled with each new revelation.

But the man was relentless.

Bowing his head, the man briefly held Cai's gaze, before announcing, "I am Merlin, faithful servant of Camelot."

Cai staggered to his camp bed, his head a whirling mess of confusion. Resting his head in his hands, he fought down a wave of nausea. "This is crazy," he told himself. "What the Hell's happening to me?" He *was* concussed, he was certain of it now; nothing else made sense...

"I know this is a lot for you to understand, a lot to take in," Merlin admitted quietly. "I know this is hard..."

Cai's head snapped up, his eyes blazing. "You know *nothing*," he shot back adamantly. "How can you *possibly* understand how I feel?"

"*I* was but a boy when I was snatched from my mother's arms and taken to stand before a King; *I* was but a boy when I was told I was going to be sacrificed; *I* was but a boy when I knew my life would never be the same again." Merlin spoke quietly but his voice was hard, detached.

Cai clenched his jaw, recalling the story he had read about the boy who had foretold the King of the dragons under his tower; could it be that it was really true and that he was now in the presence of that boy himself?

"So, you see, Cai," Merlin continued pleasantly. "You are not the only one who has had to face the reality of his destiny. It was the same for me *and* the same for your father." Merlin paused, allowing Cai a moment to gather his thoughts. "When Arthur was sixteen he, also, had to leave a life he was accustomed to; he, too, had to accept he was meant for greater things."

"But... what you're telling me is..." Cai's voice trailed off into silence, at an utter loss now...

Merlin's eyebrows arched and he smiled. "*Crazy*? Is *that* the word you would use?" he asked as he sat on the camp bed across from Cai. "I know this is hard to hear and, you're right to question what I am telling you..." He paused momentarily before adding, "But maybe you'll believe what you see..."

Before Cai could question Merlin further, he had swept his arm in front of him and the ever-darkening camp was suddenly bathed in white light. Shielding his eyes, Cai turned away.

"Cai, you need to see this."

At these words, Cai lowered his hand and turned to find himself looking at the last thing he ever expected to see.

The white light was now replaced with an image of a room; it was dark, lit only by a candle, but Cai could see it had stone walls and a desk in the corner, over which a man was hunched; he wore black clothes and seemed to blend in with the shadows around him.

The image flickered and Cai was reminded of holograms in sci-fi movies he had watched with Greg and Jules. Leaving his bed, he moved closer and dropped to his knees, his gaze riveted to the scene before him; he was so focused on the image before him that the sounds of the forest seemed to fade away.

"What *is* this?" Cai asked, overcome by curiosity and awe.

"Just watch, Cai," Merlin advised softly.

As he watched, he realised that the man at the desk was busy writing, his quill scratching as he wrote. Suddenly, there was frantic pounding on the wooden door on the other side of the room. The man at the desk turned, his quill poised in hand and, with a jolt, Cai realised the man was Merlin.

He glanced warily at Merlin who met his gaze boldly. "Keep watching..."

Cai turned his attention back to the scene and watched as Merlin crossed the room and pulled the door open. A man immediately entered, pushing past Merlin; he was much younger and wore a red tunic and black trousers. His right hand rested on the pommel of the sword at his waist.

"Wait," Cai demanded, frowning in disbelief.

Glancing at Cai, Merlin raised his hand; the picture froze and Cai stared, transfixed...

The man's face had totally caught his attention.

"Do you notice anything, Cai?" Merlin asked his voice gentle and, now, very close.

Cai tore his eyes away; looking up, he saw Merlin standing over him, studying him carefully.

He swallowed but his mouth was suddenly bone dry. Unable to speak, Cai turned his attention back to the scene, moving closer to study the man in more detail.

"He... he looks like me," he acknowledged, finally finding his voice.

And it was true. Granted, the man was broader and taller than Cai but his features were almost identical; they both had the same blue eyes and the same strong jawline. The man even had the same shade of blonde hair as him.

"That's because *he is your father*," Merlin stated gently.

"But... he can't be..." His voice was weak and small in the darkness. Suddenly, something caught his eye. "That's my bracelet," he blurted out before he could stop himself, his gaze now riveted upon the bracelet on the man's right wrist: the silver torque with the dragon etched on it. The one Greg and Jules had told him was with him when he had been found as a baby.

His father's bracelet.

"You mean this?" Merlin asked producing it from his robes.

Cai snatched it from him, gazing down at it in shock. "How did you...?" he asked, glancing up at Merlin.

Merlin smiled. "It's yours, Cai," he replied. "The first, and last, gift your father ever gave you. You were never meant to be apart from it."

Cai dropped his gaze to the bracelet once more, releasing his grip slightly, a lump forming in his throat. He had always wondered at his father's absence from his life, imagining him to be a superhero. Could it be that the truth wasn't that far removed from his fantasies after all?

He shook his head, in an attempt to clear it. What he was seeing and hearing tonight could blow apart everything Cai knew to be true, everything he had grown up believing. Sure, Greg and Jules had had weird beliefs and practices but none of them extended to *this*; *this* was a whole new level.

Cai squeezed his eyes shut hoping that, when he opened them again, all this would be gone; he'd be back home, awake, and in his own bed once more... *Sane*.

But, when he opened his eyes, nothing had changed; he was still looking at the man Merlin claimed to be his father.

As much as he wanted to deny it, to protest against what Merlin was telling him, he could no longer deny the truth to himself, it was there to see: he saw himself in the man's face, in his eyes.

Checking himself, Cai realised what he was doing but could he really believe it? Was he *really* coming around to the idea of being King Arthur's son? Before he could question himself further, Merlin broke in.

"Are you ready to see more?"

Cai frowned as he looked up at the older man. "There's more?" he asked warily.

Merlin smiled and, with a sweep of his arm, the scene continued.

Chapter Thirteen

Merlin watched silently as his lord paced before him, fear and heartbreak etched into his face making him appear far older than his years. He knew why Arthur had sought him out, knew what he was going to ask and he wasn't going to rush him; this was too painful a request. Merlin's heart went out to the young man, a man with so much responsibility on his shoulders.

So he waited.

Suddenly, Arthur turned to him; his blue eyes, usually so clear, were dark and alive with fear.

"The things you told me..." Arthur began quietly. "They were true?"

Merlin heard the fear in his master's voice; he knew Arthur was asking him to deny everything, to admit nothing was set in stone, but he couldn't, however much he wanted to.

Arthur nodded, his strength finally failing him. "And there is nothing you can do to prevent it?"

Merlin bowed his head. "Nothing, my Lord."

Arthur raised his head defiantly, the Pendragon spirit rising within him. "Then you know what has to be done."

Merlin held his gaze for a moment. "Sire, are you sure this is the route you wish to take? There can be no coming back from this decision."

Arthur nodded curtly. "It has to be done; it is the only way we can ensure my son's safety."

Merlin nodded dutifully saying nothing; there was nothing to say. Arthur didn't need sympathy, nor did he seek it; he needed to handle this as a king, not as a father. Kneeling before Arthur, he bowed his head. "I will do everything in my power to keep him safe and, one day, my Lord, he shall return to Camelot; this I promise."

A faint smile touched Arthur's lips. "I can ask for nothing more than that, my friend."

Merlin stood and the two clasped hands, sealing their agreement...

***

The scene faded and Cai's vision blurred.

Rubbing his eyes, Cai sat back on his haunches, unsure of what to think anymore. He was numb. He sensed Merlin's eyes upon him but he couldn't form a single coherent thought.

He knew his eyes had not deceived him, however much he would like to think otherwise but, in his mind, he couldn't shake the idea that what he had just witnessed had been a film, a glimpse into someone else's imagination.

He turned to Merlin, who was still watching him warily, as if afraid he might run. Cai almost smiled at that; running was still a very real possibility.

"What *was* that?" he demanded but, before Merlin had a chance to answer, he continued. "Some trick or special effect? Are there hidden cameras around here?" His eyes darted around the glade, half expecting a cameraman to leap out of the trees.

Merlin smiled. "What you saw, Cai, is the *truth*. Your father knew what he was asking when he came to me that night."

"Which was?" Cai pressed, fearing he already knew the answer.

"For me to take you away; to keep you safe," Merlin explained. "He knew he would never see you again but it had to be done."

Cai frowned. "But *why*?" he demanded. "What kind of father would send his son away?" He felt his temper rising along with his frustration; nothing was making sense.

Merlin met his gaze. "A father who loved *you* above all else; who put *your* safety before everything." He sighed sadly. "I had foreseen

Arthur's death at the hands of his nephew, Mordred. He, and your mother, understood that your safety was paramount, both as their son and as the future king of Britain, so Arthur came to me…" He waved his hand towards Cai. "You know the rest."

Cai nodded absent-mindedly. "So what happened? Did he…?" he started to ask, afraid to voice the words.

Merlin nodded. "Shortly after this, he lost his life on the battlefield defending Camelot and his people."

Cai dropped his gaze to the bracelet he was still desperately clutching, the only connection he had to a man he would never know. He had always dreamed of having a hero for a father, someone who would fight for others and fight the injustices of the world… Could all this, the scene Merlin had shown him, the bracelet… everything that Merlin was telling him… Could it all be *true?*

The rational part of him wanted to run, to put as much distance between him and the man spouting all this nonsense as he could, to return to his normal life with Greg and Jules. But there was a tiny part of him… the part that had always longed for a true family and a sense of belonging that wanted to stay and find out more.

"I understand your confusion," Merlin murmured quietly, interrupting his thoughts. "I know this is a lot for you to take in, for you to accept…"

Cai smiled at Merlin's choice of words; he made it all sound so simple, so easy. He shook his head, exhausted. "I just don't know what you expect me to do with all this," he admitted.

"At the moment, I expect you to do nothing," Merlin replied. He paused. "But... will you permit me to suggest something?"

Cai nodded silently, wondering what else Merlin had in store. "Why not?" he muttered wryly.

"I think you should see your birthright," Merlin explained. "I would like you to accompany me to Camelot."

Chapter Fourteen

"Camelot?" Cai echoed, his throat drier than ever.

Merlin nodded. "Your people await you, Cai."

"My *what*?" Cai demanded, a part of him still wishing this would all reveal itself to be a dream; there was no way he could have people waiting for him but, if there were, they would be sorely disappointed. He had heard the stories of King Arthur and his deeds and he was nothing like that great man...

"Your *mother* awaits you."

Cai's head snapped up and he met Merlin's gaze, his eyes burning with unshed tears. "My...?"

Merlin held his gaze. "Your mother, yes."

Cai dropped his gaze and stared at his hands, his mind racing. He had been so busy thinking about the impossibility of King Arthur

90

being his father that he had totally forgotten he may still have a mother.

Now, he was being told he *had* a mother *and* she was waiting for him!

His heart missed a beat and questions began filling his head. What did she look like? Did he look like her? Would she like him? Would *he* like *her*?

Suddenly, he felt a strong compulsion to accompany Merlin on his journey, wherever it took him, regardless of any doubts he had. Finally he had the chance to meet his mother, a chance he had longed for all his life and he was going to grab it with both hands.

And then he came to a realisation.

"You did this deliberately, didn't you?" he asked.

Merlin stared at him, his face giving nothing away. "I don't know what you mean."

"You knew that, by dangling the prospect of meeting my mother in front of me, I wouldn't be able to say no," he stated.

"And did it work?" Merlin enquired, already knowing the answer.

Cai sighed. "If there's any chance that I could meet her then..." He shrugged. "I have to take it, don't I?" He looked beseechingly at Merlin.

Merlin held his hands up. "I cannot answer that for you," he replied. "Only you can know what's in your heart, Cai."

Cai clenched his jaw, his decision already made, for better or worse. "OK, I'll go with you," he said.

Merlin nodded. "Very well." He stood up and began gathering things together.

Cai watched him for a moment. "What are you doing?"

"We leave first thing in the morning," he informed Cai without looking up. "You have an important day ahead of you tomorrow; you need to rest now, Cai."

Cai nodded, absent-mindedly lying down on his bed. As he lay in the darkness, listening to Merlin moving around the camp, a question formed in his mind.

"What about Greg and Jules?" The words had escaped before he could stop them.

"I'm sorry?"

"My foster parents," Cai explained. "They'll know I've gone missing and call the police."

Merlin paused in his work and turned to face Cai. "No, they won't," he murmured quietly. "You need not worry about them, Cai; at the moment, they remain oblivious to your disappearance and will stay that way until you decide what you want to do."

Cai sat up, glaring at Merlin. "What do you mean?" he snapped. "What the Hell have you done to them?"

"Nothing, I assure you," Merlin murmured. "But if you *do* decide to stay, they will remain oblivious. In fact, they will have no memory of you or your time together; nobody will. However, if you *should* decide to return, everything will be as it was." He glanced at Cai. "The choice is yours."

Cai felt a lump form in his throat at these words; Merlin spoke so dismissively, as if it didn't matter that Greg and Jules' lives would be so empty if he never returned to them. But it did. It mattered to Cai; he hated to think of them alone.

Lying down, he pulled the blanket over him, trying to ignore the ache in his chest.

***

The journey to Camelot was slow and uneventful.

Cai sat rigidly upon the mare Merlin had provided for him, gripping the reins so tightly his knuckles were white. His initial fears about riding a horse had not diminished, despite Merlin's assurances that nothing untoward would happen to him. He fully expected the worst: for the horse to bolt or throw him off.

Merlin glanced at him, amused by his obvious discomfort. "You don't have to worry," he assured him. "Your horse is trained to follow mine."

Cai didn't reply; these words did *nothing* to reassure him. If Merlin's horse bolted, would his follow? Determined to distract himself from further unhelpful thoughts, Cai turned his attention to Merlin.

"So… you said King Arthur was killed in battle?" he asked, glancing warily at Merlin.

The older man nodded. "That's correct; I did." He glanced at Cai. "At Camlann, to be precise."

"Camlann?" Cai echoed.

"Indeed," Merlin murmured. "It was a hard fought battle…" he added quietly, his voice fading away as his mind drifted elsewhere.

Cai glanced at him. "You said something about him being killed by his nephew?"

Merlin nodded. "That's right, I did."

Cai heaved a sigh; Merlin was giving nothing away and Cai's frustration was rapidly increasing. "So, what happened?" he pressed.

Merlin turned in his saddle, appraising Cai for a moment. "As I had prophesised, Arthur met Mordred and his forces on the battlefield," he explained, not once looking at the path ahead; it was obvious he had total faith in his horse. "As I said, it was a hard battle and Mordred was eventually able to better Arthur."

Cai swallowed. He was finding it harder to think of this as just a story and felt an intense rush of hatred towards the man who had been responsible for Arthur's death; he couldn't explain it, it was just there, a part of him.

"However, Arthur was not going to surrender easily," Merlin continued as he recalled what happened next. "With what strength he had left, Arthur killed Mordred…"

"So they killed each other?" Cai realised, feeling smug that Arthur had fought on, even as he lay dying.

Merlin's smile vanished. "Not quite," he replied quietly. "Mordred was carried from the battlefield by his mother, Morgan le Fay, and taken back to their castle where she set upon her heinous task..." He met Cai's gaze. In a very grave voice, he continued, "Using the darkest magic known to man, she brought Mordred back to life."

Cai frowned. "What? But how...?"

"Morgan le Fay is a sorceress, Cai; she has aligned herself with dark forces..."

Cai thought for a moment. "Couldn't *you* have brought *Arthur* back to life?" he demanded.

Merlin shook his head. "No," he replied curtly. "The fact is, Morgan has been lost to the Dark for many years; I will not risk my humanity. Arthur wouldn't have wanted that."

They rode on in silence for a while, Cai trying to digest this new revelation.

"In the wake of Mordred's resurrection, there were a few attempts to take Camelot, ones we easily put down..."

"Why didn't you just destroy them then?" Cai asked.

Merlin smiled. "It is not so easy as you may think; Morgan is very powerful." After a while, he continued. "Their forces have been dormant for many years now, but you should know, Cai: Mordred is now building an army whereby he can once again attempt to claim Camelot as his own.

He and Morgan have begun to slowly invade villages, gathering more people for their army, forcing them into their service."

Cai sat silently, letting Merlin's words sink in; to know that these two were invading villages, killing innocent people, in order to claim a castle, sickened him.

"That is why we need *you*, Cai," Merlin added.

"What?" Cai demanded, horrified. "You just said Morgan was so powerful, *you* couldn't even destroy her; so what do you expect *me* to do?" Despite himself, he felt fear turn his blood to ice and the sudden weight of Merlin's expectations settle on him.

"You are our secret weapon, Cai; Mordred, as yet, knows nothing of you," Merlin explained. "Your presence at Camelot will rally your men and give the kingdom a hope they haven't felt since your father's reign."

A secret weapon? Now he really *did* feel like he was in some kind of movie. How could *he*, Cai Freeman, be anyone's secret weapon? He couldn't even stand up for *himself*, let alone a whole *kingdom*! For years, Ethan had mocked him, bullied him, and he had done nothing; he hadn't even been able to ask for help. So how could anything change now? Cai shook his head adamantly. "But I'm just a kid..."

"So was your father when he became king," Merlin pointed out. "But he was the greatest king Britain has ever known." He paused before

96

adding, "You too, will be a great king: I've seen that in your future."

Cai said nothing. As much as a part of him would like to believe he could be great, Cai knew that the reality was far from that; he was a kid that was bullied, a kid that hid in the toilets when things got tough. He wasn't a man that could command an army; he couldn't lead men into battle. He couldn't rule a kingdom.

Suddenly, he became aware of his horse slowing its pace and he shook himself from his reverie as the two horses crested a hill.

Cai glanced around and realised, for the first time, that they had been heading towards the coast; he could hear seagulls calling out to each other in the distance. A stiff breeze began to pick up and Cai shivered, wishing he was wearing something warmer than his school shirt.

"There," Merlin said, as he reined his horse to a stop. "There is Camelot."

From this vantage point, Cai had a great view of the expansive landscape surrounding the castle, standing proud on the cliff top, overlooking the ocean and the land it ruled.

Even at this distance, Cai felt insignificant in its presence and, as he continued to gaze at it, he felt a great weight of responsibility settle on his shoulders.

A single thought came to his mind: *Camelot* does *exist.*

Merlin flicked his reins and, as they resumed their journey, a strange and unfamiliar feeling overwhelmed Cai: a sense of finally coming home.

Chapter Fifteen

As they approached Camelot, Cai continued to stare in awe at the sight before him, unable to tear his eyes away. Ragged flags, depicting a red rearing dragon on a white background, fluttered in the breeze atop the castle walls, their movements as tired as the material they were made from. The castle was the only building he could see and, in this desolate landscape, it looked even more intimidating the nearer he came.

The castle, it seemed, had been built on two levels: the lower was set further into the cliff top and, from Cai's vantage point, was almost hidden by the upper level which rose forebodingly out of a craggy, rocky landscape. The enormous stone keep, casting dark, elongated shadows across the ground, dwarfed the curtain wall that stood at least ten metres high; Cai could only wonder at the size of the keep beyond the walls. The western side of the castle fell away in a sheer drop to the cliffs and rocks below and, as Cai took in the sight, he recalled Merlin's words the previous night.

"I want you to see your birthright..."

Then it hit him: if everything Merlin had said was true, then all of *this* was his; *Camelot* was his...

And, with that thought, he almost laughed out loud; how could it be that he was the heir to somewhere that, until now, he had never even known existed; a place of myth and legend? It just *couldn't* be true... *Could it?* No, this *was* a dream; a dream from which he would wake up at any moment...

"It's magnificent, isn't it?" Merlin whispered his eyes transfixed, even after all these years.

Cai didn't reply; there were simply no words to describe the feelings he was struggling with. All he could do was nod in agreement.

Before he knew it, they met a rough, stony path that ran around the base of the upper level and, despite everything, Cai felt his heart begin to race in anticipation. From somewhere above him, he heard a shout: a harsh sound that rang out in the silence of the surrounding wilderness. He looked up just in time to see a man turn away from the battlements and disappear from sight. As he watched, he noticed a hive of activity along the walls; more men had been called to look at him, more faces appearing all the time.

"What are they doing?" Cai asked bewildered, glancing uncertainly at Merlin. "Why are they all...?"

Merlin chuckled. "They have all come to witness this great event," he stated simply. "They have come to see their King." He glanced at Cai. "They have waited a long time for this, Cai; many thought they would never live to see it."

Cai swallowed as he continued to sit silently on his horse, trying to come to terms with what was happening. All these people had come to see *him*? *Could* it be that all Merlin had told him *was* really true? He still found it hard to take in but now... *maybe*... just a little part of him was beginning to believe this strange man.

Merlin reined in his horse; reaching over, he did the same for Cai.

Cai stared at him blankly.

"I know this has all been a lot for you take in," Merlin began gently, as though he had read his mind. "I *do* appreciate that, Cai, but..." He gestured at the castle and the people gathered on the ramparts. "These people *need* you. Just as you have been living your life in perfect ignorance, they have been living theirs' in fear and poverty." He met Cai's gaze. "*You* are their hope, their future."

"But..." Cai started to protest.

Merlin sighed. "Do you think this wasn't hard for your father? Do you think *he* didn't feel out of his depth?"

That silenced Cai.

"You will not be alone in this, Cai," Merlin assured him. "There are many people who are

101

willing to help you; people who fought alongside your father. I, for one; I was your father's teacher and I would be honoured to be yours."

"You're forgetting that I might still go back home," Cai pointed out.

Merlin smiled as if he held some secret knowledge of what was to come. "Ah, yes, so I am; how remiss of me."

Cai frowned. "Why are you looking at me like that?" he asked.

"Like what?" Merlin enquired innocently, raising his eyebrows.

"Like you know something I don't," he replied, Merlin's words about his future still echoing in his mind.

Merlin smiled and nodded towards the castle. "Shall we?" he asked. Snapping the reins, his horse set off again along the path to the castle.

With no other option, Cai followed... or rather, his mare did.

The path narrowed as it entered the castle's shadow, dipping slightly as it veered to the right, alongside the castle wall. As they walked beside the wall, Cai looked up, grateful he could no longer see the eager faces staring down at him. The path suddenly turned to the left and they found themselves heading towards an archway. To their right there was what looked like a deep arena cut out of the earth at the centre of which was a wooden post; from this height it made Cai dizzy just looking at it. Focusing, instead, on the archway ahead of them, he watched as a man carrying a spear stepped into view.

He was nothing like Cai had expected. The films he had seen about knights painted them as heroes in shining armour, riding into battle on beautiful white horses, ready to cut down anyone who deserved it and ultimately saving the girl.

But this man... he was very different: hunched over and tired, dark circles ringing his bloodshot eyes, he looked almost beaten. He was unkempt with dirty clothes and looked as if he hadn't shaved in weeks. He looked up at Merlin and inclined his head by way of greeting.

"You're back." It wasn't a question, but a statement.

Merlin dismounted his horse and clasped the man's hand. "As you see."

As Cai watched, the two men smiled and shook hands.

Turning to Cai, the man asked, "So... is this...?" Although the man was looking at Cai, the question was clearly directed at Merlin.

Cai shifted uncomfortably under the man's inquisitive gaze.

Merlin nodded. "It is."

The man inclined his head respectfully, without question. "My Lord."

Cai smiled hesitantly, embarrassed by the title that had been bestowed. "Hello."

Merlin handed his reins to the man as Cai dismounted clumsily, aware of both men's scrutiny. Blushing, he glanced at the stranger as he handed his reins to him, grateful he didn't comment on his pathetic attempt at dismounting. As the horses were led away to the stables, Merlin directed him through the archway into a large empty courtyard, which opened up to their right.

"This is the Lower Courtyard," he announced.

Cai looked around; there was nothing much to see. It was empty and cold, due to the fact that, although the walls were high, there was no roof for added protection. The wall on the right rose up into the air and Cai could see a stone staircase built into it, leading to the upper levels of the castle; the opposite wall also had a staircase but this, Cai noticed, led to the battlements. The remnants of a fire were still glowing in the centre of the courtyard beside which lay two rangy dogs. Upon seeing Cai and Merlin, they got up and trotted further away, retreating into the shadows.

Cai glanced at Merlin. "Where is everyone?" he whispered, for some reason afraid to raise his voice, although what, exactly, he was afraid of, he didn't quite know.

"They will be in the Great Hall in the Upper Courtyard," Merlin replied. "Come." He turned and made his way over to the stairs.

Cai followed, surprised at how steep the steps were. By the time they reached the top, he was breathing heavily and sweating, his legs ached and his muscles were threatening to seize up; a blast of cold wind made him shiver involuntarily. As Merlin moved aside, Cai was met with a sea of expectant faces; it felt like the whole world had turned out to see him. Feeling very self-conscious, he inched closer to Merlin.

The crowd in front of them parted, as Merlin led the way, their eyes fixed on the newcomer. Cai did his best to avoid their gaze, preferring to look at the ground, afraid to look up and see the hope in the faces of the strangers staring back at him; a hope he knew he could *never* fulfil.

He soon realised they were approaching the keep; a set of double doors made of thick, heavy wood embedded with iron studs loomed ahead of them. This, Cai assumed, must be the Great Hall. The two men standing guard turned and pushed the doors open; they bowed their heads as Cai passed.

The heat inside the Great Hall was overwhelming, as was the pungent smell of sweat, made all the worse by the crush of bodies gathered within, waiting; the hall was dark, lit only by a few torches set in sconces around the room. Cai tried to ignore the attention he drew as he entered at Merlin's side but, as the older man led him through the parting crowd, he could hear voices murmuring to each other in wonder. He looked up, curiosity getting the better of him, and caught sight of people pointing and nodding in his direction. He couldn't help but notice that they, like the man at the front gate, were dishevelled and rough looking, the only difference being that their eyes sparkled with hope.

Cai had been so preoccupied with the attention he was drawing that, at first, he hadn't realised Merlin had stopped and was now kneeling on the floor, his head bowed in reverence. Cai lifted his gaze to see a man and woman, seated on thrones mounted upon a stone dais before them; he froze as he found himself looking at the beautiful woman and knew, beyond a shadow of a doubt, that he was looking directly into the face of...

His mother...

Chapter Sixteen

If later, someone had asked him, Cai wouldn't have been able to explain how he knew he was looking at his mother; it was just something he knew in his heart. There *was* no explaining it; it was as if some silent understanding, some secret knowledge had been passed between them.

He continued to stare at the woman sitting in front of him, his mind numb.

He wanted to go to her, to say something but he just stood there, rooted to the spot, as the seconds ticked by. All he could do was stare.

The woman wore a dark green dress, tied at her waist with a simple gold coloured belt; her long, dark brown hair fell about her shoulders and shone in the flickering light of the fire roaring in the hearth to the right of them. Her dark eyes sparkled with unshed tears as she squeezed the hand of the man sitting beside her.

"My son," she whispered as she stood and began to walk towards Cai.

The man next to her stood and addressed the rest of the hall; he was tall and lifted his head proudly as he spoke. "Your Queen needs a moment alone with Merlin and the boy," he announced, his voice deep and resounding. "Leave us; we shall recall you when we are ready." As he fell silent, he looked pointedly at a group of men standing at the foot of the dais and nodded.

Cai watched the crowds as they began to disperse, some of the men shooting him guarded looks; one man, in particular, seemed to be glaring at him long and hard, making no attempt to move, instead, forcing the crowd to move around him. He was rough-shaven, his hair unkempt but Cai got the distinct impression he was a force to be reckoned with.

When the man beside him put a hand on his shoulder, the surly man shrugged it off angrily and strode ahead, towards the dais; he climbed the platform without breaking stride and marched towards the man who had spoken to those gathered.

Upon reaching him, both men turned away and spoke in hushed, frantic voices. The surly man kept looking back over his shoulder, throwing Cai suspicious, angry glances; finally, he turned and stormed out of the near-empty hall, his heavy footsteps echoing loudly on the stone floor.

Cai flinched as the huge doors crashed behind him; he wanted to ask who the man was and why he seemed to have such a problem with him, but was prevented from doing so by his mother, who had now turned to Merlin.

"Merlin," she said softly, taking both his hands in hers. "Thank you so much for taking care of him and returning him safely to us."

Cai watched as Merlin bowed his head respectfully.

"My Lady, it was both my duty and my pleasure," Merlin replied.

The man, who had now returned to his mother's side, took a step towards Merlin and, holding out his hand, said, "We have a lot to be thankful to you for."

Merlin shook his head. "Think nothing of it." He glanced at Cai then back at the two people standing in front of him. "Now, I must retire to my quarters; I have much to do." Taking a step backwards, he bowed his head before turning to Cai. "I shall return soon."

Suddenly fearful, Cai grabbed his arm. "But... You can't leave..." There was still so much he needed to know; things only Merlin could explain.

Merlin gently lifted Cai's hand away. "I know how anxious you must be, Cai, but the time has come for you to face your destiny and you must do that alone. I shall return shortly and then you may tell me of your decision."

Cai watched helplessly as Merlin walked away, the dull thud of the doors echoing behind him. How could he do this? How could he just leave him here, now, when he needed him the most? He turned back to the man and woman in front of him.

"It is so strange, but now that you are standing before me, I can think of no words," the woman said, a tear escaping down her cheek.

"Allow us to introduce ourselves," the man interjected. "I am Sir Lancelot du Lac and this is Guinevere, Queen of Britain and... your mother"

Cai glanced at her and smiled awkwardly.

Lancelot looked between them and said, "I shall leave you both now; you need time alone." He inclined his head respectfully to Cai. As he turned away, he caught Guinevere's eye and smiled supportively before taking his leave.

Left alone, Guinevere indicated the throne Lancelot had vacated. "Please, sit."

Cai moved forward awkwardly, alerting himself to the fact that, for the first time since he had arrived in the Great Hall, he couldn't feel his legs. Thankfully, it was only a few short steps and he was glad to, finally, sit down.

Guinevere sat beside him and, folding her hands in her lap, glanced at him nervously. "I'm so glad you have returned to us, Cai."

Cai looked up when she said his name. "You know my name?" he asked in disbelief.

She smiled and replied simply, "Of course."

Cai smiled wryly. "Sorry, I guess that was a stupid thing to ask."

"No, it was not," Guinevere assured him. "I understand; this must be very strange for you."

"You could say that," Cai admitted wryly. "It's just that... my life has been so different from all this," he said, gesturing around at the now empty hall. "I didn't think I'd ever meet my parents and now... here I am..."

"Yes, here you are," she agreed, smiling warmly. She studied him carefully for a moment before adding, "You look just like your father."

Cai dropped his gaze to the flagstone floor, recalling the scene Merlin had shown him in the forest. He had seen his features in that man's face, had seen the truth but... could he really believe it? Could he really believe that King Arthur was his father? "I just don't know what to think," he admitted quietly.

Guinevere reached out, cupping Cai's cheek and bringing his gaze to meet hers. She smiled. "I imagine this has been a lot for you to take in," she murmured, taking his hand in hers. "I can't imagine what you've been through." She studied him carefully. "You must have many questions."

Cai glanced down at their hands and asked the question he had wanted to ask for so long. "Why did you...? Why was I sent away?"

Guinevere smiled, saddened by the memory. "Your father and I were worried for your safety; when you were conceived, we told no one except Merlin. He helped us hide the truth." She looked away guiltily.

Cai frowned. "Why?"

"Because Britain was a dark place and if Mordred had discovered that King Arthur was to have an heir, he would have searched the world for you, stopping only when he had put an end to your life and any threat you posed."

"But *why*? I was just a baby!"

Guinevere shook her head and tightened her grip on Cai's hand. "You are much, much more than that, Cai; you are a symbol and you stand for the Light that follows Arthur's death. It was because you were a baby that we *had* to protect you... you couldn't protect yourself and without Arthur..."

"But, you couldn't protect yourself, either," Cai protested. He met her gaze boldly, awaiting her reply.

Guinevere sat silently in agreement. "When you were born," she continued, "Merlin came to us... he had already told Arthur that he could protect you, as he had with him. We hated giving you to him but Merlin was a man we could trust. That very night, he took you away and that was the last we saw of you... until now." She lifted her eyes to meet Cai's. "We gave you a gift... a bracelet."

Cai stared at her too shocked to react. Recovering himself, he pulled up his sleeve to reveal the bracelet Merlin had returned to him.

Guinevere stifled a gasp, her eyes filling with tears as she stared at it. "It was your father's, I had given it to him on the day of our wedding," she explained, her voice breaking. She wiped her eyes, attempting to regain her composure. "The first, and last, thing he ever gave you," she continued, echoing the words Merlin had spoken the previous day.

Cai looked down at it numbly, tears welling up in his eyes. His vision blurred and before he could stop himself, he was sobbing; he felt Guinevere's arms around him and, soon, she was crying with him, both of them grieving for the man they had lost.

Chapter Seventeen

"There's just one thing I don't understand."

Guinevere turned towards Cai and frowned. "What is it?"

They had been sitting in silence, content just to be in the other's presence after so long apart, but now the questions in Cai's head were demanding answers.

"Well... how did no one find out you were going to have a baby?" he asked. "I mean, unless you just disappeared, someone *had* to know; it's not exactly something you could hide."

"Not ordinarily, no," Guinevere agreed. "But Merlin is a man of many powers," she added mysteriously.

"Did he do something to you?" Cai demanded, surprising himself with the sudden protective instinct he felt towards this woman, a virtual stranger.

Guinevere chuckled quietly. "Do not worry yourself; he did nothing to harm me," she explained gently, reaching for his hand. "Merlin has the power to alter a person's appearance at will; he did it to your grandfather..."

Cai nodded, his temper cooling. "I know; he told me. He made Uther Pendragon look like the Duke of Cornwall."

Guinevere glanced at him, clearly surprised by his knowledge of this event, before nodding. "That's correct; well... he did a similar thing to me," she said. "He made it appear that I was not with child when, in truth, I was."

Cai was silent for a moment before shaking his head in disbelief. "But he seems so... *ordinary*. How can he...?"

Guinevere smiled. "That is another of Merlin's many talents; he can fade into the background and no one takes any notice of him. But I have a word of advice for you, Cai; *never* underestimate him."

Cai wasn't sure how to take this; what kind of things was Merlin capable of for it to warrant a warning? But before he could question Guinevere further, she changed the subject.

"And how have *you* been?" she asked quietly, her eyes sweeping his face.

Cai was silent, debating whether to tell her the truth; to tell her about Greg and Jules and his problems with Ethan and his gang. But even as he thought about the possibility, he knew he couldn't; he couldn't tell her about what he was going through; he couldn't do that to her. It was already clear that she had struggled with sending him away; he wasn't about to add to her guilt.

So, instead of telling her the truth, he shrugged. "I've been OK," he muttered, telling himself it wasn't a complete lie.

Guinevere smiled, seemingly pleased. "And you will be staying, of course?" she asked hopefully.

Cai met her gaze; he had known this was coming but that still didn't mean he was prepared for the sudden and unexpected fear he felt when he heard the words. Staying meant he would have to accept responsibility for these people; he couldn't cope with that kind of pressure.

Looking up, he met her expectant gaze. "Um..." he floundered, trying to find the right words.

Guinevere gripped his hand desperately, as though suddenly afraid he might run. "We have lost so much time already, Cai," she began. "I cannot bear the thought of losing you again."

Cai saw the hope in her eyes and recalled the same look in the faces of those he had passed on his arrival at Camelot.

Hope he knew he could never fulfil.

Closing his eyes, he tried desperately to shut out Guinevere's imploring gaze but was greeted with the image of King Arthur looking back at him, Merlin's voice echoing in his head.

"You, too, will be a great king... I can see that in your future..."

116

Shaking his head, he opened his eyes and pulled his hand free of Guinevere's grasp. Ignoring the look of hurt and confusion on her face, he stood up, backing away, almost stumbling over his feet in his haste to get away.

Guinevere stood, tears filling her eyes. "Cai..." Her voice was small and weak, tinged with pain.

Cai shook his head adamantly, ignoring the guilt gnawing at him inside. "I can't..." he muttered. "I can't..."

Guinevere took a step towards him, reaching out for him. "Cai, don't go," she pleaded, pain etched across her face.

Cai backed away, afraid of what might happen if he let her near. "No," he said firmly. "This isn't... I can't... *I just can't!*" he cried, turning and sprinting towards the main doors.

Ignoring Guinevere's pleas, he pushed the doors open, pausing momentarily as he laid eyes on the crowd of people waiting outside. As the doors slammed shut behind him, he saw Merlin's concerned face amongst the crowd.

"Cai..." Merlin began, taking a step towards him.

Cai edged away; he needed to put as much distance between himself and these people as possible. Without hesitation, he turned and ran, pushing his way through the crowds. He fought to maintain his balance on the uneven surface of the stone steps as he ran down to the Lower Courtyard; clearing the last few steps with one bound, he sprinted out of Camelot and into the night.

Blood rushed in his ears, his heart pounded, his chest and legs burned, but he kept going, kept pushing himself, too afraid to stop, too afraid to face the truth. In the dark, he had no idea where he was going but he didn't care.

"Stop, Cai."

Merlin's voice in his head made him falter and he started to slow; unable to run anymore, he dropped to his knees. Drawing in lungfuls of the cold night air, his fingers dug into the damp earth as he tried to hold on to something solid while everything around him spun out of control.

"Cai..."

He looked up as Merlin appeared before him, emerging from the shadows.

Cai hung his head, still fighting to control his breathing. "Don't," he panted. "Don't say anything."

Merlin was silent for a moment. "As you wish," he murmured.

Bracing his hands on his knees, Cai concentrated on his breathing, forcing it to return to normal. Now that he was away from Camelot, he felt he could breathe again but he couldn't forget the pain on Guinevere's face as he had turned his back on her. He hated the fact that he had hurt her but hadn't known what else to do and, true to form, had run.

Aware that Merlin was still standing nearby, he looked up. "Why are you still here?" he

118

demanded.

Merlin met his gaze. "You should not be alone at this time."

Cai scoffed. "I've been alone most of my life," he spat bitterly.

Merlin watched for a moment before bowing his head. "Very well, my Lord," he said and turned to
walk away.

Confused, Cai got to his feet. "What, that's it?" he demanded, throwing his arms out in front of him.

Merlin turned to face him, infuriatingly calm. "You asked me to leave," he pointed out.

"Yeah, but..." Cai started to protest.

Merlin took a step towards him, studying him closely. "What else would you like me to do, Cai?" he demanded, his voice hard and unyielding. "Tell you, *again*, that you are King Arthur's heir and that people's hopes rest with you? Tell you, *again*, that Camelot and Britain are at risk of defeat and we need *you* to lead us? I think you heard it clearly the first time."

Cai's shoulders slumped miserably as Merlin's words hit their mark. "I can't handle this," he admitted quietly, covering his face with his hands.

Merlin stepped closer and placed a hand on his shoulder. "Yes, you can," he murmured determinedly. "You are your father's son in every sense, even if you can't see it yourself."

119

Cai looked up at him. "But I'm just a kid," he muttered. "I can't even..." He stopped as an image of Ethan leering down at him appeared in his mind. "I can't even protect myself, let alone all those people," he admitted. Suddenly, a swell of anger rose in his chest and he glared at Merlin. "And you have no right standing there telling me what to do; none of you do!" he cried furiously, gesturing towards Camelot, silhouetted against the night sky. "You put *all this* on me but I have *nothing* to give!" His throat tightened and his vision swam with tears. "*I'm* nothing," he finished quietly.

Merlin gazed down at him. "Do you *really* believe that?"

Cai looked up at him. "Why shouldn't I?" he asked.

Merlin narrowed his gaze. "Is this about those boys at your school?"

Cai stared at him before dropping his gaze, ashamed. "I'm nothing but a coward."

Merlin shook his head. "You're mistaken, Cai," he insisted. "When I look at you, I don't see a coward; I see a young man who has spent so long listening to the words of others that he no longer sees his own virtues, his own strengths." He held Cai's gaze as he continued. "Strength isn't necessarily about fighting others, it's about dealing with the blows life gives you and you have dealt admirably with many blows. Your strength lies in your heart, not your fists."

Cai shook his head, determined to reject Merlin's words. "I'll only be a disappointment: to you, my mother... all those people." He glanced at Camelot guiltily.

Merlin smiled. "The only way you can disappoint us is if you were to leave without even trying." He looked pointedly at Cai. "Maybe it's time you stopped running and live the life you were always destined to."

Cai turned away. Merlin's words had struck a chord deep within him; maybe it *was* time to stop running. He had spent his whole life running, hiding and living in fear but, now, it was time all that stopped. Things needed to change; he was sick of feeling worthless.

He spared a thought for Greg and Jules, guilt swirling in the pit of his stomach; this decision would mean turning his back on them forever. Looking up at the sky, he sent up a silent prayer that, one day, they would find happiness again with another child who needed them, just as he had.

His decision was made.

Turning back to Merlin, he stated boldly, "OK, I'll stay."

Merlin held out his hand.

Cai grasped it, sealing his own fate for better or worse, just as Arthur had done sixteen years ago; the only difference was that, this time, Cai was taking control of his own destiny and facing it alone.

Chapter Eighteen

Cai's return to Camelot was awkward and strained; not because he felt the weight of the expectations of those gathered but because he was embarrassed, embarrassed by his own cowardice. How could he look upon these people now, knowing he had run away? How could they look upon *him* and not feel doubt that he was their leader? They had put so much faith in him and he had already let them down.

As they walked past the guards into the Great Hall, people began to filter in behind him and Merlin as they made their way towards the dais once again. Cai looked up into the anxious eyes of his mother, relieved to see no judgement there; Lancelot stood beside her, watching him intently.

Cai held Guinevere's gaze as he walked towards her, trying to ignore the mutterings of those around him. He climbed the steps and came to a halt before Guinevere as Merlin took his place behind his queen. "I'm sorry," he murmured awkwardly, dropping his gaze to the floor.

Guinevere cupped his face in her hands, encouraging him to look at her. "It is already forgotten," she assured him kindly. She smiled. "You are here now, Cai; that is all that matters."

Cai accepted her words, knowing he had no right to be forgiven so easily.

"Are you staying?" Guinevere asked warily as if afraid of what she may hear.

Cai nodded. "Yes," he replied quietly. "I'm staying."

Guinevere smiled and hugged him.

As she released him, Cai cleared his throat awkwardly, embarrassed by the unexpected display of affection. Thankfully, Lancelot approached Guinevere at that moment and Cai hurriedly moved away; unsure of where to go, he stood beside Merlin, who smiled at him reassuringly.

As Cai stood there, he tried to ignore the fact that all eyes seemed to be trained on him; some were curious, some wary. One gaze, however, was particularly difficult to ignore: the unkempt man who had seemed to have such a problem with his arrival. Cai glanced at him; the man's eyes burned with barely concealed hatred, his hand resting menacingly on the hilt of the sword at his side.

As Cai watched he had the uneasy feeling that, for whatever reason, the man would rather stab him than have him stand on the dais.

Cai's attention was torn away from the man as Lancelot moved closer to Guinevere and whispered something to her. He watched guardedly as Guinevere listened intently before smiling and nodding.

Cai turned to Merlin. "Why is Lancelot always near her?" he asked suspiciously, nodding towards them.

"Lancelot married your mother after your father's death," he explained.

Cai frowned. "He didn't waste much time, did he?" he muttered bitterly, a rush of dislike surging through him as he watched Guinevere touch Lancelot's arm. He'd obviously taken advantage of Guinevere's grief in order to claim Camelot for himself...

"If that is what you think, then you are sorely mistaken," Merlin murmured, his gaze sweeping the crowd now gathered before them in the Great Hall.

Cai stared up at him. Had Merlin just read his mind?

Merlin's gaze slid down to meet Cai's, a smile tugging at his lips. "Your mind is an open book to me, Cai," he said quietly. "One you will learn to close, in time." He turned his attention back to Guinevere and Lancelot. "It is never wise to pass judgement upon others concerning matters of which you have no understanding."

Suitably chastised, Cai felt himself blush; he knew he had no right to judge his mother or Lancelot but he couldn't help it. How was he *supposed* to feel about the man who had married his mother? He was about to defend himself when Lancelot stepped forward, his hand raised; silence descended upon the Hall as everyone turned to face him expectantly.

"We knew this blessed day would come," he announced to the hall. "The day when the throne would be reclaimed by its rightful heir... by King Arthur's son." He turned towards Cai, his eyes alive with wonder; all eyes turned to the teenager.

Cai swallowed hard suddenly unsure of where to look; he hated being the centre of attention at the best of times.

"Cai Pendragon will lead us to victory in our time of need; he will save us from the darkness and bring us into the light," Lancelot continued. He turned and walked towards Cai, his eyes never leaving his.

Cai could only stare, completely taken aback, as Lancelot knelt before him and bowed his head respectfully. He wanted to lean forward and urge the knight to stand, to tell him that he shouldn't be kneeling before him but before he could react, another stepped forward, separating himself from the crowd.

"No," the man growled, his eyes burning into Cai. "This... *boy* cannot be our *King*!" he spat. "This is a travesty to my brother's memory!"

Cai glanced up at the man who was now drawing his sword; it was the unkempt man who had taken such a dislike to him.

Pulling his sword free and holding it aloft, the man ran towards Cai with a war cry of pure fury, hatred burning in his eyes.

Chapter Nineteen

In that moment, it seemed to Cai that the world had slowed right down; he froze and could do nothing but stare helplessly at the man running towards him brandishing his sword. The other men, including Lancelot, who was now on his feet, were so shocked by this sudden attack that they, too, stood motionless.

As the man leapt onto the platform, Merlin stepped forward, his hand outstretched; almost immediately the attacker was thrown backwards by an invisible force. He landed on his back on the stone floor at the feet of the crowd, glaring up at Merlin. Struggling to his feet, he was tackled to the ground by Lancelot.

The two men struggled for a few moments before a couple of other men joined the fray, grabbing the attacker's arms and pinning them behind his back. The man continued to struggle but Lancelot drew back his arm and, bringing it down, slapped him hard across his face with the back of his hand, stilling any further movement.

The hall was silent.

"How *dare* you stand against our King!" Lancelot yelled furiously, looming over Cai's would-be attacker.

"He is *not* my King!" the man spat back defiantly, his eyes burning bright with fury.

"Kay." A soft voice rose above the commotion.

All eyes in the Great Hall turned to Merlin, who took a step towards the group on the floor; the men looked up at him expectantly.

The attacker Merlin had called 'Kay' glared at him defiantly.

"You cannot think me foolish enough to accept the tale that has been spun in the wake of my brother's death, Merlin," he growled. He glowered at the men still holding him as he tried to pull his arms free. "Let me go," he demanded.

Lancelot looked up at Merlin, who nodded his consent. In turn, Lancelot nodded to the two men who released Kay from their grip. Kay got to his feet, and the others followed suit, their eyes never leaving him, ready to grab him if he dared attempt another attack.

Kay stepped away from them, violently stabbing a finger towards Cai. "That boy is *not* my nephew." Gesturing towards the crowd at his back, he continued, "These *fools* may be willing to believe you but *I* am not."

Guinevere stepped forward, looking at Kay beseechingly. "You think so ill of me, Kay?" she asked simply. "You think I would make up such a story? That I would betray Arthur?" Her voice faltered on her late husbands name but she held herself proud, determined not to fall apart in front of her people.

Cai wanted to go to her, to comfort her, but he didn't know how.

Kay glanced at Guinevere and his anger began to waver.

Lancelot took advantage of his hesitation and said, "Can you not see that the boy looks exactly like his father?" He glanced towards Cai. "The likeness is there for all to see, if you choose to," he added.

Kay scoffed, shaking his head in defiance.

Merlin stepped forward. "Whether you choose to believe it or not is neither here nor there," he replied calmly. "It is the truth."

"You cannot expect us to just accept him," Kay protested, slowly mounting the steps to stand eye to eye with Merlin. "He has done *nothing* to prove himself; none of us came to Camelot expecting to just take our place around the Table. *We* had to *earn* it."

Merlin and Lancelot exchanged meaningful glances. Before he knew what he was doing, Cai stepped forward, suddenly aware he was unable to feel his legs.

"Can I say something?" he asked.

Kay turned his gaze upon him. "Ah, the boy speaks!" he cried, his voice dripping with sarcasm.

Merlin glanced at Cai uncertainly. "Are you sure?" he asked quietly.

Cai nodded; everyone seemed to be talking about him, arguing over whether he should take the throne, but no one had thought to ask *him* what *he* wanted. He cleared his throat, buying time as he tried to calm his racing heart.

"I understand why you don't want me here," he said, looking directly at Kay. "I've only just arrived and now everyone's saying that I should be King. But I didn't ask for this," he continued. "I thought I was just a normal kid... but then I'm pulled through a portal, or whatever, and meet a man who tells me I'm King Arthur's son and that he's Merlin and that I'm..." He held Kay's gaze. "This is just as hard for me as it is for you."

Kay said nothing but continued to stare at him, the muscles in his face tightening as he clenched his jaw. "Is *that* why you ran away?" he sneered. "Because it was *hard?*"

Cai dropped his gaze and shifted from foot to foot awkwardly. "That was..." Words failed him; he had no defence, nothing he could say could justify why he ran.

Kay turned to face him, and was about to speak when Lancelot approached him, tearing his attention away from Cai.

"Leave him, Kay," Lancelot ordered. Kay glared at him but said nothing. "He is just a boy," Lancelot added softly.

130

"And *that's* my point," Kay retorted.

Cai lifted his chin determinedly ready to prove that, whatever had happened before, he was now ready to face whatever he needed to. "I don't know what's expected of me but all I can do is try to live up to your expectations."

Kay snorted derisively. "I don't *have* any expectations of you, other than you'll fail."

Cai smiled wryly. "Then I shall prove you wrong," he promised and paused before adding, "I know I have much to prove..."

"Exactly; you *do* have much to prove," Kay agreed. Turning to Lancelot, he added, "You cannot put this *child* on the throne without consulting *us*." He gestured towards the men who had detained him earlier.

Lancelot watched them for a moment, considering Kay's words. He sighed. "Very well," he conceded. "You have a point, Kay."

Cai couldn't help but notice the smug expression that crept onto Kay's face at hearing these words.

"It was wrong of me not to consult with the rest of you," Lancelot continued. "But we could not risk word of Cai's return getting out." He sighed wearily. "I think it best we meet tomorrow; it is late and further discussion now would be futile." Raising his head, he gestured towards the shadows at the back of the hall.

Cai followed his gaze and watched as a boy, about the same age as himself, made his way

131

through the crowd. As the boy climbed the steps and stood in front of him, Cai's jaw dropped.

"*Logan?*" he cried in disbelief.

Logan grinned. "Told you we'd meet again," he said smugly.

Cai frowned, recalling the moment at Stonehenge when Logan had laughed in his face when he had spoken about King Arthur and Merlin. "Did you *know* about all this?" he demanded.

The other boy nodded. "Of course."

"But..."

Logan held his hand up to silence Cai. "Can we talk about this later? It's getting late and I need to show you where we'll be staying while we're training." He grinned. "We're roommates."

Cai felt a hand on his arm and turned to find himself looking at Guinevere.

"This is where we part for a while," she said sadly. "You must complete your training with the Knights and with Merlin. But remember this, my love," she said cupping his face gently in her hands, "I shall always be here, should you need me."

Cai nodded mutely, unsure of what to say. She looked tenderly into his eyes before embracing him. As she released him, he stepped away and followed Logan from the hall, casting one final look back at his mother while, at the same time, trying to ignore the contemptuous glare Kay threw his way.

Chapter Twenty

Cai followed Logan across the courtyard to what looked to be an abandoned building hidden in the shadows at the far end. As they neared their objective, Cai glanced behind them towards the Great Hall; he wasn't sure what he had been expecting to see but the courtyard was now empty. The doors to the Hall were shut and Cai found himself wondering if he was still the topic of conversation.

Casting that thought from his mind, he hurried after Logan. "You made me feel like an idiot at Stonehenge when I asked if that guy was the actual Merlin," he accused.

Logan pulled a face. "Yeah... about that... Sorry, but what else could I do? Tell you the truth?" He scoffed. "Like you'd have believed me."

Cai glared at him, hating the fact that Logan was right.

He slapped Cai on the back. "Much better for you to think *you* were the crazy one," he concluded with a grin.

"Better for who, exactly?" Cai questioned.

Logan laughed, changing the subject. "It's a good job you're staying out here with me seeing as Kay hates you so much; better to keep as much distance between you as possible right now," he stated. "He's been stewing ever since he heard about you."

Cai frowned, surprised. "He *has*?" How was it that his existence had caused such hatred in someone he had never even met?

Logan shrugged, dismissing Cai's obvious concern. "Put it this way: Kay's a funny one. If I were you, I'd just let him get on with it; trust me, he'll get over it sooner or later."

That didn't sound too promising to Cai, who found himself hoping Kay would 'get over it' sooner, rather than later.

Logan stopped dead in his tracks and gestured at the building before them with a flourish. "There she is: home sweet home."

Turning his attention to the sorry excuse of a building in front of him, Cai shook his head in disbelief. The dilapidated building was made of stone but, even in the dark, Cai could see the tiled roof was weather beaten; in fact, it looked as if a strong wind could tear it off at any moment. The wooden door stood open and looked like it was about to fall off its hinges.

Cai stared at him in astonishment. "Are you kidding me?"

Logan turned to him. "What? Not good enough for the High King of Britain?"

If it had been anyone else, Cai would have resented such a comment; but this was Logan and, even though Cai had only known him a short while, he knew sarcasm was Logan's idea of humour.

"No, it's just..." Cai fell silent, searching for the right word.

Logan slapped him on the back. "Relax, Your Majesty, it looks a lot worse than it is." He glanced at the building. "To be fair, I had the same reaction when *I* first saw it; the first night, I actually thought the roof might fall down on top of me."

Cai chuckled, despite himself.

"But, trust me, it soon grows on you." Logan nodded towards the building. "Come on; it's a lot better inside." He walked towards the building, leaving Cai no choice but to follow.

As Cai gingerly edged his way through the doorway, he reached out instinctively to close the door behind him when Logan held up a hand.

"I wouldn't do that, if I were you," he warned. Cai glanced at him questioningly. Logan shrugged. "It's stuck," he explained. "Plus, I'm not sure if it wouldn't just fall off its hinges if we tried to close it."

Cai looked back at the door, his earlier fears confirmed. Releasing his grip, he stepped further inside.

It was now apparent that Logan had been trying to soften the blow when he had said the inside was better than the outside; it clearly wasn't. The building, it appeared, was nothing but a glorified outbuilding and it was all Cai could do to hide his horror as he cast an eye around the room. In the gloom, he could just make out a small wooden table and two rickety chairs in the far corner; straw was strewn across the floor, barely covering the stones.

His heart sank and he shivered as he felt a cold wind blow across his back. Looking up, he noticed two windows set high in the stone walls, neither with any glass. Cai smiled wryly to himself; he should be grateful it had a roof under the circumstances.

"And where are we supposed to *sleep*, exactly?" Cai asked, dreading the answer.

Logan indicated the straw as if the answer were obvious.

"You're kidding, right?"

Clapping him on the back, Logan grinned. "Welcome to the life of a squire, my Lord. This will toughen you up." He turned away to collect something from a corner of the room. "Here," he said, throwing a bundle at him.

Cai attempted to catch it but, as he wasn't expecting it, the bundle hit him square in the face. He looked down at what appeared to be clothes: a dark brown woollen shirt, brown trousers and a black woollen cloak, similar to the one Merlin wore.

"They're your new clothes," Logan announced. "You can hardly walk around in those, can you?" he asked, nodding at Cai's dirty uniform. "You'd stick out like a sore thumb."

Cai smiled, suddenly self-conscious. "I guess not," he replied grimly.

Grateful when Logan turned away, Cai quickly changed clothes, wincing as he pulled the woollen shirt over his head; it was very itchy and uncomfortable but at least he would be warmer now.

Turning to face Cai, Logan grinned at his friend's obvious discomfort. "You'll get used to it, trust me," he said. "You'll be living in those clothes from now on."

"Seriously?" Cai asked, scratching his neck in frustration; it seemed there was an awful lot for him to 'get used to' in this new life.

Logan shrugged. "It's too cold to keep taking them off."

Cai shook his head in disbelief. He sighed, looking around helplessly; if he had thought camping with Greg and Jules was bad, *this* was a thousand times worse.

"Oh, these are yours too," Logan added, kicking a pair of boots across the floor.

Cai glanced at Logan who was now sitting on one of the chairs, watching him carefully. Returning his gaze, Logan leant forward, resting his elbows on his knees. "Go on," he prompted. "Ask your questions; I know you're dying to."

Cai dropped his gaze, his mind whirring into life. Where should he start? He had so many questions but knew he couldn't just hit him with everything in one fell swoop.

"How long have you been here?" he asked, raising his eyes to meet Logan's once more.

"On and off, since I was seven," Logan replied.

"*Seven*?" Cai frowned. "Didn't Blu and Sapphire ever wonder where you were?" he asked.

Logan shrugged. "Never really thought about it; Merlin took care of all that. I mean, I always knew I was meant for this world."

Cai sat silently for a moment. "Do you miss them?" he asked quietly, thinking of his own situation.

Logan shrugged. "Sometimes, I guess; though I try not to think about them too often." He glanced at Cai. "You should try not to either; I mean, you've got enough to deal with and, believe me, you don't need any distractions." He shifted awkwardly in his chair, clearly looking to change the subject.

To this end, Cai continued, "So, Merlin brought you here when you were seven?"

Logan nodded. "Pretty much; I'm like you," he explained. "I don't mean I'm Arthur's son or anything, but my father *was* one of Arthur's knights. He was killed during the Battle of Camlann," he continued, losing his air of

138

confidence for a moment. "One day, Merlin just turned up and told me Blu and Sapphire weren't my real parents; he told me who I really was and that I was destined to serve you one day." He shrugged. "Didn't believe him at first, obviously... I mean, it's not every day Merlin rocks up and tells you you're from another world but then he brought me here and, over time, everything began to make sense, especially when I met you."

Cai stared at him. "Did you already know who I was?"

"Yeah and you have *no* idea how much I wanted to say something!" he cried. "I mean, you're King Arthur's son, man! *King Arthur!* I bet that blows your mind, right?"

Cai scoffed. "Yeah, that's one way of putting it, I guess."

The two fell silent, each lost in their own thoughts. After a few moments, Logan spoke. "It's strange to think that we don't exist back home now." Looking bewildered, he added, "If that makes sense."

Cai glanced at him for a moment, feeling a rush of empathy overwhelm him; their situation, this strange new world, united them both in a way nothing else could. They both knew what it felt like to be brought to a strange world, told that their fathers had been killed and that the parents they *had* known all their lives, now had no memory of them.

"So... what happened to your mother?" Cai asked warily, unsure if Logan would even want to talk about it.

Logan shrugged. "She died giving birth to me apparently."

"I'm sorry," Cai mumbled.

Logan shrugged. "It's OK; it wasn't as if I knew her or anything."

Cai was taken aback by this response, but, as Greg and Jules had always said, people dealt with grief differently and Logan didn't seem the type that would allow anything to get him down for too long.

"What was your father's name?" Cai asked.

"Sir Lamorak," the other boy replied, his demeanour changing almost immediately. "Apparently, he took on thirty knights by himself," he added proudly. "I don't know if it's true, but, if it is, it's kind of cool. I hope I'll be able to do that one day." Standing up, Logan sighed. "Look, we better get some sleep," he advised, crawling into his bed. "It sounds like you have a big day ahead of you tomorrow." He grinned at Cai. "I've never seen them argue over anything; you must bring out the worst in them," he quipped as he turned his back to Cai and promptly fell asleep.

Cai sighed, resigning himself to the truth of Logan's words; he certainly seemed to have pushed Kay's buttons without even trying. As he tried to make himself comfortable in his pathetic excuse for a bed, Lancelot's last words echoed in his mind; tomorrow he would come face to face with the knights again.

His thoughts whirled as questions came thick and fast. What would they say? Would they accept him or would they listen to Kay and reject him? And if they did, what would happen *then*? Would he be cast from Camelot without ever having the chance to know his mother, without ever being given the opportunity to discover who he really was? Surprisingly, the very thought filled him with dread but he pushed it aside, determined not to give up without a fight. He would prove to Kay, and anyone else for that matter, that he was stronger than they thought and that they should, at least, give him a chance.

With this thought in mind, he closed his eyes and was soon asleep, a renewed sense of determination filling him from within.

Chapter Twenty–One

On waking the following morning, there was a moment when Cai thought he was back home in his bed... then consciousness slowly returned to him and he felt the cold, hard reality of the stones beneath him. He sat bolt upright, regretting the sudden move instantly as pain shot through his back; he winced and, massaging his neck, cursed his newfound situation.

"Hurts, doesn't it?"

Cai looked over at Logan who was slouched against the wall, his legs drawn up, his elbows resting on his knees. He looked so at ease and rested that Cai couldn't help feeling envious of him as he massaged his own neck, trying to ease the tension.

"Don't worry; you'll get used to it," Logan assured him, pushing himself away from the stone wall as he got to his feet. He looked down at Cai. "You coming then?"

Cai frowned at him, his sluggish brain taking its time to fully wake up.

"Don't tell me you've forgotten?" Logan asked in disbelief, an amused expression creeping across his face. "You're supposed to meet with the knights this morning so they can decide your fate."

Cai dropped his head in his hands; he *had* forgotten.   The determination he had felt the *previous* night had vanished, and the tidal wave of cold, hard fear at the prospect of coming face to face with Kay again, went no way towards helping his confidence.

Logan nudged him with his boot. "Come on; it wouldn't do to keep them waiting."

Cai sighed and pulled on his boots; getting to his feet, he followed Logan outside into the brisk morning air. The sun had risen, rendering the sky a warm pink and yellow as it broke through the clouds, bathing Camelot in a strange, almost other worldly glow.

Cai glanced around; the two dogs he had spotted upon his arrival were wandering about aimlessly in the shadows while a few men and women hurried back and forth between buildings carrying out their usual morning routines.   He couldn't help but notice that they paused in their work to bow their heads respectfully as he passed and he could feel their eyes following his every move. Forcing himself to continue on his way, he tried to ignore the discomfort he felt as their eyes seemed to bore into him.

It didn't take long for them to reach the Great Hall and it was with great trepidation that Cai watched Logan open the doors to reveal Merlin pacing in front of the dais upon which Cai had stood the night before. As the boys made their way across the reed-strewn floor towards him, he turned and smiled.

"I trust you both slept well?" he enquired, his hands clasped before him.

Cai returned the smile uneasily but said nothing. Instead, he looked around the hall, taking in his, now empty, surroundings and frowned. "Where is everyone?" he asked, indignantly. If he had made the effort to arrive on time, why hadn't the rest of them? They had, after all, been the ones to call this so-called meeting; they could have at least had the decency to turn up on time.

Merlin looked pointedly at Cai. "The rest of the knights are already here," he informed the boys, his eyes never leaving Cai's. "*They* have been waiting for *you* for some time."

Cai instantly felt his stomach drop and looked away uncomfortably; that was the second time in as many days that he had had the uneasy feeling that Merlin could read his mind. It was a far from comforting thought.

"Come." Merlin stepped aside, indicating to his left. "This way."

Logan turned to Cai, grinning from ear to ear. "Wait 'til you see this; it's *so* cool," he

144

enthused as he led the way into the darkened corner.

Cai followed, intrigued, aware of Merlin falling into step behind him. He watched as Logan pulled aside a thick, heavy red curtain and disappeared behind it. Glancing back, Merlin nodded encouragingly and Cai stepped forward, following Logan into the antechamber beyond.

Torches set along the wall cast long shadows around the room revealing the waiting knights looking at them, intently; Logan stood to one side, watching Cai carefully, as if trying to gauge his reaction.

Cai ignored them all, his attention totally focused on the centrepiece of the room. All he could do was stare in wonder as he realised what he was looking at.

The Round Table...

This was the overwhelming thought that ran through his mind.

"Is this...?" he asked quietly, his voice barely above a whisper.

Logan nodded. "It sure is," he confirmed proudly as if he, himself, had built it.

"It really exists then," Cai murmured, taking a step closer, unintentionally, ignoring the five men seated around it.

He was momentarily distracted when a chair scraped against the stone floor. One of the men stood and walked towards him, his eyes fixed on Cai.

Cai stared back warily, unsure of the man's motives; after Kay's attack, he wasn't sure whom he could trust. Cai could only watch silently as the man suddenly dropped to his knee before him, bowing his head.

"My name is Galahad, my Lord." His voice was quiet but very clear and Cai had the feeling that, when this man spoke, *everyone* listened. "I offer myself, and my sword, to you; I will follow wherever you lead."

Galahad fell silent as Cai continued to stare down at the back of his head, the weight of the knight's pledge hanging between them.

Someone scoffed and Kay's voice rang out. "Get to your feet, Galah8ad..."

Cai glared at him but quickly looked back to Galahad. "Thanks, but... you can get up now," he muttered, embarrassed that Galahad remained kneeling.

The knight did as ordered and stood ramrod straight, his eyes fixed on a point behind Cai, as though unwilling to allow himself to relax. He had wavy, dirty-blonde hair and a neatly trimmed beard and he, like the other knights, was dressed simply in a leather tunic and black trousers; an empty scabbard rested against his thigh. As he studied him, Cai recognised him as one of the men that had restrained Kay the previous night.

"Cai, your place is here," Lancelot said as he rose and gestured for Cai to sit in the empty, intricately carved chair between himself and Kay.

Cai nodded, grateful Lancelot had saved him from the increasing awkwardness now settling between himself and Galahad.

Galahad bowed his head and, turning, promptly returned to his seat.

Cai glanced at Kay, who glared back at him; he looked no less pleased to see him now than he had been the previous night. And Cai had to admit, as he approached his designated place, he was less than thrilled at the prospect of sitting next to the man who, only last night, had tried to attack him.

But those thoughts vanished instantly as, on reaching his place, he studied the table; the surface was divided into twelve segments and, in front of each seated knight, lay their sword, the tips of the blades pointing towards the centre of the table. He stared in awe; never, in a million years, would he have ever believed he would be sitting here, at the Round Table, surrounded by knights, in Camelot of all places. He felt like he was on a film set.

He paused as something caught his eye.

King Arthur.

His father's name, etched into the wood. He reached out tracing the pattern of the script. His father had sat here, had ruled Britain from this very seat; it was still so hard to believe.

As his gaze swept over the table, he noticed that, at the widest point of each segment, a name was carved into the wood indicating each knight's place and, for the first time, Cai realised just how few knights sat around the table now; aside from himself, Logan, Lancelot, Galahad and Kay there were only two other men.

Cai recognised one of them as the man who had assisted Lancelot and Galahad in restraining Kay. He was a big man, broad shouldered and solid; stubble darkened his face and his black hair was shoulder length and unkempt. He stared back at Cai impassively, his face unreadable.

The second man watched Cai closely and Cai stared back at him for a moment. His chiselled jaw was clean-shaven and his dark brown hair was swept off his forehead. He was exactly how Cai had always pictured a Knight of the Round Table to be: handsome, muscular and strong. His dark eyes were watchful as he scrutinised Cai carefully. Dropping his gaze to the table, Cai realised with a jolt, that the man was missing his right hand; he stared, wishing he could tear his eyes away, but was fascinated by the deformity nonetheless.

Feeling the man's eyes upon him, Cai looked up; as he met the knight's amused gaze, Cai felt himself blush and hastily looked away.

"Do not let the hand fool you," the man murmured. "I assure you I can still wield a sword." Cai nodded, buoyed by the man's words and the iron in his eyes. The man stood and bowed his head respectfully. "I am Bedivere, my Lord," he declared.

"Don't bow to him, Bedivere!" Kay spat, rising to his feet, slamming his hands down on the table. He shot the other knight a furious look. "And he is *not* your Lord!"

Ignoring Kay, Bedivere raised his head and met Cai's gaze. "Your father was a great man; one I was honoured to serve until the very end."

Kay threw his hands into the air and dropped back into his chair, sensing the futility of his protests; despite himself, Cai felt a surge of smugness flare within him.

Bedivere stood tall as he continued, "If you will accept my sword, my Lord, I, too, would be honoured to serve you."

Cai could practically feel the fury now emanating from Kay; he bit back a retort as Kay made a disbelieving noise in the back of his throat. Instead, he nodded and said, "OK, yeah; sure." Unsure of what to say or do now, Cai sat in his chair, looking around at the knights; he found it difficult to believe these men wanted to declare their loyalty to him when he was just a boy, an untested boy at that. He briefly met Logan's amused gaze, before looking back to Lancelot. "Where's everyone else?" he enquired.

Lancelot hesitated a moment as if it pained him to admit what he was about to say. "These are the only surviving Knights of the Round Table," he said quietly.

Cai stared at him in disbelief. "But yesterday... this place was full..."

"There are many good men at Camelot, Cai... none more so than those who sat at this table." Lancelot paused, momentarily lost in his thoughts. "But not everyone can be a Knight of the Table; that honour must be earned." Cai dropped his gaze, feeling a fraud, as Lancelot continued. "We have lost many great men but, in time, and with you back in Camelot, this table will be whole again."

And just like that, the weight of expectation settled upon Cai's shoulders once more. But before Cai could reply, Kay spoke in his blunt, direct way.

"Yes, well, we are not here to talk about any of that," he pointed out. "Let us not forget the reason we *are* here," he continued, glaring round the table. "To decide just how *worthy* this boy is," he finished, pointing at Cai.

"Kay." Merlin stepped out of the shadows, speaking for the first time since entering the room. Kay glared at him. "Anger will not serve you well in this," he murmured. The muscles in Kay's jaw twitched and his face darkened but he said nothing. "Lancelot?" Merlin prompted as if Kay hadn't spoken.

Lancelot nodded, gathering his thoughts. "We all know why we are here," he said, glancing warily at Kay. He swept his gaze over the sparse gathering. "We need a leader, someone who will inspire our victory; someone who can make Camelot, and Britain, great again."

Kay studied Cai for a moment before scoffing and shaking his head. "*He* couldn't lead us to the next county let alone into war!" he spat.

The man who had yet to introduce himself leant forward in his chair, narrowing his eyes. "Lancelot, Kay has a point; he is but a child..."

150

"As his father was, before him," Bedivere was quick to point out. "Let us not forget that, Gawain."

Gawain acknowledged this and bowed his head in agreement.

Kay leant forward. "Yes, but Arthur was *destined* for this," he argued. "He was strong, a natural born leader…"

"Just as Cai is," Merlin interjected. He glanced at Cai. "Cai's future is a strong one; one that cannot be ignored… by any one of us," he added solemnly, looking at each knight in turn before finally focusing on Kay and Gawain. "What will it take for you to swear yourselves to him?" he asked.

"If I may…" Gawain began.

Lancelot nodded. "Proceed."

"Although I do not agree with Kay's actions last night," he continued, glancing pointedly at Kay, "I *do* understand where he is coming from." He shared a look with Kay before returning his attention to Lancelot. "The boy, no matter what his heritage may be, is untried and untested. I suggest we take the time to train him, to test his strength in times of crisis." He glanced at Logan. "We are still training Logan; he can work alongside him."

Logan caught Cai's eye and the two boys shared a grin.

Lancelot scowled. "You talk as if we have all the time in the world, Gawain; unfortunately, time is a luxury we do *not* have," he said, his voice betraying his impatience and frustration at the situation.

"But you must see that..." Gawain began but fell silent as Cai cleared his throat, determined to have his say.

"You're right," Cai murmured, glancing at Gawain. From the corner of his eye he saw Kay look at him in surprise. "I'm not here for an easy ride; I understand that I have a lot to learn. So give me the chance to learn the skills I need; a chance to prove I *can* do this."

As Cai finished, the room was silent for what seemed like an age.

Lancelot was the first to speak. "You are right, Gawain; it makes sense to take the time to train him now, while Mordred is still ignorant of his existence, rather than rushing in when Cai is not ready," he reasoned. "Let us not forget that Arthur, too, had to learn the skills necessary to become the great man he was." He looked at Cai and smiled. "I see no reason why his son could not be the same if he is given the right tutelage." He turned his attention to Kay and Gawain. "But if he proves himself, you will swear fealty to him?"

Gawain nodded. "You have my word."

Lancelot glanced at Kay. "Kay?" he enquired.

Kay smiled wryly and glanced at Cai. "As you wish," he muttered grudgingly.

At these words, Cai felt himself relax as an overwhelming, and wholly unexpected, feeling of relief washed over him; it wasn't until that

152

moment that he knew just how much their acceptance meant to him. He glanced at Logan who was still grinning back at him.

Lancelot turned to face him again. "You will begin your training in the morning, Cai."

"If I may be so bold," Bedivere said. "I would like to offer my services in Cai's training." He met Lancelot's gaze. "You know my skills with the sword; there is no one better placed to teach him." He spoke with a quiet confidence and it was clear he was stating the facts, as they were, rather than making a boastful declaration of his own prowess; Cai instantly found himself warming to this man and hoped Lancelot would allow him to become his tutor.

Lancelot, however, shook his head. "No, Bedivere," he replied brusquely. "I would prefer you to accompany Galahad when he leaves Camelot; he will be more in need of your skills, I think." He glanced at Kay and Gawain. "We can work with Cai..."

Cai scowled, disappointed by these words.

Bedivere looked no less pleased but said nothing. He bowed his head respectfully. "As you wish."

The rest of the meeting was lost on Cai; voices merged into the background as the knights discussed Bedivere and Galahad's quest to reach out to those people who needed protection.

Cai, instead, found himself thinking about the next stage of his new life. He was scared and excited in equal measure but one thing was for sure: he was ready for whatever came his way; ready, at last, to prove his doubters wrong.

Chapter Twenty-Two

Galahad and Bedivere's departure from Camelot was a long, drawn-out affair but one that fascinated Cai to no end; he had often seen this sort of thing on TV shows and in films but it was something else, entirely, to witness this first hand. The Lower Courtyard was alive with activity as men readied their horses, checked saddlebags and weapons and ensured they had enough supplies for several weeks away. There were so many people, it was a wonder they had room to move; everyone, it seemed, was involved - men, women and children - and there was a great sense of unity between them.

Watching the hive of activity around him, Cai felt all the more like a spare part; everyone was engaged in their own tasks and there was a renewed sense of purpose in the air, as if new life had been breathed into them. Although engrossed in their duties, people passing by would stop to smile at him and bow or curtsey, respectfully, to which he responded with an awkward smile and a nod of his head. They seemed to hold him in high regard, something he still struggled with and found difficult to accept.

Cai was pleased when Guinevere joined him in the courtyard, if only to distract him from dwelling on his discomfort and, although only a few words had passed between them, Cai felt better for her presence.

"Are you quite well, Cai?" Guinevere asked, her concern for him evident.

Cai turned at the sound of her voice. "Er, yeah… I'm fine," he replied quietly, almost ashamed to tell her how he was feeling; although this was only his second day, he didn't want her to worry about his struggle with his newfound role. Anyway, once his training started, he wouldn't have time to even think about it.

Before they could speak further, Lancelot stepped forward and the crowd fell silent. "Today, we witness a great event," he began, his voice ringing out in the expectant silence. "Today, we ride forth to offer hope to our people; hope of a better tomorrow…!"

Cai felt his cheeks blaze as the crowds burst into rapturous applause and began chanting his name; he was still at a loss to understand why *he*, of all people, could offer so much hope to so many.

Suddenly, the wind was knocked out of him as Logan clapped him on the back, the shock of the impact soon dissipating as Guinevere slipped her hand into his and pulled him to her, gently kissing his cheek. As she embraced him, he was aware of nothing but her arms around him, grounding him.

"There are places at Camelot for all who need it; a chance to fight with us, to triumph over the evil that plagues this land..." Lancelot added.

As he continued, Cai couldn't help noticing how passionately the knight spoke in front of so many people, all of whom were now listening attentively, their tasks, momentarily, forgotten; he made it look so... *easy.* Cai couldn't help wondering if, one day, he would be able to speak to as many, as confidently; he doubted it. Public speaking and attention had never been his thing.

He was roused from his thoughts as Bedivere and Galahad approached him.

"Farewell, my Lord," Bedivere said as both knights bowed low.

"Goodbye..." Cai murmured, an awkward silence hanging in the air. "Um... good luck."

The knights straightened and returned to their horses, mounting with ease before leading their men from Camelot to roars of cheering and cries of encouragement.

Logan nudged Cai, nodding towards the line of men leaving. "Just think: one day soon, this will be us," he pointed out wistfully.

Cai's gaze wandered over the scene before them; he was right, one day, this could be them. But, would that day ever come, would they ever be ready? He hadn't even started his training yet and already Logan was imagining them leaving Camelot together... and for what? Would they be going to war? Would they finally be facing Morgan and Mordred? *How do you even begin to fight magic?*

Suddenly feeling overwhelmed, and filled with an intense need to escape, Cai found himself backing away, disappearing into the crowd...

***

Cai slipped into the Great Hall, grateful to be alone; his fears had chased him to the only place he could seek solace, the only place he could be alone at that moment, while everyone was still celebrating outside.

He cringed as the huge wooden doors banged shut behind him, the sound reverberating through the hall. He paused, frozen to the spot, half-expecting Logan to have somehow heard it and come running in, hot on his heals.

But, to his relief, nothing happened. No one came. He was still alone.

In the short time since arriving at Camelot, Logan had seemed to become his shadow, a constant companion; wherever Cai went, he tagged along. It wasn't that Cai wasn't grateful, he was; it was just that, to a boy like Cai, who had never had any real friends to speak of, suddenly having this friendship thrust upon him was a big thing. He wanted to be as easy-going around Logan as Logan was around him but there was a part of him that was always expecting the worst. And the more he thought about it, the more he realised that, maybe, just *maybe*, he was expecting the friendship to be taken away or to just fizzle out, like it was nothing.

Casting these dark thoughts from his mind, Cai focused on the real reason for his return to the Great Hall. Crossing the room, he ignored everything else but the red curtain in the corner; pulling it aside, he stepped through.

The silence of the chamber enveloped him. Standing just inside, he took a few minutes to really *look* at the Round Table, in all its glory. So much had been going on earlier that Cai hadn't really had a chance to experience the real significance of the moment.

This table, something that should have been so simple and unassuming, was probably the most breath-taking, and unbelievable, thing Cai had ever laid eyes on.

It was also one of the few links he had to his father.

Stepping up to the table, he looked at the name etched into the wood in front of him.

Sir Bors.

He glanced to his left and saw Bedivere's name, followed by *Lamorak.*

Cai realised, with a jolt, that this was Logan's father's name; it was also the place Logan had taken at the table.

Moving round he read the other names: *Geraint, Tristan, Percival...*

None of these names meant anything to him, they were just words carved into the wood, memories of a time, and of people, Cai would never know.

He paused as he read the next name on the table; it was a name that sent a shiver down his spine, a name he had heard so much of...

Mordred.

"Cai."

Cai looked up at the sound of his name to see Merlin standing just inside the chamber. For a moment, they did nothing but look at each other; no words were spoken.

Merlin stepped further into the chamber, his eyes never leaving Cai's. "Your father would have been proud of you today," he murmured.

Cai frowned. "But I didn't *do* anything," he protested.

Merlin watched him, a smile touching his lips. "You didn't *do* anything?" he echoed in disbelief. "Cai, you *did* a great deal; you stood your ground in the face of great adversity." His smile widened. "Even your father wasn't one to stand against Kay without good reason." He paused, allowing his words sink in. "He would have been so pleased to see you return to Camelot; to take your rightful place amongst his knights at the table." Merlin's gaze drifted to Arthur's empty chair and he smiled sadly.

Cai followed his gaze, Merlin's words touching him deeper than he would like to admit; for years he had yearned for his mother and father but had accepted his reality, accepted he would never know them. But now that he knew his father was forever out of reach, he realised there had always been a part of him that had hoped he'd meet him one day; that he'd have the chance to get to know him. Instead, he would now have to settle for second-hand accounts of him; memories of strangers who had known and experienced something he never would.

And it *hurt*. It hurt that the man who claimed to love him had sent him away.

His eyes drifted down to the name before him, the name of the man who had started all this; he clenched his fists and moved towards the door, suddenly overcome with the intense desire to destroy the whole bloody table.

Merlin moved to block his path, preventing him from leaving; his eyes fixed on a spot behind Cai.

Cai was too tired to try to force his way past Merlin, so he waited, waited for the older man to relent and move out of his way. Realising this was not about to happen, he took a step forward, in an attempt to force Merlin's hand. "Let me out," he pleaded when Merlin didn't budge.

Merlin didn't respond, his gaze still fixed on a point behind Cai; it was almost as if he were in a trance.

Spotting his chance, Cai made his move but Merlin blocked his way once more.

"Turn around, Cai," he ordered, quietly, now looking directly at him.

Cai huffed angrily. "No; just… get out of my way," he growled, his temper rising all the more.

Merlin took a step towards him, his gaze intensifying. "I said: turn around." His voice was hard, inviting no argument.

Cai glared back at him in defiance, determined to stand his ground. He wasn't about to turn just because Merlin told him to; he wanted to go, to get out…

Despite his determination to the contrary, Cai found himself yielding to Merlin's will as he slowly began to turn around. He tried to resist, tried to fight against whatever Merlin was doing to him, but the more he fought, the weaker his will became and he soon found himself facing the table again.

But, this time, he realised that he and Merlin were no longer alone.

Chapter Twenty-Three

The man sitting at the table stared back at Cai, unmoving; his face drawn, his expression grave. Everything about him was dark, from his dark eyes to the black, loose-fitting clothes he wore. His wild black hair fell to his shoulders in a tangled mess, framing his slim face. He was younger than Cai had envisioned, probably more Galahad's age than Lancelot's.

Cai knew who he was immediately; he didn't need a name on the table to have his fears confirmed. He looked back to Merlin, seeking answers. "Is that...?"

Merlin inclined his head. "Yes, Cai; this is Mordred."

Mordred...

Cai felt the anger burn through him like wildfire as he crossed the room; all he wanted, in

163

that moment of blind fury, was to hurt Mordred, to inflict as much pain on him as he could...

To make him pay for what he had done to his family...

Without thinking, he reached out to grab the front of Mordred's shirt and, pulling his fist back, was poised to hit... but watched helplessly as his left hand completely disappeared into Mordred's chest; he recoiled in horror. Undeterred, he tried again, only for the same thing to happen.

Cai stepped away, dejected, realising he couldn't touch him.

He frowned, trying to understand what was happening; this didn't make any sense. He flinched as a hand touched his shoulder and turned to face Merlin.

"It's an image, Cai; it's not real," he murmured soothingly.

"An *image*?" Cai shook his head, still trying to understand. "But... he looks so *real*." Then, as he took the time to *really look*, he saw subtle signs that this *wasn't* real; like how lifeless Mordred's eyes were and how he seemed to flicker, ever so slightly, as if he had no solid form, just as the image of his father had the previous day.

Beside him, Merlin waved his hand and Mordred faded into nothing. "See?" he asked.

Cai rounded on him, ignoring the sympathy in his eyes. "*Why?*" he demanded angrily. "Why would you *do* that?"

"Do what?" Merlin asked, remaining infuriatingly calm.

Cai pointed at the place where Mordred had been sitting, only a moment ago. "Make him appear," he cried. "Why would you show him to me and then make him disappear?" He was aware his anger was misplaced but, as Mordred was no longer there, Merlin was the next best thing. And, to be honest, it felt good to be shouting at someone; it helped, somehow.

"It's OK to feel like this," Merlin assured him.

Cai turned away and gripped his head in frustration. "I just feel so... *angry*," he admitted, as his temper began to cool. "I didn't even know I felt this angry," he added, turning back to Merlin. "But then I saw him... and it was like..." His voice trailed away; he sighed, leaning back against the wall. "I hate him; I hate him *so* much," he admitted, glaring at the, now empty, chair.

Initially, Merlin didn't speak then took a step towards him. "To answer your question, I conjured this image in order to show you your enemy," he explained, his eyes never leaving Cai. "It is all very well hearing tales about the man and seeing his name etched into a table but you need to see his face; you need to know how you will react when you come face to face with him."

Well, I guess I know now, he thought drily. His eyes went to Mordred's name once more. "Why is his name still here?" he asked. "Why didn't any of you get rid of it?"

165

Merlin followed Cai's line of sight. "His name serves as a reminder," he explained. "It serves as a reminder of what can happen when power is coveted above all else."

"He betrayed my father," Cai reminded him. "He betrayed your King."

Merlin nodded. "He did, Cai; he betrayed us all." He paused for a moment before continuing. "When Mordred first came to Camelot, he was a lot like you and Logan..."

Cai bristled at the very idea of being considered as anything like Mordred; he glared at Merlin and was about to say as much, when Merlin spoke once more.

"It's true, Cai," he insisted, smiling. "He was young, eager and, being Arthur's nephew, had a lot to prove." Merlin's gaze was wistful. "And he did. Thanks to Lancelot, he became a strong knight, well worthy of his place at the table."

Cai frowned, his interest piqued. "What did Lancelot have to do with it?" he asked.

"At first, Lancelot and Mordred became friends," Merlin explained. "They went on many quests together and Arthur trusted him to look out for Mordred in his absence. Between them, Arthur and Lancelot taught him to be a good knight."

Cai scoffed. "Well that didn't work out too well, did it?" he muttered. Looking at Merlin, he asked, "So, if Mordred was such a good knight, what made him betray everyone?"

Merlin slowly shook his head. "The lure of power affects us all in different ways: some turn

166

from it, some respect it... others yearn for it with every fibre of their being. Mordred was one of those men for whom power, and all that came with it, was everything." He sighed. "And, despite his apparent love for Arthur, it soon became clear that he had always harboured a deep hatred of him and coveted his throne; it seemed Mordred had heard a lot from his mother."

Cai studied Merlin carefully. "I don't understand; they hated Arthur just because he was king?"

Merlin smiled wryly. "If only it were that simple," he murmured. Indicating a chair, he said, "Sit down, Cai; this is a long story."

Cai shook his head. "I'd prefer to stand."

Merlin inclined his head in respect. "Very well." He paused a moment, considering his next words. "Morgan was Arthur's half-sister; she was the daughter of Igraine and the Duke of Cornwall." He studied Cai carefully. "I trust you remember the story of the Duke of Cornwall and Uther Pendragon?"

Cai nodded mutely, recalling what he had read in the book: Uther Pendragon, a man so in love with Igraine, the wife of his enemy, had ordered Merlin to change his appearance to that of the Duke so he could trick her into returning his love.

"I am not proud of my actions that night, Cai," Merlin confessed, dropping his gaze. "And if I could go back, I would, but..." He looked at Cai. "What is done is done."

"But how does that have anything to do with Morgan and Mordred?" he demanded, suspecting Merlin was deliberately avoiding answering; which, in turn, begged the question: what was he trying to hide?

"When the war between the Duke and Uther began, Morgan was sent away from Camelot, for her own safety," Merlin explained.

"Hang on..." Cai frowned. "Wasn't Camelot my... Uther Pendragon's castle?"

Merlin smiled. "No, Cai; before Uther, Camelot belonged to the Duke of Cornwall, Morgan's father."

Cai stared at him. "But I thought Camelot always belonged to Uther Pendragon; I didn't realise he had stolen it from the Duke."

Merlin looked grave. "He didn't steal it, Cai; it was the spoils of war." He paused. "But we digress... When Morgan realised her parents' plan to send her away begged her them to let her stay but the Duke was adamant: he sent her to a convent in the north and that is where she stayed for the duration of the war." Merlin paused for a moment before continuing. "When the war ended, Morgan received word of her father's death and her mother's decision to marry Uther Pendragon; Igraine wanted her to return home but Morgan refused."

"Why?" Cai asked; if it had been him, nothing could have kept him from his mother.

"The damage was done: in Morgan's eyes, not only had Igraine sent her away but now she was marrying another man so soon after her father's death," Merlin explained. "It was something she was not prepared to forgive."

Cai nodded; when Merlin put it like that, it was easy to understand her anger. After all, he couldn't deny he hadn't felt the same resentment towards Lancelot; not that he'd ever let that get in the way of him having a relationship with his mother. "So, that was it?" he asked. "She never went back home again? But how does this...?"

Merlin held up a hand to silence him. "It wasn't quite as simple as that, Cai. As soon as Morgan became aware of her mother's plans, she started plotting her revenge. You see, while at the convent, Morgan had learnt how to control the forces of nature and she was a very good student. At that point she was at a crossroads, as I once was: she had to choose between the Light and the Dark. Her mother's news was just the push she needed..."

"She chose the Dark," Cai concluded, totally caught up in the story now.

Merlin nodded. "Indeed. Years passed: Morgan returned to Camelot and was reunited with her mother; the relationship was strained but Uther and Igraine welcomed her, nonetheless. I watched from afar and it soon became clear to me that Morgan had her own reasons for coming to Camelot," Merlin continued. "Shortly after her return, Uther fell ill; Igraine was devastated. She begged me to help which, of course, I did but it soon became apparent he had been poisoned and he was beyond my help: I could do nothing more for him."

"*Morgan!*" Cai breathed, the pieces of the puzzle now falling into place. Merlin nodded, his face grim. "So what happened then?"

"I went to her chambers but she wasn't there; a search of the castle revealed that she was gone," Merlin explained. He shook his head. "She had left before she could be brought to justice. Upon hearing of her husband's death and her daughter's treachery, Igraine fled to her chambers and, shortly after, died of a broken heart." He paused, his eyes tinged with sadness at the memory. "Morgan finally had her revenge."

Cai stared at him, unable to believe what he was hearing; this was more like a TV programme than real life. Could she really be so cold-hearted? Could she really be satisfied by the death of her mother? "Where did she go?" he asked, referring to Morgan.

"I never did find out," Merlin admitted.

"Why not?" Cai asked. "Couldn't you use your power to find her?"

"I could have but Camelot was weak; we had other priorities... *I* had other priorities."

"Like what?"

Merlin smiled. "Like the fact that we had no one to lead us; there was only one thing I could do." Cai stared at him, waiting with baited breath; thankfully he didn't have to wait long. "I had to return Arthur to Camelot; he needed to take his place here, amongst his people."

Cai said nothing, he just stared at Merlin; it hadn't been that long ago that he had said almost the exact same words to *him*.

Before Merlin could continue, however, Logan burst through the red curtain, skidding to a halt at the sight of them.

"I... um... I was looking for you," he said quietly, turning to Cai. He cleared his throat self-consciously. "You just disappeared on me." He glanced at Merlin before returning his gaze to Cai. "Lancelot wants to see you in the armoury."

Cai stared at him. "The...?"

"*Armoury*," Logan repeated, finding it increasingly difficult to hide his enthusiasm. "It's *so* cool..." He faltered momentarily, as if remembering they were not alone.

Merlin smiled. "Forgive me, boys..." He turned to Cai. " I fear I have already taken up too much of your time. We shall continue this another time," he promised as he turned and started to leave.

Cai scrambled away from the wall, reaching out to stop him. "But you can't stop there!" he protested. "I need to know what happened!" He was aware of how desperate he sounded and of the strange look Logan was giving him but he chose to ignore it; he *needed* to know more.

Merlin turned to him. "Cai," he murmured. "You have already heard quite enough for today; you need to take time to digest what you have learnt. Go with Logan. We shall continue this when next we meet." He glanced at Logan then back to Cai. "For the present, focus on what's ahead of you: you have a big day tomorrow and you need to prepare for that."

Cai was silent; he knew Merlin was right. His training began in the morning and he needed to focus on that. Reluctantly, he nodded. "OK, fine," he relented. "We'll talk soon."

Merlin nodded. "We will," he agreed. "Now, I must return to my chambers. I wish you well for tomorrow, Cai," he said, before bowing his head to Cai and Logan in turn.

"Thanks," Cai muttered grimly as Merlin lifted the curtain, disappearing behind it.

Chapter Twenty-Four

As they left the Great Hall, Cai was oblivious to everything, too preoccupied trying to digest what he had just heard. He couldn't believe Morgan Le Fay had cold-heartedly planned the murder of Uther Pendragon as if it were nothing; he couldn't understand how *anyone* could do that.

But then he thought of Mordred; of the all-consuming anger he had felt when he had seen the former knight sitting at the Round Table and he had to ask the question: if Mordred had been real, if he hadn't been an image created by Merlin... how far would *he* have gone? The man had, after all, killed *his* father, just as Uther Pendragon had been responsible for the Duke's death. Could it be that Cai, like Morgan, had it in him to kill in cold blood?

And it wasn't as if he hadn't felt a similar anger before: he had completely lost it with Ethan when, outside school, he had snatched the book from him. If Mr Grayson hadn't pulled him off...

"Hey."

Jerked back to the present by Logan's impatient voice, Cai looked at him.

"What?"

Logan scoffed and shook his head. "You didn't hear a word I said, did you?"

Cai shook his head.

Logan rolled his eyes. "I *said*..." he began deliberately, as if speaking to a particularly slow child. "When are you going to tell me what you and Merlin were talking about?" He studied Cai. "Whatever it was it seemed... intense. And you haven't said a word since we left," he added. "Seriously, what's going on?"

Cai was silent. He couldn't tell Logan what he had really been thinking; if he did, he was sure Logan wouldn't be able to look him in the face, ever again. So, instead, he shook his head and tried to appear dismissive. "It was nothing," he murmured.

Logan raised an eyebrow, clearly not believing a word. "Nothing?" he questioned. "It didn't *look* like nothing."

Cai shrugged, aware of Logan's steady gaze as they continued to cross the courtyard. "He was just telling me about Morgan le Fay."

"Oh, yeah? From what I've heard, she's a total lunatic."

174

Cai smiled; he couldn't have agreed more. He glanced at Logan, bracing himself as he asked, "What do *you* know about her?"

Logan shook his head, pulling a face. "Nothing really; just that she hated Arthur... and she hates you."

"Yeah, that pretty much sums it up," Cai agreed, matter-of-factly.

Logan grinned. "I bet it sucks knowing you're related to her *and* Mordred."

Once more, Cai retreated into his thoughts, Logan's words echoing in his head. He was right, he *was* related to them both; the only two people in the whole world who wanted to destroy him. How unlucky could he be? He almost smiled at the irony of it all. *Almost.*

His mind strayed back to his earlier questions and he was, once again, caught up in his dark thoughts; *their* blood ran through *his* veins. Maybe he and Morgan *weren't* so different, after all...

That thought, alone, made his blood turn to ice.

Thankfully, he couldn't dwell on this as Logan nudged him, pointing towards an outbuilding on the southern side of the courtyard. It, like every other building in Camelot, was made of stone with a thatched roof; a thick trail of smoke rose up into the late afternoon sky.

"This is..." Logan announced, his eyes fixed firmly upon the building ahead. He glanced at Cai, as if suddenly remembering his presence. "...My favourite place in the *whole* of Camelot."

Cai threw him a questioning look; to his eyes, the building looked no different from any other, except for its size. It was certainly larger than most, but he couldn't see what made this one so special. "Why?" he asked, his confusion evident.

Logan grinned at him. "You'll see," he replied enthusiastically.

Cai sighed inwardly, fighting the urge to roll his eyes in exasperation; he had never known anyone who liked to build up suspense quite like Logan.

Picking up his pace, Logan led Cai around the side of the building, deftly sidestepping a group of frantic chickens as he did so, before disappearing through an open doorway. Cai paused at the sound of strange noises emanating from within: rhythmic clangs of metal hitting metal, the hiss of water...

On reaching the door, he stepped inside, instantly recoiling from the intense heat and deafening noise that he tried, in vain, to ignore; the acrid smell of molten metal filled the air. Blinking, he waited until his eyes became accustomed to the semi-darkness of the room, lit only by the fire blazing in the huge forge at its centre. Around this, stood six anvils where men were hunched, relentlessly hammering pieces of metal into shape; wooden tables stood nearby, littered with an assortment of tools, scraps of metal and, much-needed water-skins. Newly forged swords lay in carts, awaiting collection.

The men working the metal were varied in age, some only a few years older than himself, but it was clear they had spent years doing this work; their muscles were testament to that. They worked with an intensity Cai had never seen before; their arms glistened with the sweat pouring off them and their clothes were soaked through, but they remained totally focused on producing weapons for the many men that would soon be arriving to swell their ranks.

Logan came to stand beside him. "What did I tell you?" he demanded. "Cool, eh?"

Cai smiled at his friend's enthusiasm; it was easy to see why Logan liked this place so much: three out of the four walls were lined with weapons and armour. Glancing around, Cai could identify numerous spears, swords, axes and longbows as well as shields, helmets and chainmail; this really was an Aladdin's cave of weaponry.

As he surveyed the weapons, the youngest blacksmith looked up from his work and did a double take, his hammer poised in mid-air, as his eyes landed on Cai. Slowly bringing his hammer down, he let it drop to the floor before unceremoniously dumping the sheet of metal he had been working on into a trough of water; steam rose and a violent hiss filled the room as he made his way over to Cai before sinking, reverently, to his knee. Distracted from their work, the other men soon followed suit.

Cai closed his eyes and sighed; he would never get used to anyone bowing before him. "Please... get up," he implored. "Return to your work," he added, ignoring Logan's inane grin.

The men rose to their feet, the majority returning to their work, only the younger blacksmith remained, his eyes fixed on Cai. His black hair fell to his shoulders, limp and heavy with sweat, and, now, Cai could see his clothes were threadbare and ragged.

"What's your name?" Cai asked.

"Osric, my Lord," he replied. "My father... he owns the forge," he continued, clearly nervous in his presence.

Cai nodded, glancing around. "It's... nice."

Osric bowed his head respectfully at Cai's words, allowing himself a brief smile.

"Where *is* Gadeon?" Logan asked. "Lancelot wanted us to meet here..."

"Ah, yes; forgive me, my Lord," Osric muttered apologetically, casting an anxious look at Cai. "He is out back... Sir Lancelot is with him..." He ran his fingers through his hair before wiping his hands on his trousers. "I'll go and get them, my Lord," he offered before bowing and hurrying away.

Logan chuckled. "That never gets old." He turned to Cai. "It must be so weird to have everyone bowing and scraping to you all the time."

Cai smiled wryly. "Yeah... you could say that," he agreed, his mind wandering back to his life before Camelot; he had only been here a day and already he had been shown more respect than he had ever received in his entire life.

His attention was soon drawn to the back of the building as Lancelot entered, followed by Osric and a balding man that was clearly Osric's father. Gadeon's clothes, like those of his son's, were stained and threadbare; he was a few inches shorter than Osric and it was clear that, in his youth, he had been muscular and fit but age had taken its toll.

His personality was vastly different from that of his son's; upon seeing Cai, Gadeon smiled and made his way over to him, dropping to one knee before him. "My Lord. I am Gadeon, at your service; my forge is yours to command." He straightened, his eyes sweeping over Cai's face before turning to Lancelot. "The image of his father," he breathed in wonder.

Lancelot smiled sadly in acknowledgement. "He certainly is," he murmured.

Gadeon turned back to Cai, placing a hand over his heart. "My Lord, it was my honour to forge weaponry for your father, the greatest King this land has ever known," he declared. "It would be an honour for Osric and I to do the same for you."

Cai shuffled his feet, finding this situation more and more uncomfortable. "Thanks..."

An awkward silence settled in the room but, thankfully, Lancelot chose that moment to speak. "I have asked you here, Cai, in order for Gadeon to provide suitable equipment for your training," he explained.

"OK..." Cai said warily, eyeing the weapons carefully as his heart started to pound. What would he do if they put a sword in his hand...? Or a spear, for that matter? His mind started to whirl at all the possible ways in which he could embarrass himself; the last thing he wanted to do was make a fool of himself in front of everyone.

"First thing's first," Gadeon announced, clapping his hands. "You're going to need mail..." He paused, catching Cai looking at the weapons, and smiled. "I know it's every boys' dream to wield a sword; no doubt you've heard tales of the glory of battle..." he said, looking pointedly at Logan. "But armour is just as important in battle. Come."

Cai followed Gadeon as he led the way and came to a stop in front of an array of mail shirts and leather armour. He watched as Gadeon selected a well-worn, stained, padded shirt.

"This should fit," he said, offering the shirt to Cai.

Cai took it, turning his nose up at the musty smell. "It stinks," he choked, fighting the urge to be sick. "It smells like something died in it."

Logan laughed, clapping Cai on the back. "Get used to it, mate."

"What did you expect? Men have fought and died in that shirt; heroes, every one," Gadeon informed him, proudly.

Cai frowned. "And you want *me* to wear it?"

Folding his arms across his ample chest, Gadeon continued, "Trust me, my Lord, you will be glad of it."

He didn't elaborate and Cai didn't ask further questions, fearing he wouldn't like the answers. Clenching his teeth, he glanced at Logan and Lancelot as he went to remove his shirt.

Gadeon shook his head. "No, put it on over your shirt," he instructed.

Relieved, Cai pulled the padded shirt over his head glad it wouldn't be touching any more flesh than was actually necessary. Looking at Gadeon, he said, "OK, so what now?"

"Now, we find you a mail shirt..." He cast a critical eye over Cai, turned and selected one of the smaller chain mail shirts. Taking it down, he brought it back to him. "Hold your arms out," he instructed before adding, "I want you to understand how heavy this is going to be..." And with that, he placed it unceremoniously into Cai's waiting arms.

Cai let out a cry of surprise as the shirt fell from his grasp and landed in a heap on the floor.

Logan doubled up in laughter while Gadeon smiled, clearly amused. Cai frowned and looked at Lancelot and Osric, the only ones who weren't smiling.

"Pick it up, Cai," Lancelot said quietly.

Cai glanced furtively at the faces watching him, suddenly very aware they were all staring at him, no doubt waiting for his next mistake. Gritting his teeth, Cai bent down and, after a few moments spent struggling with the weight of the shirt, heaved it from the floor. He met Gadeon's gaze head on; the blacksmith looked back at him respectfully.

"How does it feel?" Gadeon asked.

Cai hesitated for a moment. "Heavy," he gasped, stating the obvious, his arms aching under the weight.

Gadeon nodded, smiling. "Heavy, indeed," he agreed.

Lancelot stepped forward, drawing Cai's attention to him. "Get used to it, Cai," he instructed. "You will wear it at every training session, no matter what."

Cai gazed down at the shirt in horror. "Are you serious?" he demanded without thinking. "I can barely lift it, let alone run around in it!"

"It *will* be hard at first," Lancelot agreed matter-of-factly. "But, better you get used to it *now* rather than on the eve of battle, wouldn't you agree?"

Suitably chastised, Cai nodded. "I guess…"

Lancelot signalled for Logan to step forward and, together, they took the shirt from Cai's arms.

Cai looked questioningly at them. "What's happening now?"

"We're going to help you put it on," Lancelot informed him.

Cai shook his head, backing away. "Er, thanks, but I *can* dress myself," he protested indignantly.

Logan scoffed. "No offence, mate, but I doubt that; it took ages before I was able to put it on myself." He grinned reassuringly. "Don't worry, you'll get the hang of it, one day."

'One day' didn't sound at all reassuring to Cai; he couldn't believe the irony of the situation he now found himself in. He was apparently a King... people bowed to him and respected him and yet... he was now wearing a filthy, stinking shirt that would make even a pig sick *and* he couldn't even dress himself.

Left with no other choice, Cai allowed Lancelot and Logan to slip the shirt on over his head, tensing as the cold iron touched his neck. Bracing himself, he looked down; the chain mail hung like a t-shirt, except it was colder, and a hell of a lot heavier, and Cai found himself tensing under its incredible weight.

How was he even meant to move in this thing, let alone fight...?

"Relax," Gadeon advised. "Otherwise, you'll do yourself harm before you even get to the training field." He smiled reassuringly. "It won't always feel this heavy, my Lord."

Cai sighed and rolled his neck and shoulders, trying to make himself comfortable but it was easier said than done; the shirt was definitely not made for comfort.

Logan clapped him on the back and he almost collapsed under the weight. "You'll be fine in a few days," he declared confidently.

"I'll have to be," Cai muttered to himself before looking once more at the weaponry. "So... do I get a sword now?" he asked, hoping he sounded more confident than he felt.

Lancelot shook his head. "Not for now; you need to get used to wearing your shirt first... But we'll talk about that later," he continued. "For now, eat and rest; you have a full day ahead of you tomorrow." He fixed Cai with a stern look. "Do not take that shirt off; it's important you understand its weight so that you can work with it. It *must* become part of you."

Cai nodded mutely before bidding farewell to Gadeon and Osric, who had returned to his work.

The light was already fading as Cai and Logan set off towards the Great Hall. Once Cai was certain they were alone, he turned to Logan. "Lancelot's intense, isn't he?"

Logan shrugged. "He's OK, really." He glanced at Cai. "Kay's the one you want to watch out for," he warned. "I mean, if you think Lancelot's intense, you ain't seen nothing yet."

Cai felt his stomach drop at the prospect of meeting Kay again, especially in training, *with weapons*, but he pushed those thoughts aside, determined not to think about the knight until he had to. "Did you know Lancelot and Mordred used to be friends?" he asked, changing the subject.

Logan frowned. "No." There was a moment of silence as he took in Cai's words. "Really? Are you sure about that?" he questioned in disbelief.

Cai sighed, disappointed that Logan had nothing to add. "That's what Merlin said."

"Well, I never saw that one coming," Logan muttered as he pushed the doors to the Great Hall open. "Listen, after we've eaten, we better head back to our quarters," he advised, changing the subject. "We have an early start."

"How early?" Cai asked warily, the weight of his shirt wearing him down.

"We have to be in the arena at first light."

"First light?" he groaned. "When's *that*?"

Logan paused, before answering, "About 5:30..." Seeing the look of horror on Cai's face, he added, "Don't worry, though; I'll wake you up in time."

"Thanks," Cai muttered grimly, following Logan inside, eager to eat, at last.

Suddenly, the hall was filled with the grating sound of benches being pushed back as the entire assembly fell to their knees; even those serving or making their way to a table discarded their platters on the nearest surface and dropped to the ground, bowing their heads in reverence. In the silence that followed, Cai noticed Logan was enjoying this way too much for his liking.

Cai swallowed, uncertain what to say or do. "Oh God, not again," he breathed, mortified that this was happening again; he had never been more uncomfortable in his life.

"Tell them to return to their meals," a quiet voice behind him advised.

Cai turned to find Merlin standing behind him with Guinevere at his side; he nodded to the older man gratefully before turning back to his people. "You can return to your meals now."

Logan leaned towards him, his eyes still riveted on the scene before them. "You might want to say it a little louder," he whispered pointedly.

Cai blushed as he repeated his request and was relieved to see everything return to normal. He turned back to Merlin and smiled. "Thanks; I... wasn't expecting that to happen."

Guinevere smiled. "There is still much for you to get used to, I'm sure," she murmured.

Cai nodded, feeling suddenly awkward. "Yeah..."

Logan cleared his throat. "Well, I'll just go and get some food..." He nudged Cai. "Come find me when you're ready."

As he left, Merlin smiled. "I, too, must take my leave." He turned to Guinevere and bowed. "Good evening, my Lady," he murmured, before turning to Cai. "My Lord."

Left alone, Cai suddenly remembered how he had left her earlier that day in the Lower Courtyard, without a word of goodbye; he shifted awkwardly under his mail, hating how rude he had been but he hadn't even given it a thought, until now.

"I heard from Lancelot that you acquitted yourself admirably in the meeting."

Surprised, she hadn't confronted him about his behaviour, Cai shrugged. "Um, I guess... I was just honest," he replied, trying to recall what he had actually said; the meeting seemed like an age ago now.

Guinevere nodded. "Honesty is always the best road to travel, I find." She paused, seemingly noticing his clothes for the first time. "I see you have selected your armour." Cai nodded, looking down at himself. "And how do you like it?"

Cai suppressed a groan as he fidgeted, trying to get comfortable; his back and legs were already hurting under the weight and it was becoming increasingly harder to remain standing. "I didn't *choose* it; it was given to me," he corrected her. "I'm supposed to keep it on all the time but..." He shrugged and glanced at her guiltily. "I hate it," he confessed.

Guinevere laughed and Cai couldn't help but smile as tears pricked his eyes; it felt good to have made his mother laugh at long last, even if he *did* smell. Reaching out, Guinevere cupped his cheeks. "It suits you," she murmured.

Cai swallowed against the lump in his throat and smiled. "I start my training tomorrow," was all he could think of to say.

At these words, a look of sadness crept into Guinevere's eyes but it was gone before Cai could question her about it. She cast a look over the Great Hall and, spotting Logan, smiled. "In that case, you should eat with Logan and then retire," she stated. Pulling him closer, she kissed his cheek before making her way to her throne.

Cai watched her go, unable to shake the feeling that he had upset her somehow.

Trying in vain to push those thoughts aside, Cai made his way to Logan's table; Logan glanced up as he arrived, a leg of chicken in his hand.

"Everything alright?" he asked around a mouthful of food.

Cai nodded as he took his seat, grateful to finally relax, the weight of the shirt now taken by the bench. "Yeah, fine..." he muttered, glancing at Guinevere, who still looked out of sorts. His attention was, momentarily, pulled away from her as Logan shoved a plate of food towards him.

"Eat," he instructed. "It's good."

Cai nodded again and began to eat but the food was tasteless and he no longer had an appetite for it. His eyes kept drifting to Guinevere who seemed lost in her own thoughts, her forehead drawn into a frown...

"Just go talk to her," Logan advised, drawing Cai's attention back to him.

"What?" Cai asked, in an attempt to distract himself.

Logan held his hands up in surrender. "Look, I have no idea what happened, and I don't want to know, but... ever since you sat down, you've been looking at her with puppy dog eyes..."

188

"No I haven't," Cai protested, blushing.

Logan raised his eyebrows, clearly not believing a word of it. "If you say so," he muttered. "Look, I'm going to level with you now: you can't go into training tomorrow with your mind not on the job; they will rip you apart and they won't listen to excuses." He paused, letting his words sink in. "So, take my advice and go talk to her. For your own sake."

Cai held his gaze for a moment, knowing he was right; he *did* want to focus on his training but, apart from that, he wanted to know Guinevere was OK.

Heaving himself up from the table, he stood and slowly made his way over to Guinevere's throne, his movements cumbersome under the weight of the shirt. She looked up as he approached and, Cai was pleased to see, smiled.

"Cai," she greeted him, reaching for his hand. "I suppose you have come to say goodnight?" she prompted.

Cai nodded, taking her lead. "Er, yeah..." he began hesitantly. Bracing himself, he added, "But I wanted to see if you were OK first..."

Her smiled widened. "I am well, Cai, I assure you," she stated.

Cai swallowed nervously. "But you seemed... a bit strange when I told you about my training; I didn't know if I had said something to upset you..." He cringed inwardly at how lame he sounded.

189

She rose and stepped towards him. "You have not upset me, my son," she assured him. "I was just..." She paused, gathering her thoughts. "Hearing you talk of your training... it made me realise that things are moving a lot faster than I would like." She looked at him, tears in her eyes. "Once your training is complete, you will leave Camelot..." Cai felt a lump in his throat at the prospect. Guinevere squeezed his hand and forced herself to smile. "But it is the way of things; I cannot stand in the way of fate. And, until then, we shall just have to make the most of the time we have together."

Cai smiled. "Yeah; we will," he agreed.

Guinevere hugged him. "Goodnight, my son."

"Goodnight..."

As Cai left the Great Hall, he felt lighter than ever before in spite of the cumbersome shirt he wore; despite the inevitability of his leaving, he would make his mother proud of him.

And that, he determined, *would begin tomorrow...*

Chapter Twenty-Five

Cai awoke the following morning to the sound of shuffling. He shivered in the darkness, pulling his cloak tighter around him, even though he knew it would do no good. He cursed the chainmail as he tried to get comfortable. Just as his eyes slid shut once more, he felt a hand on his shoulder and Logan shook him awake.

"Come on, we need to get going," Logan told him. Taking hold of Cai's cloak, he tugged it to one side.

Cai groaned, propping himself into a sitting position and ran his fingers through his hair. He sighed and, with great effort, forced himself to stay awake; this early in the morning he couldn't think of anything other than getting through the next few hours.

"Seriously," Logan insisted, nudging Cai sharply. "They'll come and drag you out of bed if you're not on time. And I'm telling you now that, if Kay walks in here to get you, you're on your own."

Cai glanced at him wearily. Logan had lost all of his usual bluster; he seemed to be genuinely worried at the prospect of Kay having to come and get them. "Cheers," Cai muttered drily, trying to hide his own worries. "And here I was thinking you were supposed to serve me."

Logan snorted. "Yeah, well; Kay's a special case. I'm not going toe to toe with him for anyone, not even you," he retorted good-naturedly.

Cai smiled wryly and, pulling on his boots, got to his feet. Rolling his neck from side to side, trying to ease his tense, aching muscles, he gestured to the door. "You'd better lead the way then."

Logan obliged, leading Cai out into the crisp, morning air. He followed Logan across the courtyard, ignoring the now familiar gazes of the few people unlucky enough to have to be up at this hour. They continued past the Great Hall and down the steps to the Lower Courtyard and, it was with relief, that Cai realised they were now alone; the last thing he needed was an audience watching his every move.

As they made their way across the Lower Courtyard, Cai fell into step beside Logan. "So, this training..." he began.

"Is hard," Logan finished for him.

"What does it consist of, exactly?"

Logan shrugged. "At the moment, fighting: weapons training, hand-to-hand combat, stuff like that." He grinned. "I gotta tell you though, Cai, it's really cool!" he added enthusiastically. "It's hard but cool. I mean, where would you ever get to sword fight back home?"

Cai smiled, unsure if he was quite ready to share in Logan's enthusiasm. His eyes landed on the sword at Logan's side. "So, you know how to use a sword?" he asked warily, trying to hide his own growing nerves.

Logan scoffed. "Yeah, of course," he replied; he spoke as if the very question offended him. "It's the first thing they teach you; every knight needs a sword."

Cai nodded silently, his fear turning his stomach to ice as his worries returned with a vengeance.

"Lancelot's my mentor," Logan announced proudly, thankfully changing the subject.

Cai frowned at the sound of Lancelot's name, recalling what Merlin had told him the previous day. He still wasn't quite sure how he felt about Lancelot just yet. Sure, he had been reasonable enough when deciding upon Cai's fate and helping to arm him but there were still questions he needed answers to where the older knight was concerned; questions regarding his relationships with Guinevere and Mordred for a start.

On reaching an archway at the end of the courtyard, Logan took the lead once more. Almost immediately, the ground fell away to reveal a well-trodden path, winding around the side of Camelot and Cai realised, with a jolt, that, for a short distance at least, they would have to negotiate the rocky path of the cliff edge in order to arrive at their destination.

Cai paused and tentatively looked down to the waves crashing ferociously against the rocks far below.

Logan grinned back at him, perfectly at ease with their situation and seemingly enjoying Cai's discomfort. "You gonna stand there all day?" he chirped.

Cai lifted his gaze to meet his friend's. "Course not," he muttered, relieved he sounded more confident than he felt.

Concentrating on every step, he continued along the path, trying to ignore the fact that, if he fell, the mail shirt he was wearing would almost certainly drag him to a watery grave. Steeling himself, he focused on the path ahead, telling himself he'd be OK; after all, this part of the journey wasn't *that* long, anyway.

"You know, the more you think about it, the harder it will be," Logan called back, offering advice.

Cai glanced up, cursing to himself; Logan was already past the worst of it and was now leaning against the wall, looking smug and totally at ease. His grin widened as he nodded towards Cai knowingly. "Just don't look down," he cautioned.

In that moment, Cai hated Logan; hated the fact that Logan had been here longer, hated the fact that he knew far more than he did and hated that he made him feel stupid and pathetic without even trying.

Clenching his hands into fists, Cai summoned up every ounce of determination he had and forged on. With every step he felt his confidence grow and began to relax more knowing that, by not looking over the edge, he was able to focus on his goal: to get to the end of this path, back onto safe ground.

It wasn't long before the path rose and he found himself in the shadow of Camelot's walls, grinning triumphantly at Logan. Walking that path was only a small victory but it *was* a victory, nonetheless.

Logan put an arm around Cai's shoulders. "Better late than never, I suppose," he said, by way of congratulations.

The boys set off again, Cai's racing heart now almost back to normal. His body ached from the tension of the climb and the weight of his armour but he was determined not to focus on that; he still had so much left to focus on, he couldn't lose it so soon in the day.

It wasn't long before Logan stopped again and, Cai realised, they were standing at the top of a grassy slope. A well-trodden path led to what could have been an early type of football stadium but it was much smaller and, instead of seats, the sloping sides were grass banks; a wooden post rose from the centre. He looked up to his right and, from this viewpoint, he could see the path he had rode along with Merlin two days previously and the archway through which they had first entered Camelot.

Glancing down, he saw Lancelot, Kay and Gawain standing in the centre of the 'stadium' awaiting them.

Cai glanced at Logan. "Is this…?"

Logan nodded, his face set in grim determination. "The place where laughter comes to die," he quipped.

Cai narrowed his eyes. "Quick question: why couldn't we have left Camelot the same way we enter it?"

Logan looked at him as if he had lost his mind. "And where, exactly, would the fun be in *that*?" he asked, with a grin. Before Cai had a chance to reply, Logan nudged him. "Come on." He turned to Cai as they set off, his eyes dark. "A word of warning: don't think they'll go easy on you because of who you are." He paused before adding, "I'll be surprised if they don't knock you out in the first five minutes."

Without waiting to see Cai's reaction, he pulled ahead leaving Cai alone with a sense of impending doom.

Chapter Twenty-Six

"About bloody time," Kay growled, glaring at Cai as he and Logan approached the small group of knights. "Another minute and I was about to drag you from your beds." He spat on the ground.

Cai felt the full force of his hatred but said nothing; somehow he couldn't help but think that Kay's comments were directed more at him than at Logan and it took all his self-control not to respond.

Lancelot scowled at Kay but said nothing. Turning his attention to Cai, he said, "I trust you slept well."

Cai shrugged, not an easy feat in chain mail. "OK, I guess," he muttered guardedly.

Lancelot held his gaze for a moment and Cai had the impression he wanted to say more but was holding back. Instead he said, "As you know, Cai, this morning you are to commence your training with us." He nodded towards Kay. "Kay will be your mentor…"

Kay smirked, as he looked Cai up and down.

Cai immediately had the uneasy feeling that Kay was measuring him up for what was ahead and knew he found him wanting. Panic set in; in that moment he wanted Lancelot to know he didn't want Kay as a mentor, he wanted Gawain instead but he stayed put, choosing to stay silent, to say nothing. What good would it do to complain? He'd only end up looking like some spoilt little kid who wanted things his own way and expected an easy ride.

So instead of speaking up, he kept his mouth shut and glared back at Kay determinedly.

Cai was aware of Logan watching him but he kept his eyes trained on Kay, fully understanding that to look away now would be a sign of weakness.

"Gawain will assist Kay in your training," Lancelot continued.

Gawain nodded towards Cai, his hand on the hilt of his sword.

Cai saw the muscles in Kay's jaw clench as he looked away, focusing on a point beyond the arena; it was only a slight reaction from the knight but it *was* there. Could it be that Lancelot wanted Gawain there to check Kay and his dislike for Cai? Suddenly, he felt slightly more optimistic; perhaps he was just reading too much into it.

Lancelot cast a look around at those gathered before returning his attention to Cai once more. He held Cai's gaze for a moment and, for the second time that morning, Cai had the feeling Lancelot wanted to say something to him. Whatever it was, Cai wished he'd just spit it out; he hated these awkward moments.

Suddenly aware that everyone was watching him, Lancelot cleared his throat. Bowing to Cai, he murmured, "I wish you well," before walking away, indicating for Logan to follow him.

Logan gave Cai a quick thumbs-up before following Lancelot up the slope and out of the training arena, his hand resting upon the hilt of the sword at his side.

"What are you smirking at, *boy*?" Kay demanded, taking a step closer to Cai.

"Nothing," Cai replied guardedly, unaware he'd been smirking. His gaze slid to Gawain who was watching him warily, his eyes every bit as suspicious as Kay's. Maybe he *was* fooling himself to think things were going to be OK; these two were apparently of the same mind where he was concerned.

Kay narrowed his eyes; Cai glared back defiantly, content to wait for the older man to speak again. "If you've come here expecting things to be easy then you're sorely mistaken." Kay's eyes burned into Cai as he spoke. "If you think that saying you are my brother's son automatically earns you a place at the Table, think again." He bent down, looking Cai directly in the eye. "If you think I will let you sit on my brother's throne, take my brother's place..."

Cai held Kay's gaze, fear settling in his stomach, cold and tangible, seeping into every part of him. The world seemed to disappear for a moment; no one existed but the two of them as they were engulfed by the black cloud of Kay's anger for him.

"Enough, Kay." Gawain's gruff voice seemed to cut through Kay's hatred like a knife, jolting them back to the present.

Kay straightened up, his eyes softening ever so slightly as he broke eye contact with Cai.

Gawain guided him away from Cai. "The boy has done no wrong..." he murmured before his voice dropped so low that Cai could no longer hear what was being said.

Cai watched them carefully, waiting to pick up on anything said between them but it was no good; their voices were too low.

Turning his attention to the arena, he glanced around, studying his surroundings. It was empty except for the three of them; some way behind them was the post and, he now noticed, there were two wooden swords and shields resting against it.

Cai was about to turn back to Kay and Gawain when he sensed he was being watched. Glancing up, his gaze fell upon a dark figure overlooking Camelot's walls. Even from this distance, Cai knew the figure was Merlin; his hands were clasped behind his back, his black cloak buffeted by the breeze.

Cai held his gaze, wondering if Merlin intended to watch all of his training; he shifted uncomfortably at the thought. He wasn't sure he wanted anyone watching any of his training, let alone his first session. He had to admit though, as he continued to stare back at Merlin, it felt good to know that he was there, supporting him, even though it was from a distance.

As he continued to hold Merlin's gaze, another figure came and stood beside him on the wall. The newcomer was obviously a woman; she wore black robes and a cloak similar to Merlin's. Long black hair framed her pale face, tendrils of which were being blown by the breeze.

Cai watched as she leaned towards Merlin, who inclined his head towards her as she spoke. After a moment, Merlin turned and left his position on the wall, disappearing from sight.

The woman watched him leave before turning her gaze back to Cai. He stared back, transfixed; he was at her mercy. He wanted to turn away but couldn't. Whereas Merlin's presence had settled him, this woman made him feel uncomfortable; whereas Merlin's gaze had been watchful, the woman's gaze seemed to burn with an icy fire. It didn't matter that Cai couldn't see her face clearly; it was enough that he *felt* her eyes burning into him.

Burning into his very soul...

Chapter Twenty-Seven

"You think daydreaming is a good way to spend your time, do you?" Kay demanded, grabbing Cai's arm and yanking him round to face himself and Gawain once more.

"No, it's just..." Cai started in protest but his voice trailed away to nothing; somehow, he didn't think these two would believe that the woman had made him feel so uncomfortable. He knew if he said anything, it would only result in them laughing in his face and their opinions of him would sink even lower, if that were at all possible. And *that* was the last thing he wanted.

Kay watched him for a moment, his eyes dark and unfathomable, before gripping his arm and pulling him further into the arena.

Cai managed a brief glance over his shoulder only to find the woman had disappeared; Camelot's walls were now empty of any spectators.

He barely had time to wonder where she had gone or whether he had imagined it and she had never been there at all, before Kay shoved him forward, releasing his grip as he did so.

Under the weight of the mail, Cai stumbled but recovered his balance quickly. Looking around, he found himself standing next to the wooden post he had spotted earlier; at his feet lay two wooden swords. Turning away from the post, he focused on Kay and Gawain once more.

"Your attention needs to be focused on us and what we teach you," Kay informed him. "Otherwise you might as well just hand yourself over to Mordred and have done with it; save us all the time and trouble."

Cai remained silent.

Kay glanced at Gawain and nodded. Gawain walked over to the post and picked up one of the wooden swords. Standing before Cai, he held the hilt towards him, gesturing for Cai to take it.

Cai looked at it. "What?" he asked expectantly.

"Take it," Gawain instructed impatiently.

Cai obeyed, frowning as he did so. "What's this for?"

Kay smirked. "Haven't you seen a sword before?"

Cai glared at him. "Of course I have," he retorted defensively. "But they're usually made of iron."

"Do you really think we'd let *you* loose with a weapon that could seriously injure one of *us*?"

Kay asked. He cast a knowing look towards Gawain and the two knights laughed at the very idea of Cai holding a real sword, let alone *injuring* one of them; Cai glanced between them, his temper rising.

Clenching his jaw, Cai looked down at the sword in his hand, trying to focus on something other than his growing anger. The grip had been bound in strips of leather, the cross guard and blade smoothed down.

"No, these… are training swords," Kay announced, once he had stopped laughing. He bent and picked up the second sword; studying it, he ran his hand appreciatively along the shaft of the blade. "We give these to *children* when they start their training," he added contemptuously.

Cai stared back, making every effort to rein in his temper; he knew Kay wanted him to take the bait but he wouldn't give him the satisfaction. He knew from his past run-ins with Ethan how best to respond to threats and taunts: he *had* to ignore them. That was the only way to deal with bullies.

But, then again, he knew Kay was in a totally different league to Ethan.

Kay turned to Cai. "Are you ready to show us what you're capable of, boy?" he asked. Holding the wooden sword at his side, he started walking a slow and purposeful circle around Cai, his eyes never leaving his student.

Having no idea what else to do, Cai echoed his moves, all the while keeping his eyes trained on Kay; he wanted to keep him in his sights, to be prepared for anything the knight threw at him.

Kay held his arms out to his side and bowed his head, his gaze fixed on Cai. "Whenever you're ready... *my Lord*," he announced mockingly.

Cai felt his temper begin to boil again; he'd love to wipe the smirk off Kay's face once and for all... to show him he had what it took to fight alongside him and the other knights. But he decided to bide his time; he couldn't lose his head. He knew that to act rashly, was just what Kay wanted and he wasn't about to hand him more ammunition to ridicule him further.

Cai was vigilant, awaiting any sign of an opening. Kay held his sword loosely in his right hand as if he knew he faced no real threat from Cai; this was obviously the case but it still galled him. For Kay to be so openly unconcerned was the ultimate humiliation; what was it about him? Why did everyone see him as a laughing stock, something to be mocked?

In that moment, he was straight back in school with Ethan, Charlie and Aaron.

"Are you two going to dance all day or am I going to watch a fight?" Gawain called out impatiently, his arms crossed over his chest.

Kay let out a harsh bark of laughter that held no mirth whatsoever. "It would seem our *King* would rather wait for others to fight than to lead the battle charge himself," he taunted, sparing his friend a brief glance. Turning his attention back to Cai, he sneered, "You don't deserve the name Pendragon."

That was all it took…

Cai snapped.

Clenching his jaw and tightening his grip on the sword, he launched himself at Kay, all reason gone.

All he saw were his tormentors: Ethan… Charlie… Aaron… *Kay*. For that moment, they were all one and the same; he could make no distinction between them, he didn't want to.

They all needed to pay for what they had done to him.

Screaming with rage, he held his sword aloft, ready to strike Kay with all the strength, all the anger, he had pent up over the years. But the knight had already stepped aside before Cai got anywhere near him.

Slowing his pace, Cai brought his sword down and turned to face Kay, breathing heavily and struggling to stand under the weight on his back. He glared at the knight as he tried to regain his composure, to ignore the embers burning in his stomach, fuelling him to attack again.

"What was *that*, exactly?" Kay frowned. He casually twirled his sword in an elaborate arc as he moved towards Cai.

Cai bristled; Kay was obviously showing off, taunting him all the more. Kay grinned at him and Cai's need to wipe the smug smile off his face intensified.

Closing the distance between them, Cai gripped the hilt of the sword with both hands and took a swing at Kay, who, this time, remained steadfast, easily deflecting Cai's blade with his own.

Kay shook his head derisively. "Is that the best you can do?" he asked, clearly not interested in the answer. He looked Cai up and down. "Pathetic!" he spat.

"Then *teach* me!" Cai demanded, fed up with Kay's dismissals and put-downs. He *knew* he lacked the skill to lead men, he *knew* he couldn't stand shoulder to shoulder with the rest of the knights but he wanted a chance to *try*. "Stop giving me a hard time and *teach* me how to fight! *Teach* me how to use a sword!" he challenged.

Kay held his gaze, his dark eyes boring into Cai's. "Is that what you think I'm doing?" he asked, his voice dangerously low. *"Giving you a hard time?"* He took a step closer to Cai, forcing Cai to look up at him. "Let me tell you something, *Cai Pendragon...*" He spoke as if Cai's very name left a bad taste in his mouth. "You don't know the meaning of a hard time; you've spent the last sixteen years having it easy while the rest of us..."

Cai snapped, shoving Kay in the chest, needing to put as much distance between them as possible. "You have *no* idea about me or about what's happened to me," he raged. "I'm sorry that you don't want to believe I'm Arthur's son and I'm sorry I haven't been here but that wasn't *my* fault!" He paused, breathing heavily but he couldn't stop now; he was on a roll; his temper was burning, his rage engulfing him. "I'm sorry that Arthur never told you about me but he had his reasons and if you can't see that then..."

He got no further in his tirade because Kay stepped forward and shoved him hard in the chest; it was done casually, as if he was doing nothing more than shooing away an annoying dog.

Cai fell backwards, losing his sword as he landed heavily on the hard ground, his breath knocked out of him under the weight of the chainmail. Glaring up at Kay, he was about to get to his feet but was prevented from doing so as Kay stood over him, his sword pointed at Cai's throat.

Cai swallowed, his throat moving uncomfortably against the tip of the wooden blade.

Kay looked down at Cai, a fire burning in his eyes. "Consider this your first lesson," he murmured quietly. He pressed the blade against Cai's throat as he continued. "Never let anger cloud your judgement. An enemy will look for *any* sign of weakness and will not hesitate to use it to their own advantage." He stared down at Cai a moment longer before tossing his sword aside and walking away.

Chapter Twenty-Eight

Cai stared at Kay's retreating figure as the knight climbed the east slope of the arena, his stride never faltering. As he watched Kay's departure, Cai tried to regain his composure. He couldn't help feeling like he had had some out of body experience; he had seen himself snap and attack Kay but had been unable to do anything to stop himself. He couldn't believe he had lost it like that... *again*. What was happening to him?

He looked up as a shadow fell across him and he found himself staring up at Gawain.

"Get up," the knight ordered, gruffly, before turning and retrieving Kay's discarded sword.

Jolted back to reality, Cai obeyed without question, scrambling hastily to his feet and collecting his own sword; turning, he faced Gawain. He tried to cast everything that had just happened from his mind, tried to ignore the rawness he still felt in the pit of his stomach, but it was impossible; he still felt shaken. He had lost control, had let Kay get under his skin, something he had been determined to avoid.

He shook his head despondently; losing his temper seemed to be how he dealt with his problems now, there was no middle ground.

What kind of person was he becoming?

"Don't take it personally," Gawain advised, watching Cai carefully.

Cai glared at him and scoffed. How could he *not* take it personally? Kay had certainly made it personal when he had taunted him about Arthur; until that moment, he hadn't been sure himself whether he truly believed he was King Arthur's son but, as soon as Kay questioned it, Cai's rage had intensified and he had lashed out in defence of his father's name.

"Kay means well," Gawain continued, nodding in Kay's direction.

"Really?" Cai questioned, raising his eyebrows in disbelief. "I'd hate to see what he's like when he doesn't."

Gawain grinned; it was brief and no sooner had it touched his lips than it was gone. He took a step back, serious once more. "Your stance is all wrong," he informed him, pointing his sword at Cai's feet.

Cai glanced down at his feet self-consciously. Frowning, he looked back to Gawain in confusion. "What do you mean?" he asked.

Gawain shook his head in exasperation. "You stand with your feet too close together; you need to spread your weight." He demonstrated, planting his feet shoulder width apart. "Otherwise, it's too easy for your opponent to knock you off your feet." he concluded.

Cai blushed, recalling how easily Kay had knocked him to the ground with no more than a nudge, albeit, a hard one. He adjusted his position, mirroring the knight's stance, and immediately felt more balanced.

Gawain relaxed and approached Cai, looking pleased. "Good," he murmured. Standing in front of Cai, he raised his right hand in which the sword was held. "The sword needs to be an extension of your arm; it needs to feel natural in your hand," he explained. "It should be held loosely at first; if you hold it too tightly, you'll feel it more." He looked at Cai intently. "*You* hold it as if you're afraid it will leap out of your hand and act of its own free will."

Cai felt his cheeks flush. "But what if I drop it?" Even as the words left his lips, he was aware of how foolish that sounded and was glad Kay wasn't around to hear.

Gawain smiled indulgently. "You won't," he replied confidently, as if he knew something Cai didn't. He moved away and nodded to Cai. "Let's start with the basics: always move the sword across your body..." He demonstrated, bringing his arm up so that the blade was alongside his left ear. Cai watched intently as, slowly, he brought the weapon down so that it crossed his body; he immediately raised the weapon up along his right side before bringing it down again, across his body, to his left. "See?" he asked, looking at Cai expectantly.

Cai nodded mutely.

Gawain nodded towards him. "Show me."

Casting his nerves aside, Cai focused on the weapon in his hand. Loosening his grip on the hilt of the sword, he mimicked Gawain's movements, slowly and deliberately, careful not to make any mistakes.

"Quicker, boy, quicker!" Gawain growled, as he circled Cai.

Cai repeated the movements, picking up speed, painfully aware of how stupid he looked swinging his wooden sword at an imaginary foe. "I feel like an idiot," he growled, his arm and shoulder burning painfully under the weight of his chainmail.

Gawain stood in front of him once more, fixing him with an icy stare. "That will be the least of your worries in battle," he stated. "You wont have time to think of anything, other than how to stay alive; your enemy wants you dead," he stated plainly.

"I get that," Cai acknowledged, lowering his sword and looking up at Gawain. "But it's hard to imagine I'm fighting someone when there's no one there."

Gawain nodded curtly. "Very well; *I* will engage you."

"What?" Cai asked, a mixture of apprehension and excitement filling him. He remembered what it had been like to fight Kay, the way the knight had taunted him, had made him feel foolish; he wasn't sure he wanted to go through that again.

On the other hand, Kay had been more intent on making a point; with Gawain, he may actually have a chance of a proper sword fight.

"Come on, boy," Gawain grinned. "Don't look so scared; I'm not going to kill you." He watched Cai steadily as he added, "Or was Kay right...? Maybe you *don't* have the courage to fight."

At the mention of Kay's name, Cai bristled; he didn't want it getting back to Kay that he had screwed up twice in one day. "I have what it takes," he announced, adopting the stance Gawain had just taught him.

"Good. I would hate to return to Camelot with the news that Kay was right; he would never let us forget it." He smirked at the thought before taking his position opposite Cai. "Oh, and one more piece of advice: no matter what happens, *keep moving.*"

The words hadn't even left his lips before Gawain launched himself at Cai, his sword arcing down towards him.

Cai had only a moment to register what was happening, and to consider his reaction, before he stepped back and, clumsily, brought his sword up to meet Gawain's.

The wooden blades met in mid-air, the sound echoing in the silence. Cai winced as a searing pain shot through his arm and his hand went numb, causing him to almost drop his sword. Ignoring the tingling in his fingers, he backed away, readying the weapon as best he could.

Gawain attacked relentlessly, forcing Cai into more defensive moves. It wasn't long before Cai's entire body ached, the force of the blades meeting reverberating through him. With dogged determination, he forced himself to keep going, aware only of the man in front of him and the weapon he was wielding.

"Look for an opening," Gawain shouted. "Look for your chance."

But Cai was too busy defending himself to form a coherent thought; it was all he could do not to drop his sword and surrender.

Suddenly, just as Cai was anticipating another forceful blow, Gawain twisted out of Cai's reach, circled around his left side, and brought the flat of his blade down on Cai's lower back.

"Now you're dead," Gawain stated with a smile. "Either that or fatally wounded," he added as an afterthought.

"Is there a difference?" Cai panted, fighting the urge to drop to his knees; the only thing stopping him was the very real possibility that, if he did, he may never get up again.

Gawain grinned. "Not as far as you're concerned, you'll still be dead."

Breathing heavily, his body soaked in sweat, Cai turned to face Gawain. Despite having lost and being in intense pain, he couldn't ignore the overpowering feeling of pure exhilaration that welled up inside him; he felt like he could do anything and *finally* appreciated Logan's enthusiasm for weapons training.

He may have been clumsy, he may have lost, but all Cai could think of was how much he wanted to do it all again. He wanted to experience the rush, the total single-mindedness of the moment... it was like nothing he had ever felt before.

Suddenly, he felt an arm drape over his shoulder and turned to find Logan grinning back at him.

"That wasn't bad for a first time," he said encouragingly.

Cai felt himself blush. "You saw that?"

Logan nodded. "Of course."

From the corner of his eye, Cai caught sight of Lancelot approaching, his gaze fixed on Gawain. "Where's Kay?" he asked.

Gawain looked at the ground and said nothing.

Lancelot narrowed his eyes, shaking his head in disappointment, before turning and retracing his steps.

Cai watched him go before turning to Gawain whom, he noted, looked troubled, his eyes fixed on Lancelot's retreating figure.

Sensing Cai's gaze upon him, he turned to the boys. "That's it for today," he said abruptly, his attention clearly elsewhere. "We'll see you here at first light, tomorrow."

And, with that, he set off after Lancelot.

Cai and Logan watched in stunned silence.

Logan frowned. "What was *that* about?" he demanded. "And where's Kay?"

Cai sighed. "I don't know; we had an argument and he stormed off..."

Logan stared at him. "You had a *fight* with *Kay*?" he asked in disbelief. "OK, you're going to have to tell me everything, you know that, right?"

As they returned to Camelot, Cai turned to Logan, eager to change the subject. "I saw Merlin this morning; there was a woman with him..."

Logan glanced at him. "Tall woman, dressed in black? Freaky eyes?"

Cai smiled, recalling the uneasy feeling he had when she had looked at him. "I guess; I couldn't see her eyes," he added quickly. "She was too far away."

"That's Nimue," Logan announced. "She's Merlin's apprentice or assistant... or something. I never see her; she's always holed up in her rooms, probably concocting poisons or something."

"*Poisons?*" Cai asked, alarmed by this revelation.

Logan laughed. "Relax, I'm having you on! Do you *really* think Merlin would let her do that?" After a moment's silence, he continued, "So, you *really* had a fight with Kay?"

216

Cai nodded, slightly offended that Logan didn't believe him. "You don't believe me?" he questioned indignantly.

"It's not that," Logan insisted. "It's just... Remind me not to cross you anytime soon." He paused for a moment before adding, "God, I'd have loved to have seen you take him on."

Cai remained silent; he'd never admit it aloud, but one confrontation with Kay was certainly enough. Somehow, he didn't think the knight would let him survive a second.

Chapter Twenty-Nine

Sitting in the Great Hall, having had time to process the events of the morning, Cai was slowly coming to terms with the enormity of what he had done; he had attacked a Knight of The Round Table and, given Kay's temper, was amazed he was still standing.

"So you *really* shoved him?" Logan asked, his eyes alight with excitement.

Cai allowed himself a smile. This was new; he'd never been the object of anyone's admiration before and, he had to admit, he was quite enjoying it. Logan's non-stop questions, and obvious respect, had Cai recalling every minute detail in great depth; he knew he was over-exaggerating most of it but, at that moment, he didn't care. It felt good to finally have someone show an interest in *him*. "Yeah... I really shoved him," he replied, taking a sip of his drink.

Logan shook his head in disbelief. "I've had plenty of run-ins with Kay over the years but I've *never* had the guts to do *that!*" he laughed.

Cai lowered his gaze; despite what Logan seemed to think, he wasn't proud of his outburst. He shrugged. "None of it was planned," he insisted. "It just happened."

Logan frowned. "Yeah, about that... how did it happen, exactly? You've not actually said..."

Cai sighed. "He said some things about..." He glanced at Logan before continuing. "...My father," he finished awkwardly.

Logan raised his eyebrows, nodding knowingly. "Ah."

Cai glanced furtively at Logan. "Yeah... it was weird, though, because, until that moment, I wasn't even sure I believed I *was* King Arthur's son," he admitted. "But hearing Kay say I didn't deserve the name Pendragon..." He paused as he felt his temper flare at the memory. "I just lost it."

Logan studied him. "Maybe it was a good thing he said it, then."

Cai stared at him, aghast. How could he *say* that? Wasn't he supposed to be his *friend*? How could he look him in the eye and side with *Kay*, of all people? "How d'you work *that* out?" he demanded, struggling to keep his temper.

Obviously sensing Cai's growing anger, Logan held his hands up in surrender. "Hang on a second," he said quickly. "I didn't mean he was *right* to say it; I just meant..."

"Yeah... meant *what*, exactly?" he prompted coldly.

Logan glanced at him warily before continuing. "I just meant that, if he hadn't said it, you wouldn't have known how you really felt about everything."

Cai looked at him, stunned, realising he was right: he had instinctively reacted to Kay's words without realising the knight had actually helped him to accept the truth. "I guess you're right," he admitted thoughtfully.

Logan nodded enthusiastically. "It was the same for me," he continued.

"Was it?"

Logan nodded. "A couple of years ago, some kids started on at me about being a *'foster kid'*..." he said, punctuating the phrase with air quotes.

Cai waited and, when he didn't continue, asked, "So what did you do?"

Logan made a face, clearly trying to appear nonchalant. "Punched one of them. Don't get me wrong," he added quickly, "I'm not proud of what I did but it did send a message out – to them, and others, who thought I was an easy mark." He fell silent for a moment before adding, "You know, on the plus side, Kay now knows you're not someone to be messed with."

Cai scoffed. "I think you're giving me *way* too much credit here," he protested. The idea that *Kay*, a Knight of the Round Table, was in *any* way affected by him and his little outburst was, quite frankly, laughable.

"Hey, have you noticed something weird's going on?" Logan asked suddenly, looking around the hall.

Cai followed his gaze, unsure of what Logan was talking about; all he could see were people eating and talking – nothing out of the ordinary at all.

Logan leaned across the table. "Have you noticed... they've hardly looked at you since you came in?"

Cai frowned; since when had that become a *bad* thing? "So?" he questioned; he certainly didn't see this as a problem.

"Don't you think it's weird that, for the last two days, everyone's been watching you and now they've, what... just lost interest?" he demanded. "Well, I find that *very* strange. And, isn't it weird that Lancelot, Kay *and* Gawain aren't around?" Logan pressed, gesturing around the hall.

Cai nodded, his mind now working overtime; they had all come back to Camelot... so why weren't they here? Surely Kay couldn't *still* be angry?

"I'll go see what I can find out," Logan offered, jumping up from his bench before Cai could stop him.

Cai watched him as he moved to the next table before looking away quickly; the last thing he wanted was to actually *invite* attention by being caught staring. Let Logan ask his questions, let him try to figure out what, if anything, was going on; he'd probably come back with nothing, anyway.

Logan soon returned with a smug look on his face.

"What?" Cai asked, narrowing his eyes suspiciously; he had obviously discovered *something* and was desperate to tell Cai.

"So... the rumour is..." Logan paused, drawing this moment out as long as possible.

Cai sighed exasperatedly. "Are you gonna tell me or not?" he demanded impatiently.

"It looks like Kay's left," he stated simply.

"What?"

"You heard: he's left Camelot."

Cai rolled his eyes. "So? He's not a prisoner, he can..."

"No, you don't get it," Logan interrupted. "Apparently, he was furious when he came back," he explained. "He stormed in, saddled his horse and rode out of here... He hasn't been seen since."

Cai shrugged. "So? It's only been a few hours... I don't see what the problem is."

"Lancelot and Gawain have gone after him," Logan stated as if that changed everything. Seeing Cai's obvious lack of interest he rolled his eyes. "Don't you get it?" he demanded.

Cai shrugged. "Obviously not."

Logan sighed in frustration. "It must be something more than Kay just going for a ride, otherwise, why would Lancelot and Gawain *both* go after him?"

Cai considered this for a moment.

"I reckon your fight upset him more than he wanted to let on," Logan concluded.

Cai smirked, despite himself; although this sounded ridiculous, he kind of liked the idea of being the cause of Kay's leaving. Maybe Kay had realised he had gone too far and left because he didn't want to face the music.

"Wanna go wait for them to come back?" Logan asked, grinning excitedly.

"I don't know..." Cai muttered uncertainly. Somehow, he didn't think Kay would appreciate him being there to see his return.

Logan, however, wasn't taking no for an answer. "Oh, come on! Don't you wanna know what happened?"

Cai scoffed. "I doubt they're going to tell *us* what happened," he protested.

"Maybe not *us*," Logan agreed, "But they would have to tell *you*... *if* you demanded it. You're their King, after all; they have to do what you say."

Cai laughed at this; he couldn't see Lancelot, Kay or Gawain following his orders anytime soon; not about this, anyway.

"Come on, Cai," Logan pleaded, his desperation showing. "There's nothing else to do around here."

Cai sighed, knowing he was right. "Alright," he conceded, reluctantly. "Let's go..."

Logan grinned and practically leapt from his bench as he eagerly led Cai from the hall.

Cai wasn't surprised to find the Lower Courtyard empty, but one look at Logan told him his friend had expected something different: his disappointment was obvious. "They're probably not even back yet," he muttered, trying to bolster his friend.

Logan shook his head. "Or maybe they're back and already in the castle somewhere..." He looked around for a moment before nodding in the direction of the stables. "Come on," he said, pulling Cai in his wake.

"Where are we going?"

Logan glanced behind. "Seeing if their horses are back, of course," he explained.

"And if they're not?" Cai questioned.

Logan looked at him as if he were stupid. "Then we'll *know* they aren't here, won't we?"

Cai followed reluctantly, really hoping Logan didn't want to hang around the stables all afternoon; he could think of a thousand other things he'd rather be doing...

As they entered the stables Cai was immediately overwhelmed by the stench; he paused, trying to adjust to the oppressive smells and heat. Stable hands were hard at work caring for the many horses but, upon seeing Cai, paused to show their respect. After a brief acknowledgement, Cai turned to Logan.

"Well?" he asked expectantly, not really knowing where to look; he didn't know what the knights' horses looked like and didn't know where to begin searching for them.

Logan shook his head, indicating an empty stall in front of them. "It doesn't look like they're back; that's where they keep their horses," he added for Cai's benefit.

Cai nodded, unsure how to answer. Being this close to horses brought back unpleasant memories of his journey here and he was dreading the day he would have to learn to ride.

"Hey, Girl..."

Cai's attention was drawn to the chestnut coloured mare Logan was talking to. He watched as Logan reached out and stroked the beast's nose, murmuring reassuringly to her.

Logan caught Cai watching and grinned. "She won't bite, you know."

Cai blushed. "I know," he muttered.

"Come and say hello, then," Logan challenged, stepping away from the stall door.

Clenching his hands into fists, Cai stepped forward warily, keeping a watchful eye on the horse. Reaching out, he hesitated, as the horse jerked her head to look at him.

"Relax, mate," Logan advised, his eyes darting to Cai as he soothed his mare. "She's interested in you, that's all."

Cai swallowed nervously, finally closing the distance between himself and the horse. He placed his hand on her nose. "Hello," he said stiffly, tentatively stroking her.

Logan snorted. "This is priceless!" Reaching over the stable door, he unlocked it and slowly pushed it open, gently encouraging the horse to move backwards. He glanced at Cai who was still loitering in the doorway uncertainly. "What *are* you doing?" he asked mockingly. "Get in here."

Cai braced himself and, as he stepped cautiously inside, carefully avoiding the manure and damp straw, Logan closed the door behind them.

Returning to the horse's side, he looked at Cai. "You don't like horses, do you?"

Cai shrugged. "It's not that I don't like them," he protested weakly. "It's just... they're so big and I don't know what they're thinking."

Logan nodded, looking up at his horse. "That's true, I guess. But trust me; horses are great." He looked over at Cai. "You'll find that out when you start your riding lessons." Seeing the apprehension on Cai's face, he quickly added, "Don't worry; you'll learn how to handle them quite quickly." He patted the horse's side. "They just need to know you respect them and they'll respect you in return."

Cai nodded, taking in Logan's words. Moving closer, he stroked the beast's flank. "What's her name?"

Logan took a moment before answering. "I haven't really found one that suits her yet," he shrugged. "I just call her 'Girl' most of the time."

Before either boy could say more, they heard the faraway clatter of hooves in the courtyard. Logan's eyes darted to Cai, alive with excitement.

"They're back!" he hissed, moving to the front of the stall, Cai hot on his heels.

They watched as Lancelot and Gawain led their horses into the stables, handing them off to stable hands.

"Perhaps I was wrong to try and force it upon him," Lancelot said, once they were alone.

Logan glanced at Cai and frowned questioningly.

Cai could only shrug in return as he moved closer to the door, hoping Lancelot would elaborate.

"He shouldn't be on his own," Gawain insisted. "He needs to be *here*..."

"I know that but, you know Kay," Lancelot retorted as they left the stables. "Hard-headed at the best of times; he will return when he is ready..."

Cai and Logan glanced at each other briefly before Logan lifted the latch and they dashed out of the stall in pursuit of the knights.

"So where *is* Kay?" Cai demanded. "We heard he'd left but we expected him to come back with you."

Gawain fixed Cai with a hard stare. "Kay is none of *your* concern," he replied bluntly.

Lancelot shot him a warning look before turning to Cai. "Forgive us, my Lord, but, at present, it is paramount that your time be spent on your training and rest."

Cai sped up to match their pace. "But if he's left because of me, maybe I should speak to him..."

Gawain scoffed at the idea but said nothing.

Lancelot turned to Cai, forcing him to stop. "Cai, your concern does you credit but Kay needs time..."

Logan frowned. "Time for *what?*"

Lancelot looked decidedly uncomfortable as he spoke, his gaze landing briefly on Cai. "Time to accept recent... events." He paused before adding, "Rest assured, his absence will not be permanent; he will return when he is ready. Until that day, Gawain and I will take over your training."

And, with that, he bowed his head and the two knights walked away without another word.

Logan turned to Cai. "*Now* tell me you had nothing to do with it," he challenged.

Cai stood, confused; throughout their conversation Lancelot had been awkward and, it had been obvious he knew far more than he was prepared to say. Maybe Logan hadn't been too far off the mark when he had suggested that Cai had had more to do with Kay's disappearance than the knight wanted to let on. Maybe, coming face to face with the nephew he knew nothing of had sent him over the edge; maybe Kay really *did* hate him.

And, with that thought in mind, Cai was suddenly aware of just how much that possibility hurt...

Chapter Thirty

"Now you're dead."

Those bloody words... again!

Cai collapsed back onto the damp grass as all the tension began to drain from his body. His ankle still hurt where Gawain had kicked his legs out from under him and his head was beginning to pound.

Gawain stood over him, his face unforgiving. "And where's your sword?" he demanded. Cai glared up at him but said nothing; he was only too aware of his mistake. "Retrieve it," Gawain ordered as he turned and walked away.

Summoning what little strength he had left, Cai rolled over and got to his feet; collecting his sword, he made his way over to where Gawain stood waiting.

"Tell me what went wrong," the knight instructed.

Cai sighed. It had been a week now; a week of intense training that always ended with his 'death' and then having to dissect his mistakes with Gawain afterwards. "I hesitated in the last attack."

Gawain nodded, looking at Cai thoughtfully. "Why?"

Cai shrugged. "I don't know; I just... lost concentration, I guess."

Gawain took a step closer. "Do you think that's good enough?" Cai dropped his gaze, unable to look the knight in the eyes. "Your hesitation gave me the opening I needed," the knight continued, referring to the moment he had kicked Cai's legs out from under him. "And what happened when you fell?"

"I dropped my sword," Cai admitted quietly.

"You *dropped* your sword," Gawain echoed, clearly unimpressed. "How many times have I told you: *never* relinquish your sword, for an enemy will *never* fail to take advantage." He paused for a moment, allowing his words to sink in. "But, it grows late; we must return to Camelot."

Cai followed in Gawain's wake, determined not to replay the afternoon's lessons in his head but it was hard not to, especially when it didn't feel like he was making any progress at all.

"Tomorrow, you will learn how to ride a horse," Gawain announced as they reached the path leading into the Lower Courtyard.

Cai stared at him "What?"

"You heard me. It's about time you learnt: Lancelot and I both agree..."

Cai frowned casting an anxious look towards the stables, his mouth suddenly dry.

Gawain smirked. "Don't look so worried; learning to ride can't possibly be any worse than you learning to master the sword." And with that, he left.

Cai watched him leave, the knight's words doing nothing to reassure him; he didn't believe he would ever learn to control a horse.

They just need to know you respect them and they'll respect you in return...

Logan's words came back to him and he found himself truly considering them for the first time. He did respect horses... how could he not? They were much bigger and much stronger than him and they could do some serious damage...

"Fearing something is not the same as *respecting* it."

Cai's head snapped around at the unexpected sound of Merlin's voice. He frowned as Merlin drew near. "I don't..." he started to protest but stopped, changing tack. "How did you even know...?"

Merlin inclined his head. "Forgive me, Cai; I do not make it a habit to listen to your thoughts but... I sensed your torment."

"My torment?" Cai echoed.

Merlin met Cai's gaze. "Your time here, so far, has not been easy, I fear."

Cai smiled wryly; that was certainly an understatement.

Merlin studied him. "You fear so much for one so young."

Cai snorted. "Well, what do you expect? I've got a lot to fear!" he snapped back. "I'm getting nowhere in training so I have no idea how I'm actually going to survive my first battle and, now, I have to learn how to ride an animal that could kill me!" Throughout his outburst Cai watched, as Merlin remained infuriatingly calm. He glared at him. "Aren't you going to say something?" he demanded.

"And what would you have me say?"

Cai shrugged. "I don't know!"

Merlin continued to watch him for a moment. "It is not the sword or the horse you have to master, Cai; it is your *fear*."

"And just how do I do *that*?" he demanded, frustrated by Merlin's cryptic statements.

"That, I cannot tell you."

Cai stared at him. "But you're *supposed* to know, you're *supposed* to *help* me."

Merlin smiled. "But this is *your* lesson to learn; no one can do that for you."

Cai closed his eyes and sighed. Rubbing his forehead, he tried to calm his temper, which was rising by the second. It was all very well, Merlin standing there, telling him to master his fear but he had no idea how.

"Think of all you have achieved so far," Merlin advised softly. "Your time here has not been without success."

Cai opened his eyes, looking up at Merlin. "I guess..." he conceded.

"You cannot expect to learn everything at once," Merlin continued. "It takes hard work, determination and commitment... and *you* have all that."

"I just thought it would be..." He shrugged despondently. "I don't know... *better* than this."

Merlin smiled. "Let me assure you, Cai, I had many similar conversations with your father when he first came to Camelot."

Cai's eyes lit up at this revelation. "You did?"

Merlin nodded, smiling sadly. "If he were here now, he would be the first to say that what you are embarking upon is not easy."

Cai returned his smile, wishing Arthur *were* there to offer advice and consolation. "So he found it hard too?"

Merlin nodded. "He did; Kay would be the first to tell you."

"Kay would tell me what?" he pressed.

Merlin shook his head. "I'm afraid that is Kay's story to tell."

Cai smirked. "Well, it would be a lot easier to hear *if* he ever decided to return to Camelot," he pointed out.

"True," Merlin conceded. "But Kay must return in his own time; we cannot force him."

Cai had no choice but to accept Merlin's words; he had given up trying to figure out what had made Kay disappear, it clearly wasn't just him.

After a moment, Merlin spoke. "You cannot do this alone, Cai," he reminded him. "You must seek help when you need it. There are many here who are only too willing to help you, if you would only ask."

Cai groaned inwardly, these were words he had heard all of his life - from teachers, Greg and Jules... but he had never acted upon them; why would he? He had no answer; if he had, maybe his life would have been a hell of a lot easier.

"You are correct, your life would have been far easier... if only you had sought help." Merlin smiled knowingly.

Cai stared at him, stunned, before realising he had read his thoughts again.

"Learn from your mistakes, Cai," he advised. "Now, I must take my leave, I am expected elsewhere."

Together, they made their way to the Great Hall, where Merlin wished him well for the following day's lesson, before parting ways.

Chapter Thirty-One

When Cai awoke the following morning, Logan was still asleep. He lay in the early morning light for a while, contemplating what was to come in the next few hours, his fear increasing by the minute. He knew it was stupid, worrying about things he couldn't control; he was letting his imagination run away with him, letting himself worry about the unknown...

It is not the sword or the horse you need to master, it is your fear...

Merlin's words came back to haunt him; Cai closed his eyes, trying to make sense of them. It was all well and good saying he needed to master his fear but what did that even *mean*?

Cai glanced over towards Logan's bed as his friend began to stir.

"You up?" Logan asked groggily, unable to hide his surprise. "This is a turn up for the books," he muttered as he raised himself into a sitting position.

"Couldn't sleep very well," Cai explained, slowly sitting up, running his fingers through his hair.

Logan studied him. "Worried about today?" he asked tentatively.

Cai looked at him, Merlin's last piece of advice running through his mind: *Seek help when you need it... learn from your mistakes.* Maybe this is what he meant; maybe this was his chance to ease his fear. "Yeah..." he admitted, hating that he sounded so pathetic.

He held his breath, wondering what would happen now. Would Logan laugh at him? Mock him? Make him feel even more ridiculous than he already did?

"You'll be alright," Logan assured him, waving his hand in dismissal. "I mean, I bet you never thought you'd learn how to use a sword... Horse riding's no different; just something you have to learn how to do."

Logan's words made sense but they did nothing to ease his fear; the *rational* part of him knew he was right... it was the *irrational* part that didn't.

"Were *you* scared before your first lesson?" Cai asked.

Logan scoffed. "Obviously! I mean, you'd have to be an idiot not to be a little scared, right? And I like to think I'm not a complete idiot!" He paused, clearly recalling the event. "I remember the first thing Lancelot said to me was: *'This beast could kill you with a swift kick to the head, so treat her well.'*" Seeing the horrified look on Cai's face, he quickly added, "But she didn't kick me and the lesson was fine. To be honest, I think Lancelot just said that to scare the hell out of me; it worked too." He paused, watching Cai carefully for a moment. "Seriously, though, it's not worth worrying about; all the horses here are well trained – Lancelot broke most of them in himself; he's really good with them. And sure," he continued brightly, "the horse *could* kick you or throw you off, but then, you could also loose a hand to a sword… Nothing's guaranteed."

Cai stared at him, horrified, as Logan started to get to his feet. In some ways it was good that Logan could be so dismissive of the dangers but being reminded of the risks kept Cai's fear very much alive…

Logan grinned down at him and patted him on the shoulder. "Seriously, don't worry; you'll be fine." Heading out, he paused in the doorway and looked back at Cai. "Now, what do you say to getting some breakfast? I'm starving!"

***

Cai reluctantly entered the Lower Courtyard, becoming more anxious by the second. He hadn't eaten much, but that didn't stop him feeling nauseous knowing what was about to come.

Spotting three horses tethered nearby, he wondered if this was what Merlin meant when he said he had to master his fear; to be able to keep walking forward when all he wanted to do was run in the opposite direction...

"Good morning, my Lord," Lancelot greeted him, inclining his head before acknowledging Logan's presence with a nod.

Cai forced himself to smile, praying he didn't look as nervous as he felt. "Morning," he muttered, glancing once more at the horses. Looking around, he frowned. "I thought Gawain was going to be here..."

"He is training with the others," Lancelot said before nodding to Logan who untethered the horses.

He returned almost immediately leading a black horse, already saddled; coming to a stop before Cai, he offered the rope to him.

Taking it, Cai tried, desperately, to hide his fear and looked at Lancelot expectantly.

The knight stepped forward, patting the horse firmly on its shoulder as he looked it over. Nodding, he began, "This is a descendant of Llamrei, your father's horse; her name is Rei."

Cai stared at her, overwhelmed; another connection to his father.

Lancelot continued, "She will be a good partner for you; she is strong and reliable, quick in battle." He turned to Cai and, fixing him with a hard stare, warned, "But she could still kill you with a kick to the head, so be sure to treat her well."

Upon hearing these words, the two boys shared a knowing smile; Cai's fears momentarily forgotten. Reaching up to stroke the mare's nose, Cai hesitated as she moved her head, snorting hot air onto his hand as she did so. After a moment, he moved closer to her, gently placing his hand on her muzzle. Recalling how Logan had greeted his own horse the previous day, and ignoring how ridiculous it felt to be talking to a horse, he murmured, "Hi, Rei…"

Lancelot nodded approvingly. "The bond you begin to create with your horse today will be deep and ever-lasting; one that you *cannot* take for granted. They are intelligent animals that will carry you into battle," he added. "The two of you will become a formidable force, working together against your enemies."

Cai listened attentively, his eyes darting between Lancelot and the horse; his words stirred something deep within him, something he hadn't known was there: a belief that this could *actually* work. A belief that he would *actually* learn to ride… Turning his attention to the horse, he stroked her absent-mindedly and began to warm to the idea of them being a team…

"Hang on," Cai frowned, as something dawned on him. "I'll be riding her into *battle?*" he asked, ignoring Logan's exasperated sigh as he dropped his head in his hands.

Thankfully, Lancelot took Cai's question in his stride. Nodding, he said, "Yes, Cai; you *will* be riding her into battle, *when* the time comes. But before then, you have a lot to learn."

Cai nodded slowly, as he acknowledged this fact and felt strange as, surprisingly, he no longer felt the urge to run.

Lancelot stepped away from Rei, giving Cai space. "Lead her around the courtyard," he suggested. "Let her get used to you handling her; talk to her."

Cai hesitated a moment, his grip tightening on the rope. Not knowing quite what to do, he tugged gently on the rope but the horse remained resolutely still, her black eyes staring forlornly back at Cai.

"Come on," Cai murmured, trying to sound encouraging.

Still the horse stayed put.

Cai sighed and hung his head for a moment. Looking up, he tried again. "Please..." he begged. "Walk!" he ordered, blushing as Logan snorted with barely contained laughter. Ignoring him, Cai moved closer to the mare and tugged on the rope again, hoping that it would spur her into action.

But it didn't.

"You need to show her you have control, Cai," Lancelot advised.

"And how do I do that, exactly?" Cai demanded, beginning to lose patience.

"Look her in the eye; treat her as an equal," the knight suggested simply.

Cai met her gaze and tugged at her rope again.

Logan snorted. "She's not a dog, you know," he quipped.

Cai clenched his jaw, frustrated by the whole thing. Turning back to her, he took a moment to clear his head, to calm down... Looking Rei in the eye, he waited... and suddenly felt something happen between them.

Stroking the beast's neck, he whispered, "Ready now?" and gently pulled the rope again.

This time, she immediately began to move, slow and cautious at first, but the more Cai spoke to her, the more confident her steps became. He was aware of Logan's words of encouragement as he passed his friend but ignored them, now far too focused on his horse to pay any attention to anything, or anyone, else.

After several circuits, Lancelot finally instructed Cai to stop.

"How did that feel?" the knight asked.

Cai's victorious grin said it all. "It was... good," he replied; he had never expected to enjoy leading a horse around the courtyard so much and would have willingly continued for the rest of the day. He couldn't have been more surprised that he had managed to control the mare long enough to make several relatively uneventful rounds of the yard; there had been a moment when the horse had been spooked by the sudden appearance of a dog but, acting instinctively, Cai had managed to talk the horse down.

"See; I told you it wasn't that bad!" Logan said enthusiastically as he approached. "Now all you have to do is learn how to *actually* ride her."

Cai felt his stomach drop at this; everything had been going so well... what if he screwed up and ruined all the progress he had made so far?

Lancelot glanced at him. "Don't worry; you have already started to gain each other's trust," he said, as if sensing Cai's hesitation.

Cai looked at Lancelot, glad the knight had confidence in him because *he* certainly didn't.

"You've mounted a horse before, haven't you?" Lancelot asked, ensuring the leather straps around the horse's middle were tight enough.

"Only with Merlin's help," he replied quietly, recalling his disastrous first attempts.

Lancelot nodded. "It isn't hard once you know how to do it and it will get easier the more you practise." He indicated the horse's left flank. "First, take hold of the pommel on the saddle and take the reins in your left hand then put your left leg in the stirrup..." He demonstrated, putting his own leg in the stirrup as he spoke and looked over at Cai. "Make sure your right hand rests over the back of the saddle and then..." He paused and, in one smooth movement, leapt from the ground, swinging his right leg over the horse, easily positioning himself in the saddle. Looking down at Cai, he smiled. "Simple."

Cai smiled uncertainly as, suddenly, he realised he had forgotten everything Lancelot had just told him.

Lancelot dismounted and handed the reins to Cai. "Your turn."

Cai nodded. "OK…" He reached up and took hold of the pommel; bracing himself, he put is foot in the stirrup but accidently kicked the horse which bolted forward, dragging Cai along with him. "What the…?" he cried, only just managing to pull his foot from the stirrup, before he was completely pulled off his feet.

Lancelot was quick to react, slipping his fingers into the halter and talking the horse down as he pulled her into a tight circle in order to prevent her escape.

Cai glared at the horse. "What the hell happened?" he demanded, for some reason feeling betrayed by the animal's behaviour. "Why did she do that?"

Lancelot came to stand beside Cai, looking slightly amused. "You kicked her," he stated.

"What? No I didn't!"

"When you put your foot in the stirrup, you kicked her."

Cai paused, realising the knight was right. "Oh. Sorry."

"Try again," Lancelot said, handing the horse over to Cai once more.

This time, Cai took a moment before putting his foot in the stirrup.

Master your fear…

"When you're ready, mate," Logan muttered. "We haven't got all day."

Cai glared at him before raising his leg and resting the ball of his foot on the stirrup. He paused, half expecting the horse to bolt again but, thankfully, she stayed put. Smiling to himself, he leapt and clumsily pulled himself up, struggling to swing his leg over the back of the saddle.

Logan's laughter filled the air as Lancelot stepped forward to help, pushing his leg over the saddle.

"Shut up," Cai growled.

"But you looked *so* ridiculous!" Logan insisted.

Straightening up and settling himself in the saddle, he glared at Logan who was now creased up with laughter.

"I wish I had a camera right now," he managed to say, "This would so be on Facebook tomorrow."

"If I recall correctly," Lancelot began, "*your* first time was not nearly so graceful."

Logan blushed at this, his laughter dying.

Lancelot looked over at Cai. "Well done, my Lord; it will come with practise. Just be careful not to pull too hard on the saddle as it could damage the horse. Now, make sure your right foot is in the stirrup…"

After a brief struggle, Cai found the stirrup but it took several attempts to get his boot in it.

Below him, Lancelot stepped forward, reaching for the rope Cai had used to lead the horse. "Now, I shall lead you around the courtyard so that you may get a feel for her." Clicking his tongue, he set off at a slow, steady pace.

Cai immediately tensed up as he felt the horse move beneath him.

"You need to relax," Lancelot advised, looking back and following Cai's progress carefully. "If you're relaxed, she will be too."

Cai nodded, forcing himself to follow Lancelot's advice; it wasn't always easy but, as the lesson wore on, he found his trust in the horse growing. And, once he had stopped worrying, he realised he was quite enjoying this newfound experience.

***

"OK, tell me the truth," Logan said as they guided their horses back into Camelot's courtyard. "This wasn't as bad as you thought, was it?"

Cai glanced at him, so much more at ease now, and grinned. "It's been good; *really* good," he admitted, realising just how much he had enjoyed it.

When Lancelot had suggested moving the lesson outside Camelot, Cai had initially recoiled at the idea, anticipating the worst-case scenarios. He feared that, at the first taste of freedom, or if he were too heavy-handed with Rei, she would make a bolt for it.

But, as he had left Camelot alongside Logan and Lancelot, he had soon found that all his fears were unfounded; Rei hadn't bolted, thrown him off or challenged his command. In fact, the longer they spent together, the stronger their connection seemed to become and, it was with some reluctance, that Cai had followed Lancelot back to Camelot.

Once in the courtyard, Cai dismounted, aware of a stable hand waiting expectantly to take Rei from him. Taking a moment, Cai murmured a brief goodbye to her and found himself promising to see her later. Stepping away, he handed the reins over and watched as she was led away, noticing, for the first time, how beautiful she was; every powerful muscle was defined by the brilliant sheen of her coat.

He marvelled at how quickly things had changed; only a week ago he had thought Logan strange for talking to his horse and now he found himself doing exactly the same thing.

"Well, what do you think of her?" Logan asked.

"She's great. I really like her and, I don't know... I suppose I trust her..." Cai frowned. "Which is strange because I've only just met her."

Logan shook his head. "That's not strange," he insisted. "I totally trust Girl." He grinned. "Anyway, I think horses are better than people most of the time."

"We will continue these lesson every day from now on," Lancelot's voice broke in as he approached the boys. "You will learn how to work with your horse in a variety of situations and set pieces; in time, you will also learn how to ride alongside your men and to fight on horseback." He paused, allowing Cai time to process his words, and smiled. "There *is* a lot to do, my Lord, but you *will* learn all you need; I promise you that."

Cai smiled uncertainly; there was a lot to do...

"Take a break; get something to eat," Lancelot instructed. "Afterwards, you will meet Gawain in the arena."

Finally left to their own devices, Cai and Logan made straight for the Great Hall... and food.

Chapter Thirty-Two

Cai lost all sense of time as his training continued, each day merged into the next as his training became more demanding, challenging him in ways he didn't think possible. Every day he learnt new skills and was gradually learning to put them all together. It was at the end of one of these lessons, as they led their horses back to Camelot, that Merlin approached. Studying him, Cai immediately realised something was wrong: he looked tired and haggard, something he had never thought possible.

Logan must have noticed it, too, as he asked, "Are you alright?"

Merlin smiled at the boys as they dismounted. "I am quite well, thank you." He glanced at Lancelot before looking to Cai. "I trust your lessons are going well."

Cai nodded. "Yeah, they are actually."

248

Lancelot smiled. "He knows now that horses are nothing to be feared."

Cai lowered his head in embarrassment; he couldn't believe how much he now relied on Rei and how ridiculous he had been to fear her.

Merlin's smile widened as he turned to Lancelot. "Would you mind if I borrowed Cai for a moment?" He turned to Cai. "There are things we need to discuss, my Lord," he added solemnly.

Lancelot nodded. "Of course; we have finished for the day."

Cai turned to Logan. "I'll see you later."

Logan nodded. "Yeah, sure."

Cai turned expectantly to Merlin.

"Come, Cai," Merlin murmured, indicating the archway that led out of Camelot.

Cai fell into step beside him. "Where are we going?" he asked, his curiosity piqued.

"You'll see," Merlin replied mysteriously. After a moment, he said, "I fear I should apologise."

Cai frowned. "For what?"

"For not coming to you sooner," Merlin explained. "I should have done, but I wanted you to focus on your training without any distractions."

Cai nodded, unsure of what to say.

They continued to walk in silence, Cai's attention drawn to the training arena where he could see Gawain putting men through their paces. He watched, awestruck, as men battled each other, their weapons catching the light as they sliced through the air towards their 'enemies', each desperate to win. They fought each other with such ferocity and determination that no one, who didn't already know, would guess these men were allies and not the deadliest of enemies.

Surprisingly, he thought, *One day, I'll be amongst them.*

He smiled; that thought did not frighten him nearly as much as he thought it would. In fact, he kind of liked the idea of belonging, of being a part of something...

"We'll take this path to the top of the cliff," Merlin announced, drawing Cai's attention away from the arena. He indicated a rough path running adjacent to Camelot's walls and, as they began their ascent, Cai lengthened his stride slightly; the incline was steep but he easily managed it, something he wouldn't have been able to do a few weeks ago.

Merlin, however, was a different story.

Cai watched with concern as Merlin's pace slowed down considerably and his breathing became laboured. Turning to face him, he asked, "Are you *sure* you're OK?"

Merlin smiled weakly. "As I informed Logan, I am *fine*," he insisted, emphasising the last word.

"Well, you don't look it," Cai muttered. Indicating the path behind them, he added, "We could easily turn back; I mean, whatever it is, I'm sure you can tell me in Camelot."

Merlin paused, turning to Cai. "Cai, your concern does you credit but..."

Cai smiled wryly. "You're fine," he muttered drily.

Merlin's smile strengthened. "Exactly." He set off again. "Besides, it isn't far now."

Cai followed, watching Merlin warily, preparing himself for the very real possibility that he might have to catch him if he stumbled.

The ground soon levelled out and Cai found himself walking along the cliff edge, the sea on his left. Suddenly dizzy, he forced himself to focus on the landscape ahead of him, anywhere but the sea...

"We're here," Merlin announced.

Cai stopped in his tracks. The view before him was breathtaking; the vastness of the sea, the rugged cliff face that towered over craggy rocks far below, the coastline that went on for miles in each direction, all left him with a feeling of insignificance in this incredible landscape. He watched as waves crashed against the rocks, spray shooting up several feet high, leaving white foam in their wake that ebbed and flowed with the tide. He took a deep breath; even this high up, he could taste the salt in the air, could feel it on his skin.

The breeze had picked up and Cai pulled his cloak closer about him, never more grateful for it and his padded shirt.

"Turn around, Cai," Merlin instructed.

He did so, immediately noting how tired Merlin's voice had become.

With his back to the sea, Camelot now stretched out before him in all her glory. Her walls stood tall, surveying the landscape around her, mistress of all, and Cai couldn't help but be in awe of her from this angle. Smoke rose from Gadeon's forge as people went about their business; warriors trained and men patrolled her battlements. He took a deep breath and couldn't ignore the pride he felt knowing that his father had been the one to make Camelot what she was.

Merlin gazed wistfully at the castle as if recalling happier times; he looked refreshed just looking at the view. "This was your father's favourite place," he explained quietly. "He used to come here when he had important decisions to make."

Cai swallowed; suddenly the cold wind buffeting him no longer bothered him, nothing bothered him. *His father had come here; this had been his favourite place.* And he couldn't help wondering if Arthur had stood in this exact same spot he was standing in now; he smiled at the possibility.

Merlin put a hand on his shoulder. "I thought you should see it."

Cai nodded, unable to speak; his throat tightened and his vision swam with tears. Clearing his throat, he glanced at Merlin. "He really came here?" he asked, still trying to take it in.

Merlin nodded. "I would often find him here. This was where he stood when he finally realised he was destined to rule Camelot." He paused briefly before adding, "I felt this would be a fitting place to continue our story. Do you recall what I last told you about Morgan?"

Cai stared at him in anticipation; so much had happened since he and Merlin had last spoken about her that he had almost forgotten the promise Merlin had made. Now, everything came flooding back to him as if no time had passed. He nodded.

"So... where did we leave off?"

"Morgan had killed Uther Pendragon and you had gone to get my father back." The word felt alien on his tongue but, somehow, it still felt *right*.

Merlin smiled; Cai's choice of word hadn't gone unnoticed by him. "Ah, yes; you're quite right." He paused, allowing himself a moment to collect his thoughts. "When Uther died, your father was living a happy life with Kay's family. He had grown into a good man, sheltered and protected from the pressures of Camelot. That fact alone made me glad I had kept him hidden, for if Morgan had known of his existence, she would have surely killed him. As it was, the only thing she wanted was Camelot."

"Why?"

"Killing Uther wasn't enough for her," Merlin explained. "Just as he had taken everything from her, she wanted everything that was now his, and that included Camelot; she wanted it back in her grasp."

"How come she didn't just take it, then?" Cai asked. "With all her powers I would have thought it'd be easy."

Merlin looked grave. "She tried but she was not quite strong enough to break through my defences; she had, after all, only started out on her path... So, she did the only thing she could do."

"And what was that?"

"She vanished, Cai; I know not where." Looking at him, he continued. "But, your father was protected, at least for a short time, and *that* was all that mattered."

Cai frowned. "So when *did* she find out about my father?" he asked.

"I shall get to that," Merlin assured him. "First, I should explain how he came to know of his destiny. I set up a test..."

"A test?" Cai echoed. "But you just sprung it on me..."

Merlin smiled indulgently. "There was no opportunity to test you, Cai," he informed him. "The situation we find ourselves in now, is much more urgent; Morgan and Mordred have nursed their hatred for years and Morgan has waited long enough. She will come for Camelot whether we are ready or not."

Cai swallowed nervously, a newfound fear making his blood turn to ice; with all he was doing now, it was so easy to forget the threat they were facing sometimes. Living a life away from this world, Greg and Jules had protected him against evil: now he was staring it in directly in the face.

"To all intents and purposes," Merlin continued, "Arthur was the son of a farmer; to suddenly reveal his true heritage would have caused too many problems and, don't forget, Morgan was still at large; I had to protect him as much as I could." Cai nodded in agreement. "So I put a sword in a stone..."

Cai smiled wryly, his mind drawing comparisons between myth and reality. It was strange to think that the stories he had heard growing up had *actually* happened. But, more importantly, he now knew they were also part of *his* history.

"People came from far and wide to try their luck but it was *Arthur* who finally pulled it free." Merlin smiled, recalling the moment. "He was just as surprised as everyone else. Many people questioned it; they considered him too young, and inexperienced, to rule..."

It was hard for Cai to believe people had had doubts about Arthur. He smiled; at least he had *that* in common with his father.

"He had many problems to deal with," Merlin continued. "There's nothing like a rebellion or two to make people believe you have what it takes to lead."

Cai turned towards Camelot again, a deep longing pulling at him; not for the first time, he wished he had had a chance to know the man who had been his father. "Was Morgan part of it?" he asked quietly, a black hatred rising inside him.

Merlin shook his head. "No; these rebellions involved jealous men who were dissatisfied with their lot in life and thought they could betray their king to make a better life for themselves," he explained bitterly. "Remember: Morgan had no idea of her half-brother's existence."

Trying to focus on something other than his anger, he turned back to Merlin. "Then how *did* she find out about him?" he asked impatiently.

"It didn't take long for word of Arthur's return to Camelot to spread and, with it, the truth about his parentage." He gazed at Camelot as he spoke, recalling another time and place. "I have no doubt that, wherever Morgan was, she was keeping a very close eye on Camelot. She was no fool; she knew how many people passed through every day..." He began counting off the different possibilities. "Traders, servants, even knights... Any of them could have been her spies or been intercepted by her; any of them could have informed her of Arthur's existence."

Cai narrowed his eyes suspiciously. "Do you think one of Arthur's knights betrayed him?"

Merlin shook his head. "No, I don't; the people Arthur surrounded himself with were trustworthy and loyal..."

Cai scoffed. "Except for Mordred."

Merlin inclined his head. "Except for Mordred," he agreed. "Mordred was the chink in Arthur's armour."

"How did he end up at Camelot?" Cai asked.

"Many years passed," Merlin replied. "They were quiet years and I could only assume Morgan was waiting; waiting for the right time, when she could finally claim Camelot for herself." He paused briefly, closed his eyes, and pinched the bridge of his nose as though he had a headache. Opening his eyes, he continued, "One day, a boy arrived at Camelot; he was young, about fourteen years old, unkempt and travel weary, but eager to see Arthur whom he claimed was his uncle." He paused, as if trying to maintain his train of thought.

Cai frowned; this wasn't like Merlin at all. Something was very wrong. But before he could say anything, Merlin pressed on with his story and Cai's concerns were forgotten.

"The boy was taken to Arthur where he explained he had escaped his mother's clutches, claiming she was insane. After questioning him further, I was convinced he was speaking of Morgan and that he was telling the truth about his parentage."

"What did you do?"

"I advised Arthur to be vigilant, to be wary of the boy, but all Arthur saw was a young man in need of guidance; he thought it right to take him in, to keep him near." Merlin shook his head as if, even now, he was frustrated by Arthur's decision. "He cast my doubts aside, saying Mordred needed a chance to prove he was good, despite his upbringing; he wanted Mordred to escape his mother's shadow."

"But he didn't, did he?" Cai demanded angrily. He couldn't help thinking that, if Arthur hadn't been so eager to take pity on Mordred, none of them would be in this situation now and his father would still be alive. He would still have a father and his mother would still have a husband.

"He couldn't," Merlin replied. "Morgan had indoctrinated him; her poison, her hatred, were now his to share."

Cai felt nothing but hatred for Morgan *and* Mordred. Clenching his hands into fists, he turned his anger on the only person he could: Merlin. "Why didn't *you* do anything to stop Mordred?" he asked. *"You could have used your power."*

Merlin's face was grave, serving only to deepen the dark circles beneath his eyes, making him look old, suddenly. "Cai, when my King told me to give Mordred a chance, I had no choice *but* to obey," he told him sharply. "I had already learnt the price of interfering with fate. But, although I did it, don't think I liked it. And, let me assure you, I *was* vigilant; I waited for *any* sign, *however* small, that he would betray Arthur. I saw nothing untoward in his behaviour; he had been trained exceptionally well in the art of manipulation." Merlin's tone softened as he continued. "You must remember, Cai: he had been sent to Camelot with one thought in mind; he was not going to risk his mother's plans, his *own* plans, by revealing his true intentions. He needed to earn everyone's trust; he needed to earn *Arthur's* trust if he was ever going to claim Camelot."

Cai sighed; he could understand that. One wrong move would have meant certain death. "So when did you find out what he was up to? What tripped him up?"

Merlin was just about to answer when movement on Camelot's walls caught his attention.

Cai followed his gaze and found himself looking at a woman standing on the battlements.

He recognised her immediately...

Nimue...

He glanced at Merlin who was staring intently back at her, his face unreadable. After a moment, he nodded slowly and Cai was left with the uneasy feeling that some unspoken words had passed between them.

As he hastily set off back along the path, Merlin said, "I need to return to Camelot."

"No, you can't do this to me again!" Cai shouted as he carefully negotiated the path in Merlin's wake. "You can't just..."

But he never got to finish the sentence as Merlin suddenly faltered, reaching blindly for support, his hands clawing at the air in desperation. Cai hesitated only a moment before reaching out to grab his forearms, staring in horror as Merlin's eyes rolled back into his head leaving only the whites of his eyes showing.

"Merlin?" he cried, his voice filled with terror. "Are you alright? What's wrong?"

Merlin stiffened in Cai's arms and he let out a strangled cry before dropping to his knees; clawing at Cai's shirt, he whispered, "Dark times lay ahead, my Lord." His voice was raspy, as though he had a dry throat and hadn't spoken in years.

Cai stared down at him, unable to speak, fear and confusion gripping him.

"You shall be betrayed," Merlin declared. "One you trust has darkness in their soul... A heart buried beneath secrets and lies."

Before Cai could react, Merlin fell to the ground where he lay motionless.

Chapter Thirty-Three

Cai could only stare at Merlin's prone form lying motionless at his feet; at that moment, thought and movement were beyond him. His mind and body were frozen, too terrified to think or move.

The only thought running through his mind was that Merlin needed him but he had no idea what to do. He was outside Camelot, alone... even if he screamed at the top of his voice he doubted anyone would hear his cries.

But what if Merlin was dying?

That thought alone was enough to jolt him into action. Quickly removing his cloak, he dropped to his knees beside Merlin, about to drape it over him, but froze as a shadow passed over them. Glancing up, he stared helplessly as a black mass dropped from the sky.

"What the...?" he exclaimed, stumbling as he was knocked off his feet. He watched in amazement, as the hunched mass grew taller revealing Nimue standing before him. He stared in disbelief; she had just *dropped* from the castle wall. But how could she...? It must be at least fifteen feet high.

"How the Hell...?" he began as he turned his attention back to Merlin.

Before reaching him, however, Nimue rounded on him, her dark eyes flashing with icy fire. *"Leave him!"* she hissed.

Cai froze. "But..." he started to protest, taking a step towards Merlin; he wasn't about to turn his back on him, he needed to know he was OK.

Nimue blocked his path, her eyes burning into him. *"Don't* touch him!" she warned. Turning her back on Cai, she knelt at Merlin's side, her cloak pooling on the ground around her, like black ink.

Cai watched silently as she closed her eyes and began chanting in a language he'd never heard before. He frowned as her chanting became quieter and more intense; she bowed her head, lost in whatever it was she was doing. Just as he decided it was safe to approach, a loud crack filled the air and a blinding flash of white light caused him to recoil, shielding his eyes with his arm as he did so.

Lowering his arm, he opened his eyes... and could only stare at the ground before him.

Where Merlin and the woman had been only a moment before there was, now, only the empty path leading back to Camelot.

He was alone on the hillside.

Bursting into action, he sprinted down the hill, back to Camelot; surely someone there could help. As he entered the Lower Courtyard, he ran smack into Logan and the two boys fell in a tangled heap on the ground.

"Ow!" Logan cried, clutching his arm. Glaring at Cai, as he got to his feet, he demanded, "What's got into you?"

Cai scrambled to his feet, his body tense with pent up energy. "It's Merlin…" he spat as if that explained everything. He set off in the direction of the Upper Courtyard but Logan grabbed his arm, stopping him dead in his tracks.

"Hey, hold on," he began, frowning at Cai. "Seriously, what's going on?"

Cai yanked his arm free, almost over-balancing as he did so. "I don't have time to explain!" he cried. "Merlin… he was there one minute and then… then he wasn't." Seeing Logan's confusion, he knew he wasn't making any sense but he needed to get to the Upper Courtyard, he needed to find help… maybe Lancelot or Gawain… He tried to pull free of Logan's grip but Logan held firm, forcing Cai to meet his gaze.

"Cai, slow down," he ordered, gripping his shoulders. "Just… tell me what's going on."

Knowing Logan wasn't about to let him go, Cai told him about Merlin's collapse and everything that had happened since, finishing with Merlin and Nimue's disappearance.

Logan's jaw dropped. "They *disappeared*?" he echoed in disbelief. Cai nodded. Logan fell silent, clearly trying to get his head around it all.

Cai pushed past Logan, muttering, "I *need* to find Lancelot."

"Wait!" Logan cried, appearing at Cai's side. "I think I know where Nimue would have taken him; come on."

"But what if she hurts him?" he demanded. "We need..."

Logan shook his head. "She won't," he replied confidently.

"Are you sure about that?" Cai asked doubtfully. "You didn't see..." He cringed at the memory.

"Cai, I've been here long enough to know that Nimue may be weird but she'd never hurt Merlin," Logan insisted. "Now, you can waste time trying to find Lancelot if you want but..."

Cai shook his head; he just needed to find Merlin, to see for himself that he was safe. "No, go on; lead the way."

***

Cai followed as Logan led him through a series of corridors lit every so often by wall-mounted torches; shadows danced eerily on the walls, following their progress. Cai tried to take note of where they were going but, with each step, he felt as though he were heading deeper into a maze; each corridor looked the same as the last and he found it impossible to distinguish between them.

Eventually they arrived at an archway, through which Cai could see a spiral staircase leading downwards. He stared in surprise; he hadn't been aware Camelot *had* any lower levels.

"Where are we going?" he asked cautiously, eyeing the dark stairwell.

Logan glanced at Cai. "To Merlin's chambers, where else?" He turned and, lifting a torch from its bracket, started to make his way down, leaving Cai no choice but to follow.

"I didn't know Camelot had lower levels," he said, voicing his earlier thoughts, his words echoing in the stairwell.

"Well, when you've been here as long as I have, you have to figure things out pretty quickly," Logan murmured. "Nimue caught me snooping around down here once..." He glanced back at Cai and grinned. "Let's just say, she didn't take it too well."

Despite himself, Cai smiled; he could easily imagine Logan sneaking around in the shadows.

They emerged into a dark corridor, lit only by two torches mounted on the wall either side of the stairwell. Cai shivered; the air down here was cold and damp and he wished he could return to the upper levels of the castle, but he couldn't; he *had* to find Merlin.

Logan turned and faced Cai, torchlight flickering across his face. "This way."

Falling into step behind Logan he made sure to remain in the meagre light offered by the torch. It wasn't that he was scared, he kept telling himself, it was just the dense, tangible darkness at his back made him feel uneasy; he couldn't shake the idea that some unseen force was watching them from the shadows.

Suddenly aware Logan had come to a stop, Cai peered past his head and realised they had reached the end of the corridor. Set into the stone wall was a simple wooden door; reaching up, Logan knocked three times, the sound reverberating in the silence.

As they waited, Cai heard shuffling from within before the key was turned and the door opened, very slightly, revealing Nimue's dark figure in the shadows; at the sight of her, Cai felt an overwhelming sense of relief wash over him. Merlin *must* be here; Logan had been right.

"I'm here to see Merlin," Cai declared sounding far more confident than he actually felt.

Nimue's eyes narrowed as she looked at Cai. "He is receiving no visitors at the moment."

The door began to close, but Cai halted it with the palm of his hand.

"I said: I'm here to see Merlin," he repeated not sure where his newfound confidence was coming from. He swallowed nervously as Nimue glared at him, her eyes hard and unyielding; he knew what kind of power she had at her fingertips so *why* was he running the risk of antagonising her?

After what seemed like an eternity however, Nimue sighed and reluctantly stepped back, allowing the door to open more.

"You do not have long," she informed him coldly.

Cai glanced at Logan before stepping into the room.

Logan started to follow him but Nimue blocked his path. "*Not* you."

Cai noted the look of outrage that crossed Logan's face and was grateful when he didn't argue the point. Instead, he glanced at Cai. "I'll wait for you here, then." Looking warily at Nimue, he added, "Don't be long."

Cai gave a small nod of agreement before Nimue stepped out into the corridor, closing the door behind them.

Alone in the untidy room, Cai was aware of a strange acrid smell, reminiscent of the joss sticks Greg and Jules were so fond of. Looking around, he soon realised Merlin was not in this room and, seeing a doorway framed by two columns, went in to what he believed may be his bedroom.

He paused at the sight before him: Merlin was propped up in bed, his eyes closed; he looked relaxed, as if he were enjoying a lie in.

As he stared at the older man, Cai had to remind himself that, no matter how peaceful he looked now, he had, only moments before, collapsed in pain and been spirited here as the result of some weird and very powerful magic. Surely, even *he* couldn't have been unaffected by it all.

Standing in the doorway, Cai realised how selfish he had been to come here; of *course* Merlin wouldn't want to see anyone, considering what he had just been through. Nimue had been right all along; he had only been thinking of what *he* wanted. Merlin needed to rest and recuperate and he needed to do it without Cai badgering him.

As he turned to leave, his eyes caught sight of something on the desk: a leather-bound book, the discovery of which had changed his life irrevocably.

Unable to stop himself, he reached out and, picking it up, turned it over in his hands and flicked through its pages.

"I find it comforting to read; it reminds me of better times."

Cai jumped at the unexpected sound of Merlin's voice, feeling as if he had just been caught out. Quickly replacing the book on the desk, he turned to face him.

"How are you?" Cai asked quietly.

"I am fine now, thank you," Merlin replied. Indicating a goblet by his bedside, he asked, "Would you...?"

Cai walked over and picked it up, realising, with some alarm, that the dark liquid inside was giving off steam although the goblet itself remained cold to the touch.

"It's a herbal remedy Nimue created," Merlin explained noting the shock on Cai's face. "It rejuvenates me after one of my... turns."

Cai watched, warily, as Merlin sipped the concoction in the goblet, watching as Merlin closed his eyes obviously savouring the taste.

When he opened them, he smiled at Cai. "There's no need to look so concerned, Cai," he told him. "These... attacks happen upon me suddenly but they are not without warning."

Cai recalled how Merlin had looked earlier that day and cursed himself; he had known Merlin was ill. He should have insisted they return to Camelot.

"Do not blame yourself," Merlin insisted, as if reading his thoughts. "Nimue warned me but..." He sighed regretfully. "As I had with you, I refused to listen."

Cai was surprised to hear this; Nimue seemed so cold, so unfeeling... It was hard for him to imagine her looking out for Merlin's welfare. Maybe Logan *had* been right after all; maybe she *did* care about him. "So, what happened?" he asked. "I mean... you collapsed and..."

Merlin held Cai's gaze. "What did I say, Cai?"

Cai swallowed, recalling Merlin's exact words. "You said someone would betray me; someone I trusted."

"Ah..." Merlin said thoughtfully, setting aside the goblet; it obviously made sense to him.

"What you witnessed was a prophecy," he explained quietly.

"A prophecy?" Cai repeated.

Merlin nodded. "I'm afraid prophecies are strange things," he said. "They don't always reveal themselves completely to me. I would advise you to be vigilant; traitors come in many guises. Even those you trust can turn against you."

Cai sighed, feeling tired and frustrated; this was not what he had wanted to hear. Shouldn't Merlin, of all people, be able to offer him some answers? "I don't know what to do anymore!" he confided, suddenly feeling overwhelmed by it all. "I mean... I'm trying to be a good knight, I'm trying to prove that I can do all this... I already have Morgan and Mordred to worry about but now you're telling me I have a traitor to worry about, too!"

Merlin smiled sympathetically. "No one said being a King was easy."

Cai glared at him. "Thanks; that helps a lot," he muttered sarcastically.

Merlin's face was grave as he spoke. "Cai, in order to be great you need to understand yourself *and* those around you."

"What's that supposed to mean?" Cai demanded, his frustration growing.

"Before you can progress, you need an understanding of how we all reached this point," he informed him. "It is all well and good trying to decipher a prophecy but you need to understand your enemy; maybe in doing that, the prophecy will make *itself* clear."

Cai stared at him. "So... what are you saying?"

"You need to finish the story we started, Cai," Merlin explained. "You asked me a question not so long ago... do you remember?" Cai nodded. "The answer to that question will help you clarify some things in your own mind." He picked up the goblet again and took another sip. Cai waited, hoping he would continue with the story. "Regretfully, I am not best placed to provide the answers you seek."

Cai almost scoffed. Why didn't that surprise him? Nothing seemed to make sense, nothing was straightforward; all this was turning into a wild goose chase.

"Lancelot," Merlin continued, noticing Cai's frustration, "spent far more time with Mordred than I ever did."

"So I should speak to him?" Cai asked.

Merlin nodded, his weariness evident. "That would be advisable." He paused, his gaze shifting slightly to look over Cai's shoulder. "Now, you should leave; Nimue grows impatient and she is not one to be crossed." He smiled weakly.

Cai nodded and forced a smile as he turned to leave but paused as Merlin spoke.

"Remember what I said, Cai: *be vigilant.*"

Cai nodded one final time before turning and making his way to the door. Pulling it open, he saw Logan and Nimue still waiting in the corridor.

Without a word, Nimue slipped past Cai, closing the door behind her.

"Well?" Logan demanded. "Is he alright?"

Cai nodded grimly as he set off towards the upper levels of the castle.

Logan hurried after him, watching Cai carefully. "So, come on; tell me what happened."

Cai glanced at him. "I will," he promised. "But first, we have to find Lancelot; I need to talk to him."

Chapter Thirty-Four

From Merlin's quarters, Cai had gone in search of Guinevere; if anyone would know where Lancelot was, it would be her. However, all she could tell him, was that Lancelot and Gawain had lead a small group of men from Camelot earlier that day and she had no idea when they would return.

Disappointed he would again, have to wait before he could find out more, he suggested to Logan they await the knights' return in the Lower Courtyard.

Sitting on the steps opposite Camelot's entrance, Logan turned to Cai. "Why are you so desperate to speak to him anyway? What's so important?"

Cai sighed. "Merlin said I needed to understand Mordred better and said the best person to ask was Lancelot."

Logan frowned. "Why?"

"Do you remember I told you Lancelot and Mordred used to be friends?" Logan nodded. "Well, I bet he knows loads about him."

"Yeah, you're probably right," Logan agreed.

They continued to sit in silence as the minutes turned to hours. As the light began to fade, Logan suggested he get them something to eat and it wasn't long before he returned with two bowls of broth. Although not hungry, Cai was grateful for the warmth it provided.

"So... where d'you reckon he is?" Logan asked, downing the last of his meal.

Cai shrugged. "I don't know; I'd have thought they'd have been back by now."

Logan's face paled as a sudden thought struck him. "You don't think...?" He hesitated.

Cai frowned. "What?"

Logan tentatively continued. "You don't think anything could have happened to them, do you? I mean, Morgan *is* out there somewhere..."

Cai stood up so fast, his legs almost gave way under him; he hadn't even considered that possibility. The two boys looked at each other, transfixed.

Suddenly, they were aware of the sound of horses' hooves pounding the ground. They turned just as Lancelot and Gawain entered the courtyard, bringing their horses to a stop; a group of fifty or so men trotted in after them, all talking and laughing good-naturedly. A wave of relief washed

274

over Cai as he watched the knights dismount and hand their reins to a servant. Spotting them, Lancelot nodded in greeting.

"Boys," he murmured, a puzzled expression on his face.

"We were wondering where you were," Cai explained, hurrying after Lancelot. "We were worried."

Lancelot smiled indulgently. "Well, as you see, we are safe and well," he said, indicating himself and Gawain, obviously not in need of their help.

"I need to talk to you," Cai announced eagerly.

Lancelot held up a hand. "Not now, Cai," he said wearily. "It has been a long day." He looked at each boy in turn. "We are going to rest; I suggest you two do the same." And, without another word, he began to walk away, Gawain following in his wake.

Logan cleared his throat pointedly and nodded towards Lancelot's back at if to say: *do it now.*

"No, it *can't* wait!" Cai blurted out before he could stop himself.

Lancelot turned to face Cai, his hand resting on the hilt of his sword; he smiled, amused that Cai would speak to him in such a manner.

"I mean..." Cai floundered, attempting to sound more confident than he actually felt. He became aware of Gawain, Logan and some of the men nearby watching him, but forced himself to continue. "I need to talk to you about Mordred," he said, lowering his voice. "Merlin said..."

Lancelot stared at him for a moment before glancing furtively around the courtyard. Ignoring Cai's request, he turned and climbed the stairs, leaving Cai no choice but to follow.

As they reached the Upper Courtyard, Cai moved to block his path. "Please," he begged. "Just a few questions."

Lancelot refused to look at him. "I can't," he said curtly, his tone inviting no argument.

"But..."

Lancelot shook his head adamantly. "*No.*"

Lancelot started to walk around him but Cai, enraged by his refusal, reached out and grabbed his arm; didn't he understand how important this was? Instantly, Gawain was there, pulling Cai's hand away. Cai yanked his arm free of Gawain and glared at Lancelot.

"You can't just walk away," he insisted. "I have a right to know what happened; I have a right..."

"I said *no!*" And with that, he walked away.

Cai made to follow but Gawain blocked his path.

"Let it be," he said quietly.

Cai clenched his jaw, knowing he'd never get past Gawain. He watched helplessly as Gawain, too, walked away, disappearing into the shadows.

"Well... *that* was weird," Logan muttered, breaking the silence.

Cai turned to him. "So it wasn't just me?" he asked, "You thought that, too?"

Logan frowned thoughtfully. "It was like as soon as he heard the name 'Mordred' he just flipped out." He glanced at Cai. "Well, we *definitely* need to know what happened now..."

Cai couldn't have agreed more; to say he was even more curious now was an understatement. Casting a final look in Lancelot's direction, he reluctantly set off towards his own quarters.

Logan fell into step beside him and they walked in silence for a moment. "What do think he's so desperate to keep hidden?"

Cai frowned. "What do you mean?"

"Well, the fact he just shut you down, like that..." Logan replied. "I mean, if *that* isn't weird, I don't know what is." He glanced at Cai. "If they were friends once, maybe there's still a part of him that has some loyalty towards Mordred." He clicked his fingers as a sudden thought occurred to him. "Maybe *he's* your betrayer!"

Cai frowned. "How d'you work *that* out?" he demanded.

"Think about it," Logan encouraged. "You said they were friends..."

"Yeah, but..."

Merlin's warning echoed in his head.

Traitors come in many guises... Be vigilant...

Cai was desperate not to leap to conclusions but the damage was done; the doubts were there now. Was Lancelot truly capable of betraying Camelot and the memory of King Arthur? Despite Cai's unwillingness to believe the worst, there was a little voice reminding him that Lancelot hadn't wasted much time in marrying Guinevere after Arthur's death. Maybe his loyalties *never were* with Arthur; if that were true, how could Cai expect them to extend to him? And if he *was* in league with Mordred, he couldn't really be in a better position to help him destroy Camelot.

Cai fell silent as he entered their quarters and lay on his bed. He lay awake in the darkness for what seemed like hours, his doubts, Lancelot's sudden change of attitude and Logan's comments playing on his mind. He would not rest easy tonight.

Chapter Thirty-Five

The following day, as Cai and Logan made their way to the stables, they saw only the solitary figure of Gawain waiting for them; a stable hand waited nearby with Rei and Gawain's horse.

Logan was the first to notice. Nudging Cai, he nodded towards the knight. "How do you explain this, then?" he murmured.

Cai followed his line of sight, his brain working overtime, trying to come up with reasons to explain Lancelot's absence. He glanced at Logan. "Do you think he's not here because of last night?"

Logan stared at him as if the answer was painfully obvious. "Don't *you*?" he demanded.

Cai had to admit he had a point. Lancelot's reaction to his questions the previous night had been strange to say the least; he had been very defensive when Mordred's name was mentioned and it hadn't taken much for him to snap. Cai had gone over and over it in his head all night but he couldn't come up with any explanation for Lancelot's behaviour other than he knew things about Mordred, things he didn't want to share with anyone.

Things he wanted to *stay* hidden.

It infuriated Cai that he didn't know what they were. After all, the man *was* married to his mother; if he was hiding something about Mordred, he needed to know in case it put his mother in danger.

And then there was that *other* issue, the one hanging over Cai like a black cloud: *was* Lancelot the traitor in Merlin's prophecy? He didn't want to think that, not of the man who had once been his father's best friend, the man now married to his mother; besides that, he liked Lancelot and didn't want to think the worst of him. But, at that moment, what other choice did he have?

"Maybe you have him running scared," Logan grinned, clearly enjoying this.

Cai looked doubtful. "I don't think so." He couldn't imagine Lancelot ever 'running scared', even if his suspicions *were* right.

"Yes, you do! I mean, if he wasn't dodgy, he'd be here, wouldn't he?" Logan asked. "But as it is, the questions you were asking last night..." His gaze lingered on Gawain as he spoke. "He knew that, if he *was* here today, you'd probably start up again and he didn't want to refuse to answer you; that, in itself, would raise questions."

280

Cai looked at Logan bewildered. "I thought you liked Lancelot," he reminded him.

"I do," Logan insisted without missing a beat.

"Then why are you so keen to suggest he's hiding something?" Cai asked. "And why are you enjoying this so much?"

Logan shrugged. "It's not that I'm 'enjoying' it as such..." he replied, quickly. "It's just... anything even *remotely* interesting is exciting here. I mean, if they had a *TV* or something..."

Cai started to laugh, despite himself.

Logan glanced at him warily. "Why are you laughing?"

Cai shook his head, attempting, but failing miserably, to control his laughter. "So you're accusing Lancelot of hiding something because you're *bored*?"

"Basically... yeah, I guess I am," Logan grinned. He caught Cai's gaze for a moment before both burst into laughter.

It was times like these that Cai was glad Logan was in this world with him; Logan always knew the right thing to say to lighten the mood.

"I'm glad you two can still find things to laugh about in these dark times," Gawain called to them, clearly unimpressed.

Cai and Logan's laughter died immediately.

"Yeah, well..." Logan began lamely.

Gawain cut him off, clearly not in the mood for any of Logan's retorts. "You need to go to the armoury," he instructed, pointing at Logan. "Lancelot's waiting for you."

Logan groaned. "And he couldn't have told me that *before* I'd traipsed all the way over here?" The glare Gawain shot his way left both boys in no doubt that he was in no mood to argue. Logan held up his hands in surrender. "OK, OK, I'm going," he muttered. Nodding at Cai in farewell, he said, "See you later."

As he wandered away, Gawain turned to Cai. "Are you going to stand up there all day?" Without waiting for an answer, he turned and walked towards the horses.

Faced with no other choice, Cai followed. "What's going on? Why isn't Lancelot here?" he demanded. "Is he avoiding me?"

Gawain turned to face him, smirking. "And just *why* would he be avoiding *you?*"

Cai shrugged, his confidence wavering. "I figured, after last night..."

"Let me explain something to you," Gawain said, his dark eyes boring into Cai's. "I don't know what you *think* happened last night but Lancelot has no reason to avoid you." And, without giving Cai a chance to respond, he walked off.

"So why wouldn't he answer me?" Cai asked as he jogged after him.

"That is none of your concern," Gawain replied curtly as he mounted his horse.

"But I thought he was supposed to be my mentor," Cai reminded him, taking the reins from the stable hand. "He can't mentor me if he's not here."

Gawain slowly turned his head to look at him but Cai stood firm, determined not to back away from the knight's cold stare. "As I said: *it's none of your concern,*" he repeated firmly. "*I* shall be teaching you to ride from now on."

"But..." Cai started to protest, ignoring Rei's growing impatience.

Gawain narrowed his eyes, studying Cai carefully. "You take an unusual amount of interest in other people," he observed. "If you spent as much time concentrating on your training as you do on asking questions, you'll be battle ready in no time." Cai didn't miss the sarcasm in his voice but he held his tongue and said nothing. Gawain nodded towards Rei. "Now, mount up; we have a lot to do."

Cai glared at him for a moment before doing as he was instructed. He ignored the protests of his aching muscles as he mounted Rei and, spurring her into action, followed Gawain out of Camelot.

***

Thankfully, Cai didn't have much time to think about Lancelot as Gawain spent the whole morning running through drills and pushing him and Rei to ever-greater lengths; in addition to practising riding the horse at different speeds, Gawain also started teaching him the correct

283

positions for fighting from horseback, whilst still maintaining complete control over his steed. As usual, Gawain was hard on him but Cai, channelling all his pent up frustration, followed his instructions to the letter, forcing himself to ignore how ridiculous it felt to be doing it all without a weapon.

By the time they returned to Camelot, Cai was sweating buckets and aching all over, eager for a break; even Rei's coat was damp and slick with sweat. Dismounting, he took a moment to regain control of his body, clinging onto Rei's saddle all the while. Glancing at her, he caught her forlorn gaze and patted her neck. "It's OK, girl," he murmured encouragingly. "We did it; we survived."

After leading her to the stable, he handed her over to the stable hand before heading out to the courtyard where Gawain was waiting and the two of them set off to the Great Hall.

"You did well today," Gawain announced, in a rare moment of praise.

Cai stared at him, taken aback. "Thanks," he murmured, trying not to sound too surprised.

"You have a good relationship with Rei; it is good to see."

Cai smiled proudly; he had to admit, he understood now what Lancelot had meant when he said he and Rei would become a team. He knew they were working well together and knew that, when the time finally came to face their enemies in battle, they would do so *together*.

When they reached the Great Hall, Cai looked around, his eyes immediately finding his mother. Seeing that she was alone, he headed over to her, taking his place beside her. They ate lunch together, conversation flowing easily between them but, as the meal wore on, Cai began to feel guilty about the doubts he was harbouring about Lancelot and couldn't help wondering if he should broach the subject with her.

He immediately dismissed the idea, realising that saying anything right now would be a bad idea; after all, he had no proof of Lancelot's betrayal and telling her anything would only worry her, maybe unnecessarily.

As they spoke, he tried to push his questions out of his mind but the more he tried, the more they seemed to cling on, until, in the end, he could barely look his mother in the eye.

Noticing his strange behaviour, Guinevere studied him. "Are you quite alright, Cai?" she asked.

Cai forced himself to smile. "I'm fine," he insisted. "I just... I'm tired." He knew it was a weak excuse but it was all he had.

Guinevere began to speak but paused as Gawain approached.

"Forgive me, my Lady, but..."

Guinevere smiled at the knight. "It is quite alright, Gawain; I understand that Cai is needed elsewhere." Her gaze fell upon Cai. "Until this evening, my son..."

Cai smiled; he had never been more grateful for Gawain's interruption. So, after saying a hasty goodbye to his mother, he followed Gawain from the hall, ready to lose himself in his lesson. After all, if anything could make him forget about Lancelot, for a few hours, it was that.

Chapter Thirty-Six

Gadeon was waiting for them in the courtyard, a sword and scabbard in his hand. Upon seeing Cai and Gawain leave the Great Hall, he hurried over, bowing and handing the sword to Gawain. "As promised, Sir Gawain."

Gawain nodded his thanks as he took the sword from the blacksmith.

Cai watched the exchange, eyeing the sword with interest; it was the perfect distraction from his concerns about Lancelot and his mother. For weeks now, he had been asking Gawain when he might progress to an actual blade in training but the knight had done nothing but dismiss him, always insisting he was far from ready, much to Cai's growing frustration.

After handing the sword over, Gadeon turned to Cai and smiled. "I look forward to hearing of your success with it, my Lord."

Cai frowned, looking between Gawain and Gadeon. "What do you...?"

Gawain held the sword out to him. "It is yours, Cai."

Too shocked to speak, Cai reached out and took the sword. It was a simple design, nothing much to look at, but... *it was his first sword* and, to Cai, the most beautiful thing he had ever seen. He grinned, looking to Gawain. "Are you serious?" he asked. "This is really *mine?*"

Gawain nodded. "You have earned it."

Cai looked down at the sword again. Unwrapping the belt from the scabbard, he buckled it around his waist.

Gadeon smiled. "How does it feel?"

"Strange..." Cai admitted, readjusting its position. "But good," he added quickly.

"That is all I needed to hear," Gadeon beamed.

Gawain placed a hand on the blacksmith's shoulder. "Thank you, my friend."

"Yeah... thank you," Cai added, sincerely.

Gadeon bowed his head. "It is my honour," the older man insisted. "Good day to you, my Lord," he said, bowing to Cai before taking his leave.

Once alone, Gawain turned to Cai. "Are you ready to put that sword to good use?"

Cai grinned enthusiastically before falling into step beside Gawain. As he walked, he rested his hand on the pommel; at last, he was getting somewhere, he was *finally* earning his place here...

But the sight that greeted him when they left Camelot, however, stopped him in his tracks. He swallowed anxiously, casting a wary eye over the scene before him: rows of men lined the arena, working through drills; their blades rang through the air, accompanied by harsh shouts as men called to and joked with each other, their camaraderie easy for all to see.

"What is this?" Cai demanded, glancing uneasily at Gawain. "Why are they all here?"

"It is time you trained alongside your men now," Gawain informed him as he continued along the path.

Cai had no choice but to follow. "But..."

Gawain glanced at him. "You have learned the basics; the only way you will continue to progress is if you learn to fight alongside others with a blade of your own."

Cai shook his head, trying to deny Gawain's observations. "But I'm not ready," he insisted.

Gawain turned to Cai. "If we didn't think you were ready, you wouldn't be in possession of a sword and you *certainly* wouldn't be here." He paused, allowing his words to sink in. "A king must fight alongside his men in battle, my Lord."

Cai stared at him; in all the time he had been at Camelot, this was the first time Gawain had acknowledged him as his king. For a moment, he was lost for words, floored by the knight's unexpected recognition of him.

"You know how to fight; you know how to defend," Gawain continued. "Now, you must understand how to do that when you're surrounded by people all wanting the same thing: to win... to *survive."* The knight held Cai's gaze for a moment before turning to look at the rest of the men. "If you want their respect, you have to fight alongside them. Your father knew this," he added for good measure.

At the mention of his father, Cai lifted his head defiantly. Gawain was right; there had to come a time when he learnt how to fight with his men. He couldn't continue to hide behind his fears, otherwise he'd never leave Camelot; he would never avenge his father...

"OK, then," he said, looking at Gawain. "What are we waiting for?"

The knight smiled...

***

"You will practise the skills I have already taught you," Gawain instructed as they reached the arena.

Cai stared at him. After all the talk about fighting alongside his men, Cai had expected to do just that; not just run through the same old drills...

Gawain looked at him knowingly. "Trust me; they will feel far different now that you are using a sword."

So, under the watchful, and ever-critical, eye of Gawain, and suddenly very aware he was no longer alone, Cai ran through the techniques he had already been taught. No sooner had he started than he realised Gawain had been right: the drills did feel different now; the weight of the sword alone made his movements cumbersome and slow and the more he tried to concentrate and correct his mistakes, the clumsier he became, much to Gawain's frustration.

"You're thinking too much!" he chastised for what felt like the hundredth time. "I've told you: you have to stop trying so hard, just let it happen. Stay on your toes," he added, spotting Cai's stamina lagging.

Cai clenched his jaw and redoubled his efforts, very aware that he was making a fool of himself in front of his men.

But Gawain didn't seem to care...

"Come on; move!" he barked, his impatience growing.

"I *am!*" Cai growled.

"Stop!" Gawain ordered, coming to stand before Cai.

Breathing hard, Cai watched him carefully, wishing he were anywhere else but here. He dropped his gaze to the ground, his cheeks burning from a mixture of exertion, embarrassment and anger; anger at himself and his inability to do what he had found so easy, only yesterday. Thankfully, the men around him were still heavily engaged in their own training so he was, at least, grateful for that.

"Look at me, Cai," Gawain muttered, his voice softening.

Cai glanced up and noticed a look of sympathy in his eyes. He glared at the knight, unsure which was worse: Gawain's anger and frustration or his sympathy.

It didn't take him long to decide; not once in his life had he ever asked for, or expected, anyone's sympathy. Anger and hatred he could deal with, but the idea of anyone feeling *sorry* for him infuriated him; he had never sought an easy ride in life and he certainly wasn't about to start now.

"I don't need your pity," Cai muttered as he watched Gawain collect two shields. His heart sank and he groaned inwardly; he hated using a shield, they were cumbersome and seemed to forever get in his way, his shoulder injury was testament to that.

Gawain frowned. "Who said I was giving you any?" he retorted. Cai looked at him and was glad to see the knight's gaze had hardened. Holding a shield out to him, he said, "Take it; maybe you'll move quicker when you have reason to."

Cai did as he was told, the familiar nerves he felt at the prospect of fighting one of the knights made his muscles tense; pushing these aside, he focused instead on his determination to make a success of himself, especially in front of his men.

Taking the shield, Cai slipped his left arm through the two leather straps and, as the weight dragged his arm down, adjusted it, bracing himself against the burning pain in his shoulder...

"We will run through some basic moves..." Gawain began, before pausing to study Cai. "Because of your injury, we haven't used this as much as I would have liked but that is about to change." He indicated Cai's shoulder. "Daily use will make it stronger. Now, remember what I said in your first lesson," he continued. "Think of your shield as just another extension of your body; do not forget it's there. It could save your life when you least expect it and can also be a means of defence or attack." He met Cai's gaze. "I'm going to attack you with my sword; I want you to defend."

Gawain attacked slowly at first, giving Cai plenty of time to get his arm up so that the shield caught the blow. The contact wasn't nearly as bad as Cai had expected and, when Gawain pulled his sword back to launch a second attack, Cai was able to change position and defend himself again.

Unsurprisingly, however, it wasn't long before his shoulder began to burn with the effort but Cai forced himself to ignore it; he had to because Gawain wasn't letting up and his attacks were picking up in both speed and strength. As Gawain landed another blow on the shield, Cai swept his arm across his body, pushing the blade away, thereby giving him enough space and time to back away and reposition himself

Gawain looked at him, grinning. "Excellent; you're learning not just to accept the blows anymore."

293

Cai grinned back, pleased with himself; he wasn't about to admit that the real reason he had pushed Gawain away was because he wanted a respite from the knight's attacks, a chance to rest his shoulder, if only for a second. But, he was more than happy to let the knight, and the rest of his men, think he had planned the move.

"Now, this time, I want you to block with your shield, then counter-attack with your sword," Gawain stated, watching Cai carefully.

Cai nodded, rolling his shoulders, trying to refocus his mind.

"Ready?" Gawain asked expectantly.

Cai nodded his consent whilst, at the same time, loosening his grip on the sword in his hand, as he had been taught.

When Gawain attacked, Cai moved towards him focusing on the blade arcing through the air towards him. He deflected the blow, pushing the blade to one side as he brought his sword down. It cut through the air but was easily knocked aside with such force that Cai stumbled slightly and had to quickly regain his footing.

"Steady yourself," Gawain advised as he circled Cai allowing him time to recover. "You need to focus on the whole of your body, not just your arms. Your feet need to be strong too."

Cai took a moment to take in Gawain's advice before stepping forward and launching his own attack in the hope of catching Gawain off-guard.

Gawain was ready for him, however, and he cast Cai's sword aside as if it was no more than an annoying fly he was swatting away. He counter-attacked and for the next few minutes they were engaged in battle, albeit a very one-sided one. Cai's efforts quickly faded and it wasn't long before Gawain had the advantage and had Cai retreating.

Gawain wouldn't let him give up though. "This is the time you need to dig deep," he shouted over his shield. "When your legs are weak and you find it hard to wield your sword... dig deep and find the strength you need to finish it."

Ignoring his aching and burning limbs, ignoring the sweat that was cooling on his body, Cai gritted his teeth and tried, *tried* to do as Gawain said. But he had nothing left to give; he felt drained, empty.

"Come *on*, boy," Gawain encouraged. "Think of *why* you are here, *why* we are doing this. Are you going to drop to your knees and surrender to Mordred when the time comes? Are you going to let him win this war?"

At the mention of his enemy's name, Cai felt a fire ignite deep within; it was as if someone had flipped a switch and he was now engulfed by his hatred. He conjured up the image Merlin had given him of Mordred and, suddenly, Gawain was no longer standing in front of him...

It was Mordred himself.

Faced with his enemy, Cai lost all sense of himself. He screamed and ran at Mordred raining blow after blow on him; each blow was deflected which only infuriated Cai more. Drawing his sword back, he took aim, trying to get his sword behind Mordred's shield in a desperate attempt to cause as much damage as he could.

But Mordred understood what Cai was trying to do and brought his sword up to meet his; however, in such close quarters and, in the unexpected face of Cai's anger, he misjudged his timing and Cai's blade hit his arm, biting into his flesh. Mordred let out a cry of surprise, dropping his sword.

There was a moment when Cai and Mordred stared at each other, neither sure if they could believe what was happening.

Cai recovered first: taking advantage of his unexpected upper hand, he slashed his sword through the air, his blade coming up against the wall of Mordred's shield. Frustrated by the cumbersome shield on his arm, Cai let go of the strap he was holding and shook it off, letting it drop to the ground. With his free hand, he grabbed Mordred's shield and tried to wrench it out of his grasp so that he could get a clear shot at him with his sword.

"What the Hell are you doing?"

Cai was vaguely aware of Mordred's question but he wasn't about to stop and have a conversation, not when he was so close to getting his revenge...

"Cai, stop!" Mordred cried, anger and fear evident in his voice.

But Cai *couldn't* stop, he didn't *want* to stop; the floodgates had opened and he couldn't plug the tidal wave of anger that washed over him.

"Cai...!" Mordred's voice was desperate now as he grappled with Cai's hand; finally wrenching it from his shield, he brought the shield up, the rim hitting Cai's chin.

Dazed, Cai staggered back, dropping his sword as he fell heavily to the ground. He found himself staring up at the sky; in that moment he didn't know who, or where, he was...

But then Gawain loomed over him, his fury and confusion evident.

Looking around, Cai realised that everyone was now looking at him and Gawain, their training now forgotten; Mordred was nowhere to be seen. His eyes burned and his throat tightened as he slowly pieced together what had just happened.

Gawain held out a hand to help him up but Cai knocked it aside. Getting to his feet, he shook his head, unable to look at the knight... at *anyone*.

"I'm sorry," he muttered before running from the arena, turning his back on Gawain and whatever was happening to him.

Chapter Thirty-Seven

Cai raced through the halls of Camelot, ignoring the questioning looks he drew, only pausing long enough to remove the torch from its bracket before descending the staircase...

His lungs hurt from the exertion of running non-stop from the arena, his vision swam with tears and he had to fight the urge to cry. His face throbbed painfully and, reaching up, he winced as his fingers touched his lip. On checking, he realised he was bleeding and gradually became aware of the iron tang of blood in his mouth. Suddenly feeling sick, he pushed himself onwards...

He needed to see Merlin, needed to tell him what had just happened.

He had attacked Gawain.

He had attacked Gawain because he had *seen* Mordred.

Cai shook his head, trying to make sense of what had happened; Mordred had been there, *in the arena with him,* he was sure of it.

Wasn't he?

He felt lost, adrift, and needed Merlin to make sense of it all for him.

Exiting the stairwell, he made straight for Merlin's chambers, pounding loudly on the door. He waited for what seemed like forever... and was about to knock again when he heard the heavy lock disengage.

The door opened a crack to reveal Nimue's pale features looking out, her dark eyes boring into him. Looking disdainfully at Cai, she narrowed her eyes. "Yes?" she demanded.

Cai hesitated briefly. "I need to see Merlin." Nimue blinked, obviously in no rush to answer him. Desperate now, Cai tried again. "Please... I *need* to see him." His voice cracked as he spoke and Cai hated himself for showing such weakness in front of her.

"He is not receiving visitors at present," she informed him coldly.

Finally losing patience, Cai attempted to push past her but she easily blocked his path, took his arm in an iron grip and guided him back into the corridor, quietly closing the door behind them. "But this is *important!*" he snapped as he rounded on her.

"Is it more important than his recovery?" she demanded, her voice like ice.

Realising that he had come close, yet again, to losing his temper, he bowed his head, forcing himself to take stock of what he was doing, how he was acting; yes, he needed to see Merlin but not at the cost of his health. "Well, no..." he admitted, ashamed.

"Then *go,*" she spat. "Merlin needs no distractions and *your* time, I am sure, would be much better spent *elsewhere,*" she reminded him pointedly, her gaze unwavering. Cai stared at her, willing himself not to break under her intense scrutiny. "I will not ask again... my Lord," she added as an afterthought.

"Will you, at least, tell him I was here?" he asked. "And that I need to speak to him," he added hastily.

Nimue looked at him for a moment before smiling. "Of course; you have my word..."

Cai nodded before muttering a brief thank you and retracing his steps, eager to put as much distance as he could between himself and Nimue's cold, dark eyes.

***

In the solitude of the Lower Courtyard, Cai leant against the wall and sank to the ground, defeated; he was fast losing himself to a darkness he didn't understand. Suddenly, the dam inside him burst and he gave into his tears, finally allowing himself to release all the emotion, all the pent up anger, he had felt since he left the arena;

anger at himself, Morgan, Mordred... even Kay and Lancelot.

Mordred...

He had *seen* Mordred; he had been as real to Cai, in that moment, as he would have been, had he actually been standing in front of him. But worse than that, he had attacked Gawain as a result, had kept up his attack and had ignored his demands for him to stop.

Which begged the question: how far would he have gone? Cai had an uneasy feeling that he already knew the answer but was afraid to admit it, even to himself.

This realisation scared him beyond anything he had ever known; in that moment, he would gladly return to his old life and come face to face with Ethan in preference to seeing this new side of himself.

He glanced at his shaking hands, clenching them into fists; gritting his teeth, he willed them to be still. An image of Mordred filled his head again and, desperately, he put his hands over his head, trying to block it out. He wondered if Morgan had experienced that same blinding fury when she had seen Uther upon her return to Camelot. If she had, was it any wonder she poisoned him?

He felt sick at the thought; how had he even let himself think like that? How could he excuse Morgan's actions? There was no excuse for what she had done, just like there was no excuse for what *he* was doing. To kill in cold blood... there was no honour in that.

"Cai?"

He looked up at the sound of his name and was surprised to find himself looking at the concerned face of his mother. Relief washed over him; it was a reminder that, even as his sense of self was shattering beyond any recognition, she was something he could reach out to, a voice of reason in the darkness.

He blinked and, with the heel of his hand, quickly wiped his tears away, embarrassed to be caught crying by her, of all people. Getting to his feet, he forced himself to smile but he knew he wasn't fooling anyone.

Guinevere stepped forward her eyes showing nothing but concern and love. Reaching out, she took his hand in hers. "You're cold," she murmured, frowning. "And you're trembling..." She reached up to touch his swollen, bloodied lip but Cai moved away, ignoring the pain in her eyes.

"Don't..."

Guinevere blinked, taken aback by Cai's refusal to let her comfort him. "Cai...?"

Tears welled in her eyes and Cai turned away knowing this was hurting her as much as it was him. He would have liked nothing more than to let her comfort him, to tell him everything would be OK, but he knew he didn't deserve her kindness, didn't deserve her concern.

"Cai, please talk to me," Guinevere pleaded. "You're obviously in pain; allow me to help."

Cai shook his head. "You can't," he realised. "No one can."

"How do you know that if you don't reach out?" she challenged.

Cai turned to face her. "Maybe I don't deserve your help." He tried to keep the bitterness and anger from his voice but failed miserably.

Guinevere looked horrified at the thought.
"How can you say that?" she demanded. "What could you have possibly done...?"

Cai didn't even let her finish the question before he interrupted her and found himself telling her about how he had launched himself at Gawain during their training session. He was aware of how ridiculous it sounded, aware that a true king wouldn't lose his temper, but now that he had opened the floodgates, he found he couldn't stop; he even found himself telling her about Kay. He wanted Guinevere to know the best and the worst of him, even if it led to her disappointment. Maybe, he realised, he was testing her; testing to see if she could love the real him rather than a fantasy she may have dreamed up. He fell silent as he finished, waiting for her reaction.

Guinevere smiled. "Oh, Cai; losing your temper is nothing to be ashamed of." She took Cai's hands again and looked into his eyes. "It shows you're passionate; it shows you *care*. And *that* is testament of a good king."

Cai shook his head. "It's not just that..."

"Then what is it?"

"I'm scared," he finally admitted.

"Scared of what?" she asked gently.

303

Cai hesitated, gathering his thoughts. Was he ready to do this? Was he ready to confess his fears because, once out, there would be no taking them back?

Sensing Cai's struggles, Guinevere spoke. "You know, when your father felt overwhelmed he confided in someone he could trust, someone who would listen without judgement: myself."

Cai smiled sadly. He had never really had anyone he could confide in: certainly no friends to speak of and Greg and Jules had always been too concerned with worldwide issues to worry about him; Logan often treated things like a joke and he couldn't trust Lancelot. Even when he had tried to reach out and, gone to see Merlin, Nimue had pushed him away. It was just easier to keep his thoughts and fears to himself, rather than have to rely on other people.

Guinevere placed a hand on his shoulder, watching him carefully. "Cai? Are you well?"

Seeing the concern in her eyes, he admitted, "I've never really had anyone, you know... to talk to," he finished lamely, lowering his head.

Guinevere's grip tightened slightly. "Oh, Cai... You do now. You have Merlin; he was your father's counsel for many years and his father's before him; then there's Logan..." Her voice trailed away as she paused, studying him. "And if I may be so bold as to suggest: you could confide in me."

On hearing these words, he felt his chest tighten and his throat burn as he realised how close to tears he was. Dropping his gaze, he scuffed the hard-packed earth with his boot. "I'd like that," he murmured, attempting to sound nonchalant, but failing miserably.

Guinevere smiled warmly. "So would I," she agreed. "So, what troubles you, my son?"

Cai took a deep breath; right now, his priority was finding the right words. He was more than aware that, after hearing what he had to say, she may change her mind about him and could be so horrified by what she heard that she wouldn't want to see him again.

"I'm scared of myself," he admitted quietly. "I'm scared I might be just like Morgan le Fay."

Guinevere frowned, shocked. "Whatever makes you think that?"

"Merlin's been telling me about Morgan and Mordred... I've just... noticed things; similarities between me and her..."

"Such as...?" Guinevere asked bewildered.

Cai couldn't decide whether she was looking at him differently or whether it was his imagination playing tricks on him. "She was sent away when a war broke out between Uther and the Duke of Cornwall," he explained. "And when she found out that Uther had been responsible for killing her father, she lost it and wanted revenge. Her anger and hatred made her turn on everyone; made her want revenge no matter what the cost."

Guinevere smiled knowingly. "And you're worried you're treading the same path?"

Cai dropped his gaze. "When I attacked Gawain, I saw... I *saw* Mordred. It was like Gawain

305

had changed, right in front of me." He squeezed his eyes shut, trying to block out the memory. "Mordred was all I saw and I flipped; I couldn't help it. The man killed my father and I wanted to kill *him*." He took a breath, steeling himself against his next words. "And, it's not the first time this has happened, either," he continued. "When I got into the fight with the boy outside my school... this red mist descended and my teacher had to drag me off him." He shook his head. "If he hadn't, I don't know what I would have done."

Guinevere looked grave, but Cai was glad to see she was standing firm. "Cai, you have to stop this; you *must* stop seeing only the worst in yourself." She paused briefly before continuing. "And as for you being like Morgan... well, that's simply not true. Morgan is like she is because of the *choices* she made; it is nothing more sinister than that. You can only be like her if you *choose* to be. The fact that you *can* stop, the fact that you *regret* your actions... all these things show me that you are *nothing* like her, that you are *far better* than her."

"But..." Cai started to protest weakly.

"Cai, listen to me," she implored. "You have to remember that, although you are related to both Morgan and Mordred, *Arthur's* blood also runs in your veins and that, far more than anything else, sets you apart."

At the reference to his father, Cai heard the sadness in his mother's voice and felt his own throat tighten. Risking a glance at Guinevere, he

306

saw the power of his own emotions reflected in her eyes. Without hesitation, he did the only thing that seemed right, the only thing that made sense: he hugged her.

It was a hug that spoke of the pain of their lost years and the grief they had both suffered but it also spoke of their happiness to have finally found each other again, to finally be a part of each other's lives: a family at last.

Chapter Thirty-Eight

Cai and Guinevere sat in contented silence, neither wanting to be the first to withdraw and bring an end to whatever was happening between them; they both knew that this unexpected meeting and Cai's impromptu confession had been a big step forward in their relationship, breaking down the barrier that time and distance had put between them.

Cai sat, his hand held in his mother's grasp, unwilling to let go too soon. Occasionally, Cai would glance at her and smile; words weren't necessary for either of them. Just being in each other's presence was enough right now.

For Cai's part, he was still struggling to get his head round how easy it had been for him to talk to her; it was like he had always been meant to confide in her. He smiled to himself; it felt good to have someone he was comfortable enough with to, finally, open up to.

But, deep within him, was a guilt he was still struggling to hide. Did he have the right to accept her love, accept her help, when he suspected Lancelot of some kind of betrayal? Did he have the right to sit happily beside her when he couldn't trust the man she was married to? He glanced at Guinevere, wishing this were easier; he wished he could confide in her about his suspicions but he knew that would be taking advantage of her trust. How could he look her in the eye and then proceed to break her heart?

The silence was soon shattered by Lancelot and Logan's return, the sound of their horses' hooves clattering on the stones, echoing around the courtyard. Two manservants appeared from nowhere, ready to return the horses to the stables and bed them for the night.

Upon seeing them, Cai stood up reluctantly pulling his hands from Guinevere's grasp as Lancelot and Logan reined in their steeds. While they were still unaware of his presence, he took the opportunity to study Lancelot; the knight looked comfortable on the horse and commanded the beast with ease. Cai felt a wave of resentment towards him; he didn't even *look* guilty.

But that ease soon vanished when Lancelot caught sight of Cai and his face tensed as their eyes met briefly. Cai said nothing but he stood a little straighter, as if daring the knight to say something. Lancelot, however, remained silent and Cai noticed, with some satisfaction, that he was avoiding his eyes.

"What happened to you?" Logan demanded as he dismounted. Stepping away from his horse, he studied Cai's face for a moment.

Cai touched his lip, waving away his concern. "Nothing," he murmured distractedly. "Gawain hit me with his shield." Despite talking to Logan, his attention was fixed on Lancelot who was doing everything he possibly could to appear busy in order to avoid looking at Cai; thankfully, his mother didn't seem to notice anything out of the ordinary.

Logan, however, was a different story: glancing uneasily between Cai and Lancelot, he said, "Yeah, I know that one; he knocked me out cold doing that once." He touched his jaw as if recalling the memory. "Thought I'd lost a tooth when I woke up," he added as an afterthought. He paused as his eyes landed on the sword at Cai's hip. "Hey, you finally graduated!" he cried, clapping him on the back. "Congratulations!"

Cai smiled, grateful he wasn't asking questions or making this situation any more awkward than it already was. "Thanks," he muttered.

"Yes, well done, my Lord," Lancelot murmured stiffly as he dismounted. Handing his reins to the last manservant, he said, "But I think it's time you both went to find something to eat." He walked over to Guinevere, smiling, his eyes never leaving hers. "I shall see you both later," he murmured in the boys' direction.

As Lancelot was about to lead her away, Guinevere turned to Cai.

"Remember what I said, Cai; I am *always* here for you."

Sending a final smile her way, he turned as he and Logan began to make their way to the Upper Courtyard.

"You OK?" Logan asked, curiosity finally getting the better of him.

Cai nodded, lost in his own thoughts. "Yeah, I'm OK," he replied distractedly.

Logan raised an eyebrow. "Really? And you expect me to believe that?"

Cai glanced at him and sighed; was he really that easy to read? "I attacked Gawain," he admitted quietly. Now that he had spoken to Guinevere, and it was out in the open, it seemed easier to accept somehow; it was certainly easier to talk about.

Logan smirked, clearly impressed. "So, first Kay, then Lancelot and now *Gawain*? You don't do things by halves, do you?"

Cai frowned; did he think he was deliberately looking for trouble? "It wasn't like that," he insisted.

"No?" Logan questioned. "Then what *was* it like?"

Cai shook his head. "I'm not really sure," he muttered. "Everything was fine but then..."

"Then...?" Logan pressed.

"Then Gawain mentioned Mordred's name... and I lost it. I totally lost it." He said in disbelief. He glanced at Logan, trying to gauge his reaction; he'd left out the bit about him seeing Mordred in case Logan thought he'd lost his mind.

If Logan was surprised he didn't show it; in fact, he barely missed a beat before saying, "Can't say I blame you; I mean, if I were in your shoes, I'd have probably done the same thing."

Cai stared at him. "Really? You don't think I'm crazy for losing it?"

Logan looked at him, his face serious for once. "Cai, he killed your father," he reminded him bluntly. "If you *didn't* have anger issues about that, I'd be worried." He paused for a moment, his face hardening. "If *I* was ever faced with the man who killed *my* father, I'd make him pay too."

Cai stared at him, taken aback by the coldness in his voice; a pang of shame pierced him as he recalled that Logan's father, too, had been killed thanks to Mordred. How could he have forgotten such a fundamental thing about his friend? Had he really been so caught up in himself that he had ignored Logan's pain? What kind of friend did that make him?

Before Cai could say more, Logan had changed the subject. Clapping him on the back, he said, "Come on, let's go get something to eat; I'm starving."

Cai stared at him, shocked by the sudden change; his bitterness had vanished and standing before him was the Logan of old, the boy who

312

looked for adventure and fun, even in the darkest of times.

Shaking his head, Cai admitted, "I'm not really that hungry, actually."

Logan stared back at him. "Really? Not even after the beating you took?"

Cai absently touched his swollen lip. "No, I think I'll just go and rest for a bit."

Logan looked doubtful. "Alright, then; suit yourself. But don't come crying to me when you're hungry," he warned.

Cai smiled despite himself. "I won't," he assured him.

And, with that, Logan took off across the courtyard towards the Great Hall, while Cai headed to their quarters alone.

Chapter Thirty-Nine

As the weeks turned into months, and despite Guinevere's efforts, Cai fell into a darkness he had never known before; his mind wandered constantly as he dissected everything that had happened since his arrival. First, he had clashed with Kay, then Lancelot, then Gawain... how could he possibly fight alongside these men now? How could he ever earn back their respect?

To top it all, his doubts regarding Lancelot were increasing every day which wasn't helped by the fact that, every time Cai approached the knight or made any attempt to talk to him, he would find some excuse to disappear; something was obviously wrong and it was frustrating Cai that he couldn't find out what. He tried to keep things in perspective, tried to tell himself that he shouldn't doubt Lancelot without all the facts, but it was hard not to when he was always going out of his way to avoid him.

Everything was happening so fast; each day seemed to pick up more momentum and he was acutely aware that the day was coming when he would have to face Mordred, *for real*. Doubts had long since started to creep in: would he be ready? Could he face Mordred without running away?

And then there was his anger... Although there had been no more outbursts like the one with Gawain, Cai could still feel it in him, bubbling away just below the surface, waiting to reveal itself. He tried to hold onto Guinevere's words that he was better than Morgan and Mordred but every day just reminded him that he was more like them than he'd ever care to admit.

Logan had tried to talk to him several times, tried to keep his spirits up, but all Cai would do was push him away. In desperation, he had tried, again, to seek advice from Merlin but he was still under lock and key thanks to Nimue and, when he tried to speak to Guinevere, the words stuck in his throat and he changed the subject completely, unwilling to let her see he was still struggling.

But despite the darkness engulfing him, life at Camelot continued, unabated. His sessions with Gawain and his men continued although they had become strained and awkward since his outburst; he was grateful the knight hadn't said anything but could not ignore the wariness with which he now treated him. He wanted to apologise, to explain what had happened, but he couldn't find the words; he had alienated himself and had no idea how to make it right again.

Instead, he contented himself with putting all his efforts into his training, a newfound determination urging him to succeed, to prove to himself, and those around him, that he was better than his so-called family. As a result, Gawain had intensified his training; he was now performing ever more challenging sequences and the results had shown themselves almost immediately: he was quicker and stronger than ever, his reflexes faster.

It was following such a training session that he unexpectedly met Merlin as he was leaving the arena. The older man looked much better: gone were the signs of exhaustion and pain he had seen on the hillside all those weeks ago.

At the sight of him, Cai ran to him. "You're OK!" he cried, relief evident in his voice.

Merlin smiled. "And what else would you expect?"

"I..." Cai faltered briefly before finding his voice. "I did *try* to visit you," he explained hurriedly. "But Nimue..."

Merlin held up a hand. "Say no more," he murmured. "Nimue can be... over-protective; she takes on far too much at times."

Cai had the urge to point out that she had been more like a jailer these last few weeks but thought better of it. Instead, he said, "Well, it's good to see you."

Merlin smiled. "It's good to see you, too, my Lord." He nodded towards the emptying arena at Cai's back. "You're training has progressed well; if I am not mistaken, you are much changed from the boy you were when you first arrived."

Cai said nothing; Merlin was right, he *was* changed – in so many ways. How could he *not* be? So much had happened... he had had to learn quickly or get swallowed up in the tide.

"You have honed your skills well," Merlin commented.

"Thanks," Cai muttered, embarrassed.

Merlin studied him intently. "Your mother has been to see me; she's worried about you, Cai."

Cai stared at him, taken aback by this sudden, unexpected disclosure. Guinevere had spoken to Merlin about him? What, exactly, had she said? Cai dropped his head, waiting for Merlin to continue.

Merlin pressed on, his eyes fixed on Cai. "It seems, despite everyone's best efforts to the contrary, you are determined to let darkness consume you."

"*What?*" Cai asked outraged. He shook his head. "No, it's not like that..." Didn't anyone understand what he was going through?

"Then what *is* it like?" Merlin asked, crossing his arms over his chest.

Cai was silent, his mind whirling; the truth was it was *exactly* as Merlin described it. The only thoughts that ran through his mind nowadays were negative; not even at his lowest with Ethan had he given in, not like this. Maybe he was being self-indulgent but he couldn't help himself.

"If you cannot see the light, then you are already defeated," Merlin pointed out, simply. "If you let Mordred into your mind to the point where you shut out those who care for you... Ask yourself: what is there left to fight for?"

Cai shook his head, wishing that simple act could sort it. "This is all too much," he admitted. "As if I didn't already have enough to get my head around, you've now got me doubting everyone around me with your talk of a betrayal." He sighed before adding quietly, "And I know I'm nowhere near good enough to take on Mordred." There: it was all out in the open, at last; strangely, he already felt better, lighter, as if a weight had been lifted. Merlin, he knew, would understand; he had dealt with these feelings before.

Merlin was silent for a moment. "Cai," he began gently, placing a comforting hand on his shoulder. "All you can do in this life is deal with what's in front of you, just like you always have. Focus on one thing at a time. Right now, you need to be ready to face Mordred alongside your men."

Cai scoffed. "You make it sound so easy. You *are* aware I've only been training for a few months?" he asked.

Merlin smiled. "I am very aware, thank you. And you're right: you haven't had the length of training any boy your age would normally have had, but you are more capable than you know, Cai. You have a well of strength within you, a strength

Morgan and Mordred do *not* have." He paused briefly, before continuing. "I told you once that your strength lies, not in your fists, but in your heart; that is still true. You've just lost sight of that."

Cai dropped his gaze. "But... I'm not ready," he confessed.

"Look at me, Cai." Cai looked up at Merlin, seeing the empathy in his eyes. "Do you think *anyone* is ready for their first battle... or their second? Or third? I can promise you that every man here feels the same way you do; they just don't let their fears take over."

Cai drew strength from his words; could it really be that simple? But then, another doubt, like a black cloud, appeared in his mind, casting a shadow over him once more. "What if no one wants to stand alongside me?"

"Why would you think that?"

"Well, for a start, I haven't seen Kay since my first day here," he admitted. "To be honest, I don't think he cares whether I live or die."

Merlin frowned. "Now, that simply isn't true." He paused. "Right now, Kay is in pain; your return opened many wounds for him. He just needs time." He smiled. "You and Kay are more alike than either of you would care to admit; if you could both acknowledge that fact then..."

Cai scoffed. "I don't think that's likely..."

Merlin sighed. "Kay will return soon and, when he does, I suggest you swallow that pride of yours and make amends."

Cai bristled at the thought. Why should *he* be the one to make amends? *He* wasn't the one who had walked off and disappeared for weeks on end. "And what if I don't want to?" he asked petulantly.

"I might wonder why you are so affected by the thought of Kay not standing with you," Merlin commented. "Could it be that, despite your best efforts to demonstrate to the contrary, you *do* care about him? That you *do* wish for him to see you as what you are: his nephew?"

Cai was silent, as he considered this. No, it couldn't be that; all he felt towards Kay was anger and resentment. But before he could protest otherwise, Merlin gestured towards Camelot.

"Come, Cai; we should return. I find I grow tired; perhaps I came too far today." Left with no other choice, Cai accompanied Merlin back to the castle.

Chapter Forty

Cai sat alone in his quarters, Merlin's words still echoing in his head. Could it be he was right? Did he, on some level, want Kay to recognise he was his nephew and not someone to be shunned and vilified? If he did, was that *so* wrong?

He sighed, too tired to think about Kay anymore; he had far more important things on his mind. Merlin had asked what he had left to fight for and, after some consideration, Cai realised he and his men had something Mordred and Morgan would never have: *people to fight for.* They weren't just fighting this war for themselves; they were fighting for everyone in Camelot, everyone in *Britain*... everyone who had ever suffered at their hands.

He looked up, his reverie broken, as movement caught his eye.

Silhouetted in the doorway, Logan smiled back at him. "You done brooding yet?"

Cai scowled. "I wasn't brooding," he protested indignantly.

Logan scoffed. "Sure you weren't." It was clear from his tone that he didn't believe him for a second. "But I think you've wallowed in self-pity long enough, don't you?"

Cai had no comeback for that. Thanks to Merlin, he was coming to realise that Logan was right; he couldn't continue feeling sorry for himself, that would put him on the back foot; Mordred would have the upper hand and, he wasn't about to let that happen.

"Come on," Logan continued, beckoning Cai to follow. "And bring your sword."

Cai got to his feet, figuring the best way to get over this was to do something. "Where are we going?" he asked.

"To the best therapy session you'll ever have," Logan quipped.

***

Cai raised his sword as Logan's arced through the air towards him; there was a clash of iron as the two blades met in mid-air.

Logan pushed his blade against Cai's but Cai held fast, his feet planted firmly on the ground. The muscles in his tired arm started to burn and shake but he wasn't going to back down. He met

Logan's gaze, as each pushed against the other's blade, waiting for the other to break.

Logan grinned. "You're not bad for a beginner," he joked, trying to get a rise out of him.

Cai said nothing; he couldn't afford to. Any form of distraction right now could be his undoing. Logan was a head taller than Cai and certainly stronger and more skilful with a sword, thanks to his earlier training; he definitely had the advantage. But Cai was beginning to understand there was more to fighting than just being the strongest; he just had to be patient and wait for an opening.

"You wanna call it quits?" Logan asked, still pushing hard.

"No way," Cai growled stubbornly.

Logan stepped forward, forcing Cai to step back. "You sure?" he asked. "There's no shame in losing to a superior opponent, you know."

Cai resisted the urge to roll his eyes. Instead, he answered in a way he knew Logan would understand: with a concerted effort, he pushed hard against Logan's blade before pulling his own away and twisting away from his friend, leaving Logan standing alone.

"Nice one," Logan murmured appreciatively, regaining his footing. "I thought I had you on the ropes there."

Cai shook his head, wiping the sweat from his forehead. "So did I," he muttered.

They were alone in the training arena and had been for most of the afternoon. When they left their quarters Logan had announced it would be good if they trained on their own for a while. Cai had been doubtful at first but found that, once they began, he actually enjoyed himself; he hadn't felt this free in a long time. It was good to train without Gawain breathing down his neck or the weight of the expectations of his men.

And, with no dark thoughts clouding his head, he was able to just focus on the job in hand.

It was good to see Logan wield a sword; he was more experienced so Cai had been able to pick up a few tips and had tried to use them against Logan but, unfortunately, his efforts had been anticipated and easily deflected.

But this only made Cai more determined to beat him and, with each fight, he learnt more and felt his confidence grow. It was good to feel positive, *truly* positive about, himself and his abilities; this was something he wasn't used to.

Now, as he faced Logan, he assessed his situation. He could run straight at him, in the hope of catching him off guard, but he knew Logan was too clever for that; he would be expecting it.

Which was exactly why Cai waited, biding his time. He watched Logan carefully, waiting for an opening. It wasn't long before he saw it; Logan only glanced up at Camelot for a moment but it was enough. Enough for Cai to know he had to take the advantage.

Lunging towards Logan he feinted to his left, glad when the other boy, caught off guard by the sudden attack, brought his blade up to meet

Cai's in anticipation.   At the last moment, Cai twisted round to Logan's left, holding the tip of his sword to Logan's back; to his surprise, Logan seemed frozen to the spot.

"Surrender?" Cai asked, unable to keep the grin from his face.

Logan straightened up, sheathing his sword and holding his hands up as he turned to face Cai. "Surrender," he conceded with a nod.

"Really?" Cai asked warily.

Logan chuckled. "Sure. It's about time you won."

Cai frowned.   "Did you let me win?" he demanded suspiciously.

Logan shook his head. "No, though I'd like to say I did," he admitted. "You won that, fair and square." He held out his hand. "Well done."

Cai was taken aback but shook Logan's hand. "What happened?" he questioned. "You lost focus."

"Yeah, I know; there's a lesson for you." He glanced towards Camelot again.   "I saw something..."

Cai frowned, sheathing his sword.   He followed Logan's gaze before turning back to his friend, watching him warily in the fading light; he guessed it was early evening by now and he couldn't ignore the chill in the air, cooling the sweat on his skin, causing him to shiver. "What?" he pressed.

"Kay," Logan replied. "Gawain was with him."

"So?" Cai muttered darkly.

What did *he* care whether Kay was back within the castle walls or not? Just so long as he didn't have to see him, he'd be happy. But there was also a part of him that was curious; curious to know what would happen now he was back. Would the knight still be gunning for him or would he want to move on?

Cai felt his stomach churn as he realised that, tomorrow, Kay would probably be at his training session and he would have no choice but to face him.

Chapter Forty-One

As they walked back to Camelot in silence, Cai found himself wondering what was happening with Kay; personally, he hoped Lancelot and Gawain were giving him a hard time about his recent behaviour.

Logan came to a sudden stop as they entered the Lower Courtyard, causing Cai to almost crash into him. Grabbing Cai's arm, Logan pulled him backwards as he dragged them into the shadow of the wall.

"What the...?" Cai gasped as he fell against his friend.

Logan held a finger to his lips, imploring him to be quiet.

Cai automatically fell silent, following Logan's gaze.

Four figures stood in the courtyard: Kay, Gawain, Lancelot and Merlin, cloaked as usual in black. It appeared Lancelot and Merlin had been awaiting Kay and Gawain's return.

Cai watched from the shadows as Kay paced angrily, barely able to meet anyone's gaze.

"You have no right to suggest such a thing," Kay was saying, his rage almost palpable. "What I feel towards the boy has *nothing* to do with them."

Cai and Logan glanced at one another; Logan frowned before they both turned their attention back to the men who were standing a short distance away.

Lancelot stepped towards Kay and grabbed his shoulder, turning him to face him. "You cannot keep pushing Cai away; Arthur wouldn't have wanted that. And, neither would Ailla," he added softly.

Kay seemed to slump at the mention of the name; he looked beseechingly at Lancelot, his eyes shining.

Before Lancelot could say more, Merlin stepped forward.

"We know how much you lost that day, Kay; we know what Mordred took from you." He paused for a moment before continuing. "Do not hold Cai responsible for that."

Kay dropped his head, rubbing his forehead. "I never said he *was* responsible but..." He shook his head. "I can't... I just can't do it." His shoulders slumped and Cai couldn't help thinking he looked defeated. "I can't be what he needs me to be," he confessed quietly.

Lancelot sighed and it was clear, when he next spoke, that he was quickly losing patience. "Cai is but a boy; he doesn't deserve what is being asked of him, much less understand it..."

Kay scoffed. "And you think *I* do?" he demanded furiously, his temper flaring unexpectedly. "You think that, by throwing the boy at me, I'll just forget what I lost?" He shook his head and looked at the men surrounding him, their sorrow etched on their faces. "Well, I *can't* forget; I *won't*."

He started to walk off but Lancelot reached for him; no sooner had Lancelot's hand touched his arm than Kay was rounding on him, pushing him away.

Lancelot reacted immediately; gripping the front of Kay's shirt, he pushed him back against the wall, pinning him to the stones. Kay struggled but Lancelot was unyielding.

"Stop it, Kay!" Lancelot growled. When it became clear Kay wasn't about to obey, Lancelot shook him, thrusting him heavily back against the wall.

Kay stopped struggling and glared at Lancelot. "Let me go," he demanded quietly.

But Lancelot was adamant. "Not until you've heard this." He paused, gauging Kay's attitude and allowing him the time he needed to calm down. After what seemed like an age, he spoke again. "I am not suggesting Cai is a replacement for Kelyn; we all know she can never be replaced..."

329

From the shadows of his hiding place, Cai held his breath, watching with fascination as the scene unfolded before him. Kay glared at Lancelot, his eyes boring into his friend; Cai wasn't sure if Kay would let Lancelot continue or whether he was about to attack him.

"...But maybe, just *maybe*," Lancelot continued quietly, "his presence here can give you hope that all is not lost." He paused, slowly releasing his grip on Kay's shirt and met his gaze. "He is your nephew, Kay, and he *needs* you; don't turn away from him." He reached out and put a hand on Kay's shoulder. "And, if I'm not mistaken, you need *him* too. After all, you came back for a reason."

Cai watched with bated breath, his earlier thoughts echoing around his head.

Kay said nothing and Cai took it as a good sign that he wasn't shouting the odds at Lancelot, denying Cai's parentage.

Cai shifted his gaze to Lancelot, taken aback by the way he had defended him; he had never heard the knight speak so fervently about anything before. Sure, he had welcomed him to Camelot, but he had never sounded so... *protective.*

Looking back to Kay, Cai was struck by how broken he looked, a shadow of the man that had loomed over him in the training arena, so long ago. He watched as Kay left, leaving the other three alone.

Gawain looked to Lancelot. "Well, that went well."

Merlin looked between the two knights. "We must give him time," he advised. "As you said, Lancelot, he came back for a reason; he just needs to realise what that reason is."

Then, as if by some silent agreement, the knights and Merlin began making their way towards the Upper Courtyard.

As Merlin reached the steps, he glanced up and stared straight at the spot where Cai and Logan stood. Instinctively, Cai pressed himself hard against the wall in an attempt to step further back into the shadows but he couldn't shake the uneasy feeling that Merlin was staring straight at him. He held his breath, fully expecting Merlin to call his name.

Thankfully, however, Merlin tore his gaze away and climbed the stairs, saying nothing. It wasn't until he was out of sight that Cai was able to breathe again.

Logan stepped out of the shadows, looking back at Cai. "I wonder what all that was about," he murmured thoughtfully. "Who d'you reckon Ailla and Kelyn are?"

Cai said nothing; it was strange but, seeing the look on Kay's face and hearing the pain in the man's voice as he spoke, his anger and hatred for him were changing, becoming something else entirely.

And, as he and Logan made their way to their quarters, he realised with a jolt, that he was beginning to feel *sorry* for Kay.

Chapter Forty-Two

The following morning, as Cai and Logan arrived in the arena, they were greeted by the brooding figure of Kay flanked by Lancelot and Gawain; the arena around them was empty for some reason. Seeing the knights, Cai instantly recalled the scene from the night before, the whispered conversation between them and Merlin and the questions that had been plaguing him all night.

Who was *Kelyn? And* why *had Kay been so upset at the thought of Cai replacing her?*

He couldn't forget the look on the knight's face or the emotion in his voice as he had spoken of her, the way he seemed weighed down by whatever burden he carried.

As these thoughts engulfed him, he let his gaze wander towards Kay and froze as he found the knight's dark eyes glaring back at him. Cai swallowed nervously as he stared back, frozen with fear.

Cai knew he and Logan had stumbled across something they were not meant to have heard, something that Kay had taken great care over to keep hidden. Knowing this made Cai feel guilty, as though he had stolen his secret; he should have revealed himself then and walked away but there had been a small part of him that had *wanted* to stay, to find out more. Maybe, he realised suddenly, a part of him wanted to see his tormentor suffer.

As they approached the knights, Cai shifted his gaze to Lancelot, recalling the way he had spoken up in his defence; he had seemed so convincing, his words so heartfelt. Cai couldn't help wondering, yet again, if his recent doubts about Lancelot were misplaced; after all, would someone looking to betray him really stick up for him?

Don't be so naïve, a small voice in his head chastised. *A traitor would say or do just about anything in order to cause the most damage, the most pain.*

He heard these words in his head but he wasn't sure he could really believe them, not yet; he needed more proof. After all, Lancelot had never given him any *real* reason to doubt him... maybe he was just being paranoid, allowing his fears to get the better of him. And wasn't everyone allowed *some* secrets? But, what with Merlin's prophecy coupled with tales of Morgan and

Mordred... was it any wonder he was seeing betrayal everywhere?

Cai watched Lancelot carefully; he seemed so much more at ease now, as if the recent problems between them hadn't existed. He couldn't help wondering what had caused this sudden change in him; what, exactly, had brought him back to the training arena?

"You have a sword, I see," Kay stated gruffly, glancing at Gawain.

Cai met Kay's glare head on. "Yeah; I've had it a few weeks now, actually," he added pointedly.

"He's quite good, you know," Logan declared in Cai's defence. "Gave me the run around yesterday, didn't you?"

Cai blushed but said nothing; he wasn't about to oversell himself in front of Kay. The knight would, no doubt, slap him down if he did.

Kay raised an eyebrow questioningly. "Well, we'll soon see about that, won't we?" he murmured.

Cai couldn't help but notice he didn't sound convinced which only served to make him more determined. As he rested his hand on the hilt of his sword, he watched Kay closely. "Where's the rest of my men?" he asked.

"With Kay's return, we thought it best for you to reacquaint yourselves with each other," Lancelot explained. He glanced pointedly at Kay before placing a hand on Logan's shoulder. "Come, Logan."

Logan glanced at Cai and nodded curtly. "You got this," he muttered encouragingly before turning and falling into step behind Lancelot.

As he led Logan away, Lancelot offered Cai a brief smile that he barely managed to return. He was still unsure of his feelings towards Lancelot but that was the least of his worries.

Right now, he needed a clear head for whatever Kay was about to throw at him.

"So, you use a sword now, do you, boy?" Kay demanded, stepping forward.

Cai nodded, standing firm as he looked back at him defiantly.

Kay turned to Gawain. "And he is ready?"

Gawain nodded. "He's handled it well... so far," the knight replied.

Kay seemed to consider Gawain's assessment for a moment before turning back to Cai and holding out his hand. "Show me the blade," he commanded.

Cai hesitated only a moment before drawing the sword from its scabbard, holding it up for Kay to look at.

Kay nodded appreciatively. "Not bad," he conceded. "May I?" he asked, holding out his hand expectantly.

Cai could only nod mutely, shocked at this unexpected turn of events; he would never have thought Kay would ever speak to him as an equal, let alone ask permission to look at his sword.

Taking the sword, he turned away and, raising it, sliced through the air and ran through a series of moves. Satisfied, he handed it back to Cai. "It is a good first blade," he concluded. "One you can trust."

Cai nodded again trying to understand what Kay was talking about; to be honest, he was still stunned that Kay was speaking to him *at all*.

Kay turned to Gawain. "Will you leave us?"

Gawain glanced first at Cai, then Kay, his eyes uncertain. "I don't think..." he began to protest.

Kay put a hand on Gawain's shoulder. "Gawain, please," he murmured. "What do you imagine will happen?" he questioned, beseechingly.

Gawain glanced at Cai before heading over to Kay and, turning aside, spoke quietly to him.

Cai caught the words *'after last night'* and saw Kay drop his gaze to the ground in an effort to avoid his friend's concern.

Quickly recovering himself, Kay shook his head and glared back at Gawain defiantly. "Look, if you don't trust me..."

Cai could hear the hurt in Kay's voice and looked away, feeling awkward as he recalled what he had witnessed the previous day.

Gawain shook his head adamantly. "It's not that I don't trust you..." he insisted.

"Then leave us." Kay glanced at Cai, watching him carefully. "I need to work with him alone." He met Gawain's gaze head on. "I *need* to do this."

Cai watched silently as Gawain considered Kay's request. He could tell that the knight was caught between wanting to obey Lancelot's original orders and agreeing to his friend's wishes.

Eventually, he shook his head. "I should know better than this," he grumbled.

Kay grinned. "Thank you," he said, bowing his head in gratitude.

Gawain grunted in reply before turning and walking away, leaving them alone together in the arena.

"There's no need to look so scared, boy," Kay said as he turned to face Cai.

"I have a name, you know," Cai pointed out defiantly, glaring back at him.

Kay considered his student for a moment before turning away and unsheathing his own sword. "So... you have a sword," he mused, his sword poised and at the ready. "But do you know how to *use* it?" He gestured towards Cai. "Let's see what you have learnt in my absence."

Cai wanted to challenge him, to find out where, and why, he had gone, leaving Gawain to take over his teaching but he sensed that would be unwise considering they were about to fight with real swords. So he chose to hold his tongue and say nothing.

Instead, he circled Kay, waiting for a chance to attack. He relaxed his grip on the sword, trying to calm his nerves; standing in front of Kay once more, memories of their previous encounter came flooding back. Everything Cai had learnt suddenly vanished and he didn't know what to do; the sword suddenly felt alien in his hand and his body no longer felt like his own.

Kay watched him carefully. "What are you waiting for?" he demanded. "For me to give you a chance?" He laughed. "I can promise you, boy... *that* is not going to happen. Make your move."

Upon hearing the command, Cai darted forward without thinking. Even before he'd moved, he known he wasn't committed to it and that fact was sickeningly obvious to Kay.

Seeing his chance, Kay brought his blade up to meet Cai's; the resulting clash of iron echoed in the silence. The strength with which Kay's blade had met his own caused Cai to flinch and drop his sword.

Kay straightened and looked at Cai, studying him closely. "What was *that*?" he demanded.

Cai looked at him, unable to find his voice.

Kay shook his head and picked up Cai's sword. Holding it out to him, he said, "Somehow, I don't think that was your best, was it?"

Cai glanced at the floor guiltily.

Kay sighed. "Look, you have to remember everything Gawain has taught you; you have to trust that everything you know is still in here..." he said, tapping his own head. "No matter who your enemy is."

Cai nodded slowly, tightening his grip on the sword. He knew Kay was right; he couldn't let what had gone before intimidate him now, otherwise, what would he be like when he finally met Mordred?

Kay watched him expectantly. "Are you ready?"

Cai took a moment before nodding again.

Kay readied himself, anticipating Cai's attack.

This time, as he engaged Kay, Cai was pleased that he had started stronger, his confidence growing by the second; almost immediately, Kay was forced into a defensive position and it soon became clear he was able to hold his own against the knight. He revelled at the surprise evident in Kay's eyes but didn't allow himself to become distracted and was ready to deflect the blow aimed at his head, counter attacking immediately and forcing Kay into another defensive move.

Stepping away, seeking time and space, Kay studied him. "Not bad," he acknowledged. "Gawain taught you the *basics* of swordsmanship, I see."

Cai bristled at this; yet another thinly veiled insult aimed at him and he was determined to show he was capable of more than just a few *basic* moves. Stepping forward, he swung his sword at Kay, immediately regretting it, aware he had broken one of the first rules: he had let his emotions get the better of him.

Kay easily deflected Cai's blade but made no move to counter attack. "Take a breath, boy," he commanded, circling Cai slowly, giving him space.

Cai watched Kay cautiously, half-expecting a sudden attack; when it became obvious that none was coming, Cai rolled his neck, making a conscious effort to let his anger go.

"Remember what I said to you: anger will only be your enemy in battle," Kay reminded him. "It clouds your mind and judgement." He gave Cai a few more seconds before coming at him again, his sword raised.

Cai moved to the right, trying to bring his sword round to Kay's left but Kay was quick to anticipate the move: the knight's sword met Cai's in mid-air. Instead of giving way though, Cai held firm, pushing against Kay's blade.

Suddenly, Kay stepped back taking his sword with him, upsetting Cai's balance as he did so. In one swift movement, he slammed the hilt of his sword into Cai's jaw, sending him sprawling to the ground.

"What the...?" Cai demanded furiously, clutching his jaw and wincing at the sharp pain.

Kay came and stood over him, grinning. "You'll live," he informed him.

Cai glared up at him furiously. "Yeah, no thanks to you," he shot back, propping himself up.

"What do you think I was trying to show you?" he asked, kneeling beside Cai; there was no anger in his voice, only curiosity.

Cai shrugged, too shocked and outraged to form a coherent sentence.

Kay laid his sword on the ground, gesturing towards the weapon. "The blade is not the only weapon you have on the battlefield," he informed Cai conversationally. He ran his index finger along the blade. "Obviously, you have the blade..." He glanced at Cai. "I'm sure you can imagine the damage *that* could do..."

Cai glared at him, keeping a wary distance as he gingerly moved his jaw, wondering if Kay had broken it.

Kay glanced back at the sword on the ground, indicating the hilt. "The hilt is split into three parts: the cross guard..." He pointed to the simple bar of metal separating the blade from the grip. "The grip..." He indicated the leather bound grip before moving on to the top of the weapon. "And finally, the pommel." He pointed to the bulbous metal mound at the top of the sword. "This is what I hit you with." He smiled. "And if that doesn't work, then there's always your shield, fists or feet."

Cai frowned, only half listening, still moving his jaw from side to side, testing for damage; thankfully, it didn't seem too serious but he knew he'd feel it for the next few days.

Just another injury to add to the list, he thought wryly.

Kay looked up. "You can't be over-reliant upon your blade; your opponent will try to force you into any position where you have no space to move. If that happens, you have to be confident

341

you can get out of it. Now, I'll show you how to do that."

Cai nodded, unsure how to respond; he wanted to say 'thank you' but he really couldn't bring himself to thank the man who had just hit him in the jaw with a sword. He really wasn't prepared for this sudden change in Kay; a few weeks ago he had been yelling at him, telling him he was too cowardly to be a knight, now he was talking to him calmly and promising to show him some defensive moves. His head was spinning and he knew it wasn't just from Kay's attack.

Indicating Cai's jaw, Kay asked, "How is it?"

Cai shrugged. "OK, I guess," he muttered, not wanting to show any sign of weakness.

As Kay reached out towards him, Cai flinched, and for a split second, he saw a look of pain cross Kay's face. He paused, his hand outstretched. "I'm only going to look at it," he assured him.

Cai nodded, allowing Kay to inspect the injury.

"As I said, you'll be fine," Kay muttered dismissively after a moment. "I cannot hold back, Cai; Mordred certainly won't," he added darkly. "You *must* be prepared if you are to have any chance against him and his men." He paused. "Do you understand?"

Cai nodded, watching Kay carefully; at the mention of Mordred's name, he had seemed to retreat into himself. "What's he like?"

Kay frowned. "Who?"

342

"Mordred."

"Evil," Kay replied venomously.

Cai stared at him; his tone conveyed so much hatred it made Cai nervous.

"He is a selfish man, concerned only with his own gain," Kay continued bitterly. "He betrayed my brother..." His eyes darkened as he stared up at Camelot. "He betrayed us all..."

Cai noticed Kay clench his hands into fists, watching him warily; this quiet rage of Kay's was far more intense than the blustering anger he had experienced so far. On impulse, Cai moved closer to him; it was important to him that he let Kay know he understood what he was going through, that they weren't so different after all. Swallowing his nerves, he said, "I know what Mordred did to you..."

Kay slowly turned to look at him, his face unreadable. "What did you just say?" he demanded.

Cai froze as Kay's eyes bored into him but he needed to see this through. "I know Mordred hurt you," he explained. "I understand your loss... we *will* avenge it," he added, trying to sound reassuring.

"You *understand*?" he spat as he got to his feet. "Tell me, how could a mere *boy* understand *my* pain? How can a *boy* understand what it is like to have your whole world ripped apart and taken from you in a heartbeat?" He glared at Cai, his eyes shining. "You can't even *begin* to imagine what that's like..."

343

Cai was on his feet in an instant. "How can you say that?" he cried. "Mordred killed my father!"

"I know," Kay muttered quietly, pain etched on his face. He stared at the ground, avoiding eye contact. "And every time I look at you, I am reminded of that." He sighed, picked up his sword and returned it to his scabbard. "Every time I look at you, I am reminded of how much I have lost." He glanced at Cai briefly. "Training's over for today," he announced and made his way back to Camelot.

Cai watched him go, unable to find the right words to get him to stay. A sense of déjà-vu swept over him as he watched Kay climb the slope out of the arena.

As he disappeared from view, Cai couldn't help wondering if they would ever be able to finish a session without arguing over things either one of them could change.

Chapter Forty-Three

A few days later, Cai stood at Rei's stall, still replaying his encounter with Kay.

"I just don't get him," he was saying while the horse munched slowly on her hay. "I was only trying to ..." He paused; what had he been trying to do? Help? Sympathise? He didn't know anymore...

He smiled as Rei moved closer to him and rested his head against her warm neck, stroking her sleek coat. Everything had been going surprisingly well until he had opened his big mouth. Why had he picked *that* moment to ask Kay about Mordred? He could kick himself for even broaching the subject. After all, Kay had finally been treating him like a human being, finally seeing him as something other than a usurper, intent on claiming Camelot for himself.

But now, it seemed, they were back at square one; Kay was barely speaking to him outside of training and could barely look at him without looking like he wanted to kill him.

Inhaling Rei's scent, Cai allowed himself to relax, finally letting the tension leave his body. Between Kay and Lancelot, he was exhausted; his thoughts and emotions, still all over the place. He was still no closer to figuring out Lancelot's behaviour and had given up trying.

The knight had done so much for him when he had first arrived in Camelot: he had taught him to ride, had urged Kay to form a relationship with him and had stuck up for him when Kay had rallied against him. Cai knew that, on the surface, Lancelot was an honourable Knight of the Round Table, his father's best friend, no less, and his mother's husband.

But that was where Cai's faith in the man ended and his doubts began. Would an honourable man marry his best friend's wife in the wake of his friend's death, whatever the supposed reason? After all, surely he could have helped protect Camelot without the need to marry Guinevere.

And then there was Lancelot's reluctance to face any of Cai's questions regarding Mordred. Why wouldn't he want to talk *unless he had something to hide?* Niggling doubts kept telling Cai that maybe Lancelot still held some measure of loyalty towards Mordred, if only for old times' sake and the friendship they had once shared. If that were the case, what did that mean for him and the other knights? Could they count on Lancelot when it *really* mattered?

Unable to think anymore, the same doubts churning over in this head, he closed his eyes and listened to the noises in the stables around him as they melted into one...

He was so tired... tired of doubting, tired of all the questions...

"I wondered if I might find you here."

The soft voice broke into Cai's thoughts and he turned to see Guinevere standing beside him.

Cai straightened abruptly, the sudden movement spooking Rei, who backed away. Cai watched her for a moment before turning his attention back to his mother.

Standing before her, Cai was suddenly self-conscious of the state he was in; his hair was messy, sticking up in places, and his clothes were dirty and dusty thanks to his latest training session. Running a hand through his hair and dusting himself down, he tried desperately to make himself presentable.

"Sorry, I've just finished training," he blurted out by way of an apology.

"It doesn't matter to me," she murmured. She turned her attention to Rei, studying her. "She is a beautiful creature," she said. "So much like her mother..."

Cai smiled proudly. "Yeah... she's great."

"A horse worthy of you, I feel," she added, turning her attention back to him.

Cai bowed his head, embarrassed. "I don't know about that."

Guinevere smiled. "Will you accompany me outside, Cai?" she asked.

Cai nodded eagerly. "Sure..." He cast a final look at Rei as he followed his mother outside.

"I've spoken to Gawain and Kay..." She paused, glancing at Cai. "They are quite impressed with you, it seems."

Cai's eyebrows rose, surprised. "They are?"

Guinevere's smile widened. "You seem surprised." It wasn't a question but a observation.

Cai shrugged. If he was honest with himself, he *was* surprised; it was one thing *him* feeling pleased about his progress but quite another to hear that actual *knights* had praised him. "I guess I am," he admitted.

Guinevere's eyes softened. "Arthur had days when he doubted himself," she told him. "Not that he shared those feelings with any of his knights," she confided. She smiled fondly at a memory. "He always said it wouldn't do for a leader to show weakness in front of his men."

Cai watched her carefully; her voice had become wistful. Something else had changed too: in remembering her husband, an incredible sadness had set in; her dark eyes shone with unshed tears and she seemed, suddenly, to be carrying a heavy burden with her.

Sensing Cai's awkwardness, Guinevere smiled apologetically. "I'm sorry," she murmured, collecting herself.

348

"Don't be," Cai reassured her. "I like hearing you talk about him," he added quietly.

Guinevere's face lit up. "Do you? It's not too painful?"

Cai shook his head; he couldn't explain it but, whenever Guinevere spoke of Arthur, it was like he was there, by her side, and they were a family again.

Guinevere frowned. "Cai, what is it?"

Cai looked at her, unaware she had been watching him. He smiled self-consciously. "Nothing," he muttered quickly, shaking his head.

"Cai, I thought we had talked about this," Guinevere reminded him softly. "Didn't we agree that you would confide in me, if you needed to?"

Cai glanced at the ground.

Reaching out, Guinevere gently touched Cai's shoulder; he looked up and saw the concern in her eyes. "Tell me what is bothering you; I've watched you these past weeks and I see you are in pain. Allow me to help."

He spoke before he could think better of it. "It's Kay," he confessed reluctantly.

Guinevere frowned. "What about him?"

Cai shook his head. "This is going to sound silly…"

"Cai, please…" Guinevere pleaded. "I take no pleasure in seeing you like this."

Cai hesitated but soon found himself telling her of his most recent run-in with Kay. When he finished, he looked up at her, surprised to see her smiling back at him. He bristled at the sight; was she *laughing* at him?

"Oh, Cai," she murmured. "I've lost count of the many times your father and Kay argued when they were younger."

Cai frowned. "But... I thought they were close; I thought Kay respected him."

"Oh, he did," Guinevere was quick to agree. "But, as children, they were always arguing, apparently. Once, Arthur told me that Kay never ceased to remind him that he was younger and therefore should do whatever Kay ordered him to do." There was no malice in her voice, no resentment, only affection.

For his part, Cai found it hard to imagine Kay being a child; he found it even harder to believe that anyone could order King Arthur around.

"But despite everything, they had a deep love and affection for one another," Guinevere continued. "They would do anything for each other."

From the way Kay talked of Arthur, Cai knew he had a great respect for the man that had been both his brother and king. What he didn't understand was why he had such a problem with *him*. Having a working relationship with Kay was all well and good but he wanted Kay to trust him; he wanted to be able to call him 'uncle'; he wanted Kay to tell him about the Arthur he had known as a child, *the Arthur no one else knew*. He wanted Kay's respect.

But perhaps he was wanting *too* much.

"You do not like Kay," Guinevere observed, breaking into Cai's thoughts.

Cai shrugged.

"You know, Kay is not as bad as you think," she continued. "He is a good man." She blinked and her eyes were tinged with sadness, once more. "He has suffered much in this war," she paused, lost in a memory. "War can break us all in some way; even the strongest of men can fall."

"What do you mean?" Cai asked, his interest piqued as he recalled the conversation he had overheard in the shadows of this very courtyard. Perhaps Guinevere could fill in the blanks for him.

Guinevere glanced at him. "Nothing," she replied quickly. "I should not have said a word; I spoke out of turn."

"But..." Cai started to protest.

"Cai." Guinevere spoke firmly, inviting no further argument. "It was not my place to say anything; please, do not press me further." She shook her head and sighed, obviously regretting her tone. Reaching for Cai's hands, she said, "Forgive me, Cai; I did not mean to snap."

"It's OK," Cai reassured her, not wanting to cause her further pain.

Guinevere shook her head. "No, no it isn't; this war... it has destroyed everything everyone holds dear; it has taken so many lives... husbands, brothers, wives, mothers... children." She indicated the walls of Camelot. "This place... it was once grand..." She smiled down at Cai. "But I know

351

that, one day, under *your* rule, it shall be restored to its former glory," she murmured. "But, until that day, don't lose faith in those who will fight beside you."

"You mean Kay," he asked, although his mind wandered to Lancelot.

"In time, he will see that you are worthy," she assured him quietly. Studying him, she added, "Cai, I feel there is something else that worries you, please let me help."

Cai stared at her; he wasn't used to being read so easily.

"Um..." he floundered. "I can't tell you."

"Cai, you know you can tell me anything."

Cai heard the pain in her voice and wished he could take back his words. She waited silently for a moment and, when it became clear she wasn't giving up, he sighed. "I'm not sure I can trust Lancelot," he blurted out before he could stop himself.

Guinevere looked at him in disbelief. "What on *earth* makes you say that?"

"There's things I've heard; things from Merlin..."

Guinevere narrowed her eyes. "What things?" she asked, concerned.

"That Lancelot and Mordred were once friends," Cai informed her, watching her reaction carefully.

Guinevere was silent for a moment. "Indeed, they *were* friends," she admitted. "But that doesn't mean they still are."

"Do you know what happened between them?" Cai asked.

Guinevere shook her head. "The details were not given to me; Arthur wanted to protect me as much as possible when Mordred's intentions became clear." She paused before continuing. "Maybe you should speak to Lancelot, himself."

"I *have* tried; loads of times," Cai informed her. "But he won't talk to me; when I first asked him, he got really angry and refused to answer any of my questions."

"Well, maybe *I* could..."

She didn't get to finish as the thunderous roar of horses' hooves pounding the ground interrupted them. Cai and Guinevere turned to see Galahad, Bedivere and their men galloping into the courtyard; they looked troubled.

Guinevere stepped to one side, putting as much distance between herself and the horses as possible.

Cai watched as more men and women on horseback flooded into the courtyard. He wanted to ask who they were and where they had come from but before he could, Bedivere fell to his knee before him.

"We bring grave news, my Lord," he murmured.

"What is it?" Cai asked, concerned; he felt Guinevere's presence beside him and was grateful for it.

Bedivere stood, glancing around the courtyard warily. "We should not talk here..."

Cai nodded. "We should gather the knights," he ordered, instinctively knowing this was the right course of action. Reluctantly, he turned to Guinevere but before he could speak, she shook her head.

"Go, Cai... you are needed elsewhere."

Cai nodded, grateful for her understanding and began to make his way through the gathering crowd, almost bumping into Galahad as he did so.

Galahad inclined his head respectfully. "I shall join you after I have ensured these people are settled and fed," he said, tugging against the reins of the horse standing next to him.

Cai nodded before setting off to the Great Hall, Bedivere hot on his heels, all thoughts of Kay and Lancelot forgotten.

Chapter Forty-Four

Cai looked around the room, and still couldn't quite believe it: after months of training, of living at Camelot relatively quietly, he was now sitting in what had been his father's chair, at the Round Table, for his first official meeting with the Knights. He waited nervously for the proceedings to start, desperate to hear what news Bedivere and Galahad had brought back.

Lancelot and Kay sat deep in thought on either side of him, Lancelot to his right, Kay to his left. Beside Kay sat Gawain, his face grave and pensive; next to him Galahad's chair stood empty and beside it, sat Bedivere, his eyes darting between the knights seated around the Table. It was clear to Cai that he was desperate to reveal what he and Galahad had discovered on their travels but was holding back until Galahad joined them. Each knight, including himself and Logan, had laid their swords on the table, their blades pointing towards the centre. Merlin paced silently behind Logan, his gaze fixed on the ground at his feet.

Cai met Logan's gaze across the table and was willing to bet the fear he saw on his friend's face was mirrored in his own. Logan offered him a grim smile; one that Cai couldn't find the inclination to return. *What was the news Bedivere and Galahad brought with them? What had they learned?*

Shifting uncomfortably in his chair, Cai glanced around. Should he say something? Was *he* supposed to be taking charge of this meeting? He dropped his gaze to his lap, wishing he knew what he was supposed to do. He looked up as Galahad entered the chamber.

The knight looked at him apologetically as he made his way to his chair. Before he sat down, he bowed to Cai.

"Forgive my lateness, my Lord," he murmured.

Cai waved his hand dismissively. "It's fine, don't worry about it."

"Are the newcomers settled?" Lancelot asked.

Galahad nodded as he sat in his chair. "They're as settled as they can be, under the circumstances."

Cai looked between them for a moment before turning to Galahad and Bedivere. "What circumstances?" he demanded. "What have you found out?"

Bedivere and Galahad exchanged apprehensive glances, before Bedivere began to speak.

"My Lord, we do not bring good news," he began, glancing at each knight in turn. "Mordred has left a trail of destruction across the countryside." He dropped his gaze, shaking his head. "Countless villages have been destroyed; men and women, alike, left for dead. Children..." He closed his eyes, clearly struggling to find the words.

Cai felt an icy fear grip his stomach; as he continued to stare at Bedivere, he felt his eyes begin to burn. He swallowed, unable to find the words; he had never imagined a Knight of the Round Table could ever be this affected by war.

Galahad continued. "We spoke to those who have survived... they all say the same thing: Mordred's forces took men and boys, young enough and strong enough, to fight for them. They were torn from their mother's arms," he added quietly.

Cai felt Lancelot stiffen beside him as he heard these words. "They took *children*?" he asked in disbelief.

Galahad nodded, glancing between Cai and Logan. "Boys a year or two younger than..." He fell silent, unable to finish the sentence.

Cai glanced at Logan, whose face was ashen. It was the first time he had seen Logan so shaken.

Lancelot leaned forward in his chair, resting his elbows on the table.

There was an oppressive silence in the room and Cai felt like he was suffocating; he wanted nothing more than to leave this room and get as far away from this horror as he could.

"We spoke to anyone we could," Bedivere was saying. "But there wasn't many who would listen..." He paused as if bracing himself for what he had to say next. "They feel betrayed," he added quietly.

Kay frowned. *"Betrayed?"* he growled. "Betrayed by whom?"

Galahad cleared his throat nervously. "By us... by Arthur."

At these words, Kay exploded, slamming his hands on the table as he shot to his feet, a towering force of fury. *"Treachery!"* he cried angrily, his eyes burning. "How *dare* they say such things...?"

"Sit, Kay," Merlin commanded; his voice was quiet, inviting no argument. Kay remained standing, glancing at Merlin as if daring him to give his order again. Merlin met his glare head-on. "Anger will not serve us well here; sit down," he repeated firmly.

After a moment, Kay relented and sat down but Cai could still feel the anger rolling off him in waves. Not that he could blame him; he felt just as angry at this news.

Merlin walked towards Bedivere and Galahad, pausing behind Logan's chair. "What did they say?" he asked.

"Does it matter?" Kay growled, clearly in no mood to listen.

Merlin ignored him, focusing instead on Bedivere and Galahad.

"They resent that he couldn't protect them when it mattered," Galahad explained. "They wanted to believe in him but..."

Kay shook his head in disbelief. "And I suppose they've forgotten he was fighting for them until the very end?" he muttered bitterly.

"Kay, they are not aware of the facts," Merlin reasoned. "All they are aware of is that Mordred has torn their families apart and their King hadn't prevented it." He paused before adding, "We all know how powerless and angry we feel when someone we love is taken from us." He looked directly at Kay. "It is always easier to blame others for our loss than to face the reality of it; it isn't right, but it *is* human nature."

Kay fell silent, accepting Merlin's words.

Cai looked at them warily; he had the feeling that more was being said between them than just the words being spoken. He recalled the conversation he and Logan had overheard in the Lower Courtyard but he pushed it to one side; now was not the time to dwell on that.

"Those men and women that returned with us..." Bedivere continued. "They are willing to join our forces; they are willing to believe we have the means to find Mordred *and* save their loved ones."

"There aren't many," Gawain commented drily.

"I know, but it's a start," Galahad pointed out.

Merlin nodded. "Indeed it is," he agreed.

"My only question is: what happens next?" Lancelot asked. "Time is against us; Mordred is slowly isolating us..."

"And we are helping him, the longer we remain here," Gawain was quick to point out.

The room fell silent; no one was willing to say what needed to be said.

Unable to stay quiet any longer, Cai gathered his courage. "We have to do *something*," he announced.

Every eye in the room turned to him.

"Like what?" Logan asked, taken aback by Cai's statement.

Cai shrugged; he hadn't given any of this much thought. He had just hoped that if he acknowledged the fact they had to do something, someone else would come up with a plan; after all, they were all far more experienced in this than he was. "I don't know..." he admitted quietly. "But Gawain's right; if we stay here much longer, Mordred will turn the whole of Britain against us." He looked at each knight in turn. "All I know is, I don't want to sit here doing nothing while there's people out there who need our protection." He fell silent, his heart hammering in his chest; he had no idea where these words were coming from, no idea how he could sound so assured... He looked around, waiting for *someone* to say *something*.

360

"The boy's right," Kay announced, surprising Cai with his unexpected support. "We've waited long enough; the time has come for us to act. It's time we stopped putting off the inevitable..." He glanced pointedly at Cai before looking around the table. "We need to start making plans."

Merlin nodded in agreement and, smiling at Cai, added, "And, I believe, now is the time we make Cai known to his people; to show them there is still hope."

Chapter Forty-Five

After the meeting, Cai followed Lancelot out of the Great Hall, Logan trailing after him.

"Hey, wait up," Logan called as he fell into step beside Cai. "Where you going in such a rush? Did all that freak you out? It did me."

Cai glanced at him; he couldn't deny that being a part of that meeting had shaken him. After all, it wasn't every day he was told that the person who wanted to kill him was now building an army against him and destroying families to do it. And to know that, at last, he would be leaving Camelot to recruit people to swell his own ranks...

This was real now.

Things were starting to happen and he had no power to control any of it...

But that was not the reason why he was following Lancelot, not really.

"I need to talk to Lancelot," he said, deliberately ignoring Logan's question.

Logan frowned. "Why? What's so important that you couldn't talk to him in the meeting?"

"I need to find out about what happened with him and Mordred," Cai explained.

"But... you've already tried that," Logan pointed out. "He's shut you down once; what makes you think he won't do it again?"

"I don't," Cai admitted. "But I have to try; I *have* to know I can trust him."

If he was leaving Camelot, he had to know his mother would be safe under Lancelot's protection.

He watched as Lancelot crossed the Lower Courtyard and made his way into the stables. The knight was finally alone and Cai thought this the best time to talk to him, as there was no one else around to interrupt them.

"Do you want me to come with you?" Logan asked, his eyes betraying his concern.

Cai shook his head. "No, I'll be fine but keep a look out; I don't want anyone interrupting."

Logan nodded in agreement as he lent against the stable wall.

Cai was fully aware Logan wanted to come with him, wanted to hear Lancelot's story first hand, but he also knew that whatever Lancelot had to say had to be just between the two of them, at least to begin with.

Cai stood in the doorway of the stables acclimatising himself to his shadowy surroundings; daylight shone through the doorway but could not reach the stalls where horses stood looking at him curiously. He spotted Lancelot standing in front of a stall; his back to him, unaware of his presence... or so he thought.

"Are you going to stand there *all* day or are you actually going to say something?" Lancelot asked drily, as he turned to face Cai.

Cai forced himself to take a step forward. "I leave in a few days," he began. "We need to talk now, before it's too late." He knew that probably sounded far more dramatic than it needed to, but he couldn't help it.

Lancelot studied him for a moment before sighing and running a hand wearily over his face. "Very well." He indicated a wooden bench against the wall to Cai's right but Cai shook his head. Lancelot stepped forward but kept to the shadows. "The time has come for me to finally stop running from the truth."

"And what *is* the truth?" Cai asked.

Lancelot dropped his gaze. "Mordred was fifteen when Arthur asked me to mentor him. He was young and eager to learn..." He looked up at Cai guiltily. "It flattered me that Arthur would trust me with his nephew... it meant a lot."

Cai watched him silently; he saw the sadness in Lancelot's eyes as he spoke of Arthur, the same sadness he saw in his mother and Kay when they spoke of him.

Lancelot pushed his grief aside as he continued. "His training started well; he listened, did exactly as I said..." He smiled wryly. "He was a good student."

Cai narrowed his eyes and instinctively clenched his fists at his sides; to hear Lancelot speaking so positively about Mordred infuriated him. "How can you *do* that?" he demanded.

Lancelot frowned. "Do what?"

"Stand there and tell me how wonderful Mordred was!" Cai cried angrily. "After what he's done, how can you...?"

"You wanted the truth, Cai," Lancelot retorted. "This *is* the truth. It pains me to admit that there was once a time I welcomed Mordred into Camelot, when I supported his endeavours to become a Knight of the Round Table; I championed him, mentored him... And I'm ashamed to admit that, if Arthur and I hadn't done that, Mordred would never have had the opportunity to do what he did." He fell silent, his gaze returned to the floor. "If we hadn't... then Mordred and Morgan wouldn't have the power they have now."

Cai stood watching him, silently acknowledging his words; there was nothing he could say to placate him. But did he even want to? Maybe it was right that he carried this guilt with him.

"I was blind to Mordred's true intentions for a long time," Lancelot continued quietly.

Cai frowned. "What do you mean?"

Lancelot shrugged helplessly. "He would say or do something... And, after spending time with him, I realised he was very bitter and quick to anger. At first, I convinced myself that nothing was awry, that it was just how he was; I mean, look at Kay..." Lancelot shook his head. "But this was more than just bitterness and a quick temper; Mordred had a *rage* inside him, a rage I ignored for far too long."

"So how did you...?"

"We were on a quest," Lancelot explained. "It was Mordred's first since accepting his place at the Table."

"What happened?" Cai pressed, his frustration rising. *Why was Lancelot taking so long to get to the point?*

"One night, Mordred had taken first watch," Lancelot continued, as if Cai hadn't interrupted; he was lost in his memories now and all Cai could do was listen. "I awoke to find the camp empty; Mordred was nowhere in sight. So I went in search of him; it wasn't long before I found him," he added darkly. He paused, gathering his thoughts; it was clear he was finding this difficult. "I came upon him in a clearing; luckily there was no moon that night so I was able to remain hidden. He wasn't alone."

Cai had a feeling he knew exactly who had been with Mordred but he asked the question anyway. "Who was with him?"

"I know now it had been Morgan le Fay," Lancelot explained. "But at the time, I was not aware of her identity. I watched them from my hiding place, all the while knowing something was dreadfully wrong; aside from the fact that we had travelled alone there was something wrong with Morgan. To this day I cannot believe what I saw." He looked at Cai. "She... *flickered*, Cai; like a candle, she flickered."

Cai held his gaze, recalling the image Merlin had shown him when he had first come to this world; he remembered how confused *he* had been. "I've seen it too," he murmured. "Merlin... he showed me my father when I first got here."

Lancelot glowered and shook his head. "*Magic!*" he spat contemptuously. "This world would be a lot better off without it! This war would have been over by now."

Despite himself, Cai felt hurt by Lancelot's hasty words. "Without magic, *I* wouldn't be here," he muttered quietly.

Lancelot closed his eyes and sighed, running a hand through his hair. "I know, I know; I'm sorry. I didn't mean..."

Cai shrugged, suddenly feeling awkward. "It's OK," he said. "So... what happened then; after you saw them?" he asked, bringing the conversation back to Mordred.

Lancelot shook his head. "Their voices were hushed, but I did manage to hear a few words..." He paused before continuing. "They spoke of a plan and how, when Mordred returned to Camelot, she would be waiting for word from him; he said that, when the time was right, he would grant her admittance to Camelot and she would then take her revenge." He fell silent for a moment, his thoughts, no doubt, back in that forest clearing. "That was all I saw; I ran, *ran like a coward.*" Despite his best efforts, he couldn't keep the bitterness from his voice. He turned from Cai. "I should have done *something!*" he cried angrily. "I'm a Knight of the Round Table, *not* a coward!" He shook his head. "I should have done something that night; it was my duty. But I was confused, scared... so I chose to say nothing; I just ignored what I had seen. When Mordred returned to camp, I took second watch and, the following day, we continued with our quest as if nothing had happened." His voice was detached now, cold and unfeeling, consumed by guilt.

"So you said *nothing?*" Cai asked in disbelief. "Not even when you got back to Camelot?" Maybe he hadn't been so wrong about Lancelot, after all; by saying nothing he had certainly betrayed Arthur. But hadn't Merlin said...?

"You think so little of me?" Lancelot demanded rounding on Cai, his eyes boring into him.

Cai glared at him defiantly. "But you just said...!" He paused, taking a breath, trying to control his frustration. "And, to be honest, I don't know what to think anymore!" Cai retorted. "I mean, it's not as if you've even tried to explain any of this before now, is it?" he demanded angrily.

368

"So, can you really blame me for thinking the worst?"

Lancelot studied him, his face unreadable. After a moment, he relented and explained, "You have to understand, I had never experienced magic before that moment; I didn't know what to think or how to deal with it. When we returned to Camelot, I did the only thing I could: I went to Merlin. I knew, through conversations with Arthur, that he had... powers beyond anything I could ever understand," he explained. "I told him what I had witnessed..."

"He knew it was Morgan, didn't he?" Cai asked, relieved to know that Lancelot *had* done something, after all.

Lancelot nodded. "Merlin and I went to see Arthur and I told him everything. Arthur and Merlin came up with a plan..."

Cai frowned. "What kind of plan?"

"They wanted to test Mordred... It was announced that Arthur would be leaving Camelot, that he had heard word of unrest to the east and that he wanted to put an end to it before it became too much of a problem." He paused before continuing. "The day before we were due to leave, Arthur sent Mordred on a false errand, thereby ridding him from Camelot..."

"But wouldn't that just have been playing into his hands?" Cai asked. Surely sending him away would give him the chance to speak with Morgan more freely?

369

"That's exactly what I argued, but Arthur was adamant." Lancelot smiled. "Arthur was a great planner; he knew how to lure enemies into a trap. He wanted Mordred to have the chance to speak to Morgan and to relay all the false information he had given him; he wanted them to make their plans." His smile faded as he continued. "Later that day, Arthur called a meeting and the true nature of his departure was revealed to the remaining knights. As you would expect, there was outrage and disbelief but we all knew we had to stand together. It was agreed that Merlin and Kay would stay behind to lead the contingent charged with the protection of Guinevere and Camelot; the rest of us would ride out with Arthur and lay in wait until Merlin contacted us."

Cai listened eagerly, wishing he could have seen his father and the knights in action; it would have been an amazing sight.

"We hadn't been gone long when Merlin got word to us that Mordred had led his attack on Camelot," Lancelot revealed. "We wasted no time; we rode back to Camelot and engaged them. Merlin was able to hold back Morgan and eventually cast her from Camelot; without her support, Mordred quickly retreated, taking his men with him. As our remaining men and women tried to rebuild Camelot and accept what had happened, we were all aware of only one thing: we were now at war."

Cai sat in silence, mulling over what he had just heard. He couldn't put his feelings into words; somehow, nothing seemed adequate. "I'm sorry," he murmured wracked with guilt.

"For what?" Lancelot asked, bewildered.

Cai sighed, angry at himself. "For thinking the worst of you," he admitted. "For doubting your loyalty to my father."

Lancelot smiled wryly. "I'm guilty of many things, Cai, but disloyalty to your father *isn't* one of them." He paused. "He may not have been my brother but I loved him like one; I was proud to serve him. And..." He broke off as he looked at Cai. Taking a step towards him, he dropped to one knee and bowed his head. "And I will be honoured to serve you."

Cai blushed at this unexpected pledge; he glanced around the empty stables, furtively, anxious someone might see them. "Get up," he ordered, hastily.

Lancelot did as Cai asked. "Do you accept my fealty?"

"Of course I do," Cai said quickly. "Though I don't know why you'd want to serve me after just finding out I didn't trust you."

Lancelot's smile came easily this time. "As you say: I didn't exactly give you any reason to think otherwise, did I?"

"But I don't understand... Why did you avoid telling me any of this for so long?" Cai asked.

Lancelot hung his head in shame. "Because I felt guilty for ever trusting that man," he

371

admitted. "It wasn't something I was eager to acknowledge, especially to you."

"You weren't the only one who trusted him," Cai pointed out.

"No," Lancelot agreed. "But that doesn't make my burden any easier to bear."

Cai nodded, appreciating that Lancelot still needed time to forgive himself; perhaps this conversation may have helped him in some way.

Chapter Forty-Six

Now that they had cleared the air, and he was working closely with Lancelot once more, Cai had many opportunities to find out more about his father; unlike Kay, Lancelot was more than willing to share his memories with him. The knight was only too happy to tell Cai about the many quests they had been on together.

Cai's last few remaining days in Camelot passed quickly and he soon found himself standing with Logan in the armoury being kitted out for their journey the following day. Being in the forge, once more, while Gadeon bustled around him, reminded Cai of just how far he had come: the last time he had been here, he had been too scared to even pick up a sword but now... now, he was about to leave Camelot, he was preparing to fight for her and his father's legacy.

"You nervous?" Logan asked, casting a sidelong look at Cai.

Cai fidgeted as he watched Osric mend his chainmail. "No, not really," he lied.

Logan raised an eyebrow. "Really?" he asked in disbelief. "If it were *me* and *I* was about to meet *my* people for the first time as the High King of Britain, *I'd* be bloody terrified!"

Cai tried to smile but his mouth was suddenly dry and Logan had said nothing to help ease his nerves.

Sensing Cai's unease, Logan turned to him. "Hey, it'll be alright," he said encouragingly. "I mean, these people need someone to lead them, it may as well be you, right?"

Cai scoffed. "Yeah, a sixteen year old who's never fought a real battle before!"

"But you're *King Arthur's son!*" Logan exclaimed as if that was all the argument Cai needed from now on. "That's *gotta* carry some weight."

"The boy's right," Gadeon added. "You *are* King Arthur's son." He narrowed his eyes as he studied Cai. "I saw the boy that walked into my forge all those months ago and now he stands before me, a man. You will do Camelot and your father proud, my Lord," he added, bowing low.

Cai smiled, touched by the blacksmith's words. He wished he were as optimistic as Logan and Gadeon but he wasn't; his people already distrusted Arthur, most of them blaming him for their suffering. What could Cai possibly say or do to make them see things differently?

***

Cai shivered in the early morning light as he, the knights and a contingent of one hundred men stood in the courtyard, waiting for their horses to be brought to them. Men and women lined the courtyard, eager to see their King ride out of Camelot for the first time. Initially, Cai had been against this idea - the last thing he wanted was a fanfare - but Merlin and Lancelot had quickly made him realise his people needed to witness this; they needed to be a part of this momentous day.

Cai watched as the men assigned to accompany him bade farewell to friends and family. He found it hard to watch; this was the moment he had been dreading, the moment he would have to leave his mother behind...

Turning his attention away from his men, Cai sighed, his impatience growing. "How long is this going to take?" he demanded, his frustration finally getting the better of him.

Kay scowled at him from the shadows. "As long as it takes; *you* try saddling the horses with provisions and see how long it takes."

Merlin smiled. "Have patience, Cai," he advised, pulling his thick layers of fur closer about him. "These things cannot be rushed."

"Not if you want it done properly," Kay added pointedly.

Cai glared at him but was soon distracted as Guinevere took his hand; her hand was cold in his and, even in the limited morning light, he could see her eyes shone with tears.

"Be safe, my son," she murmured.

Cai forced himself to smile. "I will..." As he spoke, he couldn't help hearing the emptiness in his own voice.

Guinevere glanced at Merlin, who was standing dutifully beside Cai, wrapped in his cloak. "Look after him," she asked quietly.

Merlin placed a hand on his chest and bowed. "I will, Your Highness; I will lay down my life, if necessary."

Cai smiled grimly at him, glad he was going to be riding with him; it helped knowing they had Merlin's powers to call upon, if anything should happen.

"Let's hope it doesn't come to that," Kay muttered. He met Cai's gaze and the two stared at each other for a moment.

Cai knew that was the best he could hope for under the circumstances but, despite everything, found himself wishing he could say a proper goodbye to the man who was his uncle. But, however much he may have wanted to, he knew he couldn't; there was still something between them preventing either of them taking that final step.

His attention was suddenly drawn to the sound of horses' hooves on flagstones and he turned to see the horses being led out to them. He smiled at the very welcome sight of Rei, her saddlebags fit to burst; she pulled determinedly against her reins and Cai could tell she sensed something out of the ordinary was happening.

Taking her reins, he stroked her nose, making eye contact and whispering words of comfort to her; he smiled, pleased when she responded to his voice, calming, almost immediately.

Movement caught his eye and he turned to see Lancelot and Merlin deep in conversation. He watched them for a moment, noting the urgency of Lancelot's gestures and the furtive glances he cast around the courtyard. Curious, Cai angled himself and Rei so he had a better chance of overhearing their conversation...

"All I'm saying," Lancelot said, "is that it could be dangerous..."

"No more dangerous than if we waited," Merlin protested. "We cannot keep putting off the inevitable; it *is* Cai's destiny, after all."

"But..." Lancelot protested.

Merlin placed a hand on his shoulder. "Lancelot, do you trust me?"

Lancelot held Merlin's gaze. "You know I do."

"Then trust me in *this*."

Lancelot's eyes bored into Merlin for a moment before he nodded. "Very well. Do what you must."

"Thank you." At that moment, Merlin turned from Lancelot, catching sight of Cai watching him. He smiled. "Are you ready?"

Cai nodded mutely. Before he could mount his horse, he felt a hand on his back and turned to see Guinevere who was, now, openly crying; Lancelot dutifully made his way to her side. She tried to smile through her tears. "Come back to me safely, Cai Pendragon," she begged.

"I will..." Cai promised, this time with far more conviction. He gazed at her and, seeing the pain in her eyes, he said the one thing he knew would go some way to easing it, something he had wanted to say for so long now... "I love you... Mother," he whispered.

Despite her tears, a smile now brightened her face. "I have waited so long to hear you say that..." she whispered, hugging him tightly. She turned her head slightly and whispered, "I love you, too, Cai."

Cai held onto her for all he was worth; getting to know her after all this time made leaving that much harder, but he knew he had to do this. So, holding back his tears, he released her; the last thing he wanted was to lose control in front of everyone, least of all Kay who, he noticed, was still watching him intently.

Lancelot stepped forward and placed a hand on Cai's shoulder. "We shall have a feast upon your return," he declared. Cai smiled uneasily, unsure of what to say. After a moment, Lancelot added, "Your father would be proud of you."

"Thanks," Cai choked before he turned and, placing his foot in the stirrup, pulled himself into the saddle in one swift, confident move. Smiling down at Guinevere one last time, he saw the pride in her eyes as she looked up at him. Nodding in farewell, he nudged Rei forward as he followed Merlin out of Camelot.

Chapter Forty-Seven

As the days passed, Cai found himself wondering more and more about the snippet of conversation he had overheard between Merlin and Lancelot. It was obvious they were hiding something from him but the question was: *what?* What could be so bad that they felt they needed to keep it from him?

Lost in his thoughts, he gazed blankly ahead; he had no idea where they were or where they were going, for that matter, other than a vague knowledge, thanks to Bedivere, that they were heading east. The familiar countryside surrounding Camelot had long since fallen away, replaced by empty green fields that seemed to stretch on for miles in every direction. There was no protection from the mind-numbing wind that had suddenly sprung up from nowhere. Above them iron-grey clouds had rolled in, darkening the late afternoon light, threatening rain.

The initial conversation between the men had died down as everyone's concern was now about keeping warm and looking for shelter against the impending rain. Even Logan had lost his enthusiasm and now rode quietly beside Cai, his mood as black as the clouds above.

"This is rubbish," he muttered darkly for the thousandth time.

Cai smiled wryly. "What, exactly, did you expect?"

Logan shrugged. "I don't know! But not this; I thought it would be like the films, you know? With us galloping across the countryside..." He sighed dejectedly.

They fell into silence, once again, and Cai let his gaze wander to Merlin who rode at the head of the procession. He hadn't, as yet, had a chance to question him about what he had overheard but he planned to, just as soon as he could work it into a conversation.

Ahead, Merlin reined in his horse and, turning in his saddle, held up a hand. Behind Cai, Bedivere and Galahad mirrored the command, bringing the men behind them to a stop.

"We shall rest shortly," Merlin announced. He pointed ahead to a hill shrouded in shadows. "We shall cross that hill; beyond, there is a valley where we shall rest for the night."

"Thank God!" Logan muttered to Cai, his shoulders sagging in relief. "I don't think I can last much longer."

Cai couldn't help but agree. After days in the saddle, the muscles in his back, shoulders and thighs were beginning to burn; none of his training with Lancelot or Gawain had prepared him for how hard this would be.

As they continued their journey, Cai heard Bedivere relaying the news to the rest of their men. He turned in his saddle to see Galahad spur his horse into a gallop as he sped on to tell the men further down the line.

As they reached the top of the hill, Cai had an uneasy feeling in the pit of his stomach as he realised he would soon learn what it was, about this journey, that Lancelot had deemed too dangerous.

***

Once they were settled, it hadn't taken long for Bedivere to organise a hunting expedition and it soon became clear that Logan wasn't the only one who had found the lack of action, so far, frustrating. Many of the men volunteered but Bedivere chose only a few, much to the disappointment of those overlooked. Cai felt for the ones forced to stay behind; after years of waiting at Camelot, they were now forced to watch and wait for their friends to return from what would surely be, by far, the most exciting thing they had done in a while.

Cai soon forgot their plight, however, when he caught sight of Merlin sitting alone by a newly lit fire. Wandering over, he sat opposite him watching the hypnotic dance of the flames.

"You seem quiet," Merlin observed glancing briefly at Cai.

Cai could only shrug.

"I daresay you were expecting more... adventure." Merlin smiled. "Logan certainly seems disappointed." He looked around the camp. "He is not with you?"

Cai shook his head. "He talked Bedivere into taking him hunting."

Merlin raised an eyebrow. "And you did not choose to go?"

Cai looked at Merlin across the fire; this was it. "No; I wanted to talk to you... in private," he added pointedly.

"I see." Merlin settled back, waiting for Cai to continue.

"I overheard you and Lancelot talking before we left..."

Merlin smiled wryly. "You make quite a habit of that, don't you?"

Cai bristled at the observation; what was *that* supposed to mean? He rounded on him. "You know, if people told me things, I wouldn't *have* to eavesdrop, would I?" he complained bitterly.

Merlin's eyes shone brightly in the firelight as he looked directly at Cai. "No, you are quite correct in what you say..." Cai stared at him; had Merlin just acknowledged he was in the wrong? After a moment, Merlin continued, "But it is not always the wisest path to take; one can often misinterpret what one hears."

Cai narrowed his eyes. "So, are you going to tell me what you were talking about?" he pressed, ignoring Merlin's comment. "Because Lancelot said it was dangerous, so *I* think I have a *right* to know..."

Merlin inclined his head. "Very well," he agreed. "It *is* only right you are made aware of what lies ahead." He paused for a moment, studying Cai, before continuing, "When I suggested this excursion, I knew it was going to be more than simply introducing you to your people."

Cai frowned. "So you lied to me," he declared, frustrated.

Merlin ignored the accusation. "You still have much to learn, Cai; about your father, about Mordred... about *yourself.* This journey will be the first step to achieving that."

"What do you mean?"

"Tomorrow, we shall take a detour..." Merlin met his gaze. "Tomorrow, I shall take you to receive Excalibur."

Cai's jaw dropped. "You mean...?" he began.

Merlin nodded. "I do," he smiled.

Cai almost burst with excitement at the prospect; Excalibur would soon be *his*. He couldn't believe it; *he*, a boy who, not too long ago, had been a victim, was now sitting opposite the greatest sorcerer of legend being told *he* was going to receive the greatest sword of legend; his father's sword, no less. This was beyond anything Cai could ever have imagined.

Seeing Cai's expression, Merlin hurried on. "This is no time for excitement, Cai," he warned. "While it can be argued that Excalibur *should* be in your possession, Lancelot's fears are not unfounded."

His face dropped, instantly. "What are you talking about?" he asked. "I can use a sword now; I'm not going to..."

Holding up a hand to silence him, Merlin continued, "Excalibur is far from a normal sword. It is imbued with magic and intimately linked to your father, you and..."

"*And...?*" Cai pressed.

"And Morgan le Fay," Merlin finished.

"What does *that* mean?" Cai asked fearfully; nothing involving Morgan was ever good.

"It means that, since your father's death, sixteen years ago, it has been out of Morgan's reach," Merlin explained. "But as soon as it is in your possession, she will immediately be aware of it *and* of *your* existence."

Cai swallowed nervously. "Oh."

"So, you see, it is not a simple matter," Merlin concluded.

Cai rubbed his forehead. "So... you're telling me that when I get Excalibur, she'll come after me?"

Merlin nodded. "Indeed."

385

"But how will she know who I am?"

"Excalibur will only respond to the Pendragon bloodline; therefore, she will know, instantly, that a descendant of Arthur possesses it." He paused for a moment, before continuing. "Morgan may be a servant of the Dark but she is a very intelligent woman and must *never* be underestimated."

Cai shook his head, his mind working furiously. "But I don't understand. You said she was linked to Excalibur, too; how can that *be*? She isn't..."

"She stole the sword a long time ago," Merlin explained, anticipating his question. "She cast a spell upon it so that she would always know that Arthur wielded it; that way, she would know that he lived."

Cai's mouth was suddenly as dry as sandpaper. "And that goes for me too?"

Merlin nodded.

Cai leaned forward, resting his elbows on his knees, dropping his head in his hands. He heard Merlin get to his feet and walk around the fire, towards him, but he didn't look up.

Placing a hand on Cai's shoulder, Merlin said, "Rest assured, Cai, no matter what happens, you have men who will fight for you; men who will lay down their lives for you."

Suddenly, they were interrupted by the triumphant return of the hunting party and, as the camp sprang to life, once more, Cai withdrew into his own thoughts, lost to his fears of what was yet to come.

Chapter Forty-Eight

Having not slept much the previous night, Cai found he didn't feel like eating the following morning. Images of Morgan and Mordred, the deranged sorceress and her mad son, who would stop at nothing to kill him, had plagued him all night. Recollecting how he had felt when Merlin had first told him of Excalibur, his initial excitement was now long gone; all that remained was fear and nausea.

Earlier that morning, Merlin had informed Bedivere, Galahad and Logan of his plans to retrieve Excalibur; Bedivere, and a select few of his men, were to accompany himself and Cai in this quest while Galahad, Logan and the rest of the men would remain in camp. Logan, it seemed, was not happy with this plan and had argued the point with Merlin until he was blue in the face, but the older man would not be moved; realising the futility of his argument, Logan had retreated to his tent to sulk.

Despite Logan's strop and Cai's private misgivings, the news had certainly bolstered everyone's spirits. Personally, Cai couldn't see how Excalibur would help if it was going to bring Morgan to their door.

Later, after a brief farewell, Cai had reluctantly left camp with the others, hoping none of this would play out the way he feared; maybe Merlin was wrong and, maybe, after all this time, the magic Morgan had cast on the sword had worn off. Could that happen? He really needed to check this with Merlin…

He was about to do just that when… a voice stopped him.

"You seem out of sorts today, my Lord." Cai turned in his saddle as Bedivere bowed his head guiltily. "Forgive me, my Lord; I did not mean…"

Cai held up a hand; there was no need for an apology. "It's fine," he murmured. Glancing over to him, Cai noticed that Bedivere held the reins loosely in his left hand whilst his right arm rested on his thigh. He couldn't help wondering how awkward it must feel riding a horse one-handed; *he* certainly couldn't do it but Bedivere made it look so easy. "I was just thinking," he added.

They continued to ride in companionable silence for a while until Bedivere spoke. "I don't know if you are aware of this, my Lord, but…" He glanced at Cai. "Before he died, your father charged me with the task of returning Excalibur to its final resting place."

Cai stared at him. "You were with him when he...?" He couldn't bring himself to finish the sentence.

Bedivere nodded. "I was and it was my honour to fulfil his last wish." He paused before adding, "He died in my arms."

Cai dropped his gaze to his hands; a deep, overwhelming sadness engulfed him as tears stung his eyes. Gathering his courage and, bracing himself for the answer, he asked, "Did he... Did he suffer?"

Bedivere shook his head. "No; thankfully, it was quick."

"What happened?" Cai asked before he could stop himself; did he *really* want to know? Could he handle it?

Yes, a small voice inside him answered. *He* had *to know.* It *would* be painful but he *had* to know.

Bedivere glanced at him uneasily. "Are you sure...?"

"I *need* to know," Cai insisted, urgently.

Bedivere inclined his head. "Very well, my Lord." He fell silent for a moment. "The Battle of Camlann was very long and hard," he began. "We fought hard for several days but Mordred's forces would not yield; they were far stronger than we could ever have anticipated." He stared wistfully ahead as he continued. "They fought like they were possessed..." He shrugged. "Maybe they were; Morgan, I have come to realise, is capable of anything."

Cai watched him intently, loathe to interrupt or ask questions; it was important that Bedivere told his story in his own time, and in his own way.

"When Arthur finally met Mordred on the battlefield, we knew that the outcome would decide the course of the war," Bedivere said. He bowed his head sadly. "When Mordred dealt Arthur that fatal blow... it was as if he had run me through, too. But the war was far from over; Arthur still had one final attack left in him..."

Cai listened with barely concealed glee as Bedivere described how Arthur, with the last of his strength, had fatally wounded Mordred. It didn't matter that he knew Morgan later saved her son; all that mattered to Cai was that Arthur, in his last moments of life, had still been determined to fight for the lives of his people, his knights and his family. It made him proud to carry the Pendragon name and he found himself all the more determined to continue what his father had started.

"...I set about trying to save him," Bedivere was saying. "But he begged me to stop." He bowed his head. "He knew he was beyond help," he added quietly. He glanced at Cai. "I tried to convince him otherwise but he was adamant. He made me promise to take Excalibur and return it to its final resting place."

"And where was that?" Cai asked, his curiosity piqued.

"A lake," Bedivere replied.

"A *lake*?" Cai echoed in disbelief.

Bedivere shrugged. "It was not something for my understanding either; in fact, there was a moment when I refused his order," he shamefully admitted. "But Arthur was adamant; he asked me to promise I would do it and to trust what he said. So I did," he added simply. "I went with Merlin to the lake," he continued. "I remember standing on the shore, looking out over the water; I looked at Excalibur and, in that moment, I almost reconsidered what I was about to do. It was too beautiful to cast into the water..." He smiled ruefully. "It was fortuitous Merlin was with me; he reminded me of my promise and that gave me the resolve I needed. I threw it... with all my strength, I threw it..." Bedivere turned to Cai, watching him... "But, before it even touched the water, a hand reached out and grasped it."

Cai stared at him, aghast. *"Are you serious?"*

Bedivere smiled. "Quite serious, my Lord. Then it disappeared below the surface." He shook his head. "I was convinced my mind was playing tricks on me but Merlin assured me what I had seen was true. And, despite what my head was telling me, I had been witness to something far greater than I could ever comprehend." He glanced at Cai. "Your father did many great deeds with that sword; you, too, will be worthy of it... of *that*, I am certain."

Bedivere's words resonated somewhere deep inside Cai but they did nothing to quell the fear building inside him with every second that passed.

"But something still weighs heavily upon you, my Lord," he observed.

Cai took a moment, bracing himself for his confession. He glanced at the knight, bolstered by the concern he saw in his eyes. "When I get the sword... Morgan will know about me," he admitted quietly.

"I see," Bedivere murmured gravely.

Cai glanced at him. "I can't pretend that the thought of her knowing about me doesn't terrify me."

Bedivere nodded in understanding. "As well it should; you would be a fool if it didn't." He grinned. "And I am not in the habit of serving fools."

Cai smiled, despite himself, but said nothing. What could he possibly say that wouldn't make him sound less than what he was supposed to be? He was *supposed* to be King Arthur's son, the High King of Britain; he was *supposed* to fight Mordred and finish what his father had started, rebuild Camelot...

"My Lord, I cannot pretend she won't hunt you down..." Bedivere's words cut into him like a knife.

"Thanks," Cai muttered wryly.

"But, if I may be so bold... Maybe it's a good thing; you can finally be the King your father

393

would want you to be." He fell silent for a moment, then, turning to him, he added, "But, whatever happens, my Lord, my sword will be *yours* to command; whatever it takes to protect you, I shall do."

Cai found himself smiling at Bedivere. "Thank you," he said sincerely. He didn't know what it was about this man but Cai instinctively knew he was a warrior to be reckoned with, and one he would be grateful to have by his side.

Chapter Forty-Nine

"We are near, my Lord," Bedivere announced, later that afternoon.

Cai surveyed his surroundings, wondering how Bedivere, after all these years, could possibly tell; there were no notable features on the landscape to indicate where they were… none that *he* could see, anyway.

Ahead of them, Merlin turned down an overgrown path to their left and followed it as it rose over the crest of a small hill; behind them, Bedivere's men followed, keeping a wary distance and, no doubt, on the lookout for any impending threats.

On reaching the top, Cai gasped as a huge lake came into view and the desolate landscape opened up before him; the water, so still, acted as a mirror, perfectly reflecting the sky above. The lake itself looked peaceful and inviting, surrounded as it was by hills and fields, and he wanted nothing more than to rest here for a while.

"Just as I remember," Bedivere murmured, sitting back in his saddle, surveying his surroundings.

"Come, Cai," Merlin called.

Cai turned, surprised to find Merlin already standing at the water's edge. Dismounting quickly, he looked around for somewhere to tie Rei.

"My Lord... Allow me," Bedivere offered as he dismounted. Approaching Cai, he held out his hand and took the reins from him.

Smiling gratefully, Cai walked towards Merlin; Bedivere hung back alongside his men, some of whom had already dismounted and were checking their horses, making sure they were well watered and rested before their return journey. As Cai approached the shoreline, Merlin knelt down and lightly touched the surface of the water with his fingertips.

Cai watched in disbelief as the lake was lit from below with a golden light, steadily increasing in its intensity as it rose closer to the surface; small ripples appeared in the lake's centre, ever expanding as they spread across the water.

"My Lord, there...!" Bedivere cried, pointing to the centre of the lake. *"Excalibur!"*

Cries of wonder filled the air and, as Cai looked in the direction the knight was pointing, he frowned, unable to believe what he was seeing: *a sword was slowly rising from the water.* He stood, transfixed, unable to look away as it continued to rise; as he watched, he slowly realised its hilt was gripped firmly by...

A hand...

"What the...?" he gasped, taking a step closer to the water's edge in a vain attempt to get a closer view.

Sunlight glinted off the cross-guard as water cascaded from the scabbard, crystalline in the sun. The hand continued to rise, slowly revealing a slender arm and, eventually, a beautiful, young woman, dressed in a white robe, with golden hair emerged, untouched by the water; she was bathed in a bright, white light that shimmered about her.

Mesmerised by it all, Cai was unable to tear his eyes away from the incredible sight. Words failed him; he had never seen anything so beautiful, so... *magical.*

Merlin turned to Cai. "You must take the boat and go out to meet her," he instructed, his voice penetrating Cai's thoughts, bringing him back to reality.

Cai shook his head, taking a step back. "What? On my own?" he demanded, hesitantly.

Merlin smiled. "You have no reason to fear her, Cai," he reassured him. "She is the Lady of the Lake. Now go; she awaits you."

He glared at Merlin. "But aren't you coming with me?"

Merlin shook his head. "No, this journey is yours... and yours alone." He pointed to a boat waiting, not too far away, along the shore.

Bracing himself, Cai walked slowly towards it, wondering what he had to do. He had never sailed a boat before and this one certainly wasn't doing much for his confidence; it looked as though it would sink the moment it touched the water. As he reached it, he gritted his teeth and proceeded to drag it to the water's edge, thankful for the strength he had developed through his training.

Suddenly, the boat was afloat; panicking, he threw himself inside. Scrambling to his feet, he stopped, aware that the boat was rocking precariously from side to side. Noticing two oars laying on the bottom, he tentatively sat down and, picking up each in turn, placed them carefully into the water. Gripping them tightly, he attempted to row but, frustratingly, only managed to skim the surface of the water.

"No need for that, Cai," Merlin called. "Just sit still; I will do the rest."

Cai glanced back at the shoreline and noticed Merlin was now standing with his arms outstretched, palms facing out towards him, his eyes fixed intently upon Cai. After a moment, and seemingly of its own accord, the boat began to drift towards the centre of the lake.

Suddenly, Cai was jerked backwards as the boat picked up speed and, too freaked out to do anything else, he held onto the edge of the boat in a vice-like grip. Looking around frantically, he expected the boat to capsize at any moment, but, as he looked fearfully towards the shore, he began to calm down, knowing Merlin still had full control.

Cai sat as still as possible, trying his best to stabilise the boat as it neared the woman... who now appeared to be *standing on the water,* awaiting him. Incredibly, the boat came to a stop just a few feet away from her, bobbing gently on the, now calm, water.

The woman smiled radiantly as she looked down upon him. *Cai Pendragon, you come at last.* To his amazement, the woman's lips didn't move as she spoke; instead, her voice resonated deep inside his head. Her voice was clear and pure, instantly putting Cai at ease, making him feel safe.

Unsure of what to do, he just stared at her.

The lady studied him for a moment; he found himself blushing, unable to look away. *You have risen to the challenges before you and have come far in such a short time,* she observed. Her gaze dropped to the sword at his side and she smiled. *But the High King of Britain should now carry a sword worthy of his station.*

Cai stared in wonder as she lowered the sword and offered Excalibur to him. He swallowed nervously and, reaching up to take the weapon, gazed at it in disbelief as he realised that, despite its watery home, it was perfectly dry. As soon as his fingers curled around the scabbard, he felt something shoot through him, like a surge of electricity; he almost dropped the weapon back into the watery depths but he held fast, unwilling to relinquish the blade.

Now gazing upon the weapon in his hands, he noticed the pommel and cross-guard were both highly decorated with intricate Celtic designs of dragons surrounded by complicated linear patterns. Cai took hold of the hilt and pulled the sword free of its scabbard, relishing the hiss of the blade against leather and marvelling at its beauty as the sunlight glinted off the highly polished blade. Drawing the sword closer to him, he noticed the blade, too, had a Celtic design etched into it. It was also incredibly light, the balance perfect. Cai turned it over in his hand. He had never seen anything like it before; it was truly breathtaking. The scabbard, in vast contrast to the sword it housed, looked unremarkable; it was black leather, attached to a simple leather belt that had been wrapped around the shaft.

Sliding Excalibur back into the scabbard, his gaze returned to the woman who was still smiling down at him. He opened his mouth to speak but she shook her head slowly and placed a finger to his lips to silence him; Cai was instantly flooded with warmth, although no contact had actually been made.

Difficult times lay ahead of you, Cai Pendragon, she warned. *The Darkness that follows you will seek to destroy you and all you hold dear... But fear not,* she continued. *You have a great strength within you, a strength that will see you through...*

Her words echoed those Merlin had spoken to him previously but he still couldn't quite bring himself to acknowledge them.

400

I sense your fear, the Lady continued. Cai dropped his gaze shamefully but the Lady pressed on. *You are wise to acknowledge such feelings,* she added. *Men without fear are foolhardy and make poor leaders.* She paused. *Look at me, Cai Pendragon,* she commanded. Cai lifted his head to see her smiling down on him. *Your heart is strong and true. Let* that *be your guide in all your endeavours; it will steer you well.*

And, suddenly, just as quickly as it had appeared, the light from below began to dim. Before he knew what was happening, the woman began to descend and the boat started to drift back towards the shore.

"No, wait!" Cai cried frantically, instinctively reaching out to stop her and desperately clinging on to the sides as the boat began to rock, once more. That couldn't be it, she couldn't just *disappear*; he had so many questions he wanted to ask, questions that needed answers... "Please, wait!" he pleaded. He wanted to leap into the water, he wanted to find some way to bring her back, but he knew it was too late; all he could do was watch, helplessly, as she returned to the lake, once more.

Left alone, Cai gazed at Excalibur, replaying the woman's words, over and over, in his head.

You have a great strength within you, a strength that will see you through...

Cai tightened his grip on the sword feeling something inside him change; it was strange, as if an invisible bond now connected him to the sword

401

in his hand.   He felt complete, like he was suddenly, and unexpectedly, *whole*; he could feel the power already flowing through him.

This was his sword now...

Merlin was waiting for him when the boat reached the shore. "Give me your sword," he said, indicating the sword at his side.

Cai unbuckled his belt, wrapping it around the scabbard before handing it to Merlin.   He immediately replaced it with Excalibur, revelling in the feel of it against his body.

Merlin smiled as he looked down at Cai. "It is where it belongs, once more, my Lord."

But no sooner had the words left his lips than a crack of thunder rent the air and forks of lightning split the sky; dark clouds roiled above them, gathering ominously, as another jagged fork of lighting shot forth, momentarily illuminating the shoreline with a blinding white light.   The once calm lake was now dark and dangerous as waves rolled across its surface, becoming higher and more ferocious by the second.

"What's happening?" Cai shouted to Merlin, fighting hard to be heard above the sudden, deafening noise of the wind raging around them. Bracing himself against the unexpected onslaught, Cai fought the terror gripping him, trying not to panic as he tried to understand what was happening; one minute it had been calm and serene, the next...

"My Lord, it is as we feared..." Merlin replied curtly as he scoured their surroundings, clearly searching for something. *"She is here..."*

She...

Cai's blood turned to ice and his mind flashed to Morgan before he grabbed Merlin's arm and tried to pull him away from the lake. "Then we need to get back to the horses," he cried desperately. "Come on, Merlin; we need to *leave! Now!*"

Merlin shook his head and stood firm. "It is already too late," he murmured, his eyes fixed upon a point across the water. Without looking at Cai, he added, "Leave, Cai; go with Bedivere, make your escape. *I* shall deal with this." He took a step forward, placing himself in front of Cai, his arms poised at his sides.

"My Lord...?" Bedivere cried pointedly, pulling at Cai's arm.

Cai yanked his arm free, following Merlin's gaze and, as the scene was lit by yet another flash of lightening cutting through the dark, heavy clouds, he saw her: a woman standing on the opposite shore. She was dressed in black robes, her black hair whipping around her head as the wind battered her relentlessly. She seemed completely unaffected and at ease, despite the chaos around her.

"Give me the sword, boy."

The woman's voice rose above the cacophony around them, easily cutting through the roaring wind to reach Cai's ears, as clear as day.

As Merlin took another step towards the water's edge, raising his arms, Cai could only watch in fear and awe; he could feel the power raging between the two, the air practically vibrated with it. He stared as Merlin churned the water in the lake, calling it forth, creating a wall of water between them and the woman. A scream of rage split the darkness and Bedivere pulled once more at Cai's arm.

"My Lord, we must leave this place," he pleaded and, for the first time, Cai heard fear in his voice.

Turning, Cai raced after Bedivere, faltering as they reached the top of the hill. As the sky above them pulsed with bursts of muted white light, Cai watched in horror, realising his men were already engaged in their own battle; the skirmish was frenzied and bloody. Their attackers, although smaller in number, were clad in black chainmail, vicious and hell-bent on inflicting as much damage as possible. Already, some of Cai's men lay injured or dying.

Cai could only stare, fear paralyzing him...

Bedivere pulled Cai around to face him, his eyes boring into him. "Stay with me, my Lord," he ordered urgently. Cai nodded mutely but the knight held firm. "I mean it, Cai; do *not* leave my side."

"I won't," Cai promised; he wasn't sure he even *wanted* to, under the circumstances. Pulling Excalibur free, and feeling better for it, he glanced at Bedivere and saw the fury in the knight's eyes.

"We must leave this place," he said. "Whatever you do, my Lord: do *not* stop until you reach your horse."

Cai nodded but, before he could do anything, a scream of pure rage split the air; looking up, Cai only had a moment to grasp what was happening before Bedivere stepped in front of him.

The knight didn't hesitate as he brought his blade up to meet their enemy's and, sweeping it aside, quickly followed through with a thrust of his own, sinking his blade deep into his opponent's chest. The man dropped like a stone, a silent scream frozen on his ashen face.

Cai stared in horror at the sight of the dying man at Bedivere's feet, blood pooling in his mouth as he tried to fight for one last breath; he watched as Bedivere placed his boot on the man's chest and pulled, drawing his sword free.

"Cai, with me!"

Bedivere's voice cut into Cai's thoughts and he was ripped back to the present, just in time to see another man running towards Bedivere's back, his face twisting grotesquely in anticipation of his attack.

"Bedivere!" Cai screamed, pushing the knight out of the way.

Carried by the momentum of his attack, their would-be attacker stumbled on past them, only just managing to pull up short before he fell face first into the mud. He turned on them, his eyes alive with bloodlust.

Watching as the man circled them, sword at the ready, poised for attack, Cai was reminded of Bedivere's earlier words: *They fought like they were possessed... maybe they were...*

The man screamed and charged at Cai, fully committed to his attack. Cai scrambled backwards, putting as much distance between them as his shaking legs would allow, Excalibur now forgotten, useless in his grip; all his lessons, all the knowledge he had gained over the past few months, was gone...

He remembered nothing.

Seeing Cai's retreat, the man laughed manically before sweeping his sword around once more in an elaborate arc and renewing his attack, never once breaking stride. Desperate now, Cai held his ground and brought his sword up to meet the sweep of his opponent's blade just as Bedivere launched himself at the man, wrestling him to the ground.

As the two men landed in a heap, Cai's attacker released his grip on his sword; seeing his chance, Cai kicked the weapon away. Bedivere struggled with the man briefly before landing a punch on his face, breaking his nose; the man's head snapped back and, for a moment, he appeared stunned.

Suddenly, the man brought his knee up, ramming it into Bedivere's groin; in one swift movement, he cast Bedivere aside and, scrambling to his feet, delivered a vicious kick to the knight's ribs.

Instinctively, Cai moved towards the fallen knight but pulled up short as the man turned to face him.

"I'll rip you apart with my bare hands, boy," the man growled.

Not doubting his words for a second, Cai tightened his grip on Excalibur, drawing whatever strength he could from it. As the man rushed towards him, Cai brought the blade up and watched helplessly as the tip of the sword pierced his chainmail, sinking deep into his stomach. The man gasped and gazed down in shock before looking back to Cai, a twisted grin on his lips as blood ran from his mouth. Dropping to his knees, the man reached up, trying to pull the blade free, but it was no good; he fell at Cai's feet, drained of whatever strength he had left.

"Cai, retrieve your sword!" Bedivere gasped, still writhing in pain.

The knight's words spurred him into action, his stomach churning at the sickening, wet sound of the blade being pulled free. Hurrying to Bedivere's side, he knelt down, quickly checking for injuries.

"Are you alright?" he demanded.

Bedivere nodded as he sat up. "I shall be... My sword..." he gasped, still clutching his side. He glanced at Cai. "Nothing's broken..."

Cai nodded and reached for the knight's sword just as brilliant white light engulfed the battlefield; reaching out, Bedivere pulled Cai down to the ground beside him and, drawing his dagger, launched himself to his feet, ignoring his injury. "Stay down!" he ordered, his voice betraying his pain.

Keeping low, Cai followed Bedivere's gaze, scouring the landscape for any danger, but was shocked at what he saw: gone was the darkness, gone were the black clad warriors, both living and dead... everything was exactly as it had been before the unexpected attack. Cai sat up slowly, looking to Bedivere for an explanation but the knight looked back at him, just as confused.

Getting to his feet, Cai gazed around, watching, as his men slowly stood, each as stunned as the next; no one could explain what had happened or what they had been a part of. He watched as his men knelt to tend to the wounded and the dead and, strangely, despite everything, Cai felt buoyed by these simple actions.

"Cai."

Cai turned at the sound of Merlin's voice to see him striding towards him, his robes billowing around him; he looked strangely energised by what had happened and, as he took in the aftermath of battle, he came to stop beside Cai and Bedivere.

"She has gone," he declared.

Cai frowned. "What...?" He paused, trying to gather his thoughts. "Who *was* she?" he asked, suspecting he already knew the answer.

Merlin's eyes darted to Bedivere before returning once more to Cai. "Morgan le Fay."

Cai froze, his blood turning to ice in his veins. *Morgan le Fay.* After all this time, he had finally seen the sorceress in the flesh, albeit at a distance, but still…

"We must leave this place; we must get these men somewhere safe," Merlin insisted; Cai nodded in agreement. "We must return to the others and inform them of what has taken place here."

Cai stared at Merlin, wishing he understood what had happened and what this meant now. Would they have to abandon their people, yet again, and return to Camelot? Would Morgan continue to attack them until Cai finally surrendered Excalibur? Well, that wasn't even an option; he would *never* give up his father's sword.

Tightening his grip on Excalibur's pommel, Cai felt his resolve strengthen as he surveyed the scene before him; these men had put themselves between him and Morgan le Fay, protecting him, without question. As he watched them, he silently acknowledged what he had, so far, avoided: he was now ready for whatever lay ahead; he *had* to be, there was no going back. Morgan could throw whatever she had at them but he would never give up until she and Mordred were defeated.

He was, now, more determined than ever: he *would* defeat his enemies and save his people.

He would finish what his father had started; he would lead his people to victory…

Epilogue

I felt the change instantly; it was as if the very air around me became charged with power... such power I hadn't felt in a long time... power I'd almost forgotten...

I could taste it, feel it as if it were a part of me; the yearning has returned tenfold.

I rally against the fire in my veins, trying to make sense of this unexpected turn of events. They mean to cast me aside but I will not be banished so easily; they do not know my true strength, do not realise just what I am capable of.

They do not realise I have already breached their defences.

But they will... in time.

They meant to trick me, to put a mere boy upon my son's rightful throne... a boy more adept at hiding behind his mother's skirts than ruling a kingdom.

The fury rushes through me in an instant, intensifying the fire within that has burned for so long.

I have waited long enough...

They will live to regret it, each and every one of them. I shall make sure of it; I will destroy everything they hold dear...

For I am coming...

And I will not *be stopped...*

JOIN MY MAILING LIST!

Where legends come to life...

Sign up to my mailing list to receive news, updates and a FREE copy of my short story, FIRE AND ICE!

This is an EXCLUSIVE offer, only available when you join my mailing list – you won't find this anywhere else!

PLEASE LEAVE A REVIEW!

Honest reviews will help spread the word and bring my books to the attention of other readers who may enjoy them. I don't have the muscle of the big publishers so can't take out full page ads or put posters up in towns and cities... but I do have something far more valuable:

A loyal, and committed, bunch of readers.

So, if you enjoyed reading THE BOOK OF LEGEND, and want to help me spread the word, then please spare a few minutes to leave a review (it can be as short as you like).

To leave a review, click the link below.

Thank you so much!

If you enjoyed THE BOOK OF LEGEND, here's an exclusive excerpt of Book Two THE PRISON OF ICE AND SHADOWS...

Prologue

The pounding of boots on the cold hard-packed earth outside her homestead echoed her rapid heartbeat. Wide-eyed, she looked to her mother, crouching beside her in the dark; the older woman's eyes glistened with unshed tears of terror as she stared helplessly back at her. Both knew they were at the mercy of Fate herself. Her mother raised a shaking finger to her lips and shook her head, forbidding the girl from making any noise.

The girl nodded and sat back on her haunches, her breathing ragged and loud in her own ears, silently praying that she and her family would make it through this accursed night. She tried to swallow but her mouth was so dry, it was impossible. The acrid smoke in the air burned the back of her throat and stung her eyes, filling all her senses. She could only imagine the horrors taking place outside; horrors she and her mother *would soon be forced to witness, if they were to escape.*

Her father had left them with a promise that he would return but the more the girl listened to the chaos around them, the less sure she was of her father's survival... of anyone's *survival. Whatever force had invaded them seemed too powerful to hold back.*

Cries of terror and fury filled the night as villagers fought for their own and their family's survival. Men cried out in rage, overcome by bloodlust, as they fought their enemies, while mothers cried out for the lives of their children as sons were ripped from their arms and their daughters' throats slit before their eyes.

The girl's mother moved closer to her, careful not to make any noise and attract the attention of the invaders; she pulled her daughter into her arms, this simple gesture enough to make the girl feel safe and she felt herself relax even as her mother tightened her desperate hold on her. They watched, as the dancing orange flames from the torches outside grow brighter, taunting them both.

She closed her eyes, a single tear escaping; she knew enough of this world to know what was happening. The invaders were setting fire to anything they could find: carts, hay, houses... anything that could be used as a hiding place, weapon or means of escape. Nothing was sacred anymore and the girl knew it was only a matter of time before their home was set alight; every second that passed brought that moment closer.

She opened her eyes as her mother took her hand, pulling her to her feet.

"Where are we going?" the girl whispered, shooting a glance at the door, fearful that someone would burst through at any moment.

Her mother turned and faced her. "I am doing what I promised your father I would do: I'm getting us away from here." She turned and tugged her daughter forwards but the girl refused to move, yanking her arm free from her mother's grasp.

"I will not leave without Father," she stated adamantly, taking a step back. She knew she was being foolish, putting both herself and her mother in even greater danger, but she couldn't desert her father. Not now.

Her mother approached her, her dark eyes boring into her daughter's. Cupping the girl's face in her hands, she held her gaze. "Listen to me," she implored, her voice desperate. "We are living in dark and dangerous times and now the danger has finally caught up with us as we knew it would. Your father is fighting for us and this village but he needs to know we are safe." She stroked her daughter's cheek and, in a softer voice, added, "Now, you need to be brave and we need to leave." She looked deeply into her eyes. "Do you understand?"

The girl swiped angrily at her tears, pushing them away, and nodded determinedly.

Her mother took her hand once again and pulled her through the darkness towards the rear of the house, its simple layout making it easy to negotiate even in the dark.

"Wait!" the girl hissed pulling free of her mother's hold once again. She hurried over to her bedding, ignoring her mother's disapproval, and slipped her hand beneath the furs. Pulling out a silver dagger, she grinned at her mother. "Father gave it to me," she explained, retracing her steps.

Her mother gazed down at her, smiling; the disapproval she had always felt when her husband had insisted on teaching their daughter how to use weapons vanished; all she felt, in that moment, was pride. Pride that her daughter stood before her now, weapon in hand, ready to protect them; for the first time she saw her husband in her daughter's demeanour, in the steel of her eyes. At any other time, she would have pulled the girl into her arms and told her how much she loved her but that could wait for later, when they were safe.

But right now they needed to get as far away from here as possible.

Reaching out, she took her daughter's hand and, together, they made their way to the door, stopping only to peer outside before racing out into the unknown.

At the rear of the house a bank rose up towards a forest and the girl instinctively ran towards the trees, as she had done so many times before.

Behind her, she ignored her mother's ragged gasps for air as she forged ahead, only stopping when she reached the shelter of the trees; her need to find her father consumed her. From this vantage point, she scoured the village below, her heart breaking. The fire still raged, destroying all in its path, destroying everything familiar to her, everything she had ever known; flames engulfed several buildings, dancing gleefully in the darkness, while men in black chainmail stalked the night, searching for fresh victims. Bodies lay strewn over the ground, young and old alike, a testament to the evil that had finally found them. Those that weren't already dead were being rounded up like cattle and anyone trying to fight back was killed or beaten into submission.

As she desperately searched the chaos for any sign of her father, a maniacal scream rent the air, cutting through the cacophony, surrounding her like a knife. The girl's attention was snapped back to the bank below her as a woman, dressed in black robes, materialised out of the darkness. Without breaking her stride she began slowly ascending the bank, a predator of the night, finally cornering her prey.

The girl stared in horror at her mother, still halfway down the bank, clawing desperately at the earth as she tried to reach her daughter and the safety of the trees. Fear had consumed her and she was gasping for air. As the woman closed in, the girl knew it was already too late. She despised herself for abandoning her mother in her hour of need.

"You dare to escape us?" the woman demanded. She glared at the girl's mother unwaveringly, her black hair billowing around her shoulders.

The girl watched helplessly as the newcomer drew closer, suddenly aware of white lightning dancing around her fingertips; as she neared her mother, the woman closed her hands, extinguishing the light. Willing herself to move, but fear preventing her from doing so, the girl remained crouched in the shadows as she watched the scene unfold below her.

Her mother turned and looked up defiantly at the woman looming over her. The two stared at each other for what seemed like an age before the newcomer smiled, coldly, down at her prey.

"Your cowardice is priceless," the woman murmured disdainfully.

Hearing her mother referred to as a coward, the girl's grip tightened on her dagger as she inched closer to the edge of the trees, preparing to take aim.

Her mother caught sight of her and, sensing her intention, the older woman's gaze hardened as she silently begged her to remain hidden. Her eyes flicked towards the trees, signalling her daughter to go deeper into the forest but she shook her head, determined not to leave her mother to the mercy of this heinous woman.

Instead, she waited, biding her time, ready to throw at the first opportunity. Her father had always said that patience was the mark of a true hunter and warrior and she heard his voice, reminding her of that fact, as clearly as if he were with her now, hunting a rabbit.

Seeing her daughter's defiance, the older woman resumed her tortuous climb, only for her assailant to step in front of her, placing herself between mother and daughter. She knelt before her victim and grabbed a fistful of hair, forcing her to look her in the face.

The girl watched, paralyzed by fear, unable to believe what she was witnessing. For the first time in her life her mother, usually so strong, looked utterly terrified; her eyes wide, her breathing shallow.

"Please don't hurt me," she begged, failing to hide her fear.

The woman cackled. "First, I catch you trying to escape and then you ask me not to hurt you?" she murmured, studying her. "I have to admit, I admire your nerve."

Tears were falling freely now from her mother's eyes. "Please... I don't want any part of this... spare me..."

The woman cast her captive towards the ground, glaring down at her in disgust. "You're all the same," she sneered. Tilting her head to one side, she added, "Give me one good reason why I should spare you."

The girl watched as her mother glanced at her again before looking back to the woman kneeling over her.

"I thought as much," she sneered. She stood up and, before the girl could react, before she had a chance to throw her weapon, white light blazed from the woman's palm, a bolt of light hitting her mother squarely in the forehead.

The girl instinctively shrank back into the shadows, shielding her eyes from the sudden burst of light as her mother collapsed on the ground. She prayed the woman wouldn't turn and catch sight of her; no sooner had the thought entered her head than she cursed herself for her own cowardice.

Recovering her senses, the girl scrambled to the edge of her hiding place and took aim, ready to avenge her mother's death, the only way she knew how. Without a second thought, she released her meagre weapon, watching as it sliced through the air towards her target.

But... it was too late.

There was a loud crack and the woman disappeared into the darkness once more.

The dagger sailed through the air in vain, landing in the grass just past where the woman had stood only moments before.

Too shocked to try to understand what had happened and too heartbroken and guilt-ridden at the sight of her mother's prone body lying on the hillside to do anything else, the girl left her hiding place. Skidding to a halt beside her mother she dropped to her knees, cradling her mother in her arms, ignoring the tears that stung her eyes.

Hooking her hands under her mother's arms, she dragged her lifeless body up the bank to the relative safety of the forest. There, she sat, cradling her mother's body, sobbing silently, as the only place she had ever called home was destroyed.

And, later that night, as the flames died, a cold, unforgiving hatred took root in her heart.

ACKNOWLEDGEMENTS

When I first sat down to write THE BOOK OF LEGEND, I thought it would just be me and my laptop; it wasn't until much later that I realised just how wrong I was. None of this would have been possible without the help and support of my friends and family...

All the staff at Tasty Bites, who provided much appreciated relief from writing when I needed it; Charlie, for his weekly supply of spag bol (thanks for the brain food!); Mary, whose feedback was invaluable and, without whom, the title of this series would have been very different; Lisa, who, ten years ago, became my writing partner – the stories we created together are very different from my own but they put me on this path and, for that, I will be forever grateful; Siân, for her knowledge of the equine world; Dad, for keeping me supplied with much needed drinks and snacks during this process; Steve, whose technical skills helped to produce an imaginative and eye-catching book cover and, whose well-timed questions led me to create the final battle scene – hope you enjoy!; Mum, whose unwavering belief and support has given me the confidence to finally start this process. Your honest criticism continues to make me a better writer. We still have many more editing sessions ahead of us, believe me!; and to my feline friends,

Moo and Loki, who never fail to interrupt, just when I need it.

And last, but not least, you: my readers. Thank you for purchasing this book and joining myself and Cai as we embark upon our very different journeys; there's still loads more to come, so meet you in the next book!

About the Author...

TJ's love of writing began when she wrote her first story at the age of thirteen. But life soon took over and TJ trained for a 'proper job' as a teacher. She has been teaching for ten years now and, during that time, had written as a hobby with her best friend before finally having the idea for the Prophecies of Fate series, three years ago. As well as the Prophecies of Fate series, TJ also has plans for other series in the pipeline.

TJ lives in the south-east of England and, when she isn't writing, can be found spending time with friends and family, reading, visiting sites of historical interest, hiking in the British countryside and watching any number of TV shows and movies.

TJ can be found at www.tjmayhewauthor.com, where you can signup to her mailing list to receive updates about forthcoming projects and news. Alternatively, email her at: tj@tjmayhewauthor.com or contact her on Facebook and Twitter: @tjmayhewauthor.

Printed in Great Britain
by Amazon